AN OPEN WINDOW

Gwen,

Blessings as
you read!

Sara Whitley

AN OPEN WINDOW

SARA WHITLEY

TATE PUBLISHING
AND ENTERPRISES, LLC

Published by Tate Publishing & Enterprises, LLC
127 E. Trade Center Terrace | Mustang, Oklahoma 73064 USA
1.888.361.9473 | www.tatepublishing.com

Tate Publishing is committed to excellence in the publishing industry. The company reflects the philosophy established by the founders, based on Psalm 68:11,
"The Lord gave the word and great was the company of those who published it."

Book design copyright © 2014 by Tate Publishing, LLC. All rights reserved.
Cover design by Arjay Grecia
Interior design by Caypeeline Casas

Published in the United States of America

ISBN: 978-1-62854-951-5
1. Fiction / Religious
2. Fiction / Romance / General
13.11.07

DEDICATION

To my husband, Ben. You make my life an adventure.
I love you.

ACKNOWLEDGMENTS

I sit writing this while in the midst of marketing my first book. There are still so many uncertainties swirling around in my brain, and oftentimes, I have to command myself to sit back, relax, and remember who is really in control here: God. After hearing feedback from people who have read my first book, *Another Ending*, I am beginning to think that God is up to something great here. I seemed to have accomplished my goal of bringing my readers into Molly's world, of making her and her emotions seem real. I hope you all experience that again with this book.

As always, I must thank my wonderful husband, Ben. No one supports me like you do, love. Thank you for keeping me accountable, for asking me about my progress, and for giving me time to write when the words are so heavy on my heart. I think God knew that we needed to be together when we were awkward fifteen- and sixteen-year-olds walking around with crushes on each other. He knew I needed your patience and wisdom—and your awesome bookkeeping skills. I love you, hon.

Thank you to my family, all of you. To my dad, Kevin, for being my sounding board and giving me great advice, for being my biggest fan all these years, and for helping me push and sell books, of course. To my mom, Marcia, for reading my books and catching all the little things that always seem to slip by me and for encouraging me and supporting me for my entire life. Your love is an inspiration to me, to all your kids. Thank you to my siblings, Emily, Katie, and Matthew, for being excited for me and talking about my books to your friends. I love you, guys.

A shout out to my home church family, Calvary Baptist Church. You have all been so supportive—some of you will never realize how important your excitement has been to me. And the fact that so many of you approached me about editing my second book for me because you couldn't wait to get your hands on it warms my heart. I am truly inspired that my words touched your hearts. I must also take some time and thank two very special people at Calvary, people who inspired one of my favorite characters in this story: Albert. First, Dan Mather. Although you are no longer with us, your life of faith still affects me even to this day—and don't think I forgot about all the tootsie rolls you handed out on Sunday mornings! Secondly, to Norm Campbell. I can't remember one time in my life where I didn't see you smiling, one time when the love of Christ wasn't absolutely radiating from your eyes. *That* is what loving Jesus with all your heart looks like to me, so thank you, Norm, for being a role model to not only me but to everyone in our church. Because of these two amazing men, Albert was really able to come alive in this story.

Thank you to all the staff at Tate Publishing. It has been wonderful working with you all! I feel so blessed to have been led to such a wonderful group of people. Every step of this publishing journey has been such a joy. Thank you for your hard work!

And as always, thank you to my savior, Jesus Christ. He is the reason I write. More than this is a story about Molly, this is a story about Jesus. I hope the powerful story of his love changes your life, just as it has changed mine. Because if it does, I have achieved my goal.

PROLOGUE

I looked into my groom's eyes and commanded myself not to cry. I'd spent a good half hour fretting in front of the mirror this morning, making sure my makeup was flawless for this very moment. And yet I could feel the sting of tears in my eyes, so I blinked furiously to keep them from spilling over and leaving a trail of mascara down my rosy cheeks.

My groom looked like he was fighting, and losing, the same battle. His smile wobbled uncontrollably—not from deciding whether he was happy or sad but because he was so happy he couldn't hold the tears of joy in anymore. He was blinking just the same as I was, and I squeezed his hand gently, a silent way of telling him I felt the same way he did. He gave my fingers a squeeze back and winked at me, causing my heart to gallop wildly out of control. I hoped this feeling would never go away.

We both turned our heads to the pastor, eagerly awaiting the next part of the ceremony. The vows.

My groom took my hand again and cleared his throat, ready to declare to the world that he loved me and that he promised to do so for the rest of our lives together. "I, Tanner, take you, Molly, to be my wife…"

My eyes snapped open and my head flew up from the cold table. For a moment, I was disoriented, completely unaware of where I was and how I'd gotten here. The gentle hum of the one and only washer and dryer running in the musty little building reminded me that I was in the Laundromat finishing up my last load of dirty clothes. I sighed and ran my hands through my hair, still reeling from my bizarre dream. Though no one could see inside my head, my cheeks still burned in embarrassment. I'd been dreaming about Tanner! Not only that, but I dreamed we were getting married! And that would never, not in a million years, happen. He was married to Leah now.

Two minutes was all that remained on the washer, which meant I only had about a half hour left here as I waited for that load to dry. I pulled my fresh clothes out of the dryer, moved the wet ones over, then began folding the warm sheets and towels. Normally, I wouldn't take time to do the job well, but tonight, I needed to keep my hands busy. Actually, I really needed something to keep my mind busy, and this wasn't the best task for that. Didn't take much brainpower to fold sheets and towels, fitted sheets maybe, but even the small amount of brainpower needed to complete that task didn't keep my mind off Tanner. Seems like nothing could do that lately, and it was driving me crazy.

It was far, far past the time for me to get over Tanner and move on. This little rut I was in was too exhausting to keep stumbling through, and if I wanted to feel some sort of satisfaction living here in Kansas, I needed to figure out a way to pull myself out of the rut and into the sunshine above.

Forty-five minutes later, I was in my car, just sitting in the dark parking lot of my apartment building. I looked up to the third-story window that belonged to me, and I knew I should be filled with gratitude at how far I'd come in the last five months. Facing my family after three years away was the hardest thing I'd ever done, but I'd done it. I was only here because this was where my life was now. Back in Oak Ridge, the rape still lurked for me. Painful memories pricked at my heart at each corner of my little hometown, so it hadn't been too terribly hard to pack up and leave it all behind. Sure, I missed my family, but I had a new family here—in Mary Beth, Delilah, little Luke, and, of course, Albert. They'd all adopted me and rallied around me, and they continued helping me face the dark ugliness of my past and checking up on me constantly to ensure that I was healing properly.

I let another sigh slip from my lips. I hoped that as I fell into my bed later after a midnight snack that the awful dream wouldn't haunt me again. I don't think I could handle seeing Tanner's face looking back at me, vowing to love, cherish, and honor me all the days of his life. He'd already made those vows to Leah. And some way or another, I was going to have to be okay with that, no matter how much it hurt.

PART ONE

Searching

ONE

※

Molly

DECEMBER 2011

Luke looked adorable in his Christmas suit, singing his little lungs out in the front of the church. I glanced over at Delilah, his beaming mother, and saw her brushing away tears. She sniffed and gave me a sad smile, and I reached over to take her hand in mine to comfort her.

Luke was seven years old and a complete delight. He'd been one of the biggest influences on my decision to return to Jesus during my years away from Christ. He'd invited me to the church service that stopped me dead in my tracks and sent me running in the other direction, right back to Jesus. And so tonight, sitting next to his teary-eyed mother as he sang alongside all the other Sunday school kids in the Christmas program, I felt just as proud, and my throat was tightening up just the same as hers was. When I'd met Luke, he'd been a tiny five-year-old boy dressed up as a pirate on Halloween night. And now, he'd grown so much, and he was wise beyond his years. We were so incredibly proud of the young man he was growing up to be, but it was hard seeing our little angel growing and changing right before our eyes. We both wanted him to stay young and innocent forever, because both Delilah and I had been through the darkest things life could throw at a person. We didn't want that for little Luke. The world's a cruel place, and we wanted to protect him from it.

After the program, we meandered into the fellowship hall to check out the cookies and lemonade supplied by the kitchen circle ladies whose kids were all grown—and who found such enjoyment out of serving the church in this way now that their nests were empty. While we perused the overflowing cookie table, I leaned in close to Delilah and whispered, "He's got a couple more innocent years ahead of him. Just enjoy this time. It goes by in the blink of an eye."

She winced. "Guess we were thinking the same thing tonight, huh?"

I nodded. "Yup. He's got a rough world out there waiting for him. But he's got the best mommy in the world," I declared, poking her ticklish spot, "who's teaching him how to maneuver it and make the best decisions possible. And he's got a pretty rocking auntie too, not to toot my own horn or anything," I teased.

She giggled. "You're not *really* his aunt, silly."

"Yes, but his real aunties live far away. So I'm kind of a replacement auntie. He loves me the same as his real ones anyway," I countered, poking her again.

"True," she agreed, giggling.

"Mommy! Did you get some pictures of me singing?" Luke came running over to us, spilling his lemonade behind him. With cookie crumbs stuck to his face, he was grinning from ear to ear. Total boy.

"Sure did, sweet boy. You looked very handsome," she declared.

He grinned larger and gave a big nod. "I'm going to finish my 'fresments with Joey over there." He pointed to where his friend sat waiting with a couple other kids.

Delilah stifled her laughter. "Okay, buddy. Enjoy your refreshments."

He took off running again. He'd be lucky to have even a few drops of lemonade left in his cup by the time he made it over to his friends. Still chuckling at his hilarious antics, Delilah and I plopped ourselves down to enjoy our own refreshments.

"Hey look," Delilah said slyly. "There he is."

I rolled my eyes but looked over to see Greg Turner ushering his three-year-old daughter Mandy to a free table. When would Delilah stop pushing me towards this guy? Greg's wife had unexpectedly run off a few months ago, leaving him to care for their young daughter all alone. Since then, he always had this terrified look on his face, like he thought everyone here was judging him for his wife's disappearance. But if there's one thing I'd learned after settling in Green Lake and making Community Christian Church my home church, it was that the people here truly were different. No one gave me judgmental glances as more and more people heard about my dark past. Recently I'd joined a women's Bible study and briefly shared what I had been through, so my past wasn't a huge secret anymore. And yet these women, and the rest of their families, always had a smile and a kind word to say to me. I knew that they probably all had their thoughts and opinions on the decisions I'd made, but they kept them to themselves and simply prayed for me and supported me. That's the kind of church family this was.

So I felt bad for Greg. He needn't worry about people here judging him. Sure, they probably had their opinions on his situation too, but generally, everyone here had his best interest in mind and wanted to help him and Mandy through this difficult time. Delilah's idea of helping him included me, as she had a plan to set us up.

"Not gonna happen, honey," I said before Delilah had a chance to try and convince me to go and talk to him.

She made a face at me and asked, "And why not? He's a perfectly nice guy. And he's totally available," she said suggestively.

"Yeah, well, you're totally available too. Why don't *you* go talk to him?" I replied saucily.

"Oh no," she said with a vigorous shake of her head. "I don't think so."

I leaned forward and teased, "And why not? He's a perfectly nice guy!"

Delilah laughed. "Too serious for me. I hardly ever see him smile. I need someone to make me laugh, someone to joke around with and make me feel like a teenager again. I never really got to feel like a teenager in love, you know?" Her voice began to take on that dreamy, far-away tone to it—the tone she often took when thinking back to her high school years. It was a tone that was often mixed with regret, and I could hear it dripping from her voice now. "Luke takes up all the love my heart has to offer anyway," she said with a shrug.

Delilah had only been fifteen when she'd gotten pregnant. So even though she was now twenty-two years old, gorgeous, and an amazing catch that any guy would be lucky to get his hands on, she felt old and used up. She'd never had the chance to fall hopelessly in love as a teenager, to write out her first name with the last name of her crush and dream about what it might be like to one day get married and then start a family. She'd only dated one guy, David, and had wound up pregnant from him. David hadn't wanted anything to do with the baby but had been against abortion and adoption, so he simply watched Delilah grow round with his baby while he went out and began dating other girls.

Still, Delilah was one of the strongest, most confident young women I had ever met. And yet, deep down, I knew she longed for something more in life. She loved Luke with every ounce of her being, but her life was a constant battle to survive. The world wasn't kind to single mothers, that was for sure, as she lived in a tiny run-down house and struggled to pay her monthly bills. She'd never gone to college; she worked as a secretary for a law firm in town. In high school, she had dreamed of going to school to study architecture, but when she got pregnant, those dreams dissolved like sugar in iced tea on a hot summer day. Luke always

came first. Always. Any money she could have used for her education, she instead invested in him, and her mother didn't have
the money to help her out either.

Now she never even considered dating. She could joke with
me about needing someone to make her laugh, but I knew her
better. She'd never date because that would take time away from
Luke, and no one came before him.

I leaned close and reached my hand out to squeeze her arm.
"You have so much to offer someone, Delilah. I know you think
you're not worthy or that you can't take time away from Luke
to date someone. But Luke can't be your whole life, hon. You
deserve some happiness too. You should *allow* yourself a little
happiness," I advised gently.

She shook her head sadly. "You can't understand, Molly. It
feels so wrong to date when I have a baby waiting at home for
me, needing me."

My eyes darkened. "You're right," I said a bit too sharply, and
her eyes registered the mistake she'd just made. "I don't understand. Because I don't have a baby waiting at home for me. I
should, but I don't."

"That's not what I meant, Molly. I forgot," she said sincerely,
and I nodded, a sigh slipping out from the saddest place in the
bottom of my heart.

"Sorry," I apologized, and an awkward silence settled over us.
But before the silence settled in and ruined our good night, Mary
Beth, Delilah's energetic mother, came bustling over and broke it
for us. I silently thanked God, knowing that I could always count
on Mary Beth to come in and overtake any conversation.

Thoughts of Greg and Mandy faded from our minds as Mary
Beth plopped herself down and began chattering away. "Oh, baby,
I just can't get over that handsome young man of yours. Every day
he makes me fall more in love with him."

We spent the rest of the evening discussing little Luke and
catching up. In the few short weeks since I'd moved back to

Kansas, I'd been crazy busy working on my GED. I wanted to get it done as soon as possible because I wanted to start spring classes at the community college close to Green Lake. I still worked at Mary Beth's little restaurant but not as much as I had before I'd spent a few months back in Iowa. Mary Beth wanted every single detail of what I'd been up to, how my family was, and how studying was going. I smiled as I filled her in, her head bobbing in excitement. Crazy how she could make my boring life seem so exciting.

Alone in my apartment that night however, I let myself feel a little blue. Things had turned out far better than I ever imagined—but it wasn't how I always dreamed my life would turn out. I was living miles and miles away from my family in a new state, apart from every familiar thing I had grown up around. Yes, this was a new adventure for me, but if I'd made smarter decisions my senior year, I could be living out a different adventure. Instead, Leah was living out my adventure with Tanner back in Iowa. She was married to the man I had once thought I would get married to. They were probably thinking about starting a family soon too. Leah's degree in radiology technology had only taken her two years to earn, and she already had a stable job at the hospital in Oak Ridge. It made sense that they would start thinking about starting a family.

If things had worked out for Tanner and I, we'd be a family of three already. Me, Tanner, and our little baby girl. Not Tanner's biological child, but he had been more than willing to marry me and adopt the baby, to love her as his own daughter. While I never found out the sex of the baby—I'd gotten the abortion before my appointment that would have told me—I was positive it was a girl. That's what my gut told me.

Thoughts of the abortion and my deceased baby always made me feel sick, so I pushed those thoughts out of my head. *Take these thoughts from me, Father*, I prayed. *I know I'm forgiven...so help me forgive myself. Tell my baby I love her, Lord. Tell her I can't wait to hold her and kiss her one day. Please, Lord.*

I swiped the single tear that trickled down my face away with my sleeve. *Enough crying.* I'd done too much of that in the past few years. I needed to keep moving on; I needed to figure out how to live my new life even with my dark past looming behind me.

To get my mind on brighter things I let my thoughts wander to Greg Turner. He was good-looking enough, but Delilah was right. He *was* pretty serious, and he didn't smile much. But who could, after what had happened to him? I should know better than anyone how hard it was to smile when life handed out blow after blow. And no one buys a fake smile anyway. I knew that all too well. So why try to pretend with people? We all knew he was dealing with a huge trial and that it was extremely difficult to handle. You just can't hide something like that, not in a town this size.

I hadn't had much luck in the men department through my whole ordeal. Jason had been a nightmare, sending me spiraling into a pit so deep it had taken three years to even begin climbing out of it. I was still climbing out, still dealing with the effects of the rape every single day of my life. Tanner had been a brief glimmer of hope in my dark world, but I'd run away from the false assumption that he'd told Jason about the pregnancy behind my back. Then there'd been Tyler. He was a sweet guy, and he'd made me feel better, but it had been the farthest thing from a godly relationship. And I hadn't dealt with the rape when I'd been with him, so I'd been unable to love him the way he longed to be loved. It had ended before it ever really began with Tyler. And he wasn't a Christian. It would have never worked out for us. Now Greg, he *was* a Christian. He was nice, and he was good-looking—all that curly, brown hair was just adorable. But he had a past, just like me. I wasn't sure if it would ever work between us, two people with so much heavy baggage to sort through.

Still. If he ever asked me out, I would probably say yes just to see where things would go. I deserved some happiness after what I'd been through, right? Sure, it would be difficult to deal with his divorce and his little girl, but we were both strong Christians. We could make it work if we tried hard enough.

So I drifted off to sleep with Greg's handsome face swirling around in my head, allowing myself the luxury of dreaming of the what ifs. Life was waiting for me, beckoning me to move on and take a few risks—not the kind of risks that I'd taken in the past three and a half years, those had been mistakes—risks like allowing myself to really love again, good risks with happy endings. I deserved a happy ending after all I'd been through. And so did Greg.

Who knew? My happy ending was out there somewhere. Maybe it was with Greg. I'd just have to wait and see.

TWO

❖

Molly

DECEMBER

I felt like a high schooler again. I couldn't get Greg out of my head! I woke up thinking about him, and I fell asleep dreaming about what could be. He hadn't even really talked to me yet, but the more Delilah hinted and suggested, the more I felt like dating him was a good idea. We both deserved some happiness, so why not?

When I finally confessed to her that I had a little crush on him, she squealed with delight and clapped her hands. "Yay!" she celebrated, taking my hands in hers and spinning me around. "I'll help hook you two up, okay?"

I laughed. "Whoa, calm down. Don't you go saying anything to him, okay? This isn't high school…you can't go ask him out for me or give him a note that says, 'I like you, circle yes or no if you feel the same!'"

"I know!" she said, feigning hurt. "But…I'll do what I can to coax. Help it along in any way I can. Without being creepy and stalkerish, though, I promise. That's no way to start a relationship," she declared with a wag of her finger.

I shook my head. She was just like her mother, wanting to stick her nose in my business and hook me up with Greg. But, no matter how overwhelming she could be at times, I loved her spunky personality. She made my life crazy and fun. I simply couldn't survive without her.

That next Sunday at church, Delilah made good on her promise to help spark Greg's interest in me. She gently steered me to the row that Greg and Mandy sat in waiting for the service to start, and the three of us, me, Delilah, and Luke, plopped down next to them. Greg looked up in surprise but allowed a soft smile to spread across his face. It transformed him, and my heart fluttered a bit. If he let himself smile more often, he'd be that much more handsome, and every single woman our age in the church would be after him.

We chatted casually for a bit before the worship team made their way to the front to begin morning worship. As we stood singing, I couldn't help but appreciate Greg's deep baritone voice. He was an amazing singer, and so was little Mandy. Even at three years old, she sang clearly and with confidence, never missing a single word of the worship songs. Perhaps the two sang together at home.

I shook my head and refocused on worship. This was not the time for those thoughts. Out of the corner of my eye I saw Delilah grinning, so I reached out and poked her. I must have hit a ticklish spot, however, because she let out a loud guffaw. Greg and Mandy turned sharply to investigate, only to find both of us trying to stifle our loud giggles behind our hands. Greg grinned, and my face heated up. He was simply adorable when he smiled like that.

I found it hard to concentrate on Pastor Dennis's sermon, sitting so close to Greg. Mandy sat between us, but his arm rested on the pew behind her little head, so his fingertips were close to my shoulder. And I could faintly smell his cologne, which didn't make focusing on the sermon any easier. I was relieved when the worship team took the stage once again for a final song.

As everyone shuffled their way to the doors to exit the sanctuary, Delilah stepped in again. "So, Greg, we're going out for lunch. Care to join us?" she invited.

I gave her a pointed look, but she raised her eyebrows at me, amused. Greg's cheeks tinged an adorable shade of pink, but he managed to stammer out an agreement.

"Great!" Delilah gushed. "We're going to that little place downtown, the Griddle. It's Molly's favorite. She *loves* breakfast food, no matter what time of day it is. Is that okay with you two?"

Little Mandy bobbed her head shyly and stuck two fingers into her mouth. She wasn't a talker, that was for sure. Greg smiled softly, "I love breakfast too. In fact, we have French toast for dinner at our house quite often. This one has a sweet tooth. Absolutely drowns her pancakes and French toast in syrup." He tousled his daughter's curly hair playfully, his love for her radiating off his face.

Lunch was amazing; we got to see a side of Greg we never knew existed. He smiled and laughed the entire time, clearly enjoying the escape from his daily routine, which was no doubt emotionally exhausting. Being a single dad to a little girl must be extremely difficult, but from how polite and sweet Mandy was, he seemed to be doing an awesome job. She was a remarkable little girl, and my heart hurt for her. No child deserved to endure what she was enduring. Mothers were so important to little girls. She needed her mommy.

My cheeks burned as I considered the idea of becoming her mommy someday. *It could happen!* If Delilah was successful at setting us up, we might one day be a family.

It was silly to have these thoughts so early though. I needed to take this slow and get to know both of them first. One lunch together was hardly enough time to start picturing becoming a family. Besides, the leaving of Greg's wife was still so fresh in their minds. Perhaps they were still waiting for her to return, and lunch meant nothing to them. Maybe they just liked the company, the way it felt to spend a carefree afternoon laughing and enjoying life with friends.

When Greg left to take his daughter to the restroom, Delilah turned to me and urged, "Give him your number! Tell him to call if he ever needs someone to talk to."

"I don't know," I said begrudgingly. "That feels so…forward. Isn't it the man's job to pursue the woman?" I asked.

She waved her hand dismissively. "Giving him your number hardly counts as pursuing! It simply lets him know that you are there for him, that you want *him* to call you…to pursue you. *You* won't have his number unless he calls." She raised her eyebrows at me, and I laughed.

"Okay. Maybe. If I get brave enough. And don't you dare step in and give it to him for me! How embarrassing. He'll know for sure you're trying to set us up!"

"Well, I *am* trying to set you up! If you're too chicken to give him your number, it becomes my job to help out."

"No, don't!" I said with a giggle. "I'll do it. It just…feels awkward."

We quickly changed the subject as Mandy and Greg returned, but my heart began to pound after the bills were paid and it came time to leave. Delilah wasn't going to let me off the hook though. I needed to give him my number if I wanted to keep her out of this, but she knew I was feeling uncomfortable, which she found amusing. She stifled a giggle when I stuck my tongue out at her.

I took a deep breath and decided to just go for it. "So, Greg…" I began hesitantly. "I, um…I wanted to give you my number. You know, in case you ever need someone to talk to. Or if you get lonely hanging out with Mandy and need some company ever."

I watched the shock pass through his eyes, but he nodded and shrugged. "Sure. Sounds great." He fished his phone out his pocket for me to program my number in. My hands shook from nerves, but I managed to get my name and number pro-grammed in, and when I returned the phone to his hand, our fingers brushed, sending a zing up my spine. It had been so long since I'd felt like this, since I'd been truly excited about something. I loved this feeling.

I was at home Wednesday night finishing up some studying when my phone started singing. The ringtone was one I used for unknown numbers, but the area code matched Kansas, and my heart jumped at the possibility of it being Greg.

"Hello?" I stammered.

"Hey, uh, Molly? It's Greg."

I spun around and grinned like a teenage girl in love, my palms beginning to sweat out of excitement. I hadn't expected a call so soon.

"Hi, Greg," I tried to speak casually, not wanting to sound desperate. "What's up?"

"Well, Mandy's been asking about you every day since Sunday, and she was wondering if you wanted to come over and watch a movie with us. She's obsessed with Disney princesses right now, so if you're not interested, we understand."

"Oh no! I'm a big fan of princesses." My mind wandered back to Ellen, Tanner's little sister. She loved Disney princesses too, and we'd watched and re-watched princess movies with her all the time as teenagers. I could still probably quote every line from every princess movie ever made.

"Cool. Well…let me give you directions to my house, and you can come on over as soon as you want. We'll get started on snacks while we wait, right, sweetie?" Mandy agreed somewhere in the background, and I grinned.

Scribbling the address down at the bottom of my workbook, I decided studying could wait. With schoolwork quickly forgotten, I jogged to my bedroom to change out of my sweats and make myself a little more presentable. I slipped on some jeans and pulled on my favorite navy sweater. Then, studying myself in the mirror, I pulled my hair from the loose ponytail it was in and let the soft waves fall around my shoulders. I applied a little powder to cover up the shine that I never could quite get rid of and slid a soft, pink gloss over my lips, not too much, not too little. On the way out the door, I decided to spritz on some perfume, something I hardly ever wore. It had been a gift from Tyler, the boy I had dated back in Minneapolis, and it usually brought back painful memories, but I saw no sense letting the expensive bottle go to waste. And tonight was a special occasion—it was my first date with Greg, sort of. His daughter would be there, and we were only watching a movie. But still.

His house was easy enough to find. Green Lake was a very small town, so even though I hadn't lived here for long, I knew my way around pretty well. His brick house was small, but even from the outside, it looked cozy and inviting. I could see Greg and Mandy sitting at the kitchen counter preparing our snacks when I pulled in, and when my headlights flashed into the room, Mandy craned her head out the window. She scrambled down from the tall stool and ran to the door, flinging it open wide for me. I stifled a giggle as I walked up the driveway. She was adorable and about the age my little girl would be if I'd kept her. My heart tightened a bit, but I refused to let those memories ruin my night. Tonight wasn't the time to think about that. Tonight was for getting to know Greg and Mandy better. Tonight was a happy night, and I wouldn't let those sour memories ruin it for me.

I was enthusiastically welcomed in, and Mandy grabbed my hand to show me the snacks they'd prepared. While Mandy had been shy and reserved at lunch on Sunday, now it was as if she'd transformed into a whole new little girl. I shot Greg a surprised look, and he laughed.

"Looks can be deceiving! This little girl is all spunk once you crack open her shell. And she's decided she really likes you, isn't that right, Mandy?"

"Yup," she agreed. "We made popcorn cups."

"Oh?" I asked, shooting Greg an amused smile. "And what are those?"

"You've never had a popcorn cup before?" she asked in surprise. I giggled. "No, I don't think I have."

"Oh," she said with bewilderment in her voice—as if it was a complete shock that I'd never enjoyed a popcorn cup before. "Well, popcorn, a 'course. But we put in our favorite snacks too. I put in M&M's. Daddy put in pretzel sticks and marshmallows."

"Well, that sounds wonderful. I can't believe I've been missing out on popcorn cups my whole life!" I teased, tweaking her little button nose.

We settled into the living room to watch *Sleeping Beauty*, Mandy's current obsession. Apparently, this was the fourth night in a row she had requested to watch this one, Greg informed me with a grin. He sat on one end of the couch, Mandy snuggled up on his lap, and I took the opposite end. Mandy sang along to all the songs, but as the movie wore on, she grew sleepy, and soon she was snoring softly in her father's lap. When the movie ended, Greg excused himself to put Mandy to bed, and I sat there awkwardly on the couch in the silence. Ten minutes later, he tiptoed back and resettled on the couch, closer to me now that Mandy was gone.

"You wouldn't believe how hard it is to put a sleeping kid in pajamas. I should get paid to do what I do," he teased.

"No kidding," I replied. "Parenting is hard work." I thought about all that Delilah did for Luke, while at the same time working. Being a single parent was the toughest job ever.

"Definitely," he agreed. Silence once again settled over the room, and I shifted uncomfortably. "Would you like some coffee?" he offered, trying to break the silence.

I relaxed. "I'd love some."

We were both more at ease with mugs in our hands. I decided to just let the conversation flow naturally—I didn't want to force it.

"So you probably know the whole sad story, don't you?" he asked.

My cheeks burned. *Everyone knew.* Things like this traveled fast in a small town. And working at the diner, I heard every bit of the town gossip. The tongues of the old ladies I served coffee and rolls to in the mornings flapped faster than you ever thought possible. There was simply no way I could avoid hearing them talk about Greg and his runaway wife.

I nodded. No sense lying to him. He obviously knew that people talked about him, so it didn't seem to surprise him that I'd overheard people's conversations about him.

"Pretty sad, huh? We build this amazing life here, and Sophie just up and leaves it without looking back. How does someone leave a little angel like Mandy? I just don't get it," he said, completely defeated. I sat glued to my seat and didn't move a muscle; I didn't know how to react as he completely deflated in front of me. But then he shook his head and sighed. "Sorry. This is too heavy to bring up."

"No, no," I quickly interjected, wanting him to feel comfortable enough to open up to me. I relaxed and gave him a smile, trying to put him at ease. "I said I was here to talk. I'd love to listen…I've been through some pretty tough stuff too, and I know how helpful it is to release it all to someone. Really. It's not a problem."

He smiled, and my heart flopped. "All right. It *does* feel good to talk about it." He collected his thoughts, then really opened up. "I just don't understand it. We were *so* in love when we got married! And then we have this beautiful baby girl…but that's when it all changed. When Mandy was born, Sophie went off the deep end," he explained, completely flabbergasted.

I nodded. We'd all noticed it at church. Sophie never held her baby girl at church. Mandy always stayed in her carrier, or Greg would hold her through the service. Sophie hardly looked at her, let alone touched her. And she always had this empty look in her eyes—she looked dead, completely uninterested in her daughter. It was the strangest thing.

"I don't know what it was. When we were dating, Sophie talked all the time about how much she loved kids and how she wanted a big family. She was *elated* when we found out she was pregnant. I made enough money for her to stay at home when Mandy was born, but from the first week after her birth…I don't know what it was…Sophie changed. I'd come home to find Mandy screaming in her crib. Sometimes Sophie went three or four hours without changing her diaper, and Mandy had the worst diaper rash ever. I'd go in and pick her up…her face would be beet red from crying for hours on end. My heart would break when I'd change her and see that awful rash. It was horrible…I can't even describe it.

"I started worrying that she wasn't even feeding her, but she managed to at least do that, just to get her to stop crying. But it was like she couldn't stand touching her, like it physically hurt her to do so…she'd feed her and immediately put her back in the crib or playpen. I finally told Sophie that I was putting Mandy in day care, even though it broke my heart. I wanted my wife to be the one taking care of her, but she didn't seem capable of doing so. And for a while, things got better. I thought we were gonna be okay, I really did."

I nodded, encouraging him to go on. He let out a sigh but continued, "One night, she never came home. I called and called, but her phone was off. I waited up all night but fell asleep on the couch. When she came home the next morning, she was completely wasted, which was crazy because she's never been a drinker. She'd been at the bar all night, and then she'd driven home! I was furious. She could have killed someone, driving drunk like that.

"We started going to counseling, and again, things got better. She seemed to be doing better not having to care for Mandy during the day, and even though things were tighter because we were paying for day care, we were figuring it out. So we struggled along…until she pulled another all-nighter. I waited up for her to return, but she never did, not the next day or the next. She called me later to tell me she wasn't coming back. When I asked why, she just said this wasn't the way she pictured her life turning out. She wanted more adventure…said I was too boring. I haven't heard from her since…except for the divorce papers she sent me. So that's what I'm dealing with right now—a divorce. After only five years of marriage."

I sat in silence after his long explanation. "I'm so sorry, Greg," I finally whispered. I gently laid my hand on his arm and squeezed. The touch lasted for only a moment, but it still sent a zing up my spine.

"Yeah, me too. I don't know what went wrong. We started dating when I was a sophomore in college, and we never had any big dreams to travel the world or go on any big adventures. We wanted the same things…marriage, kids, a nice house with a fenced in backyard and a vegetable garden. Just a simple life, ya know? Guess she got bored and changed her mind though. I think she's living in Vegas now, doing God knows what. I don't really want to know," he spat, completely disgusted with his wife's life change.

"Yikes. I had no idea," I admitted, surprised. I didn't think the old ladies knew what Sophie was up to now either, though it was just as well that they didn't. Their lips would burn for weeks with that little piece of the story.

He sighed again. "Yeah. It stinks. But what can you do? I've had to move on quickly, for Mandy's sake. I *hate* that she's in day care, but what can I do?" he asked sadly, not really looking for an answer.

I nodded. Delilah felt the same way. She hated that Luke was in day care, but like Greg, she had no choice. If she wanted to pay the bills and put food on the table, she needed to work during the day. She did her best at night with him, but she wanted to do more. It killed her.

"Enough of this heavy stuff. We'll have plenty of time to talk through all this later," he declared with a wave of his hand.

I smiled, because that meant he wanted to spend more time with me talking and getting to know me. We finished up the night discussing the GED. Greg thought it was great that I was finishing school and looking forward to college. I skimmed over the details of why I had never finished high school though because, like he'd just said, we had plenty of time to talk about those things later on.

Greg later walked me to my car in the chilly December air, our breath coming out in friendly, little puffs. Thick clouds hung low in the night sky, and I anticipated waking up to a fresh blanket of snow in the morning. He thanked me for making Mandy's night and for taking the time to listen to him. We shared a brief hug, and then he gently shut my car door. I turned the key, and he waved as the ignition started up, and I waved back as I drove away. I glanced in my rearview mirror to watch him walk back up the driveway, his hands in his pockets. I wondered what was going through his mind.

I knew what was spinning in my mind. I was falling for this man. Butterflies fluttered in my stomach as I thought back to our cozy evening, our first date. Delilah would want all the details, so I made a mental note to call her tomorrow to tell her all about it.

I drifted off to sleep thinking about Greg. Hopefully, my dreams would be filled with his face.

THREE

❊

Molly

JANUARY 2012

"She's a natural ice skater, Greg. Holy cow," I marveled in delight.

Little Mandy was skating circles around me as I clumsily hung onto Greg's gloved hand. It was the first time we'd held hands; not that this really even counted. I wasn't holding his hand—I was clutching it with my entire being. I hadn't been on skates in years, and even back then I'd been horrible at it. I simply didn't have the balance to do it. Or the courage to stretch my legs out and go for it. Nope. I was content to clutch Greg's hand and slowly make my way around the little frozen pond.

Mandy giggled and spun, showing off her skating skills. Greg shrugged. "What can I say? I make talented kids!"

I laughed. Being here with them was so much fun. It felt so natural, like we were really meant to be a family. I knew Greg was just as good a skater as his daughter, but he stuck by my side anyway. But then suddenly, he skated out in front of me and began skating backward.

"What a showoff," I teased.

He raised his eyebrows playfully, then took my hands and began pulling me while he continued skating backward. In his glasses, I could see my reflection, my wavy hair spilling out the bottom of my knit cap and my cheeks flushed from the cold.

I hoped he found me attractive because I certainly found him attractive. Today his chin was sporting the perfect amount of stubble, and he wore a simple brown hat to protect his ears from the cold. His hazel eyes lit up from the excitement of skating backward so fast, and his cheeks were just as flushed as mine. And with that smile of his…it was almost too much for me to handle.

When the three of us could no longer feel our fingers and toes from being out in the freezing January air, we decided to call it a day and head back to Greg's house for hot chocolate. Little Mandy's head drooped on the car ride back, however, and she was soon fast asleep. Greg carried her sleeping form to the couch and settled her in for a nap, popping in *Cinderella* just in case she woke up early. With the volume turned down low, he tiptoed out of the room and joined me in the kitchen just as the kettle began to sing.

A cozy silence settled over us as we sat sipping our steaming mugs of hot chocolate. It's funny how at the beginning of a relationship, I always felt so anxious when silence halted a conversation. But the more I get to know someone, the better I feel about silence. It means that we're comfortable enough with each other, that we don't have to force conversation. We can simply enjoy each other's company.

But as I glanced over at Greg, he didn't seem as okay with the silence as I was. He was fidgety. And he kept swallowing, like he was trying to say something but he wasn't sure how to bring it up.

"Something wrong?" I asked quietly.

He gave me a lopsided smile and shook his head slightly. "Not wrong, exactly. But I do have something to run by you."

"Okay," I said slowly. It's impossible not to feel anxious when someone says something like that. "We need to talk," or "I need to run something by you," are usually followed by bad news. And I didn't want bad news, not now, not when everything seemed to be going so perfectly!

"Well, actually, I need to ask you a favor."

"Sure, anything."

"Will you…watch Mandy for me next Friday night?" he asked sheepishly.

I blinked in surprise. *Why would he need a babysitter? He never has anything to do on the weekends. And lately, he's been spending all his weekends with me. What could he possibly be doing?*

"Of course. May I ask what it is you're doing?" I asked.

He hung his head and sighed. My heart did a little lurch because this clearly was not good news. When he didn't answer right away, I had to bite my tongue from making a cutting comment. I waited for him to speak.

"Don't take this the wrong way, Molly. I've really enjoyed getting to know you, I really have. You're a wonderful woman. But right now, I feel drawn to someone else. And I'd like to take her out on Friday, just to see what happens. I don't want to have feelings for someone else while I pursue you, that wouldn't be fair. So I need to check it out, see if I really do feel something for this woman," he explained.

My head began to swim. *He felt drawn to someone else? How could he feel drawn to someone else when we were falling in love? We were falling in love…right? Or was it only me who was falling? I couldn't be sure. He looked like he really liked me, but then again, we'd been taking things so slowly. We'd never really gone out on a real date. We always hung out at his place with Mandy.*

"Oh," I said simply. "I see."

I took a swig of hot chocolate, but I'd lost my appetite for the sweet drink. Besides, it was lukewarm now and didn't taste as good. I pushed my mug aside and stood to leave.

"I should go." I reached for my coat, but Greg stood up quickly.

"Molly, don't. Please don't. I probably shouldn't have asked you. But you're the only friend I really have…I don't know. I'm sorry."

"Why don't you ask Delilah?" I asked with an edge to my voice.

He shrugged and gave me a weak smile. And that's when it dawned on me. Delilah was the woman he felt drawn to. She was the one he wanted to take out on Friday night to see if his feelings for her were real!

"She's my best friend!" I responded angrily. I felt like a high schooler; this weird twist of events screamed teenage drama. *I fall for a guy, but then he wants to ask out my best friend?*

"I know," he said sheepishly. "I feel bad. But like I said, it's not fair to you if I don't look into this. If the date flops, then I'll know it was just a little crush, and we can see where our relationship goes."

"Oh, I get it. You have a little crush on my best friend, but if things don't work out between you two, you'll just come waltzing back in here and pick up where we left off? You never really gave us a chance, Greg. You never took me out for a real date! Going ice skating with your three-year-old hardly counts!" I responded angrily.

I shoved my arms into my coat, threw my scarf around my neck, and yanked my hat over my ears. "I'll think about babysitting, okay? I'm a little too upset right now to promise that I'll do it."

"Wait!" He grabbed my arm before I stepped out the door. "I haven't asked her yet. So please don't go over there to rant to her about this. Please," he pleaded.

I softened a bit. "Fine." I gave him a halfhearted smile, and he returned it, but the smile never quite reached his eyes. My heart sank. "Good night, Greg," I said softly.

He didn't come after me as I stomped angrily to my car. And when I looked back, I didn't see his face peering out the window after me. So that was it. I knew exactly how he felt about me. I was simply a friend, someone to talk to when the nights got too lonely after putting Mandy to bed, someone to make him laugh and forget about his runaway wife.

I couldn't stop the tears from leaking out my eyes as I drove back to my apartment. I was tired of getting my heart broken, tired of putting myself out there only to end up even more messed up than I already was. Before Greg it had been Tyler, and things had turned sour with him too. Back then, I hadn't been capable of loving him, but still, it hurt when he dumped me. And before Tyler, there was Tanner. That had sort of been my fault too, but he could have tried to stop me from running. He could have shook some sense into me and made me stay. But…well, things simply hadn't turned out that way.

And of course, the start of all this had been Jason. That snake. He'd seen the innocent, naïve, and trusting young girl I'd been—a girl who had wanted to believe in love, who had wanted to change his negative outlook on life and make him laugh and smile again. I'd been the perfect target for his little game. And when I refused to move in the right directions, he'd taken the game into his own hands and forced himself upon me.

Maybe that's why I could never seem to make a relationship last. I was still so broken and damaged from what Jason had done to me. While I wasn't the same broken girl I'd been when I first arrived in Kansas, I was still healing, still trying to figure out who I was after all this happened. Maybe this wasn't the right time to try and make a relationship last. Maybe I just needed to take some time for myself and figure out what I really wanted and needed. I was still young; I had plenty of time to find someone to spend the rest of my life with.

So I decided not to be angry with Greg about this. After letting myself cool down, I could see that he truly did have my best interest in mind. I would be crushed later on if he continued leading me on, only to dump me when I was more attached to him. It was better that he had told me early, before I had begun making plans for us.

I wandered restlessly around my apartment for a bit before I decided to call my mother. I really needed someone to talk to about all the crazy thoughts swimming around in my head. And my mother responded in the perfect way. She knew me well enough to simply listen to me rant about Greg. She never tried to talk sense into me or explain why it was better for Greg to tell me now rather than later. She knew I knew that.

"I'm sorry, sweetie. He sounded like such a nice guy when we talked last week. It would have been wonderful if things could have worked out," she told me.

"Well, if things don't work out with Delilah, he might realize that he likes me," I responded. "It could happen."

"I suppose...but doesn't that feel a little weird to you? He dates you for a month, goes after your best friend, and then comes back to you when it doesn't work out? Honey, do you really want a guy like that? You deserve someone who knows with everything in him that you're the girl for him. A guy who doesn't have to go chasing after someone else to confirm his feelings for you...when the right one finds you, he'll know it, and he'll never want to let you go."

"I had that once," I answered sadly.

"Oh, baby. I know. I wish it could have worked out for you and Tanner. Dad and I always hoped you two would figure out your feelings and end up together. But God had different plans I guess," she said.

"I guess. Still hurts though." I sniffed sadly.

I could picture my mother sitting at the kitchen table with a steaming cup of tea, smiling encouragingly. I wished more than anything that I could be sitting across the table from her discussing this. While I knew that my living in Kansas, away from all the painful memories back in Iowa, was a good thing, I still missed my family like crazy. It was hard being away from home, especially with my baby sister Savannah now being in high school and experiencing all those firsts and with my brother Josh planning a wedding. I called home as often as I could for updates, but I still ended up out of the loop much of the time. I hated that.

We finished up on the phone, and I honestly felt better after talking with my mother. We hadn't always had a good relationship. While I was in high school, my parents' marriage had been so strained that they hadn't even slept in the same bed. To escape all the stress at home, my mom had taken a second job. Because she was out of the house so often, she hadn't been there for most of my high school days, and we simply hadn't had the time to chat about things like boys. I loved that it was different now, but it was ironic that it had taken my running away to draw my parents closer together and to mend our broken relationship. God works in mysterious ways, I supposed.

I resisted the urge to call Delilah during the next few days, but I could tell on Sunday morning that Greg must have asked her. When she saw me, her eyes widened in panic, like she was afraid I was angry at her. I smiled and shook my head.

"Are you okay?" she asked, very concerned.

I laughed. "Of course. He's not the right guy for me. If he was, he wouldn't have to go chasing after you to figure it out. He'd know."

She let out a big puff of breath, relieved.

"So…are you nervous?" I asked excitedly. Delilah hadn't gone out on a date since David, her first high school boyfriend who'd gotten her pregnant.

"For what?" she asked, her brows furrowed in confusion.

"Your date! Silly girl."

"Oh." She responded simply. "I told him no."

"What!" I cried, shocked. "Why?"

"Well, I don't know. I don't have a babysitter," she answered lamely.

"Really?" I asked sarcastically. "And what am I? Chopped liver?" I splayed my hand across my chest.

"Come on, Molly. I can't ask you to babysit while I go out with the guy you have feelings for!" she protested.

"*Had.* Key word: *had*. And Greg didn't have a problem asking me to babysit Mandy while he went out with you. So I might as well," I said with a shrug.

"Seriously? He asked you to babysit Mandy while he took me out? That's kinda weird." She wrinkled her nose, clearly unimpressed.

I laughed again. "Kinda. But he doesn't know or trust many other people here. I'm okay with it. Really. You should go!"

"I don't know…" she answered begrudgingly. "He's a nice guy, he really is. But…he's just not my type." *Excuses, excuses.*

I shook my head. "Yeah, he is. I've spent the last month falling in love with him. Once you crack through his sad shell, there's a treasure hiding underneath. Trust me. He's…amazing." There was no better word for Greg. He really was amazing. "I know you, Delilah. He's exactly the type of guy for you. Give him a chance."

Funny how I had been so upset over Greg asking Delilah out and here I was trying to set them up.

"I don't think so, Molly. Besides, I hate leaving Luke," she whined.

I gave her a face. "He's almost seven, hon. He *likes* when you leave him with me. It's like an adventure."

"Thanks," she replied, feigning hurt. "Nice to know he loves me."

"He loves you! And I love you too! That's why I want you to go out and do something fun for yourself, for once! You deserve some happiness."

"I *am* happy," she assured me. "And I already said no."

I rolled my eyes. "Fine!" I said, giving up. "But you know what? I'm coming over Friday night to hang out. I'm not letting you sit around all mopey. I'll bring supper over. We can dress up all cute…what do you say?"

"I'd love to," she agreed. "It's a date." She grinned mischievously at me.

"Ha, ha, very funny. Now come on. We're gonna be late for the service." I said, pulling her into the sanctuary.

The week flew by, but I still had spare time to hatch up a plan for Friday night. I wasn't going to let my best friend keep thinking that just because she'd gotten pregnant in high school, she was worthless, that she wasn't allowed to fall in love and split her attention between a man and her son. She deserved someone to love her. And she deserved to fall in love, to experience that rush of emotion when she looked at a man, to feel that zing up her spine when she touched him. She deserved to fall asleep dreaming about the what ifs and wake up to find them all coming true. Falling in love is so magical, and I wanted her to experience it for herself, for real this time. She hadn't really loved David, and he'd never loved her. And once Luke came along, she never had time to really fall in love; but Luke was older now. He could handle it if she started dating.

So on Friday night, I pulled on some sweats, threw my hair into a messy ponytail, and headed out the door empty handed. I drove across town to Delilah's place with my heart pounding—she was going to be so angry with me. But she'd get over it. I was doing this for her own good.

I wish I could have had a camera to snap a picture of her face when she opened the door. I watched the shock turn into a scowl as she pulled me in. I laughed, but she just shook her head and swallowed her giggle.

"What are you wearing, Molly? I thought we were having a date?"

"You are," I answered smartly. "But I don't like being the third wheel."

"What do you mean?" she asked, confused.

"Come one. Get Luke, and let's go."

"But—

"No buts. Let's go."

Delilah shut her mouth and whirled around. She packed up Luke and let me drive her all the way to Greg's house. She'd never been there before, but her eyes widened when she peered in the big picture window and saw him wandering around his living room.

"Molly!" She exclaimed. "What are we doing here?"

"Well, Luke and I are going to spend the evening with Mandy, probably watching Disney princess movies. And you…you and Greg are going to go out on your date."

She just looked at me, her eyes as big as saucers. "This is embarrassing. I don't want to do this. You can't make me," she said smugly, settling back into her seat and crossing her arms.

"Suit yourself. Let me just go talk to him. Be right back."

I unbuckled my seatbelt and slipped out the door before Delilah could smack me. I giggled all the way to the front door, delighted at my clever idea. Greg would agree to this; I was positive. He'd be thrilled to see Delilah sitting in my car, all dressed up and ready to go out.

Greg was genuinely surprised to see me. He stepped out on the front porch and gently shut the door behind him. "Are you okay?" he asked, concerned.

"I'm fine." I laughed. "I heard that Delilah said no."

He nodded, surprised at my bluntness. "Yeah…I don't know." His cheeks reddened with embarrassment. Being shot down must have hurt like no other.

I laughed again. "She's a handful all right. And she has a tough past, but she's great, she really is. And if you want this girl, Greg, you're going to have to work for her. Make her believe she's worth loving."

He cocked his head at me, amused. "Wow. I, uh…didn't expect this from you. I don't know what to do…she said no." He shrugged.

"Yeah. But she's sitting out in the car, all dressed up with nowhere to go. Luke's there too…and I'm here. Might as well stay and babysit while you two go out and get to know each other."

Greg broke out into a grin. "You're sneaky." He laughed, waving a finger at me.

I shrugged. "I know. It's fun."

He rubbed his neck and bit his lip. "Well. Guess I better go talk to her, huh?"

"Guess you better," I said with a grin.

I watched as Greg leaned into the car through the driver's window to say something that made Delilah tip her head back and laugh, the sound spilling out into the bitter cold night air. She nodded, and Greg stepped back to celebrate, pumping his first into the air, and then turned to me with a thumbs up, which I returned with a grin.

Ten minutes later, I was sitting on the couch, Mandy on one side of me and Luke on the other. Tonight, we watched *Snow White* while Greg and Delilah went out for dinner. Later I ordered a pizza, entertained the kids, and smiled as their heads began to bob and their lids began to droop. I tucked Mandy into bed after I wrestled her sleeping body into flannel pajamas, then settled Luke into the guest bedroom. I wasn't sure what to do once the kids were sleeping, and I had no idea what time Delilah and Greg planned on returning. So I snooped through his DVD collection and slipped in a movie I'd wanted to see for a long time. I must have fallen asleep though, because I jerked awake when the front door opened. I glanced at my phone—1:45 a.m. Guess the date had gone well.

Delilah was exhausted on the drive back to her place, but a small smile played on her lips as she closed her eyes and rested her head on the seat. I'd get all the details from her later.

In my own bed that night, I warred with my emotions. I was ecstatic that the date had gone so well for the two of them. But my heart also hurt, because Greg hadn't responded to me that way. I wondered if the date had ended with a kiss. I'd never even come close to a kiss. We'd never had any kind of physical contact, except for that one afternoon at the skating rink, and that had been through gloves and only because I needed him to keep me from falling flat on my behind.

I fell asleep remembering what my mom had advised though. Somewhere out there was a guy who when he met me, he'd know without a doubt that I was the one for him. He'd respond to me the same way Greg responded to Delilah. Someday, I'd get to fall in love again, with the right guy. That someday simply was not now, and I would just have to wait for it.

I would be happy for Delilah. She truly deserved it. And I knew that when my someday rolled around, she'd be just as happy for me.

FOUR

❀

Delilah

JANUARY

Even though I was exhausted after my date, I carried my sleeping son into his room and tucked him into his bed. It baffled me that even at his age, almost seven years old, I could still pick him up while he slept, tuck him in, and kiss his cheek all without waking him up. But I knew all too soon that he'd be grown and moments like this would be over forever, so I brushed back his curly hair and stayed by his bed a few moments longer to drink in the picture he made—my little baby, sweet and innocent and protected from the harsh truths of reality for a few more years, dreaming peacefully of puppies and magic and still believing that the world was a good place.

I crept out quietly, painfully aware of the fact that I hadn't been able to fully enjoy his baby years because I'd been so young and stressed out. It had taken me months to even accept the fact that I was pregnant with him. When I first found out, I was more worried about David. I hadn't wanted him to get mad and leave me. When I finally told him, he'd freaked, just like I knew he would.

I gave in and let my mind wander back to that crazy time, back to all the pain and confusion that comes with teenage pregnancy. I couldn't help it. My date with Greg had been beyond amazing, but I worried. Why would an amazing Christian man take any interest in a single mother struggling to pay the bills and care for her son? I was just another statistic, another teenage girl who'd had sex when I wasn't ready and wound up pregnant.

I had been terrified that night with David and all the nights after that first time. My mom had always been so honest about her past, and we'd talked openly about how sex wasn't wrong—that is, if it was done within the boundaries of marriage. My mother had wasted almost two decades of her life living with the father of my two sisters, always wishing that he would marry her and make a commitment to be there for the three of them. But it never happened, and my mom had felt empty and used when he ran off. That's how she'd ended up with me at age thirty-seven. She had a one-night stand with some loser guy because she was feeling so sorry for herself. How mortifying for her, to find herself pregnant when her other two daughters were in high school. So when I was old enough to understand what sex was, she began telling me how important it was to wait until marriage; that sex was more emotional than what the movies portrayed it to be. It was serious, not to be played around with.

I never expected things to get so out of hand that night. David and I had started dating when I was only a freshman, and he was a junior. We'd met at church, so I never worried that he would try to take advantage of me in any way. And that's not what happened that night, not exactly. It was just that his parents trusted us so much and didn't have a problem going to bed and leaving us alone in the house. David's two brothers had already graduated and were living on their own, and his bedroom was in the basement. Usually, we'd hang out upstairs in the living room, watching late night TV and holding hands. Occasionally, we'd start kissing, and then time would really get away from us. For normal teenage girls, their mothers would be up waiting for them to come home; they'd set a curfew and enforce it. But by the time I was fifteen, my mother was fifty-three years old. She was tired.

She didn't want to wait up for me, not after working all week. And she trusted me too. She liked David, and like me, she never imagined that things would get out of hand. She simply told me to remember all of what we'd talked about and to use good judgment. I think she thought that if she trusted me and we kept talking about sex, I'd never do it until I was married. That had backfired on her, big time.

On the night of the homecoming dance, things had played out as usual. We hung out with his parents for a bit, and once they went to bed, we settled on the couch to watch TV. But David soon grew tired of TV and suggested that we go to the basement to watch a movie on the big screen. I agreed quickly; the couches in his basement were big and comfy, and I loved stretching out next to him while watching a movie. But he soon grew tired of that as well, and suddenly we were kissing, the movie all but forgotten. When the movie ended and the screen went dark, David didn't suggest taking me home. I wanted to say something, but at the same time, lying next to him on the couch kissing felt so good, I didn't want to leave. So I kept quiet. Even when things began spinning wildly out of control, I didn't say anything. I didn't protest. While everything was happening, I knew deep down that it was wrong, so wrong, but at the same time, I loved it. I loved being in love. I loved that David loved me and that he was just showing me how he felt. And before I knew it, it was four in the morning, and I woke up in David's bed, our clothes scattered on the floor. The reality of what happened that night didn't hit me until three months later when I finally took a pregnancy test to confirm my suspicion. I was pregnant at fifteen years old. Fifteen.

I didn't tell him right away. I just ignored it and continued seeing him. And since I was already pregnant, I didn't have a problem sleeping with him a few more times. The damage was already done, and for those hours spent in his arms in his bed, I felt really loved. The things he would whisper in my ear made me feel like the prettiest girl in the world, so I thought that maybe I could finally tell him and he wouldn't freak out. Maybe he'd want to marry me.

But oh, was I wrong.

I told him as he held me late one night in his bedroom. I had to. He stroked my hair and whispered, "You know, I've been thinking that maybe we should cool it down a bit. I mean, we're both Christians, you know? It just feels wrong to keep doing this and then going to church on Sunday and Wednesday, pretending we're not doing anything. What do you think?"

I sat up and pulled the sheet up. "David, I need to tell you something."

He cocked his head and squinted at me, waiting for me to say whatever was on my mind.

"I'm pregnant," I blurted.

Even in the dim lighting of his bedroom, I saw all the color drain from his face, and he shot up. "What? Seriously?"

I narrowed my eyes at him. *Why would I lie about something like that? If I wasn't pregnant, he'd know in a few months when there was no baby!* "No, David, just kidding. Ha-ha…good joke, right?" I spat sarcastically.

"Not funny, Lilah. You're sure?" he demanded.

"Yes. I'm serious."

He threw the covers off and began pulling his clothes on, then threw my clothes at me, disgusted. He shoved his feet into his shoes and grabbed his jacket, but I just sat in his bed, staring at him.

"What are you doing? Let's go," he spat coldly.

"Where?" I asked, confused.

"I'm taking you home. I can't believe you let this happen."

My heart clenched inside me, and I began to panic. "Wait… David," I stammered. "You can't believe *I* let this happen? What's that supposed to mean?"

"It means, if we were having sex, you probably should have thought about getting on birth control!" he hissed.

I was feeling vulnerable sitting there in his bed with only a sheet covering me, so I pulled on my clothes before I fought back.

"Hold on. It takes *two* people to have sex, David. What about condoms, huh? If we were having sex, you probably should have thought about getting some condoms!"

"Hey, don't pin this on me, okay? *You're* the one who's pregnant, not me. It's your body, your problem," he said, pointing a finger at me accusingly.

My eyes stung from the tears threatening to spill over. He was blaming this all on me, even though neither of us had taken the necessary precautions to prevent pregnancy. It wasn't all *my* fault…if he was worried about pregnancy, he should have suggested I start birth control or he should have picked up some condoms for himself. Sure, it would have been awkward going into a drugstore to pick them up, but things were about to get a whole lot more awkward in the coming months.

"Come on, Lilah. Let's go. I don't want to deal with this right now."

I sighed and hung my head, but I followed him anyway. I didn't know what else to do. The car ride back was silent as tension hung thick in the air; David tapped one hand nervously on the steering wheel and raked his other hand through his hair. When we pulled up into my driveway, I sat there, unsure what to do. David didn't say anything.

"I'm sorry," I whispered. I thought maybe if I took the blame and apologized, he would stay and help, stay by my side as my belly swelled and my feet disappeared from my view, hold my hand during labor, wiping the sweat from my brow. I leaned in and gave him a kiss on the cheek, but he winced and turned away. I sighed and climbed out of the car, hoping more than anything that he'd stay with me.

I was wrong again. He didn't call me for the entire weekend, and he wasn't at church on Sunday morning. I didn't see him at school on Monday morning either, which was incredible because our school was tiny, and it was next to impossible to go a whole day without seeing everybody at least once. I knew he was there, though, because he was taking really tough classes, and he never wanted to miss a day. It wasn't until Wednesday that I finally saw him walking as fast as he could across the parking lot to his car. My desperation level had reached an all-time high, so I ran to catch up with him and grabbed his arm.

"David!"

He spun around, and his eyes darkened when he saw me. "What do you want, Lilah?" he hissed, angry and defeated. It was like my very presence drained all energy from him, like a little kid slowly letting the air out of the balloon he'd just blown up.

I sniffed and wiped the tears that had slipped onto my cheek. "I just…I'm scared, David. I don't know what to do." The wind whipped my hair into my mouth, and I swiped it away.

He sighed. "Lilah…I can't do this right now. I don't *want* to do this! I'm going to graduate and move away next year. You know I want to go to California. And I'm not going to let anything get in the way of that, okay? So I won't even be here to help you with anything."

I swallowed and nodded. "You don't even…want to see the baby? To meet him or her?" I asked sadly.

He shook his head. "No…I think that would make it harder."

I nodded again. "Okay. Well. I guess…I guess I'll just take care of it. I don't want to slow you down or anything."

And that was that. He didn't give me a good-bye hug, nothing, no apology for ruining my dreams; he'd just made me feel guilty about getting in the way of his. But I still loved him; I thought that maybe if I gave him some space he'd realize that he loved me too and that he wanted to be involved.

No such luck. A month later, he was walking around school holding hands with another girl, making plans to go off to California with her after graduation. I was devastated, and it was then that I felt totally and utterly alone, the weight of what I'd done crashing down on me. When I'd see him in school, he'd look the other way, and I eventually had to stop going to church because I couldn't handle seeing him anymore. Simply the sight of him made my heart drop to my toes and my head spin in panic and desperation. He didn't look sorry at all, not in the least bit. He just looked disgusted that for a moment I had stood in the way of his college dreams.

I was alone. I didn't want to tell my mother. I *couldn't*. She'd done her best to teach me about sex, telling me how special it was and how important it was to wait until marriage. Plus, she was so active in the church, and it would be so embarrassing to have to tell all her Bible study ladies that her fifteen-year-old daughter was pregnant.

So I kept it a secret. At fifteen, it was easy to hide a pregnancy. I could just throw on some sweats, and no one suspected a thing. And I was lucky, I didn't gain much weight, and I didn't suffer through much morning sickness. The only problem was I felt like I was spiraling into a black hole, falling farther and farther away from reality. I felt awful and so alone. David didn't want me, and I couldn't talk to my mom or sisters. I felt guilty and beyond scared; I wasn't ready to be a mom at fifteen. I didn't want to give birth, as I knew it would be painful. And adoption wouldn't happen unless I told my mother, and abortion—well, that was impossible too. I didn't have the money, and even though David didn't want a thing to do with the baby, he would never in a million years take me to a clinic or give me the money for a visit alone.

Eventually, it all became too much for me. I felt so worthless that I gave cutting a try, hoping that it would provide some sort of escape. That was something I never told anyone about, not my mother and not Molly. I don't know why. I'd been so honest with them about everything else. For some reason, I still felt shameful about it. The scars were still visible on my ankle; I could never escape from them. Still. I didn't want people to know that I had once thought that harming myself would solve something.

When cutting stopped making me feel better, when it failed to provide an emotional escape for me, I didn't know what to do or where to turn next. Perhaps I was being a little overdramatic, but one Saturday afternoon, I grabbed my mother's bottle of aspirin and shut myself in my room, ready to down the entire bottle and end this whole nightmare. I poured half the bottle in my hand and fingered the little white pills, knowing that it would be easier for everybody if I was gone, easier for David and easier for my mother. She shouldn't have to worry about me and a new baby at her age. And David would be free to go off to California and start his exciting new life without having to feel guilty that I was sitting at home with his baby.

But then my mother burst into my room with a basket of laundry, which she promptly dropped, and screamed when she saw me holding all those pills. I promised her that I hadn't taken any of them, but she didn't buy it. She made me go to the hospital, where I had to take a urine test. It was then I knew my little charade was over. The test would show that I was pregnant, and my mom would know soon enough.

I sat on an examination table, shaking, and my mother sat in a chair wiping away tears as she tried to distract herself with a magazine. A nurse wandered in later with a perplexed look on her face, and my mother put her magazine down and looked at her expectantly.

"Honey," the nurse said, turning to me. "Do you know that you're pregnant?"

My mom's attention snapped to me, a look of horror on her face.

I nodded, and my mom's breath caught in her throat, and her hand flew to her chest. She allowed herself to freak out for a few moments, but after that initial moment of shock, she was nothing but supportive. We worked through my suicidal thoughts by meeting with Pastor Dennis, and my mom made sure I was eating right, taking prenatal vitamins, and getting plenty of sleep. It was still humiliating, but with the support of my mom, it got easier.

There really was no way to hide who the father was. David and I had been very open about our relationship; we'd held hands in school and had even been caught sneaking kisses the night of the homecoming dance. And I was a good Christian girl, not one to sleep around. People would know that David was the father; it didn't matter that he wanted nothing to do with the baby.

My mom agreed with me to just let David go. It would be a big nightmare to try and make him be involved with a baby he didn't want. He agreed to send money when he could, and he made good on that promise. It hadn't been much in the beginning, but once he was out of college, the checks started getting bigger and bigger. I appreciated that he sent money, I really did. But still…

He hadn't been there for the months when my back ached and my feet swelled. He'd never gotten to put his hand on my belly and feel Luke kick and hiccup. He never came with for any appointments, never got to hear Luke's heartbeat. And he hadn't been there for the birth; it had been just me and my mom welcoming a screaming, healthy baby Luke into the world.

He hadn't been there during the midnight feedings. He never felt the desperation of trying to calm Luke down when he screamed for hours on end; he never had to figure out how to balance being a parent and a student at the same time. My mom did the best she could, but it was still really hard. She was just getting her restaurant up and running right after Luke was born; she spent her entire day there and then was too exhausted to help me with Luke at night. I did it all on my own.

But worst of all, David never, not once, came over to meet Luke. That was enough to break my heart. I didn't care that David hated me and never wanted to see me again. But I *did* care that he seemed to hate Luke, that he never even wanted to meet him—his own son. It was unfathomable to me.

I knew it would be impossible for David not to fall in love with Luke. If he had just stopped over once, I know it would have happened. Luke *looked* like David; he had his dark, curly hair and chocolate brown eyes, eyes that were easy to fall in love with, to get lost in. He had his cute, little dimple that appeared only when he smiled really deeply. And he even had David's quiet demeanor, his ability to sense people's emotions and to always know what to say to reassure and calm people down. I just hoped that as Luke grew and made his own mistakes, he wouldn't treat people the way David had treated me when things didn't go his way. I hoped that he would be more mature and sensitive to people's feelings, to own up to his mistakes and face them head on instead of running away like David had.

I pulled myself out of those soul-sucking thoughts. I couldn't afford to waste time thinking about that dark time in my life. I *hated* that memories of Luke's first year were so negative. But it had been a sad, very difficult time for me. I'd been dumped and left to fend for myself and a baby while at the same time going to school. I'd sat home every weekend while my classmates went out on dates, fell in love, and made memories that I would never have. I spent every dance, including the prom, rocking my infant son to sleep while all the other girls got all dolled up and took pictures with their friends. And I watched every guy pass me by because I had a baby to take care of. No one wanted to date a teenage mother, not in my tiny, little town.

It got easier as Luke got older, but when graduation rolled around, it was bittersweet. My classmates cried at the ceremony, sad to part from the deep friendships they'd made over the years. I wasn't sad. Once I had gotten pregnant, I had no time for friends anymore. The few close friends I'd had at the time stuck with me for a while, but when I continued to turn down invitations to go out with them, they slowly faded away. When you don't spend time with someone and invest in the relationship, it simply dies. And that's what had happened to me. My friendships had slowly died, so I was one of the only girls in my cap and gown with dry eyes on graduation day.

Three months later, I watched all of them leave for college. I stayed home and took care of my three-year-old. My dreams of going off to college shattered once Luke came along—I simply couldn't afford it. It just wasn't fair. In a few years, I knew most of my classmates would start thinking about marriage and kids, doing it in the order that made the most sense—college, marriage, and *then* kids. And I'd still be in Green Lake, a single mother with no college education.

But now—Greg had entered my life. Our date had gone better than I ever dreamed. We clicked right away; he was easy to talk to, and he made me laugh. And he was charming in a way David wasn't; I knew that Greg would never take advantage of me or speak to me the way David had when I told him I was pregnant. He didn't put on masks like David had, simply going to church to play the part but acting like he couldn't care less about God during the week. Greg lived and breathed his faith; I knew it from the way he prayed so genuinely at dinner and from how he looked at me. How he *really* looked at me, honestly interested in what I had to say and listening to each word, keeping silent when I just needed to talk and offering comments only when appropriate.

It was like we were supposed to be together from the very beginning. Greg had moved here after college; he had already been married to Sophie. But if he had gone to my high school, we probably would have dated, gotten married, and started our own family. There would have been no Luke or Mandy. Strange to think about. And it was probably crazy for me to assume this after just one date, but that's just how well it had gone tonight.

It had started out a little awkward, thanks to Molly. I'd originally said no to Greg, feeling slightly unworthy of a great guy like him. I knew he'd done it right with Sophie. They'd dated, gotten engaged and married, and *then* had a baby. I knew Greg had waited until his wedding night to have sex, unlike me. So what that things hadn't worked out with Sophie? It wasn't because he was abusive in any way, it was because she'd had some sort of mental breakdown. He'd done everything right. And I didn't deserve him.

Molly had seen right through me though. She knew that was why I'd turned him down. So she'd taken matters into her own hands, and what I had *thought* was going to be just a nice dinner between me, Luke, and Molly turned into a romantic date with Greg. I'd been a little mad at first and beyond embarrassed, but Greg was cool about it, and by the end of the night, we were laughing at our crazy friend Molly.

I thought back to dinner, how Greg had stirred his soda with a straw and said quietly, "I feel really bad about Molly."

I smiled and nodded. Molly had been through just as much as I had, ten times more, actually. Our stories were only similar because we'd both gotten pregnant in high school. But Molly had gotten pregnant through rape, not from being sexually irresponsible. And she'd gotten an abortion. I couldn't imagine trying to heal from something as traumatic as that, and yet she was doing great. She'd started casually seeing Greg, only to discover that Greg had feelings for me. How awkward for both of them. He'd even asked Molly to babysit while he took me out! Probably not the smartest move, but hey, men sometimes do the stupidest things.

"Molly feels things really deeply…she's probably feeling a little weird about this, especially because she thought things were going so well between the two of you. She's been through a lot, Greg," I explained. "She's still hurting from things that happened in the past few years, still figuring out how to deal with it all."

He sighed. "We, uh, never really got to talk about anything that she went through."

I smiled. "It takes her a long time to trust someone enough to tell them about it. Don't feel bad that she didn't open up to you.

And it's a really tough story to hear. It would have been hard for you to know how to respond."

He nodded, but I could still see that he was struggling with the fact that he'd hurt Molly's feelings by asking me out.

"Hey," I said gently. "Molly may feel things deeply, but she's also very aware of others around her. She could obviously sense that you really wanted to see where things would go between us…why else would she push us together on this date?"

"True," he said slowly, still not convinced. I tried again.

"And you know what else? After all Molly went through, she tries really hard now to listen for God…to watch for his hand in every situation. I honestly think that since she pushed me so hard toward you she truly believes that God is behind all this, that maybe things were never supposed to work out between the two of you because—" I stopped, suddenly embarrassed. I shouldn't be talking so seriously about our future on this, our first date. I could feel my cheeks turning pink.

He looked at me shyly and finished my thought. "Because… *we're* supposed to be together?" he asked.

I nodded.

"So…do *you* think that?" he asked, a small smile spreading across his face. "That we're supposed to be together? That God's behind all this, and Molly was just supposed to, you know, help us realize that?"

I shrugged and tried to contain my smile. "Well, if she didn't feel that way and she actually resented what you did, I don't think she would have tried so hard to get us together. She would have told me what a jerk you are and to stay away."

He cracked into a huge smile. "Well, I'm glad she didn't say that about me."

I giggled. "Me too."

Because if she had, I wouldn't be sitting across from this man with my heart pounding and butterflies fluttering around like crazy in my stomach. And my heart wouldn't be changing one of my mind's most powerful convictions, a conviction I'd been so sure of for my entire life—that it was impossible to fall in love as fast as I was falling in love with Greg.

FIVE

※

Molly

FEBRUARY

The ring was small but elegant, just a simple solitaire diamond on a white gold band. Delilah sat with her hand on her kitchen table, and we both just stared at it. It had been only a month since their first date. Greg didn't want to waste any time, I guessed.

My heart kept doing weird clenches. I wasn't sure how I felt about their whirlwind courtship and engagement. Delilah wasn't either. She'd said yes out of excitement, but now here with me, she was having second thoughts. It was awfully soon to get engaged.

"It's too soon. Right?" she asked, concern shining in her eyes. But a small smile crept onto her face as she moved her hand to watch the diamond catch the light and send sparkles dancing on the wall. Even though she had doubts, she was excited about this, I could tell.

"Oh Lilah...I don't know," I said.

She cocked her head at me and furrowed her brows. "Did... did you just call me Lilah?"

I shrugged. "Yeah. Guess so."

She sighed. "The last person to ever call me that was David," she said, gazing out the window, her mind wandering back to that stressful time in her life.

"Oh," I replied simply.

She nodded. "I went through stages with my name. I don't know what my mother was thinking when she named me Delilah. I don't know one other person that shares my name! I mean, it's a Biblical name, but she's not exactly a positive role model! She's not a hero. She's a villain. And it's a big name for a little girl. So... my sisters shortened it to Lilah, and that's what I went by as a little girl. It's what my teachers and friends called me in school. But when I hit age twelve, I must have thought the nickname was too childish or something...you know how preteens are."

I laughed. "Oh yes. I dealt with that with my little sister. She was a little drama queen, let me tell you."

"Yeah. I was quite the drama queen too. So I had everyone start calling me Delilah again, to try and sound older, more mature. But when David and I started going out, he adopted my old nickname. And I let him because I really liked him. I thought it meant he really liked me too. But after I got pregnant and he left me, I couldn't stand it! I was so angry with him, and when anyone called me Lilah, it just reminded me of him." Her face was getting red; these memories were obviously still very painful for her. I understood completely. Back when I was dealing with the rape and abortion, I stopped listening to music for that very reason. I hadn't wanted to hear those songs later and be brought back to that very painful time in my life. Music has that power, to take you back to specific times in your life. I never wanted to go back to that dark time, so I'd cut it out completely. I guess the nickname had that same power. Simply hearing it brought her back to the painful time of losing a boyfriend due to an unplanned pregnancy.

"Sorry," I whispered. "I had no idea."

She waved her hands, dismissing my apology. "No, it's fine. I'm being silly. I really do like that old nickname. It's easier, and in my opinion, it's prettier. I just...Greg has been calling me that too, and I didn't tell him about David ruining it for me."

"You should," I encouraged. "If you're gonna get married, you need to be able to talk to him about everything. Even the hard things." I cocked my head and squinted at her. "He *does* know the whole story about Luke, right?"

"Of course," she reassured. "He knows everything about my life, and I know his whole story too. That's what we talked about for so long on our first date." She smiled at the memory of that night. She'd fallen in love with Greg that first night, I knew it. She had it written all over her face that entire first week. And from that night on, those two had become inseparable. They spent every spare moment together, falling more and more in love each time they were together.

Some people were just meant to be. When I looked at Delilah and Greg, I knew in my heart that they were just that—simply meant to be. They completed each other, and even though it had only been about a month since they'd started dating, I knew this was supposed to happen. Marriage was absolutely the next step in their relationship. Besides, Luke needed a daddy, and Mandy needed a mommy. When I saw Luke and Greg at church, I could tell that Luke adored him. Besides Albert, he'd never had a strong male figure in his life, and he was just basking in the attention he was receiving from Greg. Luke adored him. And Mandy was the same way with Delilah. Her mommy left when she was so little, and she hadn't been a good one to begin with. So to have Delilah pick her up and snuggle her close, to love her the way she needed to be loved was just what Mandy deserved. She needed a mommy, and Delilah was the best mommy for that little girl. And it was about time that Delilah shared all the love she had in her heart with someone besides her son. I couldn't think of two more worthy recipients than Greg and Mandy.

I reached out and took Delilah's hand in mine. "You're the greatest friend I've ever had, Delilah. I mean that. I couldn't have gotten through the rape and abortion without you encouraging me to return to Jesus. He knew I needed you, so he led me here to help me heal. And I'm so glad we can help each other heal, because if I've learned anything from you, it's that healing is a lifelong process." She smiled at me, tears shining in her eyes. "And we're supposed to keep helping each other maneuver through this crazy thing called life, right?" She nodded. "So let me help you with this decision, okay? You deserve this, honey. You do. I know you think that getting pregnant out of wedlock tainted you in some way. And I can relate to that to some degree. The rape made me feel like the lowest, dirtiest creature on this earth. But we both know that's not true. And it's not true in your situation either. Getting pregnant didn't taint you. You're forgiven, and it's wiped away. You know that, right?"

She nodded, the tears coursing down her cheeks now and splashing onto the table. "I do. Of course I do. But…I don't know. I've spent the last seven years dealing with it alone. Somewhere along the way, I came to the conclusion that my punishment for going outside the boundaries of marriage was raising Lukey alone. I know that's not true, that's just how it ended up. But…I couldn't ever get it out of my head."

"Okay, well, you clearly know that's not true. But again, I can relate. When I found out I was pregnant, I wanted Tanner to slam the door in my face and abandon me. I wanted him to punish me for being such a bad friend. When he didn't…it felt so *wrong*. I felt that I didn't deserve his loyalty. So I ran away and punished myself since Tanner never did it for me. That's what you're doing now, don't you see?" I pleaded.

She squeezed her eyes shut and tried to choke back a sob. "You're right. But…I don't know how to stop. I know I'm forgiven, and I've forgiven myself too. And I know with all my heart that my son is not a punishment. He's the exact opposite…he's the biggest blessing that came out of something so awful. It's just how I am…I did something I know was wrong, so naturally I feel like I deserve punishment, just like you." She gave me a weak smile. "Why do we do this to ourselves, Moll? We both deserve so much after all we've been through."

"We sure do," I agreed, giving her hand a gentle squeeze. "So…do you feel better about your yes now? You deserve this!"

She laughed, the sound of it like music echoing through her little house. "Yes. I really do. Thanks, Molly. What would I do without you?" she asked in an overly sappy voice, holding back a giggle.

"Oh, I don't know," I said with a shrug. "You'd tell that wonderful young man no and then spend the rest of your life punishing yourself for something that's been forgiven for years. So it's a darn good thing you *do* have me," I teased.

We spent the rest of the afternoon gushing about the ring and Greg's sweet proposal. Greg wasn't super outgoing and flashy, but he was definitely a romantic at heart. Delilah was a much better ice skater than I was, so the two had spent many of their dates at the skating rink with the kids. Today he'd brought a thermos of coffee with and given Delilah a special ceramic mug to drink out of. As she and Greg rested on a bench watching the kids chase each other around on their ice skates, Delilah tipped her mug back to finish off her coffee, and that's when she saw it. At the bottom of the white mug he'd had "Will you marry me?" printed on it. When she saw those words, she'd choked on the coffee in her mouth, and Greg had laughed. He then got down on one knee and gave Delilah the beautiful ring that now graced her lovely hand. When the kids saw Greg on one knee, they'd rushed over to join in the fun, laughing and celebrating as a new family. It was an adorable story; I found myself choking back the tears as she told it to me. She was glowing too as she told it. She loved him. She really did, and they made a beautiful couple.

We stood in her doorway later that night locked in a hug, rocking back and forth together. It had been a long, exhausting, incredibly exciting day for her and for me too. Excitement was tiring!

As I drove home that night, I sort of felt like Tanner. Tanner always did the right thing; he was always the good guy, the hero. He was always the calm, cool, and collected one in our friendship. When I freaked out about an assignment at school, he was the one who calmed me down and got me through it. And when my parent's fighting made me want to crawl out of my skin, he was the one who listened to my ranting and never tried to give advice about something he couldn't relate to, having parents who seldom fought about anything. When I started chasing after a boy he disapproved of, he gave his two cents about the relationship, but ultimately, he'd let me make my own decision about it. Granted, it had been the wrong decision and I now wished he'd tried harder to keep me away from Jason. At the time, however, I had appreciated him backing off to let me live my own life. And finally, when I told him I was pregnant, he didn't slam the door in my face. He held me, stroked my hair, and whispered that everything would be okay. He pledged to stand by my side through it all, even though it broke his heart.

That's what I was doing with Delilah and Greg. This was a happy time for them, but it was incredibly hard for me. I loved them both and was ecstatic that they were getting married, but it was hard watching my best friend fall for a guy I had fallen so hard for. Delilah had been through some tough stuff in her life as well but nowhere *near* what I had gone through. *She deserved happiness—but didn't I deserve it too? Why had Greg chosen her over me? Would I ever find a guy like him, someone to spend the rest of my life falling in love with?*

I had to keep trusting that God would lead me down the path that was right for me. Clearly Greg had not been the right way for me—but he was for Delilah. I would be happy for them and keep walking, knowing that God had it all planned for me. I knew after all I'd gone through that his way was the best way, and that whatever I planned for myself was nowhere near as good as what he had in store for me.

I could live with that. And what an exciting next couple of months were in store for me! I would have the honor of planning a wedding for my closest friend. It would be such a joy watching her experience all this happiness—picking out a dress, choosing wedding colors, making a registry. I'd get to plan a shower for her, watch her face glow with all the happiness she so deserved. It would be an amazing next few months.

And when my turn to experience all this happiness rolled around, I knew Delilah would do the same for me.

SIX

❖

Molly

MARCH

I was up to my elbows in lavender ribbon when I absolutely couldn't take it anymore. When I told Delilah I would help her with her wedding decorations, this really wasn't what I had in mind. This morning she'd shown up at my apartment while I was still in my pajamas and bathrobe to hand me a box full of wedding favors she wanted me to construct. She smiled sheepishly and shrugged. Behind her, Luke was pulling at her sleeve and hacking his lungs up at the same time.

"They won't let me bring him to day care until after a doctor visit. And the firm is dealing with a big case right now, and I really can't afford to miss work to take him in. But I have no choice, and he has a big school project due in a few days that we have to work on tonight, plus a spring concert for the school on Friday night. I'm totally swamped! I was supposed to have these done two weeks ago...but I just haven't had the time. Please?" She looked at me with her big brown eyes, and I caved. I rolled my eyes and grabbed the box.

"You're the best!" she gushed.

"I know. Now go live your busy life. I'll look at of the ones you finished already for direction, but I think you explained it to me well enough I could probably do it blindfolded."

My job was to fill these little baggies with a few Hershey's Hugs and Kisses candies, then tie them shut with a thin lavender ribbon. Once that was done, I nestled them into little boxes and tied them up with another thicker lavender ribbon, complete with a big, fluffy bow. Finally, I was to attach a little sign that read "Hugs and Kisses from the New Mr. and Mrs." But the boxes were so little and the bows so big…it was frustratingly long work. Each one took over five minutes because I had to keep redoing them over and over again. That's what being a perfectionist got me though. I wanted each one to look amazing, but that was taking forever.

So about an hour and a half into making the boxes, I threw my scissors down in defeat, at least for the moment. I needed to take a little break and come back with a better attitude. As the maid of honor, I was delighted to help the glowing bride-to-be, but it was still frustrating work that I needed a tiny break from. I'd only completed about 15 of 130 boxes.

I decided to take a visit to my favorite coffee shop with my laptop to do some schoolwork. Earning my GED was taking a bit longer than I anticipated. But hopefully I could complete the online preparation course and take my test before this summer so I could register for classes at the community college near Green Lake. It was probably for the best that things hadn't worked out for me and Greg. My dream was to go to school and major in psychology so that one day I could help other victims of sexual abuse work through the pain and confusion. A relationship would have slowed me down big time.

A large mocha calmed my nerves almost immediately. I settled into my favorite booth in the corner of the shop, away from all the hustle and bustle of the front counter and coffee bar. That's where most of the teenagers hung out after school, sipping frappes and gossiping. I much preferred a booth to the coffee bar.

I pulled out my laptop but got distracted by my Facebook page. I really needed to set my homepage to something other than

Facebook, but I had a friend request, so I ignored that annoying voice of reason in my head that told me to log out. I'd just check it out and then get to work.

But even the best of plans don't work out at times. One click of the mouse over the friend request made my heart drop all the way to my toes. Never in a million years would I have believed that Tyler Sanderson would add me as a friend on Facebook— Tyler, the boy I'd dated in Minneapolis during the darkest days of my life, the boy who'd been so sweet and kind, who would have done anything for me, the boy who dumped me when he finally realized that I was incapable of loving him back the way he so desperately loved me.

Are you sure it's the same guy? I asked myself. But one click on his name confirmed it for me. It was him all right. Tyler Sanderson…and he wanted to be friends with me on Facebook. *Why?*

Our breakup had been ugly and painful. We'd had a big fight, and I walked home from his apartment. He didn't even argue with me when I told him I'd walk—he just let me go, not that I had expected him to. Tyler had put up with so much crap during our relationship. I was actually relieved when he finally broke up with me, because I knew he deserved so much more than I was able to give him. The last time I saw him was in the alley behind the diner I worked at. He'd given me the photograph of me he'd taken and framed for the art wall in his apartment. Guess he didn't want the reminder of our failed relationship on the wall he walked past every single day of his life. He'd wanted so much more for us than I did. He wanted marriage and kids, a commitment that I simply wasn't ready to make. And I wasn't willing to change either. I had been stuck in some weird life-sucking hole back then, unable to move forward or make positive decisions for myself. It had all been about running away back then.

So why, after such an ugly, not to mention extremely awkward, breakup did Tyler want to have any kind of contact with me? If the tables were turned, I would never waste my time seeking out someone who took so much from me without giving anything in return. Never in a million years.

Tyler's security settings were pretty tight, so I couldn't see much of his personal information, but his profile picture was only of himself. I assumed there was no girlfriend, fiancée, or wife in his life right now. I knew this because Tyler was the sort of guy who wanted to show off his girlfriends. He hated it that I would never hang out with his friends, that I never even let him introduce me to them. He *really* hated it that I never let him introduce me to his family. So if he had a woman in his life right now, it would be on Facebook. I was 99 percent sure he was single right now. Not that it really mattered, I guessed. We were over; there was no hope of us ever getting back together.

The only puzzling thing I found was under his "About Me" section. The only piece of information he let nonfriends see was his religious views. And to my complete and utter shock, I saw that he had "Christian" listed as his religious belief. When we had been dating, he never said anything about being a Christian. We'd slept together quite often, so I simply assumed he wasn't. Most devoted Christians stay away from premarital sex. I'd spent the night on many a Saturday night back then, and he never mentioned anything about missing church.

Interesting, I thought. Maybe he'd had a big change of heart, and out of guilt, he wanted to make things right with me. I figured there was no harm accepting his friend request. He'd message me if he wanted to talk about what had happened between us. If not, we'd be Facebook friends and nothing more.

Still, I struggled to get Tyler out of my mind the rest of the afternoon. I sipped my coffee and tried to focus on my schoolwork, but my mind kept wandering back to all the happy times I'd had with Tyler. Our meeting had been like something out of a movie. I had been out for a walk trying to waste time before going into the abortion clinic when it had begun to downpour.

I ran to a picnic shelter to hide, and Tyler had done the same. Being the incredibly social and outgoing guy that he is, he struck up a conversation and began flirting with me. He ended up walking me home, but he never asked for my number. A few months later in May, he came into the diner and recognized me, then surprised me by returning at the end of my shift to take me out on a date.

That first date spot became a regular hangout for us. I loved that coffee house, where they always had some kind of live music playing and the lights dimmed to create this amazing atmosphere—one that was hard to explain. I felt so at peace there. Calm. But I never went there again after the breakup. It would have felt so wrong to go there without him.

There had been plenty of happy times for us during the time we'd dated. Tyler was fun; he made me laugh. And we *did* have fun together, exploring the city, going to art museums, and taking picnics. If I had figured out how to deal with everything back then, we would have made a great couple. But of course I'd ruined that too. Like always.

When my coffee grew cold and my head was about to explode from trying to focus on studying and sorting through my feelings about Tyler, I packed up and headed home. I had 115 more wedding favor boxes to get done anyway. No sense wasting time thinking about past love affairs when there was so much stuff I needed to get done now. There would be time to sort through all that later. Right now, it was all about Greg and Delilah and their April 14 wedding. So much to do in so little time.

⁓

"Oh, Molly…you look gorgeous! I love that dress on you…I *knew* we made the right choice with this style." Her eyes were shining with unshed tears and her lips were quivering. Delilah had been so emotional lately; it was slightly amusing. Usually, Delilah was the one laughing at all my drama and pulling me back down to earth.

The dress hit me right below the knees; it was fun and swishy and beautiful. It was lavender of course, and one shoulder was embellished with three little roses right where the shoulder met the top of the dress. It was something I could probably wear again, and it hadn't broken my pocketbook. Delilah had been very considerate of that when we shopped for dresses in February.

"We definitely made the right choice," I reassured. "And your sisters will love it too."

"I hope so," she mused. "I *hated* the bridesmaid's dresses at Hannah's wedding. But I never said anything," she said, locking her lips with an imaginary key. "I just put it on and smiled the whole day. Well, I don't want that to happen at *my* wedding. I want them to love this dress!"

"And they will," I replied. I gave her a little spin to send the dress flying, and she giggled. Planning this wedding was the best thing to ever happen to Delilah. She was transforming right before my eyes.

She'd always been so confident in herself, so committed to healing from her painful past and moving forward so that Luke could have a good life. But after hours of listening to her pour out her heart to me over coffee, I also knew that she always felt like less of a Christian after getting pregnant. She felt undeserving of the kind of love that Greg was giving her now. So since I'd ended up here, we'd been helping each other deal with these deep issues. Normally, it felt like she helped me more than I helped her, but lately, the tables had turned, and I felt like I was the one reassuring her, trying desperately to get her to see that getting married was the right thing to do, that she deserved Greg, and that he was lucky to have a woman like her.

With my reassurance, wedding planning became her life. I'd never seen her more excited about something in all the time I'd known her. She went out and bought a stack of wedding magazines and began searching for the perfect gown, which she'd found in this little shop a few towns over from Green Lake. It was a gorgeous charmeuse dress—a lightweight, satin gown with a lace keyhole back. The lace cap sleeves added just the right amount of coverage, which Delilah loved. She wasn't comfortable showing off a ton of skin. Being a mom, she wanted her dress to be very modest. This dress was definitely modest but still very young and pretty, perfect for my gorgeous best friend. A lovely sweep train completed the dress, and when Delilah put it on the first time, we both immediately knew it was the one. No question.

"Put yours on now," I urged. "I can't wait to see it with the alterations finished."

"Okay," she squealed, her face lit up and her eyes sparkling. I just shook my head. She was so adorable.

"No peeking," she reminded me for the eighth time from the dressing room. "I've almost got it all zipped up."

"Are you sure you don't need my help?" I asked, choking back a giggle.

"No! I don't want you to see it until I'm standing right in front of you. For the full effect, you know."

"Oh of course," I teased.

"Okay, close your eyes! I'm gonna come out now!"

I shook my head and closed my eyes. "Okay. Open up," she said breathlessly.

My own breath caught in my throat when I took in the finished dress for the first time. It fit her like a glove, totally showing off her amazing figure without going too over the top. It was stunning, simply stunning.

"Oh, Lilah. He's not gonna be able to hold back the tears when you come walking down that aisle. And I mean that. You look…I can't even think of a word to describe you in this dress."

Delilah let the tears spill onto her cheeks. "Thank you," she whispered. "That means a lot, Molly."

I stood up to give her a hug. "I mean every word, honey. He's a lucky guy."

She laughed. "Enough of this heavy stuff and crying. This is supposed to be a happy time!"

"You're right," I agreed. "Let's get this dress bagged up and back to your house."

On the drive back to Green Lake, I shared with Delilah my shock of finding Tyler's friend request on Facebook. She squinted and wrinkled her nose, clearly unimpressed with him. From the way I'd described him to her, it made sense. He wasn't a bad guy, and most of the problems with that relationship had been my fault. Still, it hurt that he had refused to give me the space I needed to figure out everything I was going through. And the fact that he pressured me into sleeping with him, well, that hadn't won him any points with Delilah either.

"It's weird though because the only thing I could see on his profile before we became friends is that he's a Christian," I told her.

"Really?" she asked, just as surprised as I had been. "Was he a Christian when you dated him?"

"I have no clue," I said, shrugging. "I assumed he wasn't. He never talked about church, and he never made it a priority to go on Sunday mornings. And I never told him that I was a Christian either. I honestly have no idea."

"Weird. Wonder why he searched for you after all this time," she said with concern dripping from her voice. Since I had moved back to Kansas to stay, Delilah was fiercely protective of me and clearly didn't like the possibility of Tyler reentering my life and hurting me again.

"I know! When I saw it for the first time, I was convinced it had to be a different person. But it's him."

Conversation stalled as we both processed the news of Tyler's sudden return into my life. When we finally made it to town Delilah dropped her dress off at her house, picked up Luke from

Greg's, and then we headed back to my place to work on the favors for a few hours. I'd been working on them every spare chance I got, and once I got the hang of it, I could pound them out in no time. We only had about fifty more to finish—a major accomplishment in my book.

Thoughts of Tyler lingered in my mind long after Delilah and Luke headed out. I logged back into Facebook to check out his profile again, struck at how different he looked from when I saw him last. There was something about his eyes. I squinted hard and brought my face close to the screen for a better look. Definitely his eyes; they absolutely shone with the inner light that only comes from a relationship with Christ. There was no question about it. Tyler was a changed man, a man who had found Christ.

A knock at the door startled me out of those thoughts, but I welcomed the distraction. *So what that he had added me as a friend?* It probably meant nothing, and I needed to just forget about it. Still. I couldn't get those eyes out of my mind, couldn't get over how different he seemed.

But as I opened the door, suddenly it became a lot harder to convince myself that he was a changed man because the eyes looking back at me from the other side belonged to none other than Tyler himself.

SEVEN

❖

Molly

MARCH

I stood there with my mouth hanging open for what seemed like an eternity. I swallowed a few times although it was difficult because one look at Tyler had dried up all traces of saliva in my mouth. Slowly I brought my hands up to my face and covered my mouth, shaking my head. "What are you doing here, Tyler? How did you find me?" I whispered, now shaking.

He gave me his signature lopsided grin. That was just the type of person he was. Even though he'd almost made me faint by suddenly showing up at my apartment unannounced after two and a half years of no contact, he couldn't help grinning. "I had to find you," he explained softly. "I hate how we left things. It doesn't feel right."

I let my head fall back and huffed. I didn't know what to say, so I stayed silent.

He sighed. "Look, Molly. I know this is awkward. I'm sorry. But will you let me come in please so we can talk? So much has happened since we broke up. Please?"

My head was telling me no, absolutely not. I'd gotten my heart broken from him before. No matter how many issues I'd brought to our relationship, the breakup hadn't been all my fault. And even though I'd forgiven him long ago for the pain he caused me, those feelings hadn't just disappeared. And I was alone here. It was never a good idea to invite someone in without being sure of their intentions.

My heart battled back just as strongly. In all the time I dated Tyler, I never once feared that his intentions were dangerous or untrustworthy. Even from that first day, I never questioned it. If I had, I wouldn't have let him walk me to Melissa's apartment. I had no reason to fear inviting him in and hearing him out, plus I couldn't resist his sincere eyes, eyes that no matter what had happened between us I still trusted. So I let him in, much to his surprise. His eyes widened in shock, but he rewarded me with another signature grin.

"Nice place," he commented, trying to make small talk. I knew my little apartment was nothing special, and I felt heat creep up my neck and into my cheeks. But it was very affordable, and the neighbors were friendly. It got the job done.

"Thanks," I said, trying not to make him feel bad for complimenting my simple home and battling the desire to stick up for my little place. Tyler's apartment in the Cities was breathtaking, something straight out of a movie. The old historic building had been converted to an apartment, and it was chocked full of charm. Combine that with Tyler's natural artistic flair, and the place was stunning. I always loved spending time over there. It had made me feel less cheap.

"Uh, would you like something to drink?" I stammered. "Tea, coffee…hot chocolate?"

"Tea would be great," he said absentmindedly, still sweeping the place over with eyes that couldn't help but criticize. *Artist's eyes.*

I nodded and busied myself with the kettle, which took all of two minutes. Tyler had already made himself at home at my kitchen table, but I just continued standing awkwardly by the stove, waiting for the kettle to start singing. He tapped his fingers on the tabletop and was still, much to my chagrin, scrutinizing every single detail of my place. Suddenly, I wished more than anything that I had taken even a little bit of time to decorate more. I wanted to break into his thoughts and defend my choice of apartment, but I bit my tongue. I didn't have to explain anything to him. I had nothing to hide, nothing to be ashamed of. This is the type of place I could afford, and it was nice. Nothing fancy, but I wasn't that type of person.

I was relieved when the water finally began to boil. I pulled out two mismatched mugs from the cupboard and grabbed my box of tea and a bottle of honey. As I poured the steaming water into our mugs, Tyler began sifting through the box of tea, searching for a flavor.

When we both had our tea bags nestled into our mugs, the silence really got awkward. As a dating couple, silence had never been awkward. We had been so comfortable with each other that we didn't feel the need to fill the silence with useless chatter. But things were different now. We weren't a dating couple, and the silence was suffocating. I cleared my throat, encouraging him to say whatever it was he came here to say.

He smiled at me. "So how have you been, Molly?"

I cocked my head at him and frowned. "Tyler…I don't want to waste time on small talk. What are you doing here?" I asked bluntly.

Tyler laughed. "I've always loved your spunk, Molly. You're not afraid to say what you're really feeling. I love that."

I shrugged. "I like to be real. So let's not beat around the bush here. It was a big enough shock to see a friend request from you on Facebook. And then you show up on my doorstep a week later? What's that about, Tyler?" I tried to keep my voice from rising, but I was getting worked up.

He put up a hand as a signal to stop and calm down. I took a deep breath, and he explained. "All right. Here's the truth. After we broke up…something changed in me. I never ever felt normal after that…it was like a part of me was missing, but no matter what I did and no matter who I spent time with, I couldn't fill that hole. I've been in and out of four relationships since we broke up…four! And normally I don't date around. I don't like dating just to date, you know that. I want a commitment. So it was weird…I don't know why I did it."

He took a deep breath and continued, "After I broke up with the fourth girl, I went to drown my sorrows in our little coffee shop." His eyes softened. "You know, I never took any of the girls I dated to our spot, Molly. Didn't feel right."

I couldn't help but smile. He was sweet, he really was. I felt my heart clench, because even though our relationship had been rocky, he was an amazing guy. I'd lost something great when we broke up. And that hurt, even after all this time.

"Anyway, I went there that night, and there was this guy sitting at a table all by himself. He stuck out like a sore thumb, the poor guy. He was wearing blue jeans, a T-shirt, and tennis shoes. And you know how the people who normally go there dress…not like that! You gotta be hip to hang at that place, and this guy… whew. He was far from hip.

"I wondered what he was doing there all alone, but I didn't think much more about it—that is, until he plopped down at my table."

I giggled, deciding to let my guard down. "Who was he?"

"A pastor!" Tyler exclaimed.

I laughed and thought back to my youth pastor at my church in Oak Ridge. He was just like the guy Tyler had described. He was in his forties, he was losing his hair, and he was always dressed in out-of-style jeans and tennis shoes. But with a wife and five kids to take care of on a preacher's salary, it was the best he could do. And he was one of those guys who were so hopelessly in love with Jesus that he really didn't give a second thought about what he looked like. It was probably the case with the pastor Tyler had met.

"I couldn't believe the nerve of this guy. He just plops down and starts blabbering away, talking about Jesus, and the whole time I'm thinking, 'When's this guy gonna leave?' But then he invited me to his new church. He was just starting a church plant in my neighborhood, and for some reason…I said yes," he admitted with a shrug.

I sat back, startled. *Maybe his Facebook information really was accurate. Could he have become a Christian?*

"So I went. I sat in the back, feeling really out of place. I went to church as a kid, but I stopped going in middle school when my parents stopped going. My church as a kid had been so stuffy and boring, so I had this really bad attitude about church. But this place…man. It was incredible. They meet in one of the old buildings in the neighborhood, and it looks like an art gallery in there. The walls are painted black, the lights are always dimmed. There are no pews, just these really cool vintage-looking chairs. And they have a band! For someone who grew up with organ music and church choirs, that was a shocker."

"I bet," I said, intrigued. I leaned forward and took a sip of tea, encouraging him to continue.

"I was going to slip away after the sermon was over, but just as I was halfway through the door, the pastor caught me and invited me to lunch with his family. And I said yes…I have no idea why! Normally, I would make up some excuse, but…I don't know. For some reason, I felt compelled to talk with him."

"What did you say his name was?" I asked.

"Jeff. Pastor Jeff. And man, he is just amazing. He and his wife adopted two little girls from China, Annabelle and Claire. Cutest little things I ever saw. His wife, Julie, is incredible too. She stays at home with the kids and writes for a women's magazine. I've never seen a more determined woman than Julie. She has a degree in social work, and on Saturday mornings, she volunteers at a Children's Home, talking with kids whose parents have died or abandoned them. She loves those kids, Molly, absolutely loves them. Sometimes she brings them cookies or brownies, and you should see the looks on their faces. They never get treats."

I could already sense that the shelter was special to him from the way he talked about it and how his eyes got this weird, faraway look. "Did you ever go with her?" I asked softly.

"Yeah. Actually, I started volunteering with her, and I'm there all the time now. It changed my life, Molly. Those kids are amazing. Even in their bleak situations, they have such joy. And they love with no regrets. They love each other, and they love the volunteers. It's a remarkable place, filled with remarkable people. And that's where I met Christ," he said, a grin stretching across his face.

"Tell me about that, Tyler," I said softly.

"Well, I'd been going to the home for a few months with Julie, and I was falling in love with this little girl. Her name is Genevieve, such a big name for such a little girl. I nicknamed her Jenny, and at first, every time I called her that, she'd correct me. Eventually she gave up and just adopted the nickname. She still pretends to resent it, but from her smile, I know she loves it."

"She sounds sweet," I said. "How old is she?"

"Four. Gosh she's cute. Her parents were killed in a car accident while she was at her grandparents for a weekend visit. She was only three when it happened. When I first started coming, sometimes she would start crying, telling me she couldn't remember what her mommy and daddy looked like anymore. She has a few pictures of them…but it's not the same, you know?" he said sadly. "She couldn't picture them in her head anymore at night, and it broke her heart. And it broke my heart too. I got so angry with God for doing all these awful things to such a sweet little girl…I told her that one day—that I was angry at God. And she got so mad at me.

"So then she took her chubby, little hands and put them on my cheeks. She told me that Jesus never does things to hurt us. That bad things happen to us because the world isn't good. It's not the way God wanted the world to be, and because we all sin so much, bad things just happen. But I didn't like that answer. And I was shocked that she was talking like that, that she was accepting her parents' death because the world is full of sin. I know the world's a bad place, but she's just a little girl! It shouldn't have happened to her.

"But she insisted. Every time I tried to argue with her, she'd put her little hands on my face and explain that bad things happen to good people because of sin. It was just so hard for me to grasp..."

I nodded, thinking back to my own experiences. I'd been a Christian all my life, and yet some of the worst things a person could go through had happened to me. It wasn't fair; I agreed with Tyler. But I also agreed with little Jenny. The world is a bad, dark place simply because of sin. It truly is the devil's playground, but all Christians have the hope of a renewed world when Christ returns. Little Jenny seemed to understand this even at her young age. Seems like it's always easier for little ones to embrace the tough teachings of Christianity. It had been that way with Luke last year. He had been the one to teach me that trusting God and not running away was the right path for me. He'd encouraged me to return to Jesus.

"One day it finally sunk in," he continued. "God wasn't punishing her by killing her parents, like I thought she was trying to tell me. They didn't die because of any sin *she* committed. They died because the *world* is full of sin...and bad things happen in a world filled with sin. Jeff preached a sermon about it one week...and I started crying right in the middle of that church. It finally clicked.

"He lets bad things happen not because he doesn't care or because he is punishing us. I know now that the punishment for sin is death and eternal separation from Christ. But Jenny's hope comes from her faith. She knows she will be reunited with them when Christ returns."

I nodded, tears forming in my eyes. This is always a hard subject for nonbelievers to grasp. It's hard to come to grips with the fact that bad things happen to good people. Too often we think that God punishes us for our shortcomings. But I don't believe that. Yes, we have to deal with the consequences of sinning. But the ultimate punishment for sin is eternal separation from God. God doesn't keep punishing us each time we sin. We simply deal with the consequences. Jenny's parents hadn't died because she committed some sin. She was only four years old, for goodness sake! They had died simply because the world is dark and full of sin.

I didn't even know this girl, and my heart broke for her. But I was every bit as proud of her as Tyler was. Stories like this really tug at my heartstrings, because I had wrestled with some of the exact some emotions. I too often wondered why God had let awful things happen to me. It doesn't seem fair, and it sure isn't fun. But oftentimes we must pass through the fire to come out stronger and purer than before. Sometimes it takes a tragedy to snap us out of our doubt and pull us closer to Christ. That's how it had happened for me. From a different perspective, a tragedy can turn into a blessing after you see how the difficulty made you stronger. Granted, it's hard to say that to a four-year-old who's lost her parents…but who knows? Perhaps one day she'll look back on her life and realize that her experience drew her closer to God and made her a stronger Christian. God works in mysterious ways, after all. I knew that all too well.

I refocused on Tyler because he was gearing up to continue with his story. "Jeff saw me crying like a baby during the sermon, and we went for a walk after church was over. I poured my heart out to him…told him everything. I told him about you, how I loved you and how heartbroken I'd been since we broke up."

Tears began slipping down my cheeks as Tyler went on. "I told him about all the girls I had dated, trying to fill the hole I thought you'd left me with. But as I told him about Jenny and her faith, I realized the hole wasn't from you. It was from the absence of God. My whole life I'd been missing him. And the hole had grown and grown…when you left, I really felt it for the first time. That's why I thought it was your fault. But…it wasn't your fault. I just needed God…so badly.

"When I said it out loud for the first time, I stopped in my tracks and told Jeff I needed Jesus. He laughed and hugged me right in the middle of downtown Minneapolis, so happy I had finally realized this. We prayed right there on a dirty, little bench. I told Jesus I needed him. And I've never been the same Molly."

I sat back in shock. "Wow. That's awesome."

His smile stretched from ear to ear, and his eyes definitely shown with the love that only comes from Christ. There's nothing quite like the first few months of knowing Christ, being so deeply in love with him and soaking up his Word and every sermon so eagerly. I hoped Tyler's zeal never diminished, like it had with me during my three-year journey into the wilderness.

"I know. I feel…like a whole new person, Molly. But finding Christ didn't take you out of my mind. In fact, once I became a Christian, I had this deep need to find you again and make things right."

He leaned forward and took my hands in his, sending my heart pounding. He said so sincerely and tenderly, "I didn't treat you the way I should have, Molly. I asked way too much of you, and I didn't give you enough in return."

I shook my head. "That's not true," I said, choking on a sob. "I didn't give enough either. I just expected you to help me forget about all my junk. That's all I was after, Ty. I was selfish."

He smiled softly and began tracing circles on my hand with his thumb. "That may be true, but I knew something was wrong. I didn't ask about what happened to you because I wasn't sure I could handle it. I thought it would be easier to just be left in the dark. But the longer our relationship went on, the more frustrated I got when you *wouldn't* let me in. So I figured I needed to try harder to break you open, to make you let me into your world. But…you never would."

"I'm sorry," I whispered, ashamed.

"No, no," he soothed, squeezing my fingers gently. "I didn't handle it right. I would just get angry when you closed up. I should have tried harder to help you, Molly. I'm sorry about that. Whatever you went through, I know it was deep. I could see it in your eyes, but I didn't try as hard as I should have to pull you out of whatever darkness you were in."

Tyler had obviously come here for closure. He wanted my forgiveness. So I offered him the best smile I could muster and told him, "I forgive you."

He let out a sigh that was more laugh than sigh. "You have no idea what your forgiveness means to me, Molly. I've lived with this guilt for so long. That's why I came here. I'm sorry that it freaked you out...but once you accepted my friend request, I knew God was telling me it was time to find you. You'd be surprised how easy it is to find people on the Internet!" he said with a smirk, and I just shook my head at him. He was so silly.

I took a deep breath and said, "I have plenty of my own guilt about what happened between us too. And since you were so honest with me, I'm going to do the same for you. It's time I told you about my past, Tyler. I never quite trusted you with it before, but now, after you've found Christ, I feel that it's right. So...let me tell you my story."

It's always hard to watch people's faces when I share my story. No matter how many times I tell it, it's always incredibly hard to say out loud that I was raped. The shame never quite leaves, even though I know it wasn't my fault. But that's just how it is. The wound may have healed, but the scar would be there forever, a constant reminder that it had happened to me. No amount of time could change that. I simply had to keep working at it, keep believing that Christ was bigger than anything that ever happened to me.

It was no different with Tyler. His face contorted in pain when I told him I was raped, and his eyes grew watery with unshed tears. His lips quivered as he worked to keep the tears from spilling onto his cheeks. I went on to tell him about my misunderstanding with Tanner and my first runaway. I told him about meeting Melissa and starting at the diner. I told him that the day we first met, I had later gone into an abortion clinic to set up an appointment.

And that's where it all clicked for him. He finally understood why it had been so hard for me to love him the way he wanted me to love him. I really hadn't been able to. Not then anyway. My heart was incapable of love back then.

"I knew you needed more from me. But I couldn't give you more," I explained. "I know that it was wrong of me to stay with you and expect you to keep loving me, but you were the only good thing in my life during that dark time. You made me forget about the rape and the abortion, if only for a bit. I couldn't escape from those things at night, when nightmares plagued me every single time I closed my eyes. But when I was with you…I could forget."

"I never understood, Molly. I couldn't figure out why you wouldn't let me in. It makes sense now," he said tenderly.

"Yeah. So if it makes you feel better, I probably wouldn't have opened up even if you'd tried harder to help me. It would have only pushed me away faster. I had a hole too, Tyler, a hole that also needed to be filled with Jesus. I was a Christian during that time, but I was a runaway Christian. I was angry at God…I didn't want anything to do with him. But that all changed when I moved to Kansas," I said with a smile. I loved this part of the story.

I went on to tell him about my second runaway after my fight with Melissa and about the early days in Green Lake, about meeting Mary Beth, Delilah, Albert, and Luke. He smiled as I told him about that Easter Sunday that had changed it all for me. And I told him about that rainy night in the little rental house… the night I had returned to Jesus…finally.

We sat in silence as the weight of both our stories settled in around us. So much had happened to both of us, so much pain, so much darkness. But in the end, both of us had found the true light—Jesus Christ. We sat across from each other not as past lovers but as brother and sister in Christ. What had once been a broken and sinful relationship was now pure and full of Christ, a beautiful relationship at last.

I sighed. "So what do we do with all this, Tyler? Where do we go from here?"

He rubbed his neck. "I'm done with school now. I've been doing pretty well getting my name out in the community…doing family photo shoots, a few weddings, stuff like that. I like taking pictures of people, getting a glimpse into their lives for a few hours. But I also love taking still shots…you know, landscape pictures and whatnot. I'd love to get into some galleries."

I cocked my head at him, confused. "I'm not so sure where you're going with this."

He gave me his lopsided grin. "What I mean is…I could pretty much work from anywhere. I mean, it's beautiful out here. Living in the Cities, I don't have the opportunity to take pictures of rolling fields and wide open skies. I'd have to go home to do that, and it's still pretty intense with my family. So…what I mean is…I wouldn't be hesitant about moving here."

I chewed my lip, contemplating the possibility of starting over with Tyler. Things obviously hadn't worked out with Greg, and Tyler was a Christian now. An awesome guy who must still have some sort of feelings for me if he was willing to pick up and leave the Cities to move out to boring, old Kansas.

I decided to be honest with Tyler, like I'd never been before. I wasn't sure if I was ready for this. After getting my heart broken as many times as I had, I was a little more than hesitant to invite Tyler back into my world.

"I don't know, Tyler. I'm…I'm scared. I've put myself out there so many times, and it hasn't ever turned out well for me. And I just went through such a hard time…my heart is still healing. I still don't know if I'm ready to love for real."

He leaned forward, a touch of mischief sparkling in his eyes. "Tell you what. I'll wait a few months before I decide anything, before *we* decide anything. And in the meantime, I'm going to treat you like I should have treated you while we were together. What do you think?"

I wasn't really sure how he was planning on treating me better while we were living so far apart, but I knew Tyler would think of something. So why not see where this would go? I really had nothing to lose. He'd be living in Minneapolis; it's not like he'd be here for me to get really attached to and then have him realize it's not what he wanted—like Greg had just done to me.

I nodded slowly, a smile spreading across my face. "Yeah, that sounds like a good idea. We'll just see where this goes. And we'll take it nice and slow this time," I added.

"Perfect!" He clapped his hands together, then stood up, rounded the table, and pulled me into a hug, sending me into a fit of giggles. It felt so good to be in his arms again. It felt so *right*.

He decided to stay for the weekend, so I took him on the grand walking tour of Green Lake. This town was so tiny you could walk the entire length without breaking a sweat. But it wasn't like other small towns, all broken down and full of aging couples whose kids had left to find jobs in bigger cities. This town was flourishing, and the people really took care of it. They were proud of their pretty, little town, and it showed in the way each yard was perfectly manicured, and each business looked friendly and inviting. Storekeepers spent their downtime outside enjoying the sunshine and waving at passersby. It was charming; there was no other word for it.

If I had stayed in Oak Ridge and Tyler would have found me there, I would have taken him to my little bench down at the lake—that had been my spot, my escape from the world when it all became too much for me. But here, in Green Lake, I didn't really have a spot. The town was named after a tiny, little lake on the edge of town, but I'd only been there a few times and hadn't been very impressed. There were no cute, little nooks to claim out at that lake. It was really more of a glorified pond, not a lake. So after we finished the tour, I had nowhere else to take Tyler. And I really didn't want to invite him back to my house, not when it was starting to get dark. I didn't want to set us up for failure, to put us in a situation to fall into the sexual sin we'd once been living in. From our conversation about our faith earlier, I knew I probably didn't have to worry about that, but I didn't want to risk anything. Just because you're a Christian doesn't mean you're not capable of making that mistake.

I think Tyler picked up on my thoughts because when we returned to my building, he said, "I think I'll head back to my hotel for the night. It's been a long few days on the road."

"Sounds good," I replied, relieved that he hadn't made me try to explain myself. He pulled me into his arms for one last hug and then planted a tender kiss on my head. I smiled and breathed him in, my mind instantly brought back to our first date. He smelled the same as he had that night, and it was just as intoxicating now as it had been then.

And right then, I knew it would only be a matter of time before I was once again falling head over heels in love with Tyler. If just the smell of him made my head spin and my heart pound, I knew I was done for. I would fall hard and fast.

And I would enjoy every second of it.

EIGHT

❖

Molly

APRIL

Greg's voice was strong and sure as he spoke his vows to his gorgeous bride on their wedding day. The day was cold and drizzly, but inside the church, it was warm and full of sunshine from the smiles on the faces of the people sitting in the church. Mary Beth had a hankie at the corner of her eye the entire ceremony, unable to stop her tears from flowing—happy tears of course. She was ecstatic that her youngest daughter had finally, after all she'd been through, found a man to really love and care for her.

"I Greg Turner, take you, Delilah Danielson, to be my wife, my constant friend, my faithful partner, and my love from this day forward. In the presence of God, our family, and friends, I offer you my solemn vow to be your faithful partner in sickness and in health, in good times and in bad, and in joy as well as in sorrow. I promise to love you unconditionally, to support you in your goals, to honor and respect you, to laugh with you and cry with you, and to cherish you for as long as we both shall live."

Delilah couldn't hold in her tears either. No one had ever promised to love her unconditionally, to support her in every adventure life threw her way, or to cherish her. After one mistake, David had dropped her like a hot potato. But now, this amazing man was pledging his entire life to her. Of course she was crying!

She composed herself and repeated the same vows back to Greg, whose lip was quivering. He wasn't crying, but his eyes were shiny, and he was blinking an awful lot. No doubt he was trying as hard as he could to keep the tears from falling as well.

This whole week had been such a blur, a very emotional blur. Delilah's sisters were both in town with their families. They were staying with Mary Beth, and Delilah was over there every night catching up and helping her mom feed their large family. During the day, they furiously worked to finish Mandy's flower girl dress and construct the last of the wedding decorations. Then it had been the rehearsal dinner yesterday, which had been extremely chaotic. It was the first time Delilah had met Greg's family, awkward, and Mandy was exhausted and crabby. She'd thrown a fit right in the middle of the rehearsal—the first time many of us had seen that little girl upset.

We'd stayed at the restaurant until almost 11:30 last night talking with Greg's family and getting to know them. I would have left, but Delilah wanted to stay the night at my place, and she'd driven with me. So I had been stuck there all night, talking with a family that might have been mine if things had worked out differently. They were very nice people, a little hectic and crazy, which was surprising because Greg was so quiet and reserved, but nice.

Greg had three older brothers and one younger sister. His brothers were all married with kids of their own, so with Mandy, Luke, and Delilah's nieces and nephews, there were twenty kids running around. The kids had been well behaved during the wedding rehearsal, but at the dinner, they were crazy. Everyone had been talking and laughing all at once, and after they finished eating, they'd begun chasing each other around. Luke was delighted; he was gaining a sister and twelve cousins because of this wedding. For a kid who'd lived with only a mother for his entire life, this was all new and exciting for him.

Today, he proudly stood up front in a little tuxedo as the ring bearer. His hair was slicked back, and he had a very serious look on his face, closely paying attention to each word the pastor said. He didn't understand why everyone was crying.

This morning had been chaotic as well. Delilah and I were up at eight o'clock for a large breakfast; we didn't want to have to bother with lunch while we were trying to get the last-minute details figured out. We showered and then headed over to Mary Beth's to pick everyone up for hair appointments, which took over two hours. We made it to the church by noon to get changed into our dresses and do our makeup, and then it was pictures at 1:30 until almost 3:00. Finally, at 4:00 the wedding started. After a stressful week and frustrating rehearsal dinner, the wedding went on without a single mishap. Mandy flounced down the aisle after the bridesmaids and groomsmen and very carefully scattered white flower petals onto the aisle runner. Luke solemnly made his way down with the rings, and everyone oohed and ahhed over the beautiful picture we made at the front of the church.

Once Delilah and Greg both said their vows and exchanged the rings, they lit the unity candle and signed the marriage license. Pastor Dennis said a few more words, Delilah's sisters sang a song, and then they finally shared their first kiss as husband and wife. Together they walked down the aisle hand in hand, ready to start their life as man and wife after their fairy tale wedding.

The reception was small and intimate, nothing fancy. Mary Beth had cleared out her restaurant for the event, which only lasted for a little over three hours. Once dinner was over, we gave the toasts, which was extremely emotional for me. As the maid of honor, I was to give a toast, and I'd been stressing over it for weeks. I wanted it to be meaningful, and I wanted them both to remember it forever. I wanted them both to know that I loved them, especially Greg. After he'd proposed to Delilah, we had a nice chat where I'd reassured him that I was totally okay with the two of them getting married. While it was still a lot to handle, especially after how easily I'd fallen for him, I knew with all that I was that their relationship was from God. It was meant to be. And who could argue with that? After awhile, the awkwardness had slowly disappeared, especially when Tyler reentered the picture. Once we reconnected, I'd gotten over Greg faster than I'd fallen in love with him. So now, at Delilah and Greg's wedding night, I could stand up and honestly tell both of them that I loved them so much and that I truly wished them the best.

I raised my glass and began, "Delilah, you're more than a friend to me. You are a sister and a best friend all wrapped up in one amazing package. You've been there through the darkest days of my life, helping me see that through Christ, nothing is impossible. And you've seen me in the brighter times as well, celebrating with me at all the blessings God just continues to shower on us. Meeting Greg was definitely one of those blessings." I smiled at Greg. "I am so thankful that God brought you two together. You are perfect for each other.

"Today you have brought two families together and made one three-year-old girl and one seven-year-old boy the happiest kids on this earth. I am beyond excited to see you both parent these amazing kids." I swallowed the marble in my throat and willed the tears away. "I love you so much and wish you the best of happiness. And Greg…take care of her. Because if you don't, well…I know where you live." The crowd laughed. "You're a kind, sweet man, and you deserve her. So cherish her and show her every day that you love her. If you do that, I know you two will make it through anything."

Greg's brother Brian gave a more humorous speech, sharing stories from their childhood and awkward teenage years. After his speech, the happy couple moved on to cut the cake, then shared their first dance together. They decided to skip the father/daughter and mother/son dances since Delilah didn't really have a father. And since most of the guests were married with kids of their own, they had a short hour of dancing and then called it good. There was no bouquet and garter toss, no awkward chicken dance because someone requested it. We simply blew bubbles in their faces as they held hands and made their way to Greg's car, excited to spend a few days away on a honeymoon. The money they saved on a simple reception was used to fund a more extravagant honeymoon—five nights in the Florida Keys. Luke and Mandy would stay with Mary Beth, and when Greg and Delilah returned, they would all move into Greg's little house. But my hunch was they'd start a family together soon, and that little house would be too crowded for five, and they'd probably have to move into something larger. Maybe they'd even have a honeymoon baby!

I flopped into my bed that night exhausted, both physically and emotionally. I'd been up so early and had been on my feet most of the day. And I'd been the one that Delilah came rushing to when something hadn't gone the way she planned or she forgot an important detail. Not only had I taken care of those little meltdowns, but I'd been the one to calm her down and reassure her that everything would be fine. It had been exhausting—there was no other word for it.

The rest of the week wasn't much better because I knew Delilah and Greg were having the time of their lives while I was just carrying on with my normal life, working at the diner and studying for my GED test. They were probably spending their mornings eating breakfast on a balcony overlooking a beach—a beach they'd lounge on all afternoon. No doubt they were probably eating gourmet food and delicious desserts, then enjoying the sights and sounds on late-night walks on the beach. And the hardest of all…they'd be enjoying sex the way it was supposed to be enjoyed—within the bounds of marriage. And that's all I wanted. I'd abused it in the past, and it had become cheap and meaningless. I imagined that when it was enjoyed properly, it was special and very meaningful. I was a tad jealous.

But of course, Mary Beth knew my feelings exactly, like always. "Honey." She approached me gently on Wednesday afternoon after the lunch rush died down. "Are you okay?" Her eyes were kind, compassionate. That's what I loved so much about Mary Beth. When she asked questions like that, she *really* wanted to know. And if I tried to wave it off or simply say I was fine, she never bought it. I really had no choice but to be honest with her, because if I tried to lie, she'd see right through me and keep pestering me to open up. She meant well; it was just a little over-whelming at times.

"Well, I guess I'm just a little…jealous," I admitted with a sad smile.

"Oh, baby girl. I know just how ya feel. I really do…each time one of my daughter's gets married, I feel the same way."

I cocked my head at her. "Really?"

She nodded. "Yup. My girls all found the loves of their lives. But I never did. I wasted so many years of my life with their father…he was a lowlife, Molly. He really was."

"Mary Beth!" I exclaimed in surprise. I'd never heard her talk negatively about anyone before.

"Well," she said saucily, "he was! He never ever thought about getting married. Not really. I mean, he proposed to me because I kept nagging him about getting married, but he didn't really want that. Even after I gave him two beautiful daughters—" she clucked.

"Did you really want a serious commitment with him?" I asked gently.

She sighed. "No, probably not. He never was the man I needed him to be. And the fact that he just up and left us…" She stared off into space, being drawn back to that painful time in her life. After Rachel and Hannah's father left Mary Beth, she'd really spiraled downward. She'd hooked up with some guy and ended up pregnant at age thirty-seven, making the girls big sisters when they were in high school, probably humiliating them. But it had been very hard on Mary Beth. It was totally understandable that she was feeling every bit as jealous as I was. We'd been mistreated by men, and no one had ever vowed to love and cherish us for the rest of our lives.

However, my blue mood changed drastically when I opened up my mailbox on Thursday to find a letter from Tyler nestled inside. I felt my heartbeat speed up, and I couldn't stop the silly grin from spreading across my whole face. He'd taken the time to write me a letter! In a world run by texting and instant messaging, a real, honest to goodness letter was a treasure.

The paper shook in my hands as I read Tyler's beautiful words. He was charming in real life, but on paper, goodness. My heart was melting.

> My lovely Molly,
>
> I can't believe you opened your door and let me into you home three weeks ago—back into your life. I don't deserve the second chance you're giving me…but boy am I glad you're giving it to me anyway. And I so enjoyed talking to you about all the changes we've been experiencing over the past few years. It's been a rough road, to be sure. But this rough road has gotten a lot smoother now that you're walking beside me. I couldn't imagine a better walking partner.
>
> I didn't tell you how beautiful I thought you looked that weekend I dropped by. I didn't feel it was appropriate. But I can tell you on paper because you can't swat me through paper! You looked so beautiful, Molly. I'm not going to say you looked hot or even pretty because those words are cheap and lame and don't come close to what I saw three weeks ago. So I will stick with the word *beautiful*. And after hearing all you went through, I know without a doubt that you deserve someone telling you this every day of your life. Maybe if things work out for us, I could be the one to do that…and it would be the greatest honor of my

life, being able to see that face and tell you how beautiful it is every single day of forever.

I know *forever* is a scary word. But I've always wanted forever, Molly girl. Always. Even back then, when we were living our crazy lifestyle, I wanted forever. I still want it. So please keep me in mind, sweetheart. I promise this time around I will be the man you need, with God's help. I want to cheer you on when you finally enter college and then one day walk across the stage to receive your diploma. I want to hear you talk about the girls you're helping. I won't be able to offer any advice, but I will listen and encourage you when things look bleak. I want to stand by you through thick and thin because I failed so miserably at it before.

I'm so excited for the months ahead, Molly. I feel like God has something amazing in store for us. And I will wait for you as long as you need, sweetie. I promise.

Much Love,
Ty

I set the letter down with a sigh, that silly grin still plastered on my face. I could not get over how sweet Tyler was! The fact that he was willing to wait as long as I needed was enough to make me cry. It reminded me of Tanner, in a way. He'd waited over twelve years to tell me how he felt about me, and then it had only lasted for a few months before I took off to Minneapolis. This time, I wanted things to be different. This man had poured out his heart and soul to me in our visit and now in this beautiful letter. I'd do it right this time around.

Mary Beth pulled off her reading glasses and sighed. I let her read the letter, and it had clearly impressed her as much as it had impressed me. "Wow. No one writes letters like this anymore, Molly girl. You sure you didn't just write it yourself to fool an old woman like me?"

I laughed. "No, I swear! That's just how Tyler is! He's so… sweet and charming. *So* charming."

She raised her eyebrows. "Well yes, he certainly is charming." She didn't sound convinced. She still thought Tyler was the selfish, young man I'd described him to be.

"He really is different, I promise. I've gotten my heart broken too many times before to take a risk on someone who might mistreat me again," I explained.

"I know. It's just…well, I've done stupid things before too, believe it or not. I've trusted people I shouldn't have. I've allowed myself to love men who only wanted one thing. I don't want you to get hurt again, sweet girl. It would break my heart," she whispered.

I rounded the diner counter and gave her a long hug. "I promise you, Mary Beth, that if I feel he's going to mistreat me, I'll drop him like that," I said with a snap of my fingers.

"You're a smart girl, Molly. I believe you. But love can do crazy things to a woman. It can cloud our minds, lead us to make stupid choices. Just be careful," she warned.

"Yes, ma'am," I said with a chuckle, and she swatted me with a dishtowel.

~

Delilah came back from her honeymoon absolutely glowing, on the inside and out. Her skin was perfectly sun kissed from long hours out lounging on the beach and building sandcastles on the shore with her new hubby. The happy couple came home with gorgeous pictures of the sand and surf, a mason jar full of white sand tied up with a lavender ribbon, and smiles that stretched from ear to ear. From the adoring looks that passed between the two of them, I knew that this time alone had drawn them closer together and probably made both of them fall more in love with the other.

But back here, it had been a tough week not only for me and Mary Beth but for Luke and Mandy as well. I'd gone over every single night to help Mary Beth with the kids, which was exhausting. It was beyond me how Delilah and Greg had been such amazing single parents. Their kids were darlings—in small doses, of course. But when you spend more than a few hours taking care of another's kid, the thrill begins to wear off...big time. And don't get me wrong, I love both those kids with everything in me, but babysitting is tough work. Discipline is next to impossible, because no kid likes to be disciplined by anyone other than their parents. And even though Mandy and Luke were normally very well-behaved kids, they also both had a mischievous side.

Not only did we have to deal with their mischief, we also had to deal with them missing their parents. Neither kid had ever been away from their parents for this long before. They were all those kids had in the world. Luke had never had to share his mommy with anyone else before, and Mandy was really too young to remember much of her mommy. For their entire lives, it had just been Luke and Delilah, Mandy and Greg. Sharing a parent was a brand-new concept for these little ones, and they didn't handle missing them very well; they complained night and day. It was all Mary Beth and I could do to keep them occupied and distracted...which when successful never lasted more than a few hours. And to make matters worse, it had been rainy all week, and we were stuck inside. Out of desperation one night, we went out and bought each of the kids a raincoat and boots so they could go out and splash around while we tidied up the house and then collapsed onto the couch in exhaustion.

"I'm out of practice, Molly girl. These bones are too old to be runnin' after youngsters anymore. I'm wiped!"

I gave her the best smile I could muster. "Me too. I've never taken care of little kids for this long before. And I'm not even here in the morning to help! I could stay, if you need me. If you're feeling too tired," I offered.

"Naw," she said with a wave of her hand. "I should be fine. I like taking care of them, no matter how tired it makes me. And besides, Mandy wakes up at the crack of dawn, and for a few hours, we have some good alone time to connect. She's my grand-baby now…I need her to know I love her."

"She'll know soon enough, trust me. You're the best grandma ever. All your grandbabies are drowning in the love you shower them with."

"Well, good," she said with a nod. "That's the way it should be. They have parents to tell them what to do and make them eat their veggies. It's my job to just spoil them. That's why I'll be glad when those two lovebirds are home…I need to get back to spoiling."

So we both breathed a collective sigh of relief when Delilah and Greg pulled into Mary Beth's driveway on Friday evening. Mary Beth and I gladly handed Mandy and Luke over to them and promised to catch up later that weekend to look at all their pictures and hear about how wonderful it had been to run and splash in the water.

Three weeks later, though, the magic began to wear off for Delilah. Married life was proving to be more difficult than she'd imagined it to be. The couple had done the required marriage counseling to get married in our little church, but because their engagement had been so short, it had been an accelerated version. They hadn't had as much time to talk through some of the more important issues that other couples with a longer engagement would have.

One major issue for them was handling money. Delilah had pretty much been on her own since age sixteen as a teen mom, and Mary Beth had seen to it that she know how to handle her own money. She had become a pro at keeping track of expenses, writing each purchase into her check book, and making every penny count. She was the master at stretching out a dollar and was the greatest bargain shopper I'd ever seen. Money was one of the only areas of her life that Delilah had some sort of control over…she could see the money come in, make sure it covered all her bills and bought all the groceries she needed, and then tuck the rest of it away to save as a cushion when things got tough. And she loved that control.

Greg came in and messed that all up. They of course had combined their accounts, but he wasn't as strict with money as Delilah was. Greg sold insurance, and he had a steady client base in Green Lake. He was constantly bringing more people in, especially from the tiny, little towns from around the area. His house was small, and the payment wasn't overwhelming each month, so he didn't worry about finances as much as his new bride. And this bothered her...a lot. She'd find receipts lying around all the time—in his pockets when she did his laundry, in his wallet, and in their checkbook. It drove her crazy that he never recorded what he spent, that he never really kept track of how much money was coming in and out.

And while doing his laundry had seemed romantic and fun at the beginning of their marriage, she was finding that she enjoyed it less and less with each load she shoved into their creaky, old washer. It was all beginning to pile up on her. She'd gone from single working mom in charge of only two people to full-time stay-at-home mommy in charge of four people. That was a big adjustment for someone basically living on her own and answering to only her son for seven years, kind of like culture shock.

I knew all this because Delilah never stopped talking about it. Whenever she saw me, she unloaded it all onto me. And it was beginning to wear on me. She looked tired; it was clear that she had little to no time to herself anymore, not with Mandy up at 6:30 every morning. If she wanted to shower in the morning, she had to do it quickly while Greg fed Mandy breakfast. She had a window of about seven minutes to get in and out of the shower before Greg needed to finish getting ready and make it down to the office. She simply wasn't used to the demands of taking care of a three-year-old. She was out of practice.

Luke was pretty self-sufficient and was in school all day; she didn't have to worry about taking care of him so much. But even with Luke out of her hair during the day, she found that the tasks still managed to pile up on her, smothering her. "I used to think that stay-at-home moms were simply lazy women who mooched off the money their husbands made. But man, was I wrong. It's hard work, Molly. The hardest job I've ever done," she kept repeating.

"Harder than taking care of a newborn while finishing high school?" I asked with a smile.

She huffed and shook her head. "I honestly don't know! When I was dealing with that, of course it seemed like the toughest job in the world. But once he was old enough for daycare, it got a little better...and my mom helped me out a ton. Plus I could put him down fairly early and then spend the evening doing school-work. The first year was tough when he woke up at night...but after that, it wasn't so bad.

"But this...I don't have a mother helping me take care of both Mandy and Luke. It's all me during the day. *I'm* the one who gets Luke up and ready for school while trying not to trip over Mandy, who holds onto me from the minute I walk out of the bathroom. *I'm* the one who wrestles them both into the car and rushes them to school in the morning, where we barely make it in time before the bell rings to go inside! And then I go home and do the endless piles of laundry and dishes, fix lunch for Mandy, and then try and put her down for a nap. When I *do* get her down, she only naps for like twenty minutes, hardly long enough for me to get anything accomplished. And before I know it, it's time to pick up Luke from school and start dinner! After dinner, it's a tiny break because Greg's there to help. I love nights. Bath time, bedtime, and then we finally have a bit of time alone before we do it all again the next morning," she said with a sigh.

"Gee, you have a knack at making the fairy tale sound...kind of like a bad dream," I said with a wince.

She laughed. "Sorry. It's just...I don't know. It's not what I expected."

"Do you regret it?" I asked, kind of frustrated because once again someone else was living the life I was supposed to be living. First it had been Leah; she was living out my dream life with Tanner back in Iowa. And now, here in Kansas, Delilah had married the one man I had once thought I might actually have a shot with. So even though it might be overwhelming, she should be counting her blessings. I would have given anything to be in her shoes right now, married to a man that adored me and raising two amazing kids together. It was my dream life, and since I couldn't live it and enjoy it, it made me angry that all she seemed capable of was complaining about it.

"No, no. Of course not. It's just gonna take a few weeks to fall into the swing of things. We'll be fine…and I'm really happy. Just stressed, is all," she reassured.

But it was taking much longer than a few weeks for Delilah to fall into the swing of things. I found myself pulling away from Delilah and drawing closer to Mary Beth because at the moment, we connected much more than Delilah and I did. We didn't have husbands and young children to take care of. We weren't stuck at home with piles of laundry and dishes to take care of. We worked and worried about just one person: ourselves.

And then, in the midst of all the stress with Delilah and Greg, I received news from home that would rock the comfortable little world I'd built for myself in Kansas.

PART TWO

Storms

When the storms of life come, the wicked are whirled away, but the godly have a lasting foundation.

—Proverbs 10:25

NINE

❀

Delilah

MAY

A crash and a cry snapped me out of the nap I'd been trying to take after putting Mandy down for her own nap. I rushed to the kitchen to find Mandy kneeling on the countertop and the vase full of roses that Greg had brought home yesterday smashed into a million pieces on the floor, water spreading across the tile and the roses strewn about. I breathed a sigh of relief that Mandy wasn't hurt and that it had only been the vase that had broken and not my mother's antique cookie jar sitting on the opposite side of the kitchen that she'd given to me as a wedding gift. As a kid, I used to rip open packages of cookies I'd bought at the store just so I could fill up that pretty jar and feel fancy each time I took a cookie from it. Knowing how much I loved that jar, Mom had given it to me as a wedding gift, my most prized wedding gift out of all of the ones we'd received.

"I'm sorry, Mama." Mandy hiccupped around her sobs. "I just wanted to reach the cups so I could get you some coffee for when you woke up."

My heart melted each time Mandy called me mama. When Greg and I had gotten engaged, we'd sat both Luke and Mandy down and explained to them that because we were getting married, they were both going to have a new parent. Luke had been delighted immediately; he'd never had any sort of father figure in his life. Albert didn't really count; he was more of a grandpa than a father, so Luke had celebrated right away, no conflicting feelings whatsoever. Mandy, however, had struggled. She knew she had a mommy; Greg talked about her often so Mandy would grow up knowing that once, Mandy had a mommy who'd given her life and loved her, if even for a short time. It was important to Greg that she knew about Sophie even though she'd ripped out his heart and stomped on it.

We'd let Mandy work through her feelings during the engagement, but the first day I stayed home with her, she'd called me mama, making my heart go crazy with flutters. I couldn't believe how fast she'd adopted me after struggling for so long with the idea. Greg and I weren't really sure where that name had even come from; she'd called Sophie mommy. Maybe it was her own way of dealing with suddenly having a new woman in her life, even at her young age. "Mommy" belonged to her real mom; "mama" belonged to me, her new mother. Made sense to me even though Mandy never explained it to me. It was just her way of dealing with this change.

"It's okay, sweetie," I soothed. "I'm glad you're not hurt, and we can put daddy's roses in another vase. But next time you want to get something from the cabinet, you need to ask me first, okay? I'll help you, and when you get taller, you can do it all by yourself. How does that sound?"

She sniffed and nodded, her lower lip stuck out in a pout. She wanted to be independent so badly, but there was so much she couldn't do. Everything was too tall, too heavy, too complicated. The world wasn't made to cater to the needs of a three-year-old, and this frustrated Mandy. And it caused me unneeded stress as well. I had to constantly be on my toes, watching for the next thing she'd get into.

This was a whole new world for me. For one thing, I was out of practice with a three-year-old. Luke was old enough now that once I got him up in the morning for school, he could pour himself a bowl of cereal, shower, and pick out clothes for the day and make sure his hair looked somewhat appropriate without my help. I had been so young when he was little that he'd had to grow up faster than other kids, learning how to take care of himself when I was unable to do it. I took that for granted when I was unmarried, the fact that Luke could get himself ready in the morning without much help. But when I got married and moved into Greg and Mandy's world, we'd decided that I would stay home with Mandy so that she didn't have to go to day care. Greg hated that he'd had to send her to day care when Sophie left, but he'd had no other choice. Now he *did* have a choice, and it was the smartest choice financially. I wouldn't be working, but what we'd lose in income we'd save on childcare. Plus, I regretted sending Luke to day care as well when he was little. I hated that other people had had such an influence on my baby when I should have been the one teaching him my morals and values. It had been a good day care, but still…you never quite know what your kid will be hearing and seeing from the day care workers. Kids pick up so much from simply watching and listening, so I wanted to make sure Mandy would be seeing and hearing what we wanted her to see and hear. I hadn't been able to do that with Luke, but I could do it with Mandy now.

I had been more than okay with packing up my office at the law firm and saying good-bye to everyone. I appreciated that job, I really did. It paid very well for a desk job, and they'd given me medical benefits and had been understandable when emergencies with Luke had arisen over the years. But it was a high stress job, and I'd gotten burnt out quickly. I'd had no hope of quitting that job until things had taken off with Greg. So I was beyond excited for my first day home as a stay at home mommy after the honeymoon.

Things had not gone exactly as planned however. It was a thousand times harder than I thought it would be, definitely not the fairy tale life I'd dreamed of as a little girl. For some reason, I thought when I got married, things would be easier, and I'd certainly thought that staying home with only one child would not be hard. I thought it would be a piece of cake compared to trying to take care of a newborn while juggling schoolwork.

But from the minute I got up in the morning, my days were chaotic. Mandy was always up at the crack of dawn, and I had to rely on Greg feeding Mandy breakfast while I showered at lightning speed, or else I wouldn't get to shower at all. Then Greg would kiss me good-bye and head down to the office, leaving me to wrangle a sleepy seven-year-old and an overwhelmingly energetic three-year-old into the car to drop Luke off at school. I'd always prided myself on having Luke to school on time every single day, but lately, it seemed like we'd barely make it before the last few kids were disappearing into the school building to begin the day. My heart would break as I watched Luke sprint across the playground before the doors closed on him. Usually, some teacher would see him and wait for him, welcoming him in with a smile and a wave to his mama to reassure me that he was fine.

But things were no less chaotic when Luke was at school, like I'd expected. I don't know where my days disappeared to; it seemed like they always evaporated before they even really began. I'd work on laundry when Mandy and I got home…there was *always* laundry. But when you have kids, it makes sense. Mandy spilled often, and usually, I'd end up changing her outfit a few times a day, and when Luke got home from school, he always wanted to change out of the clothes he'd gotten sweaty and dirty at recess into his relaxin' clothes, as he called them. I probably could wait for the weekends to do laundry, but then it would begin to pile up on me, and I'd be completely overwhelmed. So, every few days I'd throw a load in, and then not feel like folding it, procrastinating until the next day. In truth, I didn't always have a pile of dirty laundry to wash each day, but the days I didn't start a load, I'd be ironing, folding, and putting away. It was a never-ending cycle, and an exhausting one at that.

Entertaining Mandy was harder than I thought too. I just didn't understand how she could get up so early in the morning and barely take a ten minute nap in the afternoon after running around all day. I was at my wits' end trying to keep her occupied. We'd already gone to the library and picked out books to read together and movies to watch together. She loved getting her nails painted, so we did that quite a bit too. Lately we'd been experimenting with baking, which she also loved, and it was easy for me to measure out ingredients for her to dump in, making her feel like she was really helping. Luke and Greg loved that we'd been baking for them too…it was beginning to show on Greg's waistline. Perhaps we'd cool it with the baking for a while.

The truth was that I was running out of ideas. And patience. I loved this life and I knew I didn't deserve it, but it was still hard, and I was struggling. And to top it all off, I could feel Molly pulling away from me. I was at the point now where I felt like I couldn't say anything to her about how hard this was because I was afraid she was going to get mad at me. She longed for this life, I knew she did, but she didn't know how hard it was, how much it wasn't like how the movies and books portray this life to be. It's messy, uncomfortable, and chaotic. I needed balance; I needed to fight for joy when the world gave me a million reasons to throw my hands up and quit. It would be nice to have my best friend helping me work through this, but she kept pulling farther and farther away. Her friend Tyler had been in contact with her; he'd even visited for a weekend before the wedding, and I was interested in how things were going with him. I knew he wanted to see if things could work out between the two of them, but Molly hadn't shared any news with me in a while.

On a rainy Saturday afternoon, I called up Molly to ask if she wanted to hang at the coffee shop for a bit. I missed her so much, and yet I could hear the hesitancy in her voice when I asked.

"Please, Molly? I'll leave all my home struggles where they belong…at home. I miss my best friend, and I need to see your face ASAP or else I will go insane. Please?"

She gave me a small giggle and agreed, and I inwardly celebrated. I kissed the kids and my husband good-bye and practically ran out the door, eager to spend an afternoon talking to someone outside my family. The day was chilly and damp, but inside, I was glowing. This small escape would be just what I needed to recharge for another week at home with Mandy.

I could feel the space between Molly and I; I could feel her holding back. I kept our conversation free from drama at home, but that was my whole life right now, and I quickly ran out of things to talk about. Molly was oddly silent today. I didn't know what to do. Molly and I had never had this problem. We'd been such a big part of helping each other deal with everything; we'd never had a problem talking about anything and everything. Something was up.

I looked her straight in the eye. "Molly. I know you better than anyone else. Something is up, and I'm not leaving until you tell me what it is. If you're still feeling weird about my new life, that's getting old. I haven't brought it up all day."

She shook her head quickly. "No, that's not it." She sighed and ran her hands through her hair. "I'm sorry about that. It wasn't fair to make you feel bad about talking about what's going on in your life. I mean, you listened to me talk about some of the darkest things anyone could go through! I should be able to listen to you talk about how hard this all is for you."

I gave her a small smile. Molly was always so understanding, so quick to look back on her thoughts and behaviors and let God convict her of her shortcomings. I admired that so much about her. "Thanks, Moll. And I *am* sorry I was such a bummer. I am beyond grateful for this life God has given me…for the second chance he's given me. It's just…I need to vent once in a while. Maybe I need to join a mother's group at church or something, somewhere I *can* vent to people who are going through the same stuff as me. I don't want to burden you with this stuff or to give you the impression that I'm not grateful for this. Because I am. I really am."

Molly laughed. "I know you are! It's only hard for me… because…well, I've always dreamed about being a mother. About staying home and taking care of my family. When college was still an option for me in high school, I couldn't decide on a major…I had no big dreams for myself. But the dream of having a family was always an option for me. At least, I thought it was. Doesn't seem to be working out that way for me right now, but…that's okay. I'm gonna go to college now and get my degree, and if God chooses to bring someone into my life later on and bless me with a family, I'll accept it gladly. All in his good timing, Delilah. His timing is better than mine. I know that."

I shook my head in disbelief. "I don't know how you do that, Molly. How you can be so rightfully upset about something and yet still come back and apologize for *feeling*! It's okay to be upset about things, Molly."

"I know. But I also know that being upset about something as little as that isn't worth getting in between our friendship."

I nodded. "So…what's going on then? I know something's bothering you."

I saw the hesitation in her eyes, her mind's quick decision to keep whatever it was that was bothering her locked up inside for a while longer. I'd seen this look often at the beginning of our friendship. I'd tell her about some hardship I'd gone through and how I was working through it, and for a brief moment, I could see her desire to share with me, but I could also see the hesitancy in her eyes, her fear that opening up to me would change my mind about her or cause me to judge her. I had been patient with her back then, knowing from the dark look in her eyes that she was suffering from some pretty heavy stuff. I knew she would open up to me when she was ready to, and I'd been right. After that, it had been easier for us to connect, to help each other heal from our dark pasts. And I knew that I'd have to do the same this time around as well. I could see in her eyes that something big was bothering her, but she wasn't ready to tell me yet. She'd tell me when she'd had enough time to process it and work through it a bit. That's just the type of person Molly was; she was a thinker, and she needed to work through all the details first before bringing it to me.

That was fine with me; I had enough of a full plate to deal with at the moment. This afternoon had been just what I needed to return home recharged and ready to tackle the next week.

"I'm just a tad overwhelmed, that's all," Molly said with a sigh. "I thought I would've been done with the GED by now and enrolled in classes. But it's already May, and I'm nowhere near ready for it." Her answer didn't match the pain in her eyes however. I knew something bigger was going on, something that she didn't want to share with me. Not yet, anyway. I wouldn't prod her; I'd let her come to me in her own time.

I reached out and squeezed her hand briefly. "You're doing fine. I'm so proud of all you've accomplished in your time here. You've had such an impact on me and my mom and Luke too. He still talks about you all the time, asks when you're going to come babysit him again. Just remember that God's timing is perfect, Molly, like you *just* told me. Maybe he's keeping you from the GED for a while longer because he's about to bring something big into your life. Just keep trusting that God will lead you down the best path for your life."

"It's hard," she said with a shrug, her voice cracking a little.

"I know. Believe me, I know. But all the little twists and turns he takes you on will make sense once you make it to wherever it is he's taking you." I stopped and thought about how my words of advice to Molly applied to me as well, and I laughed. "Listen to me, giving you advice that I need to take myself. Proof that I've been spending way too much time with a three-year-old and not enough time with my best friend."

Molly laughed, and I could tell that she'd finally let her guard down. We steered the conversation away from heavy stuff, knowing that we'd have plenty of time to talk through our issues later on. What both of us needed was an afternoon free of stress and drama, laughing and giggling and enjoying life. So we sat in the coffee shop for a while longer, then spontaneously decided to go see the new chick flick playing in the little movie theater. We ordered a big bag of popcorn and two large sodas and giggled at how our treats pretty much disappeared before the movie had even started. We went home full of both popcorn and joy, a joy that only comes from fellowshipping with another believer.

Molly and I would be able to deal with whatever life decided to throw at us for that very reason. We had each other, and we had God, and that was enough.

TEN

❁

Molly

MAY

I left the movie theater with a light heart and a spring in my step. Spending time with Delilah always did that for me, even if things were tense between us. We had this uncanny ability to talk through things when necessary and to let other things alone for a later time. What was on my mind right now was definitely something I wanted to leave alone for another time. I felt good that we'd been able to talk through my struggles about listening to Delilah complain about her home life. It was understandable that she needed someone to vent to, but we'd decided that maybe I wasn't the best person for the job because I couldn't relate… and because it kept bringing up memories of the abortion and my baby that never was. I would give anything to be struggling through life with my baby right now…anything.

In the privacy of my own apartment, I let my mind wander back to the phone call I'd received from my mom earlier this week, about the news I didn't really feel like sharing with Delilah just yet. I knew the news would come sooner or later, but still, it hit me like a ton of bricks.

Tanner and Leah were pregnant.

There was only one thing on my mind lately—that it wasn't fair. It wasn't fair that I'd gotten raped at eighteen. It wasn't fair that I'd gotten pregnant from it, that because of a stupid assump-tion I'd run off and destroyed the one good thing that had come from the rape—my baby girl. And it wasn't fair that Delilah had snatched up the man I'd thought I might have a future with, that she was living out my happily ever after. When would it be my turn?

Just before my mom called, I'd finally been able to sit down and really focus on studying for the GED. The cheerful ringtone I'd assigned to my mom snapped me out of my little world, and I gladly picked up the phone; it was a welcome distraction to all the hideous studying I'd been doing. "Hi, sweetie!" she replied after my hello. "How are you?"

I sighed. "I'm good, Mom. Tired, but good. I spent all day at the diner. Mary Beth was running this crazy special, and we were swamped all day. I didn't want to leave her there with just Albert helping. He's been struggling with his heart here lately. Anyway, I ended up working a double shift. Now I'm just doing some studying."

"Good for you. You'll get there."

"I know," I said with another sigh. "It's just taking so much longer than I originally planned. And I'm tired of studying!" I threw my highlighter across the table, where it clattered to the floor. I rolled my eyes in frustration but let it continue to roll across the floor. When you're in a bad mood already, even the littlest things upset you, things like a highlighter falling off the table and rolling across the floor. Never mind the fact that *I'd* thrown it…now it was all the way across the room, and I was frustrated. Stupid GED.

She laughed. "I bet. But you know, once you start taking col-lege classes, it'll be more of the same thing!"

"Yeah, but I'll be studying what I want to study!" *Hopefully.* With my luck, I'd be stuck doing generals for an entire year. I trapped my sigh, not wanting my mother to worry about me.

"True, very true." Conversation stalled for a moment, and I heard my mom sigh on the other side of the line. "Well, hon, I called for a reason. I have some news for you…good news, but I think it'll still be hard on you. And I wanted you to hear it from me, not find out on Facebook or something."

My heart skipped a beat. The fear of bad news always looms when someone starts out with a phrase like that. But I steeled myself for whatever it was that my mom needed to tell me. I'd been through so much already; I was pretty sure I could handle almost anything.

"Okay. What's up?" I asked, trying to sound brave and confident.

She took a deep breath and cut straight to the chase. "Well, Tanner and Leah announced the other day that they're expecting. I guess they wanted to wait until after the first trimester to tell people outside the family. She's due in October, I believe."

I chewed the inside of my lip, silent. I knew this day would come eventually, but still. It was just another reminder that Tanner and I had no hope for the kind of future we'd once wanted together. Coming back to find him married had been one thing. But now that he was having a baby, it sealed the deal. He had completely and totally moved on. He'd once been so excited for the birth of my baby, which I'd snatched away from him. Now he was looking forward to welcoming his own baby into the world. Leah once again was giving him something I could never give him. She gave him all the love he deserved to have; she was able to give him that love unlike I had been able to all those years ago. And now, she was giving him a baby to love, something I'd also been unable to do because I'd run away and taken the easy way out. Well, that decision was turning out to be a whole lot harder than I'd originally thought. It really hadn't been the easy way out, like I'd expected. It was something I could never escape from, no matter how strong I was in my faith now. Wounds heal, but scars remain forever.

The abortion was that scar that would never fade. Ever. And the news of Tanner's baby brought back all the memories of my own pregnancy. Leah's pregnancy would be far different than mine had been. No doubt she'd told Tanner in some cute and creative way, and he'd probably twirled her around in joy. Maybe he'd even cried.

And she'd gotten to tell her parents knowing that they'd be thrilled and excited. I'd told my parents the news with a knot in my stomach, knowing they'd be disappointed. Of course, once they found out three years later that the baby had been conceived out of rape, the situation changed. If only I'd just told them from the very beginning—how different my life would be right now. They would have helped me through it, gotten me the help I had so desperately needed. And Tanner and I would be together, raising my baby and probably planning our own family. It would be *us* telling our friends that we were pregnant.

Babies were and always would be a touchy subject for me. I put my hands on my belly, remembering how it had once been just beginning to swell with new life. I'd only seen my baby once at an ultrasound appointment, only gotten to hear her heartbeat that one time. I'd never ever gotten to hear her cry…her laugh… her beautiful voice. I'd never get to brush my fingers through her hair or hold her close, cuddling her. So many things I'd never get to do because out of desperation, I'd gotten an abortion. I honestly have no idea what I had been thinking back then. *How had I let myself believe that the life inside me was nothing but a clump of cells, an inconvenience that could easily be taken care of?* Had I given it a few months, I would have felt my baby kick and move… certainly a clump of cells cannot kick and move. That had been a life, a life I'd taken out of selfish desire to escape my troubled past. The worst part was, though, that things hadn't been that bad. Yes, I'd been raped. But Tanner had stuck by my side and so had my parents. Eventually, I would have told them about the rape, and they would've helped me through that as well. And we could have figured things out with Jason, made sure he stayed far, far away. I'd given up far too easily, and I was still paying for that selfishness to this day.

"You okay, sweetie?" My mom's voice snapped me out of my thoughts.

"Oh yeah. I'm fine." She was right. This was good news, it really was. New life was always a cause for celebration. But it was still hard for me. "Thanks for telling me, Mom. It would have been tough to find out on Facebook."

I could hear my mom's heart breaking for me across the phone line. We were so close now; she sensed my pain and felt it alongside me. "Oh, honey. I'll be praying for you. I always am, but I'll be praying harder now. This day will come for you too. I know it will. Someday, God will bring the right guy into your life, and you'll get to tell us again that you're pregnant. And this time, it'll be happy and all in God's good timing."

All in God's good timing. That was a subject that was on my mind a lot lately. I had just told Delilah earlier today that I would wait for God's timing in my life. I would wait as long as I needed to for God to bring a husband and a family into my life. But that was an easy thing to say, an easy way to reassure Delilah that I was okay with the fact that she had everything I ever wanted when I really wasn't. I didn't want her to worry about me when I knew she already had so much on her plate. And now, my mother was telling me to do the same thing, to trust in God's prefect timing. But it was so much easier said than done. I didn't *want* to wait. I was tired of waiting.

To help me get my focus back where it needed to be, I wrote out a verse that was pretty much summing up my life right now. Psalm 37:4, "Take delight in the Lord, and he will give you the desires of your heart," was written in bold letters on a blue sticky note, hanging from my bathroom mirror. It was my little daily reminder that God knew what I really desired, and that if I delighted and focused on him and his plan for my life, he would one day grant me those desires. And I was finding out too that sometimes those desires can change. The more time you spend with God, the more you realize that your greatest treasure is him. So maybe, just maybe, he was *already* giving me the desires of my heart—himself. Truly he was the greatest treasure anyway, and since I'd rededicated my life to him, my greatest desire was to draw closer to him, to delight in him every single day of my life.

Still. The desire to have a husband to love and a family to care for burned deep within my heart. It probably always would. I would fight for joy in this difficult time in my life, constantly reminding myself that compared to any other desire in my life, Christ was by far the greatest and most prized. And I would hold onto the hope that God would see the other great desires in my life and one day, hopefully sooner than later, grant me them. Surely I'd been through enough already. God couldn't really expect me to remain single and childless the rest of my life...right?

Thoughts of Tyler popped into my head. I hadn't heard from him in a while; it was easy for me to forget that he'd waltzed back into my life. Maybe God had brought him back for a reason; maybe he was the future I'd been hoping and praying for like crazy these days. God was constantly doing the unexpected in my life, so it wouldn't surprise me if that was his plan. He was always one step ahead of me, surprising me with the next twist and turn in my journey. All I could do was simply hold on for the ride and trust that I'd end up exactly where he wanted me to go.

In the meantime, I had to go on living. Life couldn't stop just because others were experiencing the things I so desperately desired. God had given me this beautiful, new second chance at life, and I couldn't waste time feeling sorry for myself. Enough time had been wasted wishing for things to be different. The truth was things weren't different. I needed to figure out how to deal with the difficult things in my life so that I could move on to the next chapter. For me, that meant finishing studying for the GED and taking the test. That would open up a brand-new door for me, a whole new exciting chapter that I couldn't wait to begin living.

I wrapped up the phone call with my mother, then squeezed my eyes shut. *Lord*, I prayed, *you know the desires of my heart. You know how much I want to be married…how badly I want a baby to fill my empty arms. But I want you to always be my number 1 desire, my only reason to live. I need your peace, Lord…so badly. Keep leading me down whatever path is best for me. I will gladly follow you wherever it is you're taking me this time, I promise. Fill me with the joy that only comes from you, Father. And help me to be joyful for all the people in my life right now…you know how hard it is for me to be joyful when they're experiencing what I so badly want to be experiencing too. Help me to keep fighting for joy.*

To some, fighting for joy seems to defeat the purpose of joy. Fighting is a harsh word; it brings to mind struggles, violence. Joy, on the other hand, is light. It's peaceful. The two words just don't seem to go together, fighting and joy. But I disagreed. I knew that desiring anything more than Christ was a sin, and it must be fought. To find the joy I so desperately desired in Christ required me to fight my natural desire to esteem God less than anything else. It was a constant battle, but one that I would wake up fighting every single day of my life. Because at the end of my life, all the other treasures that I'd stored up for myself would fade away. Another one of my favorite verses popped into my head, found in Matthew 6:19,

> Do not store up treasures here on earth, where moths and rust destroys them, and where thieves break in and steal. Store your treasures in heaven, where moths and rust cannot destroy, and thieves do not break in and steal. Wherever your treasure is, there the desires of your heart will also be.

I knew too many people wasted their lives chasing happiness in what the world said was worthwhile. Well, I refused to be one of those people who stood before the Lord one day and had to explain why I'd spent so much of my time chasing after meaning-less treasures when the greatest treasure available was right there in front of me—his son, Jesus Christ. To me, it was a no brainer. A relationship with Christ was far better than anything the world could offer me. No matter how tempting it was to chase after all that, I wouldn't do it. Instead, I'd keep falling in love with Jesus, trusting that he'd provide me with everything I *really* needed. He could see the end of my journey; he knew what was best for me. If that meant a husband and a family, I would gladly accept it. But if not, I'd figure out a way to deal with it, how to remain joyful even if I didn't agree.

I closed my book and shoved my studying aside. Pulling a piece of loose paper out from my pile of GED stuff, I decided to try something one of my favorite Sunday school teachers had said worked for her when she was feeling anxious or unsatisfied. I started listing out all the blessings God was currently shower-ing on me, hoping that if I could see in writing all that God was doing in my life right now, I would realize just how blessed I really was; I could stop wishing for all that I thought was missing. I took a deep breath and tapped the pen on my head, thinking. Even if the blessings were small, I decided they deserved to go on the list too. Every little blessing counted; they were what brought the joy in the dark times. And sometimes it's the littlest things that make the biggest impact.

After I was done, I sat back with a sigh, satisfied at what a sur-prisingly long list it was. I needed to do this more often. I needed to keep these lists and reread them again and again, reminding myself that God was constantly taking care of me. So I pulled out a shoebox and folded up this first list and decided that each month I needed to make a new list. This would be my little box of blessings.

It bothered me that so many Christians think that joy means happiness. I don't think the two words mean the same thing. To me, happiness is just a feeling, and it is fleeting. Happiness is eating your favorite flavor of ice cream or getting a new haircut. But joy...joy lasts. Joy overcomes temporary circumstances that aren't fun, that don't make you feel happy. I could relate to this big time, because right now, I wasn't exactly happy with my life circumstances. If I had my way, I would be living back in Iowa with my baby girl and Tanner. I would be surrounded by my family. But that's not how it was, and I couldn't change that. I could, however, fight for joy because joy was deeper and more meaningful than happiness. And the little blessings I'd just listed out *did* bring me happiness. The two *could* go together, happiness and joy. But they aren't the same thing. And I would take the lasting feeling of joy over the fleeting feeling of happiness any day. It just took a bit more work to fight for joy. But it was worth it.

I knew firsthand that it takes work to fight for joy. You don't just wake up feeling joyful every single day. Some days, it would probably feel a whole lot better to pull the covers up over my face and go back to sleep. Some days I didn't feel like fighting for joy. But hiding gets me nowhere; I'd learned that much in my "running away" years. If I wanted that lasting joy, I needed to pursue it. So I posted scripture verses throughout my house, verses that had always spoken to me throughout the years. And I changed the way I prayed; I decided to take some of the focus off of me in my prayer life. I knew it was okay to pray for myself, to bring my concerns and desires to God, but I also knew that if I prayed for *others*, my mood would probably change. It's just like Christmas; its way more fun to watch someone open up a gift you've given them than to open up your own presents. In prayer, it was very satisfying to pray for others, to take the focus off me and my unhappiness. I found that I was happier when I lifted up others to the Lord first. It was a simple way to fight for joy.

Maybe I needed to do some volunteer work too. I thought back to Tyler, how his eyes had lit up when he talked about his little Jenny. Volunteering at the Children's Home brought him immeasurable joy; maybe it could do the same for me. I wasn't sure if there were many volunteering opportunities in this tiny town, but Pastor Dennis could probably hook me up with any that he knew of.

I would do whatever it took. I wanted more than anything to be satisfied in where God had placed me, even if it wasn't where I'd thought I'd be at this point in my life. But I didn't want to waste my life thinking about what *could have* been...I wanted to keep moving forward, excited about what *could be*. And who knew what twists and turns God would throw in my path; he'd done it before. I didn't doubt that he could do it again. All I could do was hold on and enjoy the ride, each and every step of the way. Somehow, I would get exactly where I needed to go. I was sure of it.

ELEVEN

Tanner

MAY

The past few months had been the happiest yet craziest months of my entire life. I never knew it was possible to feel so many different emotions in such a short amount of time.

Leah and I decided to start trying for a family a bit earlier than planned since it had only taken her two years to finish her degree. She already had a few years of work under her belt and was eager to have a baby to love. And yet, I was hesitant. It still seemed liked yesterday that Molly had told me she was pregnant. The baby had been more my baby than Jason's baby; I'd been so excited to welcome that little one into the world. Now, four years later, that baby was only a memory—the only time we'd seen her was through an ultrasound. Her life had been ended before it even began, and her absence left a hole too big to fill. A hole so big, I was worried that even my own baby wouldn't fill it. I didn't want to hold my baby for the first time and wish that I'd been able to hold Molly's baby, to see her face, to hear her coo and laugh, to hold her on my chest while she slept. I'd wanted to do all those things so badly with Molly's baby. I'd be able to do that with my own baby, of course. But I knew I'd be thinking of the other baby. And that scared me…a lot.

Leah had told me about the pregnancy in the worst way possible. In her mind, it had probably seemed cute and romantic, but it caused me to respond in a way that had broken her heart. It would have been wise to tell her how Molly had told me she was pregnant—because they were eerily similar. But how could I have known? There never seemed to be a reason to tell Leah about that. I probably wasn't as honest with Leah about Molly and all that we'd been through as I should have been, but it was a painful time in my life that I didn't like revisiting. And Leah was never too happy to hear me talk about Molly anyway. It's not that she didn't like Molly, but I sensed some jealousy. In my mind, it was best to leave what was in the past in the past. There was no reason to bring it up.

But then again, I desperately wished we'd talked about it more before Leah told me she was pregnant. It had been a gorgeous Saturday morning in February, unseasonably warm and sunny. We hadn't bothered to set the alarm the night before; we just let the sunlight stream in our window to wake us up. When I rolled over, Leah was already awake, smiling tenderly at me. "Good morning, sleepyhead," she whispered, brushing my hair out of my face.

"Morning," I croaked. She looked so beautiful. I didn't deserve her.

She sat up and ran her hands through my messy hair, her eyes twinkling in excitement. "So. I'm bringing someone over today… someone I really want you to meet."

I sat up too, cocking my head. "You're bringing someone over today? Thought we planned on doing absolutely nothing today. Big, big plans, hon. You sure it needs to be today?" I gave her my best pouty face because I knew it always made her giggle.

And she did. I loved listening to her giggle. "No, really. It's important. You'll love him. Or her. Not sure which yet."

"Wait, what?" I asked, confused.

"Yeah. Hey, you know what? I can introduce you right now."

"Hon…" I shook my head, still confused. "Are you sleep-talking? Do I need to pinch you and wake you up?"

"Just, *sh*." She put her finger to her lips, a smile stretching across her face. Then she took my hand and guided it to her belly, and suddenly, my mind went racing back to February 2008. To the night where Molly, unable to say out loud that she was pregnant, had taken my hand and led it to her belly in the exact same way that Leah had just done. It had taken me a few moments to process it back then, but this time, I knew exactly what Leah was trying to tell me. She was pregnant.

That's where it all turned sour. Instead of a smile bursting across my face like she probably expected, my eyes began to dart, and the blood drained from my face. I couldn't stop my mind from thinking about Molly, about the baby that never was. And I couldn't speak.

Leah's brow crinkled, and she pushed my hand away sharply. "What's wrong?" she demanded. "We stopped trying to prevent it! What did you think would happen, Tanner?" She threw the covers back and quickly left the bed. I saw her swipe a tear from her check, and my heart sank. If only she'd told me any other way!

"Hon! Leah, wait." I jumped out of bed and ran after her, grabbing her arm and turning her around to face me. "I'm sorry. Let me explain."

"Yeah. Please do," she snapped, yanking her arm away. Leah is a pretty chill person; it took a lot to get her riled up like this. I really messed this up for her. This was supposed to be one of the happiest mornings of our lives, her telling me for the first time that I was going to be a daddy. Now it would always be a tainted memory. One thing I'd learned in the short time I'd been married was that women do not forget things easily. For example, I'd forgotten about a date once, staying at the school late to work on a project that I was stressed out about. My phone had died earlier that day too, and my charger was at home on the nightstand. When I got home that night, Leah was furious and refused to talk to me. I calmed her down, and she was fine eventually, but every time I did something wrong after that, she always brought it up. She'd never forget it as long as we were married, I was sure of it. And now, this was just another thing she'd be upset about and bring up every single time we had an argument, something she'd never forget and never quite forgive me for. She'd *say* she forgave me, but I knew better. She wouldn't forgive me, not really. And this time, I wasn't sure I deserved forgiveness.

I sat her down on our unmade bed and took her hand in mine, deciding to be honest about me and Molly for the first time, going deeper into details that I never wanted to tell her before. "When Molly told me she was pregnant all those years ago, she did the same thing you just did," I explained. "She didn't want to say it out loud, so she just…took my hand and put it on her belly. Just like you did. So…I don't know. My mind flew back to that time. I'm sorry. I'm *so* happy, babe. I really am." I cradled her face in my hands and kissed her gently, and I felt her smile under my lips.

She pulled back, breathless. "Okay. I believe you." But her eyes fell short of her smile, and she sighed. I then gave her the response she was expecting, showering her with hugs and kisses and talking excitedly about our little gift from heaven.

Luckily for me, Leah was pretty forgiving about this one. At least I'd thought so, after how quickly she let my horrible reaction go. But as her pregnancy progressed, I was discovering a side of Leah I wasn't too impressed with. Leah had dark jealousy issues with Molly. I'd seen a bit of that during the short month Molly spent at home after being gone for three years, and it had bothered me then too, but I let it go. I'd known Molly would be leaving, and I really wanted to make sure we were okay before she left. I knew Leah would be fine eventually; Molly would leave, and we could carry on with our normal lives. So Molly and I'd spent quite a bit of time reconnecting, which Leah never liked. Each time I left the house to take Molly out for coffee or to go sit down by the lake at Molly's favorite spot, Leah's eyes darkened, and she clammed up. She never wanted to tell me that she didn't like me spending time with Molly, but she didn't need to. I could sense it.

Leah's sour attitude really was kind of my fault. This pregnancy kept sending me back to the spring of 2008, to Molly. I couldn't help it though. Molly and I had been so close and so in love at the time. And the last memories I had of Molly when we'd been so in love were when she'd been pregnant. It was the happiest I'd ever been, even though she was pregnant with another guy's baby. Because after she found out she was pregnant, that's when both of us had finally stopped dancing around the very plain truth that we loved each other. *How could I not think about Molly now, during Leah's pregnancy?*

I was afraid Leah was going to get in her car and drive as far as she could away from me one morning. I really messed up, big time. She'd spent an entire Saturday morning running back and forth between our bed and the bathroom, struggling with morning sickness. She told me to stay in bed, that she was fine, but I could see that she was really having a tough time. So when she crawled back in around eight o'clock, I was still working on waking up but wanting to comfort her. In my half-asleep state, I whispered, "It'll be okay, Molly girl. Anything I can do for you?"

She wouldn't speak to me the entire rest of the day. I let her stay mad at me though because I knew I deserved it. No matter how many times I apologized and tried to explain myself, I knew she had a right to be angry. I'd be angry too if she couldn't shake off memories of a past love. It would drive me crazy. I really needed to work through these feelings, to prove to her that Molly was in my past, that she would stay in my past, because Leah was my present; she was my future. She meant absolutely everything to me, and now that we were having a baby, I was even more in love with her than ever. I hated that I was doing such a horrible job showing it, but I didn't know how to shake these memories of

Molly, how to pull myself out of that time and bring myself into the present.

But the truth was—Molly still held a gigantic part of me. She always would. We'd been inseparable from the very first day we met, and then I'd spent the next twelve years falling hopelessly in love with her. When she ran away, she ripped out a huge chunk of my heart and took it with her. And though we'd reconnected and worked through all the drama, she never quite released it back to me. Not that I'd really wanted her to. Yes, I was married to Leah, and I loved her. But a part of me still loved Molly and always would. When you spend that many years loving someone, those feelings don't just disappear. I'd moved on, figured out how to deal with her absence, but I could never completely shake the hold she somehow still had on me. I wanted to keep her in my memory, all our happy times together. I just didn't know how to do that without completely pushing my wife away from me.

That afternoon while Leah was still mad at me for my little name mishap, I decided that I needed to give Molly a call. So I slipped out of the house while Leah was napping and headed out to Molly's spot. It was more of my spot now; I went out there quite frequently to clear my head or to simply quiet myself, listening to God. Today, I needed Molly. Because even after all we'd been through, Molly and I still had a deep connection. Most relationships fade and die after trauma and distance, but not with us. Something deep held us together, something that Leah and I simply didn't share. It's not that I couldn't talk to my wife…it was just that Molly *knew* me. She *got* me. Leah could do that to an extent, but nowhere near the level that Molly still could.

So I settled myself on the bench, which was damp and chilly because of the early May showers that had fallen all morning. I zipped my jacket up and pulled my phone out of my pocket, hoping and praying that Molly would answer. She was still on my speed dial—not number 1 anymore, not after I'd gotten married.

Leah wouldn't like that in the least bit, and it was a battle that I didn't want to fight.

It rang a few times, and my heart picked up a bit, nervous that she wouldn't answer and this trip out to the lake would be all for nothing. But she finally answered, breathless.

"Hey, Tanner. Sorry, my phone was of course in the deepest, darkest corner of my purse. What's up?"

I smiled and closed my eyes, picturing her relaxing on this lazy Saturday morning. She probably had her hair pulled back, little tendrils escaping and curling around her face like it always had in high school. She sounded relaxed and happy, and I was glad. I knew that even though things had turned out fairly well for her, she still struggled to find satisfaction in Kansas. I knew she wished things had turned out differently between us, that we were still together and raising her baby. The last time we talked, she'd opened up about how difficult Delilah's wedding had been for her, especially since she'd married the man Molly had fallen for. From the sounds of it, Molly thought it was unfair that everyone else was getting their happily ever after while she was struggling to earn her diploma and save up money for college. My heart hurt for her.

"Well," I began awkwardly, not sure how to tell the girl who'd once meant everything to me that I was going to have a baby. We both knew this day would come eventually, but now that it had, it was weird. I was happy, but I also knew that I was finally closing a chapter of my life, the chapter that included Molly. She'd still be a part of my life, but not in the same way. My marriage, and now this pregnancy, meant that we were completely and totally separate, going different ways. We both had to keep moving on.

"I just wanted to let you know," I continued, "that Leah and I…we're, uh…expecting." There was silence on the other end, and my heart began to pound. I knew her heart would be clenching, thinking how unfair this was. Molly could never think of babies the same way after the abortion, so I didn't know what she was feeling.

"I know, Tanner," she said quietly. "My mom called me the other day to let me know."

I cringed inwardly a little. Molly's mom had probably wanted to warn her, which meant that she too had known that this news would be hard on her. It was better than her finding out on Facebook or something, hurt that no one had thought to tell her this big news. Not only was it a big change in me and Leah's life, but it was a big change in me and Molly's life too. It just meant that things were continuing to move forward, leaving absolutely no hope of a future for us anymore. There hadn't been that hope for a long time of course, but this was just another confirmation. Tanner and Molly were over…and from now on, it would be Tanner and Leah and baby.

"Oh," I said lamely, unsure how to go on now. I'd prepared this big long speech on the way over here, but since she already knew, I didn't really know what else to say. I almost wanted to apologize, but that wasn't fair to Leah. This pregnancy was a happy occasion, something to celebrate, not apologize for.

Molly let me off the hook and jumped in. "I appreciate the call, Tanner. I'm happy for you guys. But…it *is* a little hard for me still. I just…have so many regrets. If things had happened differently, this could be us."

I let that sink in. She was right. If things had turned out differently, we'd no doubt be married by now and thinking about a family of our own. The baby would have been a little over three years old by now, ready for a little sibling to love. I sighed. "Yeah. That's weird to think about."

She let out a small laugh. "I try not to think about it too much. I *hate* living in the past. I've been trying really hard lately to figure out how to really move on, how to be content with where I'm at. It's tough." She sniffed, probably trying not to cry.

It blew me away that in the midst of this news, Molly wasn't allowing herself to be angry. Instead, she was using it to better herself, to figure out how to find joy even when life gave her a million reasons to throw her hands up in frustration. Those years away from us, away from God, had really transformed her. She was a much stronger Christian now than she was her senior year, much more willing to look at her mistakes and hardships and use them to draw closer to God and grow deeper in her faith. Nowadays, it seemed that she used everything to strengthen her relationship with God, something I deeply admired. It made this whole ordeal that much easier. I knew it would still be difficult for her, but I also knew that she was using this in a good way.

"I'm proud of you, Molly girl. I don't know if I'd be able to respond in the way you are. I can't believe the change in you. It's amazing."

I could hear her smile through the phone line. "It is. Every single day I wake up so thankful that I'm back in a good place. It's not the place I expected to be in when I was younger, but after all I've been through, I know I'm lucky. I could have turned to worse things…drugs, alcohol. Who knows what would have happened to me if I never made my way to Kansas. God has the craziest way of working things out though. It's nuts."

"For sure," I said, still impressed. I shuddered just thinking about what *could* have happened to Molly, and I sent a silent thank you up to God for keeping my girl safe and away from the traps that so many people fall into.

When I first learned that Molly had gotten raped, I thought my heart was literally going to break into a million pieces. I'd been so disappointed in Molly when she told me she was pregnant, so hurt that she'd thrown her morals out the window and slept with Jason. After she told me the truth, I walked around for months with so much guilt, sick to my stomach that I'd been angry at her for something she'd never asked for.

Molly has this uncanny ability to read my thoughts though, and I'd received a letter in the mail one day from her, telling me I needed to let go of my guilt and begin the healing process, just as she was doing. I knew she still went in to talk with her pastor about it, always working to put this behind her and live her life to the fullest, even after that trauma.

> There is no need for guilt, Tanner. What happened was nobody's fault. If you'd tried harder to keep me from Jason, it probably would have pushed me into his arms quicker. There was this rush I got from being with him. I felt rebellious hanging out with someone you and Kristina didn't approve of. Any attempt to keep me away from him would have made it even more fun for me, even more of a thrill. So please don't feel guilty about this. Looking back, I so appreciate that you let me make my own decisions, that you let me make mistakes. I take some responsibility for what happened, even though there was no way I could have known what would happen of course, and I know it's not my fault, but still. I should have listened to my gut that night, insisted that Jason take me home. But I didn't. And I can't change it now. What's done is done, and wishing things could be different just makes it harder. I want you to move on and heal, just like I'm doing. Guilt prevents that from happening, so I'm giving you permission to release your own guilt.
>
> I don't blame you for not chasing after me either. I never left a note, but I know it would have been fairly easy to find me with the technology we have today. I once struggled with that, wondering why you never tried harder to change my mind. But I really needed to make my own choices, to figure out who I really was. It might seem like that if you'd tried harder, we might still have the baby, but we simply can't think like that. I was terrified of Jason, terrified that if I didn't get the abortion, he'd come after you and my family. It seems silly now, but my emotions were all mixed up back then…my brain was scrambled.

The combination of fear and frustration just pushed me over the edge, and I would have done anything to protect you guys from Jason. It stinks that the price I paid was the life of my child, but God and I have dealt with that. What I want you to grasp is that no matter what you might have done...I probably still would have done it. Something snapped in me that spring. I became someone I now hate. By the grace of God, that person is dead, and I have been reborn. God is good, and I am thankful for this new life, that I'm no longer on that destructive path.

And finally, I want you to know that I'm not upset that you didn't wait for me. How crazy of me to ever expect that when I returned from a three-year absence you'd be right where I left you, arms open wide to welcome me home, picking up where we left off. I'm so happy you found a way to move on, Tanner, to survive without me. Even though I only experienced your love for a short time, I know it was deep. It was real. It's hard to move on after a love like that. But when I saw you with Leah that month I was home, I was so happy to see that you'd found a love like that again. Yes, it's hard to see you loving someone again, but you deserve it, Tanner. You are an amazing man of God who deserves all the best in life. I just want to thank you for loving me even though I could not love you back the way you so deserved back then—I was just too empty, and I'm sorry you got hurt in the process. You've always been so much more than I ever deserved, and I'll cherish the memories of our friendship forever.

I pulled out that note often to reassure myself that what happened wasn't my fault. I knew that an essential part of Molly's continued healing was that I find a way to deal with my own guilt, because I knew it upset her that I felt guilty. I'd done quite a bit of soul-searching and praying on this very bench, trying to work through all these painful emotions. It wasn't something that happened overnight; it was a long, exhausting process that consisted of tossing and turning at night, haunted by regrets, struggling to love my own wife in a Biblical way because I felt like I'd fallen short with Molly. Going through long dry spells, unable to open my Bible or utter a single prayer because God felt so distant. But I felt Molly's prayers for me, her eager desire for me to heal like she was healing. And eventually, it had begun to sink in. Guilt was a roadblock to healing, and it was time for me to throw it out of my path.

A cold drop of rain landed on my nose, and I jumped, startled out of my thoughts. "Well, I'm out at your spot, and it's starting to rain again. I just wanted to tell you the news myself...make sure you were all right."

"Thanks," she whispered. "Means a lot."

"I miss you," I admitted, not sure if it was appropriate because I was a married father-to-be, but I *did* miss her. It would have been nice if she could have stayed in Oak Ridge, but I understood why she didn't want to. Oak Ridge held a weird mix of good and horrible memories. It's where we'd grown up, where we'd had so many adventures. It's where we'd fallen in love, where we'd dreamed up so many plans for our future, clueless that Jason would swoop in and destroy those dreams in a matter of months. But it's where she'd been raped, where she'd found out she was pregnant. It was where Jason had threatened her and scared her clear out of her mind, forcing her to make the rash decision to bolt to Minneapolis. And it's where she'd come back to find the rest of her dreams shattered—a future with me impossible. I probably wouldn't want to stick around either. She'd made a good life for herself in Kansas, made strong Christian friendships and found a good church family to care for her. Still. I missed her.

"I miss you too. But I'll be home in June for the wedding. Let's make plans to hang out for a bit, the three of us." As a woman, Molly knew that Leah would have issues with me, her husband, spending alone time with someone I once loved.

"I'd like that."

"Me too. Talk to you later, Tanner. And congratulations on the baby. That's gonna be one cute kid. And a lucky one too. Can't imagine better parents than you two."

I smiled. "Thanks, Molly. See you in June." I shut my phone, and the rain picked up, now falling in a steady drizzle. But I stayed put, reflecting on Molly's last comment. She thought Leah and I would be great parents, and for the first time, it hit me that I was going to be responsible for a life. I was going to be expected to care for and provide for this little one, to protect and make the best life possible for him or her. The enormity of my situation settled onto my shoulders. No longer was I worried that I would look into my baby's eyes and feel sad about Molly's baby. Molly didn't want that for me, and I wouldn't let that happen.

Now, I was just worried about the huge job ahead of me. Fatherhood was something I didn't want to take lightly; I knew what an influence a father has on his child's life. I needed to get serious about this, make sure Leah knew I loved her with all my heart and that I would give my all to our child. They needed to be my number 1 concern now. I'd wasted too much time feeling guilty about Molly and her baby that I'd been letting down my *own* wife and baby. I didn't want to look back and feel guilty about this either, so it was time to step up my game.

I drove home from the lake feeling good about my phone call to Molly. It had given me the closure I needed, and now I could go home with a new attitude, ready to love my wife and prepare myself for fatherhood after wasting all this time. And best of all, this phone call had reassured me that Molly was okay with this, that she was dealing with it in a healthy way.

It was time for me to do the same.

TWELVE

❖

Molly

MAY

I slid my phone shut and instantly felt guilty. I was getting increasingly good at telling people I was okay with where I was in life, that I was working to find satisfaction and contentment. That part was true; I was working extremely hard to find satisfaction and contentment in my life. But I didn't feel okay. I wasn't happy with where I was right now, even though I knew I had so much to be thankful for. Like I'd just told Tanner, I could have fallen into a much worse path, I could have turned to drugs or alcohol to cope with what had happened to me. I could have found myself addicted, spending all my money supporting a drug habit and living in the streets of Minneapolis. Or, like Delilah, I could have gotten so distraught and tried to end my own life. By the grace of God, Delilah's mother had stopped her just in time, but back in Minneapolis, no one would have checked up on me. *How awful would it have been for one of the girls to walk in and find me dead on my tiny little bed?* It would have scarred them for life. And I'd never told them about my family back in Iowa. They would have had no idea how to contact them, to let them know I'd taken my own life.

What a mess that would have been. I could picture it all, when news finally got to Oak Ridge. A police officer would come knocking on the front door to tell my parents that someone they believed to be their daughter had committed suicide, and they needed to go identify the body. And Josh and Savannah…if I'd taken my life, we never would have gotten the chance to work through our deep issues. They would have been forced to drag around the weight of my suicide for the rest of their lives, full of bitterness and anger.

Upon my return to Iowa after my three-year-running-away spree, I was faced with a side of Josh I never knew existed. Savannah and I had reconnected pretty easily; she forgave me quickly, and we moved on with our lives. But Josh…man. He put up a fight. Throughout our whole lives, Josh and I had been close even though I was three years older than him. We just clicked; we got along better than most siblings do. We spent our summers running through sprinklers with Tanner during the day and chasing fireflies with him at night. The three of us used to beg our parents to let us sleep in Tanner's ratty, old tent on those hot summer nights as well, where we'd usually come tromping back in around two or three in the morning because we were hot or some loud noise had scared us. In the winter, we'd spend Saturday afternoons constructing snow forts and pulling each other around on sleds, then sip Evelyn's homemade hot chocolate on the island in Tanner's kitchen. It was always the three of us growing up, and it was a blast.

We rarely fought either, something that always surprised my mom. But we figured that it was a much better use of time to be playing and getting alone than being angry and fighting. If we did get into little spats, they never lasted long because neither of us had anything to do if we were fighting. Tanner hated to be in the middle of fights and refused to take sides, so we quickly figured out that we needed to resolve our fights if we wanted to get back to the fun.

So when I returned that fall, I never expected Josh to hold such a strong grudge against me. I expected that he be angry at me, but I thought we'd be able to talk through it fairly easily and move on. We had made a great effort to talk through things, but Josh still had a tough time accepting what had happened and the choices I'd made during that time.

It frustrated me to no end that no matter how many times I tried to explain all the pressure I'd been feeling after the rape and pregnancy, he still thought I should have been smarter and able to make the right decision. He thought I was just making up excuses, that I should have known that Jason couldn't really force me to get an abortion or that he probably wouldn't have come after Tanner or the family. I tried to explain to him that yes, any normal person would have looked at the circumstances and known those things were true, but back then, my brain was all scrambled up. I hadn't been able to think clearly because so many emotions were swirling around in my brain. I was ashamed of the rape, ashamed that I'd let things get so out of hand with Jason. I thought the rape had been my fault and that I should have known he'd do it once we were alone. That simply wasn't true; there was no way I could have known. But you can't understand unless you go through it. It seems silly that rape victims blame themselves, but that's simply what happens much of the time. Josh didn't understand. He'd never understand, and that hurt. To him, I was just using the rape as an excuse for my poor decisions. But I *knew* that it had damaged me, that it had been partly to blame for my inability to think straight. I was a victim, and I wish Josh would get that through his brain.

Josh also struggled with the abortion, probably more than I did. I lived with that decision every single day of my life, fully aware that I should have a three-year-old singing and skipping through my house. But I'd worked through it, come to grips with the fact that I'd aborted my baby, and I could never undo that. I knew God didn't like what I'd done, but he'd forgiven me. And I'd forgiven myself. The hurt would never go away of course, but wallowing through guilt and shame every single day was exhausting, and I refused to do it. *God had forgiven me, so why not forgive myself as well?* When the guilt and shame welled up again and tried to choke me, I'd battle back with scripture and prayer, refusing to let my past get in the way of a bright future.

Josh seemed incapable of forgiving me for the abortion, incapable of moving on like I'd done. He let the anger consume him, refusing to deal with it like I had. To him, I'd always had the option to give the baby up for adoption, but back then, it hadn't seemed even remotely possible. I remembered back to the day Jason trapped me in the janitor's closet, telling me that even if I gave the baby up for adoption, one day the child would get curious and come looking for him. Jason told me that he never wanted that baby to come looking for him, probably because he was planning on having his own family by then and he didn't want to have to explain to a wife and family that at eighteen he'd fathered a child and then refused to have anything to do with it. *Talk about awkward.*

Back then I'd been terrified of Jason. I believed him when he threatened my family and Tanner. I knew what he was capable of after the rape...I knew he'd do anything to keep himself safe. Josh thought that was ridiculous and that I should have reported him. But again, he simply didn't understand. He didn't understand the shame, why I desperately wanted to keep the rape a secret. Reporting him would have meant telling the truth about the rape. It would have meant explaining why Jason had such a problem with the baby. He had a problem with it because he knew what he'd done was rape. And I think he'd been proud of it too, that he'd been able to have power over me. But once others found out about it—that would have been the end for him. All his dreams shattered, just like he'd shattered mine.

So I ran. And I got an abortion just like Jason wanted me to. In some weird way, I thought I'd been protecting the baby, from Jason and from all the dark, horrible things in this world, like rape. At that point, I was so bitter and angry at the world, angry at God, that I truly thought that the baby was better off dead. After all, I'd felt like dying every single day, but I was too scared to ever do it. In my mind, I was doing the baby a favor. I was doing what I wished I could do but wasn't able to.

Now, I knew the truth. God is able to take every situation, no matter how dark, and turn it into something beautiful. After all, he'd stooped into the dust and made beauty in the form of man. How much more proof did you need? Cynics might say that man is not beauty; man is capable of evil, of doing horrible things. This is true. And yet, I know different. I know this life is beautiful. I see it every single day in the sunrise and the simple rolling hills of Kansas. I see it in the face of little Luke, who is always so full of joy. Everywhere I turn, I see the beauty of life, and I know that no matter what horrible things man is capable of doing, God is bigger. One day, God will right all the wrongs, and the world will be the way he always meant it to be, perfect and filled with his holy presence.

I heaved a giant sigh, sad that no matter how much Josh and I talked, he'd never quite forgive me. He was stubborn, and he thought he was right. So no matter how much it hurt me that he refused to look at things from my point of view—a terrified eighteen-year-old rape victim—I couldn't dwell on this. In my heart, I knew I was forgiven by God, and his forgiveness was the only forgiveness that mattered anyway.

I jumped off the couch, needing to do something, anything, to get my mind off all these confusing thoughts. I told Mary Beth I'd be in later this afternoon to help her since Albert was struggling with his health right now. She really needed to hire some more people, but she was prideful and wasn't too keen on letting others come in to mess up her system. She must have really felt God telling her to hire me that day I landed in her diner, and for that, I would be eternally grateful. But in these few hours until work, I needed something to keep my hands busy and my mind off the past.

My apartment hadn't been cleaned in a while, so I pulled the vacuum cleaner out of the linen closet and tackled the living room, hoping to clear my mind a bit. As I went past my stereo I pushed play and let the praise music blast, loud enough to be heard over the vacuum, turning this cleaning session into a dance party. But I guess I got a little too into it because I rammed into my little wooden stand, the stand that the picture of me and Tanner as happy, carefree teenagers sat on. I hit it hard enough to send the picture flying, where it clattered to the kitchen floor. I heard the cheap glass shatter, and when I picked it up, I saw a crack split right up the middle of the picture, a crack now separating Tanner from me.

I don't know why this hit me so hard. But I stood there for the longest time, staring at the jagged line now separating me and Tanner. I couldn't help but think this was some sort of sign. I'd broken the picture frame holding a picture of me and Tanner on the day he called to tell me about Leah's pregnancy. *Could this be God telling me that it was really and truly over between us? That I needed to finally figure out a way to move past this?*

Right above my wooden stand, the picture Tyler had taken of me was still hanging, perfectly intact. Ever since I'd rededicated my life to Christ, I tried really hard to listen to God's voice in everything. I knew God doesn't always give us the answers in the ways we wanted him to, like randomly opening up the Bible to find a verse that answers our question or a back shiver to let us know we've made the right decision. We don't always know if we're making the right decision or which way we're supposed to go in life. But I did know that sometimes…he *does* give us signs, little hints of his will. If our hearts are open to those little hints, we can see our prayers being answered right before our eyes. But in this case, I just wasn't sure. One picture was shattered, one still hung beautifully intact on the wall. *Was it finally time for me to close this chapter of my life and open up a brand-new one with Tyler?*

I hadn't heard from him in a while; I was beginning to wonder if he'd changed his mind about restarting a relationship. *Was that chapter being closed too? What other plans could God have for me anyway?* I'd always dreamed of being a wife and a mother. *Would he really deny me of those dreams to take me down a completely new path? Or was I being punished for my reckless past few years? Was I being denied marriage and a family because I'd gotten an abortion, because I'd misused sex over and over again?*

I quickly dismissed those thoughts from my brain. I knew God didn't punish us that way. There were certainly *consequences* of sinning, but the ultimate punishment for sin is an eternity separated from God. And Christ had overcome that punishment by laying himself down on the cross and taking all that sin away. Deep down, I knew that I wasn't being punished for what I'd done all those years ago, but I had to keep reminding myself over and over again. It *felt* like I was being punished.

Maybe there was something big I was supposed to do, a life I was supposed to touch for Christ that couldn't happen if I was married. Maybe I needed to remain single for a bit longer so I could go wherever it was that God wanted me to go, without having to ask a husband to leave familiarity behind.

The ringing of my phone snapped me out of my thoughts. I jumped up from the couch and padded over to the table. The name I saw on the screen made my heart jump up into my throat. It was Tyler.

"Hey!" I said excitedly, kind of weirded out that five minutes earlier I was wishing for some sort of a sign that I was supposed to be with Tyler. *Could* this *be a sign?*

"Hey, Molly. What's up?" Just the sound of his voice was enough to lift my spirit. Tyler always had this uncanny ability to make me smile, even in the midst of all that had been happening to me while we were together in Minneapolis. That's the main reason I let myself have a relationship with him. He made me laugh; he made me forget about all the horrible things that had happened, even for just a little while. It had been wrong, so wrong. But that was because our relationship hadn't been built off Christ. Now though, it could be. If we restarted our relationship, we could make sure that this time it *was* centered on Christ. Then, it would be okay that he made me laugh and smile because it wouldn't be simply to make myself feel better or forget about my situation. I could laugh and smile simply because I liked him and I enjoyed his company.

"Well, a whole lot of nothing! My life is less than exciting right now," I joked.

"Hey now...can't be *that* bad, can it?" I could hear his smile through the phone lines.

I sighed. "Just doing a lot of working and a lot of studying. I think I'll be ready to take my GED test by this summer. But I'd hoped to already be taking classes right now. I've just been busy, not able to do as much studying as I wanted. But...it'll happen."

"Sure will. You're smart. That test will be a piece of cake for my Molly. And this way, you can start the year in the fall. It'll probably be easier than trying to jump in at semester anyway," he offered.

"True," I said with a shrug.

Silence overtook the conversation as small talk stalled. But since he called me, I wanted to let him steer the conversation. I assumed that he had something specific he wanted to talk about. Ever since we'd decided to see where things would go for us he was very deliberate with his intentions. Letters were filled with emotion, letting me know that he thought about me all the time and that he was excited for whatever it was that God had in store for us. And phone calls weren't just to talk about how my job at the diner was going or how annoyed I was at studying. It was always about something specific that he wanted to talk about. So I waited.

"So. I wanted to talk about something kind of big." I grinned. I knew it.

"Shoot." I settled into the couch, ready for whatever it was that Tyler needed to talk about. Because maybe, just maybe, God was showing me a new path to take, a path that included Tyler.

"Okay. Well, you know Jenny, of course, and how much she means to me."

"Of course," I replied. Each letter and phone call also included talk of Jenny. Tyler couldn't get enough of her. She'd been such an influence in his decision to become a Christian, and I could relate to that. What Jenny meant to him, Luke meant to me. We'd always have a special bond with those kids because they'd helped us so much more than they'd ever know. And not only did he love her for showing him the love of Christ, but he also had this deep longing to help her. She was still living in the home for children after her parents died in a car accident, and he wasn't sure what would happen to her. He desperately wanted to get her out of there, to see her placed in a loving home.

"Okay. So obviously kids can't stay in the home forever, not with foster care and all that. But Jenny's parents didn't want her to be shuffled around from home to home like that. Her grandparents are still around…but her grandpa just had a stroke, and her grandma takes care of him. They'd take her, but I just don't think it's the best thing for her. I mean, who knows how much longer he'll last? And once one spouse dies…it probably wouldn't be long until the other goes as well."

"Okay…" I said slowly, unsure where he was going with all this.

"Just hear me out. Her grandparents agree with the volunteers at the home. They're too old to take in a four-year-old. But Jenny's mom was an only child. There are no more relatives to take her in. And her dad came from South Korea when he was nineteen. He's the only one that came. There are relatives there, but we don't want to send her to some foreign country where she doesn't speak the language and she doesn't know anybody. She'd probably adjust…but it just doesn't seem like the best thing for her."

My heart was breaking for him, but to me, it sounded like he simply didn't want to lose this little girl. He didn't want her gone from his life. Maybe it would be good for her to go live in South Korea, learn her heritage, and meet her family. In the States, they missed seeing her grow up. But if she went back, she'd have the support and love of a family she'd never met. It could be a very good thing for her, even if Tyler disagreed. He shouldn't let his feelings get in the way of what was best for Jenny. I knew firsthand how hard it was trying to survive in this world without a family. It was awful, those three years without any contact with the people who loved and supported me most in the world. *Didn't Jenny deserve that love and support too?*

"Ty," I answered, trying to be gentle, "you don't know that. It could be the best thing that ever happened to her, reconnecting with a family that probably loves and misses her."

"Maybe," he said sharply, and I recoiled. It took a lot to get Tyler riled up; he didn't usually raise his voice unless something really bothered him. Jenny was a sensitive topic right now, and I knew it was best not to push Tyler about it. I knew he wanted the best for her, but he was also probably scared to death of losing her. Tyler needed someone outside of the situation to tell him that what was best for Jenny was to be with a family. And she had a family back in South Korea.

"She needs a family, Ty. You can't give her that, if that's what you're thinking." Tyler was kind of like Tanner in this way; he'd get some big idea in his head, and it took me explaining to him why it wouldn't work to finally see that maybe it wasn't the best idea. From the way Tyler was talking about this, I could sense that he was thinking about adopting Jenny.

"Are you thinking of adopting her?" I asked. "Because I don't think that's the best idea right now. You just got done with school. You don't have a ton of money saved up…" I trailed off, though I could have gone on and on about why Tyler wasn't a suitable parent for little Jenny. He didn't know the first thing about kids!

Helping out with Jenny and the kids at the home might give him the idea that he could handle raising a child, but that was in a controlled atmosphere, with trained professionals and dozens of volunteers. On his own, it would be tough…very tough. He'd have to do it all alone, and there'd be no volunteers to call when things got out of hand or messy.

"I could be a family for her. It just depends on one thing."

My heart did a weird little dance, and I didn't respond. Any words that my brain might have come up with to answer him would have gotten stuck in my throat anyway because it was closing up.

I swallowed and tried to stop my head from spinning long enough to formulate an answer to what Tyler had just said. "And just how might you be a family for her?" I asked timidly, hoping beyond hope that his answer included me.

"I'd be the daddy, of course. And the mommy. Well. You… could be the mommy. If you wanted to…"

I broke into a smile. "Are you proposing to me over the phone?" I teased.

"No, no!" he jumped in. "That'd be beyond lame. I'm simply… proposing the *idea* of us getting married so that we could adopt Jenny and be her family. If you say you'll at least think about it, I'll propose to you in the sweetest, most romantic way any guy has ever proposed to a girl in the history of forever," he promised.

I giggled. "Oh wow. The history of forever? That better be one epic proposal!"

We talked for the next half hour, dreaming and planning of all that might be in store for us. But when we hung up, I had this weird pit in the bottom of my stomach. Something didn't feel right about this whole deal. It had been beyond sweet of Tyler to call me up and give me hope that my dreams of being a wife and a mother might actually come true. But I had to wonder if his sudden interest in a relationship had everything to do with his desire to help Jenny and nothing to do with the fact that he was falling in love with me again. I knew he still had feelings for me, but a few months ago, he had been willing to wait as long as I needed to figure out my feelings. Now though, he was really pushing me to make up my mind.

"I only have a few months to get this all figured out," he said urgently as we were wrapping up the conversation. "They have to contact the family in South Korea, if they can even find them. But in the end, her grandparents will decide. And I think once I meet them, I can convince them what good parents we'd be for her. I know they'll fall in love with us.

"So…I'm gonna need an answer sooner than later, Molly girl. If you feel even just a little bit that God is leading you down this path with me, please listen. And let me know as soon as possible, okay? I don't want to lose her. She means everything to me."

I promised him I'd do some serious praying and that I'd listen closely to what God was telling me to do. While I didn't want to be one of those people who just sat around and waited for God to tell me exactly what to do on every single detail of my life, I knew that this situation was different. Sometimes we have to just make decisions and go with them knowing that if we take a wrong turn, God will get us back where we need to be going. We have to just *do* things once in a while, trusting that God will lead. But in this case, I wanted to take some time and make sure it was his will. Marriage was a huge deal, and I refused to just walk into something that wasn't going to last.

I grabbed the shattered frame and settled onto the couch again. Things hadn't turned out the way I'd always imagined for going on four years now, and yet today, it felt like my whole world had turned upside down. The chapter with Tanner had long since closed, but the announcement of his pregnancy made it that much more final. And now, this picture was broken, perhaps a gentle nudge that I needed to forget about Tanner and move on with Tyler…and with Jenny.

Tanner had said on that first day we talked after my return to Iowa that my new life was just beginning. During those three years, I seemed to run into dead end after dead end, and finding him married and happy had seemed like just another ending to me. And it didn't really feel like a new beginning, not really, up until recently, that is. Because now Tyler had just called and offered me a new life, complete with my dream of marriage and a family.

But if this was the start of my new life, why wasn't I jumping and singing for joy? Why didn't I feel like calling Delilah to share this amazing news with her? Something just didn't feel right, and I wasn't sure what it was. Maybe it was because he'd said that *Jenny* meant the world to him, that he would do everything in his power to keep *her*. He hadn't said that *I* meant the world to him or that he'd do everything in his power to keep *me* in his life. Or maybe I was still feeling sad that things were really and truly over between Tanner and me. In a few months, he'd be extremely busy with a new baby; he wouldn't have time to sit down and call me. He had a responsibility to his family now; it was time for me to let go and let him live his life free from my drama.

But I didn't want to let go. Deep down, I knew that Tanner still held a part of me. He always would. It didn't matter that he was married and expecting a baby. I still loved him. And I wasn't sure if I could go off and get married to Tyler when I still loved Tanner.

I put my head in my hands and sighed, defeated. *Why did I still love Tanner?* There was no hope of us ever getting back together, period. He was married. He was having a baby. It was over between us; it had been over for years. This obsession with him was simply getting in the way of a potentially amazing future with Tyler and Jenny.

My brain couldn't handle making a big decision just yet. I knew Tyler would want an answer within the next month or so, but that was awfully fast to make such a life-altering decision.

And once I told him I was ready for a commitment, he'd come out and propose, so the surprise element of it went sailing right out the door. That made me a little sad because every little girl dreams about the day where her Prince Charming gets down on one knee and asks her to be his wife. I didn't want to know that the next time he came out would be to propose! He *said* he'd do it in the sweetest and most romantic way in the history of forever, but the fact that I knew it'd be coming made the sweetness and romantic factor dwindle significantly. It simply wouldn't be all I'd dreamed it would be.

I shook my head, refusing to think about this anymore today. It was time to go in for work anyway, so I changed, threw my hair in a ponytail, shoved my feet into my ratty little tennis shoes, and headed to the diner. As I drove, I reassured myself that God wouldn't let me make the wrong choice this time, not since I was being so open to his will. I desperately wanted to do things right this time.

God, I prayed, *I need you. I don't know what to do here. I hate that I can't get Tanner out of my heart! Here you've possibly opened a new door for me, and yet…I'm still torn. Please let me know if I'm supposed to walk through this door. I so want to do this right this time. I'm open to whatever you have in store for me, God. I just need a little help knowing exactly what that is.*

I walked into work confident that God would answer that prayer for me. Somehow, someday, I'd finally get to where God wanted me to go. I would be patient this time though, knowing that when I took matters into my own hands, things would end up going terribly wrong. I'd learned that the hard way before. I refused to do it again. Tyler would need to be patient too, because this wasn't just about rescuing Jenny. It was also about me.

～

Work wasn't relaxing me like I'd hoped. If anything, my anxiety level was skyrocketing. The diner was crazy busy, and it was apparent that we didn't have the help we needed to take care of all the customers. Mary Beth and I were frantically taking orders and trying to make all the dishes at the same time. Eventually, we had to enlist Albert's help as a waiter though he hadn't taken orders for years. But he was okay at it, a little slow but amazing with customers. Every table we put him in charge of was happy and smiling; he had a special bond with people and an incredible ability to make them laugh. Each child he served also received one of his signature caramel candies as well.

When the rush died down, I collapsed into a booth with a cup of coffee and a sticky roll, one of Mary Beth's famously delicious baked goods. It was soft and gooey and just what I needed to unwind and relax after this excruciatingly busy shift. I closed my eyes and savored the cinnamon sugar coating, and when I opened my eyes, Albert was grinning at me from across the booth. I sat up quickly and giggled.

"Hey, Al. You scared me."

He chuckled. "Yeah. These wrinkles tend to do that to people."

I waved my hand dismissively. "Nah. Wrinkles just show the world that you're wise and have experienced so much in your life. Right?"

"Oh, I suppose," he said with another chuckle. He took a sip of coffee, and for the first time, I realized just how old he looked. He was in his eighties now, and up until a few weeks ago, he looked healthier than many people twenty years younger than him. He refused to let anyone help him carry that big bucket of dishes to the back room when it was overflowing and much too heavy for him to handle himself. And every night, he lifted chairs onto tables and mopped the floors until they shone—manual labor that he really shouldn't be doing at his age. But he, like Mary Beth, was stubborn and proud. He wanted to do all that himself, wanted to prove to us and everyone else in town that he was still young at heart and fully capable of completing those tasks.

His last doctor's visit hadn't been good however. His heart was beginning to fail him. He seemed to tire much more easily now, and Mary Beth and I were constantly fretting over him, which he hated. So I was glad to see him taking a little break with me. Usually when it slowed down like this, he'd find some little project to do, be it cleaning the windows, sweeping out crumbs from underneath the booths, or shining up the silverware. He was constantly on the move, always wanting to keep busy. But he needed to do this more often. His body would only break down quicker if he refused to slow down and rest for a bit.

He put his arms on the table and leaned forward, looking me square in the eyes. It always made me feel a bit awkward when he did this, like he was trying to look into my soul and read my thoughts or something. I smiled and asked, "What?"

"Something's on your mind, isn't it, Molly?"

That was just about the biggest understatement of the year. A *lot* of things were on my mind lately. Between dealing with Delilah, sorting out my feelings for Tanner, and the upcoming wedding for my brother, my head was about to explode. And once again, my GED was getting pushed to the side so I could take care of all that was going on. Plus, after Albert had told us he wasn't doing well, I'd come in to the diner pretty much every single day, sometimes for the entire day to make sure he wasn't overdoing it. There simply weren't enough hours in the day to get done all that needed to get done.

I nodded. "You could say that."

"Anything I can help with, kiddo?" he asked sincerely, and my heart began to melt. What a sweet old man he was, burdened with severe health problems and yet still wanting to do whatever he could to ease my burdens.

I gave him a small smile and took his hand. "Not really, Albert. I'm just a little stressed out is all. There's so much going on right now, and I still haven't found the time take my GED test yet. All this is just kinda weighing me down…I'm having a little trouble keeping up the joy," I admitted with a shrug, and he gave my hand a gentle squeeze.

"I can relate to that, sweet girl." He gave me a questioning look. "Have I ever told you my story?"

I shook my head no. "I don't believe so."

He gave a strong nod. "Well, I reckon it's about time I did! If nothing else, maybe it will help you remember that even in the toughest circumstances, God is faithful."

Albert's story did that and so much more. I sat back in awe as he launched into a heartbreaking story about how he had lost his wife as she gave birth to their second child, a little boy who'd also died shortly after birth. He'd held his young wife's hand as she struggled to push out their breech little baby boy, but the long labor and loss of blood had taken its toll on her, and she died minutes after their son made his entrance into the world. She never got to hold him or even see him. The labor had taken its toll on their son too. Doctors had tried to get him turned around, but in the process, the umbilical cord had wrapped around his little neck and strangled him on the way out. So Albert had been left in the room with the disheartened doctors, holding his perfect son in one arm and desperately clutching onto his wife's hand with the other. They had slowly filed out to let him say his good-byes. Meanwhile, his four-year-old son was waiting just down the hall with both sets of grandparents, eager to meet his new brother and to see his mommy after the long labor.

I couldn't hold in my tears as Albert described what telling his family had been like. His wife's parents had of course broken down in tears; her mother even fainted and had to be admitted to the hospital. And Paul, his son, simply didn't understand. He keep asking to see his mommy over and over again, and Albert had to explain to him that mommy didn't live on earth anymore. She lived with Jesus.

The thing that struck me most about this story was Albert's unwavering faith. Not once did he blame God for what had happened. He was hurt and confused, but he knew that God must have a bigger plan for his life than Albert had for his own. I couldn't wrap my mind around that as I wouldn't have been able to respond in that way. I was pretty sure most people wouldn't respond that way either. It was so much easier to blame God and be angry at him than to get down on your knees and admit that his plan is bigger and better. It was hard to praise God in such big storms, and yet that's what Albert had done.

Just when I thought the story was over, it got worse. Albert struggled to raise his son by himself as Paul had deep anger issues growing up without his mother. Paul hadn't been able to accept the fact that the death of his mother and brother was part of God's plan. He didn't agree with that plan, and he didn't like it, so he became angry and bitter instead. Albert refused to think about getting remarried; he instead focused all his energy making sure Paul would be okay. But things started getting worse and worse, and Albert was at a loss. Paul had been suspended from school a number of times for violence and even punching his hand through a window. Albert began to worry that he might get expelled. So the summer that Paul turned thirteen, he sent him to a camp for children who'd lost loved ones. He hoped that maybe the counselors and fellow campers would be able be help Paul in a way that he'd been unable to do for his entire life.

On the last day of camp, Albert received a phone call from the camp telling him he needed to come up immediately because something had happened. They wouldn't tell him over the phone, so Albert dropped everything and made the two-hour drive in a little over an hour. When he got there, everyone was crying and shaking their heads. The director of the camp ushered him into the office, where Paul was stretched out on a cot, a sheet pulled over his body.

Paul had been doing exceptionally well at camp. He clicked with his cabin mates immediately and loved his counselor. On that last day the boys had decided to go swimming in the little lake on the edge of the camp because it had been so hot that week. There was no lifeguard on duty, only a few counselors supervised the kids, not closely enough though because Paul had drowned that day. He had been swimming on the edge of the lake where a few big trees grew and stretched over the water. Some of the boys had been climbing up the trees and jumping off into the water, and one of the boys jumped in not knowing Paul was right below the trees under the water. He'd landed right on Paul's head without realizing it, thinking it must have been a rock or a stump instead.

A few minutes later though, a girl screamed and pointed. Paul was floating face down in the water. One of the counselors rushed into the water and pulled him out, but he wasn't breathing. While someone ran for help, they performed CPR, but by the time an ambulance made it out to the camp, Paul was long gone.

Albert described pulling the sheet down and looking at his son's face for the last time, immediately wishing he hadn't. Paul's face was blue and angry looking, not how he wanted to remember his son at all. He quickly pulled the sheet back up and covered his face, unable to stop the tears from coursing down his cheeks.

And just like that, Albert was all alone. He'd lost his wife and baby, and then…God had taken the only thing he had left in the world—his son, Paul. It was too much for one man to endure in one life! And yet when I looked in Albert's eyes, I never would have guessed that he'd gone through all of that. There was no sadness; there was no anger or bitterness. There was simply joy and love for Christ. Again, I couldn't wrap my mind around that. Tragedy after tragedy, Albert was still able to say to the Lord, "Not my will, but yours, oh, Lord."

I sat there speechless after Albert was done talking, unable to come up with anything appropriate to say. He just smiled. "It's like I said earlier, sweet Molly. Even in the toughest circumstance, God is faithful. I didn't abandon him because I knew he hadn't abandoned me. Things didn't go the way I wanted them to. But…

sometimes God takes us into the rough waters not to drown us but to cleanse us, to make us better. When it was all happening I couldn't see it, but eventually, I did."

"How?" I asked quietly, still in awe of the man sitting across from me.

"Well. I've always been a man of faith. But I loved the world way too much. I was one of those people who always dreaded hearing sermons about eternity because I thought it never could compare with what I had on the earth. I had a beautiful wife and son and another on the way…I didn't think my life could get much better! But maybe their deaths were a reminder that this world isn't what I think it is. It's bad, Molly. Bad things happen.

"At the end though, we get Jesus. And he's better than a beautiful wife and big family, by far. I think that's what God was trying to tell me. Maybe I never would have understood that if they'd lived…who knows?" he said with a grin and a shrug. "What I *do* know is that one day, we will be together again. I look forward to that."

I laughed. "Yes, I'm sure you do. But…what about Paul? I mean…you'd already lost so much! How did you get past that one?"

He let out a big sigh and nodded. "Yeah. That one was tough. But Paul struggled his entire life. I don't think he was ever going to fully heal from the loss of his mom and little brother. That's a lot for a little kid to deal with, and I just don't think his little heart could handle it. But I have to believe that in those few days he was at camp, God did something big in his heart. The people at the camp said he'd changed right before their eyes. I'll never know for sure…but something tells me that he met Jesus at that camp. And maybe God knew that things would always be hard for my boy. That even with Christ, he'd always struggle. So maybe he took him home so that he didn't have to live without his mom and brother anymore.

"I tried to be everything he needed…but maybe it wasn't enough. Maybe God knew that and to make both our lives a bit easier, he took him back and gave him what he really wanted anyway."

I felt my eyes widen in shock. I couldn't help it. Albert just said that maybe God took his son from him to make both their lives easier. To me, the loss of yet another loved one seemed harder, not easier! I shook my head in both amazement and disbelief. This man was truly something else.

He went on to explain that after Paul's funeral, he packed up and left town. Too many sad memories lived there, which I could relate to. He moved across the state and ended up here, where eventually he met Mary Beth and her two daughters. Mary Beth had been pregnant with Delilah when she started going to church and meeting with Pastor Dennis, and Albert sort of adopted all of them after that.

"I love those sweet girls more than anything in the world. You know, I was there the day Delilah was born. I held her just minutes after she came into the world, all pink and screaming. She had the darkest head of hair I'd ever seen on a baby!"

I giggled. Delilah had gorgeous, dark, curly hair. So did Luke. Her father must have been darker skinned too because her skin was a bit darker than her mom and sisters.

"And they became the family I never got to have. Instead of sons though, I got daughters. Well…more like granddaughters, really. They always say how I saved them, but they're wrong. They saved me. Without them, I'd be a lonely, old man pining for the days I'd lost."

Sometimes all it takes is hearing someone else's story to remind yourself that the storms happen to all of us. It's so easy to look at someone like Albert, someone who has so much joy and peace radiating from their eyes, and assume that nothing bad has ever happened to them. Maybe that's because some of us just like feeling sorry for ourselves. We want people to see that we're hurting, that we have it so rough and everyone should feel sorry for us too. So we walk around harboring so much bitterness and anger because of what has happened to us, and when we see those joyful, peaceful, and content people, we say it's not fair that they have it so easy. That's simply not true. Those people haven't avoided hardships and storms. They've instead dealt with them correctly; they've given up their situations and decided to trust that God knows what he's doing. They know he has plans—good plans. Sometimes those plans include hardships and trials that we don't necessarily want to walk through, but we *all* have to walk through the crashing waves. The best thing is though that Jesus is right by our side as those waves try to take us under.

So although Albert's story was heavy and sad, my heart was encouraged and lifted up from his incredible journey of faith. If he survived all those losses and was still able to live for Christ, I could certainly do the same.

THIRTEEN

❖

Molly

JUNE

As I was frantically trying to pack for an entire two weeks home for Josh's wedding, Delilah was hovering over me and getting in my way. She'd left the kids at home with Greg for the afternoon, telling him I needed her to help me pack for my trip home. But that was a bold faced lie because I'd never asked her to come and help me. She basically invited herself over.

"I really need to get away sometimes Molly. It's exhausting being around the kids 24-7," she explained, flopping onto my bed and sending a pair of my socks flying to the floor.

I tried to be understanding, but it still grated on my nerves when Delilah came over to unload on me. She'd made good on her word to get connected with some other moms in the church, which helped. Still, sometimes she came over just to talk about how tired she was of staying home day after day. But I let it roll off my shoulders and swallowed all the snarky comments I really wanted to make. Delilah was my best friend, a friend who'd once listened to me talk about some of the heaviest, darkest things in this world. I could listen to her talk about her stresses at home.

She lapsed into more positive talk, launching into an in depth story about something cute Mandy had said to Luke the other day. But my mind was spinning too many different directions to pay much attention to her. It took Delilah basically shouting my name to snap me out of my little world. "Molly! Hello? Earth to Molly!"

"Huh?" She gave me a mock annoyed face. "I'm sorry," I said with a sigh. "I wasn't expecting you to drop by, and I have so much to get together before I leave tomorrow. It's gonna be a long two weeks in Iowa."

I couldn't say, "It's gonna be a long two weeks home," because Iowa wasn't home anymore. I hadn't *really* lived there since the spring of my senior year, and since then, things at home were different. My room had been converted into a guest room; they had completely removed all traces that I'd lived there after one year went by without any contact from me. My mom had needed some closure, so they painted the walls, hung up a few pictures, and stripped my bed of its cheerful blankets and pillows to be replaced with guest bedding. It looked like a completely new room.

And yet no matter how different that room looked, it was still my old bedroom. It would always hold so many memories, both happy and horrible—happy memories of growing up with Josh and Savannah and Tanner, horrible memories of coming home after the rape and finding out I was pregnant. Those memories had haunted me that month I lived at home before I decided to move back to Kansas, and I really didn't need those memories this time around, not with all the emotions that were sure to surface because my baby brother was getting married, not to mention the fact that I'd be seeing Tanner and his pregnant wife too. That was sure to cause conflicting emotions as well. It was simply going to be a rough two weeks.

There was so much that needed to get done in these two weeks as well. Caitlin was very artsy, and all her decorations were homemade. But she'd gotten so busy with finals, papers, and projects these last few months at school that she'd fallen behind in the wedding planning. So in these two weeks, we had to construct all the centerpieces for both the rehearsal dinner and the reception, as well as all the ceremony decorations—all in two weeks' time. Plus, we had to pick up all the bridesmaids dresses and tuxes, which were sitting in a shop two hours away from Oak Ridge.

Ideally, Caitlin would do this with her mother and sisters, but her parents were divorced, and she didn't have the best relationship with her mother. And she didn't have sisters, only two brothers. So all of the projects were to be completed by me, my mother, and Caitlin. My mom and I were glad to help; it was just a tiny bit stressful. And Mom was also overly emotional right now because she was losing her baby boy, so that would make things interesting in the midst of all we had to get done.

But all that paled in comparison to the other thing I had to face. Even with all that going on, the hardest thing for me on the trip home would be seeing Tanner and Leah. Tanner and I had obviously parted on good terms and kept in touch, but I knew Leah had always had a problem with me. She tried to hide it, but she was a terrible actress. In that month I was home reconnecting with Tanner, she'd given me dark looks every time she saw me. She really was a sweet woman; the situation was just awkward. I completely understood her issue with me though; I was her husband's past love, a past love that never seemed to go away. If I was her, I'd have a problem too.

Needless to say, I wasn't too thrilled to be going home. I would smile and bear it though, just like I always did. That's who I was now—I had to make sure everyone else was all right. I'd caused so much damage by running away that now I felt like I had a responsibility to make sure everyone was happy, healing, and moving forward. That's why I could never tell Tanner I was still in love with him. I could never tell him that moving on was proving to be impossible because I couldn't let go of the fact that I'd given up the two positive things that had come from the rape—Tanner's love and my baby girl. So I simply told everyone I was fine, that I was moving on. But I wasn't so sure that I was.

I'd come a long way, yes, for never getting connected with a rape counselor I had and still was doing a remarkable job putting the rape behind me. It was one of those things of course that I'd never ever forget, but it was under control. I still had nightmares occasionally, but nowhere near the brutality that they'd once been. As for the effects of the abortion…that was getting better too. I didn't look in the mirror in the morning and want to punch my reflection anymore. That was a positive step in my book. I was still guilty and remorseful but not in the way that some overly dramatic prolife people portray women who've gotten abortions to be. Yes, I was sad. And yes, I regretted it. But life went on, and I'd forgiven myself, just as I knew Christ had forgiven me. If I became unexpectedly pregnant again, I wouldn't make the same choice of course, nor would I ever advise any woman in the position I'd been in to make the same choice. Abortion hadn't solved anything for me. If anything, it had created *more* problems for me. But I also knew that not every woman feels that way after an abortion, and I couldn't help but think that it has to do with where they stand with God. Growing up in the church, I'd come to value life as a precious gift from God. I hadn't been following Christ at the time of the abortion though; I'd been running as far away as I could get from him. Maybe that's why I had felt it was okay. I'd fallen away from God and forgotten that the life growing inside me was *his* child, not mine.

After it was over, the gravity of what I'd done had hit me almost immediately. Even as a runaway Christian, I'd known that what I'd done was wrong, very wrong. I didn't feel relief like I'd expected. I'd taken a life, and I couldn't ignore that fact. But if you research "abortion side effects" online, physical side effects pop up right away. You have to do a little digging to find the emotional side effects. And there are two extremes of course. Some women really do feel better; it's a relief to have the pregnancy taken care of. But it makes me wonder what their relationship with Christ is like. I regretted it every single day of my life. Every. Single. Day.

It hadn't been just a clump of cells. It had been a living human being, crafted together by the very hands of God. Did the women who felt relief truly believe that their unborn babies weren't really humans yet? I knew that many people claim the abortion issue isn't centered around the sanctity of life but on the right of women to control their own bodies. Many prochoice people will argue that they value life too, but they also value the freedom to choose. In a way, I could respect that. Still...it felt hypocritical to live in a country that promised equal rights—life, liberty, and the pursuit of happiness—and yet denied millions and millions of children those rights by letting their mothers end their lives.

As a future psychologist, the main thing I wanted people to know was that God doesn't withhold forgiveness from anyone— rapists, sex abusers, child molesters, murderers...women who get abortions. God forgives them all if they come to him. *That's* what I wanted people to know. We of course can't continue to do sinful things knowing he'll forgive us in the end, but if we *do* mess up and come to him, he'll forgive...always.

Those were the thoughts swirling around in my head all the way back to Iowa. I hated that so many prolife people made it sound like women who'd gotten abortions were heartless and beyond forgiveness, that we were unworthy of Christ's love. I was living proof that that wasn't true, not in the least bit. You *could* move past an abortion; you *could* be forgiven for it, just as you can be forgiven for every sin. The problem is that so many women don't think they need forgiveness. And abortion will always be accepted in America as long as people keep thinking that it's not wrong and that you don't need to come to God with it.

I could only think about stuff like that for so long without wanting to drive right off the road. There were just so many conflicting emotions when it came to abortion. So I allowed myself to dismiss those thoughts and go back to me and Delilah's conversation earlier this morning.

"I'm getting worried. What if it never happens?" she asked, referring to the fact that she wasn't pregnant yet. Her voice was getting all high and panicked, so I put down the pile of shirts I was trying to sort and put in my suitcase and sighed. She was sitting on the edge of my bed, and I joined her, giving her my full and undivided attention even though I was stressed out and running behind.

"It's only been two months, Lilah. It doesn't always happen that fast." In my mind though, I knew that sometimes it did. In my case, it had happened the first time I'd had a sexual encounter.

She nodded and swallowed. "I know. But I got pregnant with Luke on the first time. And he and Sophie got pregnant with Mandy almost immediately after they stopped using birth control. I think it should have happened by now! We never ever tried to prevent it!"

I raised an eyebrow. "Not even on the honeymoon?"

"Nope. We didn't see the point in waiting!" she said with a shrug. "I mean, Luke and Mandy already consider themselves brother and sister. But…they're really only step-siblings. When we have a baby of our own though, it'll be like we're sealing all of us together as a family. That baby would be a real sibling to both of them…part of me and part of Greg."

"Honey," I replied soothingly, "you're still a family even without a baby. You don't have to come from the same parents to be brother and sister. I consider *you* a sister, and we certainly don't share the same parents!"

That made her smile, but it faded almost as quickly as it appeared. "I know. You're right. But still. I really want it to happen for us. I mean, Luke had been an accident. I hadn't wanted him at first, and I feel guilty about that even to this day. But this time…I *really* want a little one!"

I covered her hand in mine and gave a gentle squeeze. "It's still early. Just…keep doing what you're doing," I said with a giggle, and she flushed. "It'll happen when God thinks you're good and ready. It's still kind of overwhelming for you right now. Maybe God is preventing it for a bit longer so you can have some more time to prepare for a little one. And Mandy seems to really be enjoying spending time with you during the day. She missed out on a lot of special mommy time that she's finally getting with you. That could be why it hasn't happened yet too. You never know what God's up to."

She nodded and agreed, but I could see the doubts lingering in her eyes. But that's how fear works, I suppose. Once the idea gets into your head, it torments you day and night. I'd found too that even if I bury myself into the Word and devote more time praying about a fear it can still find a way to creep back in. My fear of being single and childless for the rest of my life continued to rear its ugly head and keep me awake at night worrying. I'd given it to God, trusted that his plan for me was good, even if it was different from the plan I had. Still. That fear continued nagging me, and it was frustrating. And no matter what anyone said, no matter how many times I prayed and tried to release it to the Lord, it lingered. It was probably the same with Delilah. No matter what I said, no matter what passage of scripture I gave her to ease her mind, the fear would remain. It takes a lot of work to overcome a fear that large. I knew that firsthand.

I'd had to come face-to-face with the biggest giant of a fear ever when I returned home that first time. The last time I'd driven this road home, my hands had trembled, and my heart had pounded the entire way. I'd blasted praise music the whole way to try and distract myself, which helped some. Facing fears is easier with God though the uncomfortable feelings can still remain. But God never promised us an easy life. No, we are called to daily pick up our cross and follow him. He never promised comfort and security. Sometimes we just have to face our fears, with all the uncomfortable feelings that come, knowing that Christ is standing by our side to catch us if we start to drown.

SARA WHITLEY ❖ 168

The long drive home seemed to drag on and on as I battled all these emotional thoughts. But a hug from my dad right as I came inside the house did wonders for my soul. I allowed him to hold me for a bit longer than I was usually comfortable with, knowing that he still harbored regrets about my running away and abortion. My dad and I hadn't been too terribly close when I was young mostly because he worked so much. His strained relationship with my mom hadn't helped either. During my "running away" years though, he and Mom drew so much closer together, and dad had finally developed into the spiritual leader my family had always needed so desperately. He began spending much more time with Josh and Savannah, something I'd missed out on, which stung a little. It had taken my running away to wake him up; he'd realized that maybe if he'd been there for me more, I would have felt comfortable coming to him with the rape.

On one of my last days before returning to Kansas, my dad opened up about the regret he carried around from not being there for me more as a child. We were at Emma's for a late night pancake feast when he set his fork down and looked me square in the eyes, tears welling up in his own. "It shouldn't have taken you running away for me to wake up, sweetheart. I always knew I wasn't the dad you guys needed. But I didn't know how to change it. And I think I didn't really want to change it. Being a good dad is hard. Really hard. I was lazy back then and too okay with the fact that my kids never came to me with anything," he admitted.

Tears started filling my eyes as well, and I felt my throat constrict with emotion. Dad and I never talked like this. He'd never admitted his failures to me before. I knew there was some truth to his words. I'd never felt comfortable coming to either my mom or dad with any problem I had. I felt that they were too busy with their own lives to care much about what was going on in my world. Tanner had been my go-to guy, the one I confided in.

"That was wrong," he continued. "I should have listened to those thoughts long before you ran. If I'd spent more time with you…maybe you would have told me. And we could have taken care of you, made sure Jason paid for what he did to you…"

He trailed off, unable to voice his next thought. He didn't have to though. We both knew what he was thinking. If I'd been able to come to him about the rape, we would most likely still have the baby with us today.

I reached across the table and took his hand. "Daddy," I whispered, my voice cracking, "it's not your fault. It's no one's fault but my own. The choices I made were my own. We can't let regrets eat us alive. I've lived that way for three years, and believe me, it's not fun. You can't heal from this if you let the regrets rule you. You have to let it go."

He swallowed hard and nodded. "I know. I'm trying. I'm just… so sorry, baby girl. Please forgive me."

A single tear slipped down his cheek, and I swear I felt my heart break in two. "Of course," I whispered, giving his hand a squeeze.

So I let my dad hold and rock me now, trying to make up for all the years he hadn't been there for me. This was part of his healing process, and I would do whatever he needed to help him. Because there's nothing like breaking free from the chains of regret and moving forward, and I wanted that for him.

I got to Iowa late in the evening, so we decided to just relax and not worry about wedding stuff until the next day. They didn't even let me catch up on any sleep though; we were up bright and early heading to pick up the dresses that first morning. Caitlin chatted nonstop the whole way there, unable to contain her excitement about finishing up the decorations and marrying Josh. I couldn't help but smile at her; she was so head over heels in love with Josh. I knew my baby brother was marrying an amazing young woman of God. They had many happy years ahead of them.

I was surprised to find that I didn't struggle with this wedding as much as I'd struggled with Greg and Delilah's. Maybe that situation had felt different simply because Delilah married a man I'd been interested in. I expected that the same feelings of jealousy would well up as we prepared for this wedding, but they never did. My heart was simply overflowing with happiness for this young couple. I still desired what they had—someone to love and laugh with—but it wasn't a sharp jealousy. God really *was* working on my heart, helping me see just how truly blessed I was even though I wasn't living out the life I always thought I'd be living by now.

I also think that the talk Josh and I had a few nights before the wedding helped too. From that first night home, I could sense that something was different in Josh. I could see it in his eyes. He was treating me differently too, better. For months now he'd been holding me at a safe distance, happy I was home and yet beyond angry that I'd run away and that I'd gotten an abortion. He *said* he'd forgiven me, but I wasn't too sure about that. Now though, I truly believe he had.

We were sitting up one night watching *America's Funniest Home Videos*, a show we'd both enjoyed watching together as kids when he said, "I talked with Justine."

My head snapped to face him. Justine was the other girl Jason had raped. The girl who'd been brave enough to realize that what happened wasn't her fault and that she needed to tell someone. We used to talk quite a bit but had fallen out of touch recently. I made a mental note to give her a call sometime soon.

"Why?" I asked, surprised.

He shrugged. "She gave a talk a few weeks ago at the church about what happened. She talked about the same stuff you did. She felt that it was her fault; she didn't want to tell anyone at first. When she *did* speak up about it, a lot of people didn't believe her. I can't believe some of the horrible things people said to her!"

I nodded. Justine had shared with me all the hurtful things people had said to her, and it broke my heart. Many of her friends told her that it was all her fault, that she'd asked for it by going out with Jason and leading him on. Some of them had even stopped being friends with her because they thought she was making it up, simply crying rape to get Jason in trouble. They thought she'd willingly had sex with him but felt guilty about it and called it rape to make herself feel better. The sad part was that it could have been any one of those girls. Jason was a charmer. He was able to make girls feel special and get them to trust him. Once he had their trust, he went after what he really wanted. And I couldn't decide if he knew that what he'd done to us was rape. Because the world we live in pretty much tells rapists that it's the victims' fault…that we asked for it by flirting and letting that person get close to us.

"I don't know why I even went that night, to her talk," he admitted. "I was sitting on this very couch fully aware that the talk was about to start and refusing to go. Then the next thing I know, I'm in my car and walking in the church. I sat in the back, but it was like she was looking right at me the whole time, like she *knew* I needed to hear what she had to say because I just couldn't forgive you for what happened."

I swallowed and nodded, encouraging him to go on. Josh didn't usually open up to me about stuff like this, and it sounded like Justine's talk had finally changed his heart about my situation.

He let out a big sigh and continued, "I stuck around after it was over to talk with her, and it all came spilling out. I told her all about how I had doubted that you'd been raped…that you must have been making it up and you really did have sex with Jason and just felt guilty about it. I realized that I was being just as cruel as Justine's friends were to her. But still…I just need to know for sure, Molly. I can't let it go unless I know without a doubt that what you told me is true."

I nodded. "It's true, Josh. Jason *really* did rape me. He convinced me to go home with him one night…he told me that his dad might be there, and I wanted to trust him so badly. Tanner and Kristina thought he was just a big jerk, and I wanted to prove them wrong by trusting him. But"—I shrugged—"it didn't happen that way. His dad wasn't at home, and once he had me alone, he tried to have sex with me, but I resisted. And when I resisted he forced it on me." I took his hand and looked hard into his eyes, willing him to understand. "I didn't want to have sex with him. I knew that was wrong. But when I wouldn't, he raped me. And that's the honest truth, Josh. I swear."

He sat in silence for a few moments, nodding and processing all I'd said. I'd never given him details about the night of the rape. I probably should have long ago, but I hated telling the story. It was a night I wanted to forget, but it would have helped him see that what had happened really was rape, not just an attempt by me to get Jason in trouble.

"I believe you," he said slowly. "I do. And I'm sorry for reacting so badly. It makes me sick to think that I was to you what those girls were to Justine. I guess that's why you never wanted to tell anyone, huh?" His eyes were soft, kind. For the first time since I'd come home, Josh was looking at me with compassion and understanding, not hatred and disbelief.

"Exactly. Justine was so much braver than I was. She realized that even though people would react badly and not believe her, it was better than letting it eat her up inside. I was locked in a prison for way too long by not telling anyone. And I let Jason get away with it and do it again to Justine. If I'd spoken up when it happened to me, it never would have happened to Justine."

The weight of that realization settled in around us, and we were silent. But then Josh pulled me into a hug and whispered, "It's not your fault, Molly. You were scared. You couldn't have known that not telling would allow Jason to do it again. You have to let it go."

I sniffed and nodded, my tears wetting his T-shirt. It amazed me that here he was, comforting me and giving me advice when weeks ago he thought I was lying about getting raped. I was speechless, so I let him hug me and comfort me, in awe of the work that God had done in his heart and beyond thankful that

Justine was using her story to impact lives and change hearts. Justine would probably never know what an impact her story had had on Josh. He told me later that one of the reasons he felt that he needed to forgive me was because if something like this ever happened to his daughter, he wanted to believe her. He wanted to take care of her like he hadn't taken care of me.

Since that night, things were a million times better between me and Josh. I no longer felt like running out of a room that he was in because of the tension his disbelief and unwillingness to forgive had caused. That tension was completely gone now, replaced with the peace and joy of forgiveness and understanding. I could now proudly stand up in front of the church at his wedding with nothing but love and joy radiating from both my face and my heart.

And that's what I did. After two weeks of crazy preparation, I watched Josh pledge to love, honor, and cherish his beautiful bride Caitlin through sickness and in health, for richer or for poorer, in good times and bad. I also got to give the speech I'd been planning since December, a speech filled with hilarious memories from our childhood.

Later that evening at the dance, Caitlin tossed her bouquet, and to my surprise and shock, it landed in my arms. Everyone oohed and ahhed and teased me that I'd be the next one in my family to walk down the aisle. I just laughed it off and pretended that my face wasn't burning with embarrassment and took a seat at an empty table, playing with the bouquet and wrestling with my emotions. Tanner's voice startled me out of my thoughts however, thoughts of marrying Tyler now that I'd caught this bouquet.

"Nice bunch of flowers you got there," he said as he settled in across from me.

I smiled and shook my head. "Guess so. People keep telling me that I'll be getting married next. I guess we'll see," I said with a shrug, trying to play cool.

Tanner's signature crooked smile faded, and he nodded slowly, like the thought of me getting married bothered him a little bit. Or maybe I was reading into it too much. I really wanted to ask him if the idea of me getting married bothered him. I wanted to ask if, like me, he was still having a tough time accepting the fact that it was over between us and we'd never have a future together now that he was married. But I didn't. I couldn't. Because even if he *did* feel the same way as I did, he couldn't tell me. He was married, for goodness sake! He couldn't sit across from me and tell me he still loved me while wearing his wedding ring. It would be totally unfair and unreasonable to ask him, so I kept my mouth shut.

It hit me though that Tanner was here alone. I'd been so busy today getting ready and making sure everything was perfect that I hadn't had time to say hi to Tanner before the wedding started. Once the ceremony ended, the wedding party drove out to the lake to take a few more pictures, so I hadn't had time after to talk to him either. Now though, I realized that the few times I had seen him during the day, he'd been alone.

"Where's Leah?" I asked curiously. She wasn't too pregnant to enjoy a night out dancing with her husband.

Tanner's eyes fell; his face twisted up with emotion, and he sighed. "I don't want to tell you today, not at your brother's wedding. I was gonna come over here and ask you out to coffee sometime in the next few days to talk about it…"

I shook my head. "I'm leaving tomorrow afternoon after Josh and Caitlin are done opening presents. Mary Beth needs me to come back and help. Our busboy isn't doing well, and she needs all the help she can get."

His face fell. "I see. Well…I hate to ruin this happy day for you, but…something awful has happened. I don't…I don't know if I'm going to make it through this one, Molly," he whispered.

My heart skipped a beat, and I got all hot and panicky like I always do when someone's about to give me bad news. "Okay.

Let's hear it," I said hesitantly, wanting to be brave, but judging from the look on his face, I knew this was serious, and it would be tough to be brave. I didn't want any more bad news. *We'd endured more than our fair share of tough times. Wasn't it about time for some happiness?*

Tanner sighed, closed his eyes, and let his head fall back in defeat. When he composed himself, he simply said, "Leah has cancer."

Immediately, I felt like I'd been run over by a semi. My eyes widened in shock. "Cancer?" I asked, horrified. "Wha…? What kind?"

"Breast cancer," he replied with a crack in his voice. Big fat tears began rolling down his cheeks and falling off his face; he didn't even bother wiping them away. I looked around, concerned that people were going to notice and come over to ask what was wrong. "Hey," I said softly. "Let's go outside, okay?"

He nodded and followed me outside to the deck. The reception was in a country club, and we had a breathtaking view of the golf course from the deck. The weather outside was perfect; it was cool because the sun was just starting to set, which was gorgeous but hard to enjoy with the news Tanner has just given. A gentle breeze blew the curls in my hair into my face and made goose bumps pop up on my skin. I shivered a bit, but it was more from the shock of what Tanner had just told me than from actually being cold. My stomach felt all tangled up and I was confused.

I didn't know what to say, so I just stood there fiddling with my bracelet. But eventually after a few minutes of silence, Tanner launched into an explanation, "It's bad, Molly. Leah didn't know the lump was from cancer. She thought it was just a side effect of being pregnant. The doctor told us that during pregnancy, hormone changes cause the breasts to get larger, tender, and lumpy anyway. It's harder to notice a lump until it gets pretty big."

He stopped and looked away. As I waited, I felt my heart shattering into a million pieces. Here I'd been pining for what could have been and wondering if Tanner regretted getting married to Leah. Meanwhile, Leah was fighting for her life while carrying their child.

"It's really advanced, Molly," he said sadly while rubbing his neck. "And it's spreading like wildfire. They're worried that it might spread to her lungs too."

"What can you do?" I asked. "I mean…won't treatment hurt the baby?"

He nodded. "Yeah. It can. If we'd caught it earlier, we could have had surgery to remove it, but now that its spread…that's not really an option anymore. It's too advanced. They gave us the option of chemotherapy, but Leah doesn't want to do it. Most of the baby's internal organs are still developing right now, and we could easily miscarriage with chemo. It gets safer the farther along the pregnancy is, but I don't think she wants to pursue it even then. You can't really study this stuff without harming babies, you know?" he said sadly.

I nodded. "Well, what about radiation?" I asked. I didn't know much about cancer treatment or how that might affect their unborn baby.

He shook his head. "Can't. Doctors say it's awful for the baby. It can cause harm during each stage of pregnancy. Miscarriage, birth defects, slow growth, and development…that's what we'd be dealing with if we pursued radiation. Plus, there's a higher risk of childhood cancer. Leah would never forgive herself if later in life our child developed cancer of their own."

"So what do you do?" I whispered.

He sighed again. "Leah really doesn't want to pursue treatment right now. I'll try to convince her to go with chemotherapy later on in the pregnancy, but she's so stubborn. She loves this baby more than her own life, Molly. She's willing to die so the baby can live. She hasn't said that, but I know it's true. And nothing I say will change her mind." He squeezed his eyes shut in pain, and I felt my own tears start running down my face.

This wasn't supposed to happen to a young, healthy, mommy-to-be. Leah was supposed to be worrying about gaining weight and how she was going to lose it once the baby was born, not worrying about what cancer treatments would cause the most harm to her precious little one. She was supposed to be shopping for cute mommy clothes and enjoying the glow of pregnancy, not growing weaker and wasting away to nothing as the cancer spread. It simply wasn't supposed to be like this.

"I'm so sorry, Tanner," I whispered, knowing it wasn't my fault but at a loss for what else to say. "I'll be praying harder than I ever prayed about anything in my whole life."

He gave me a weak smile, and I pulled him into a hug. I held him and let him cry, not knowing what else to do to offer comfort. When he calmed down a bit, he explained to me that Leah hadn't felt up to coming out and celebrating today, not when she'd just gotten the worst news of her life. And she was already feeling pretty weak due to the advancement of the cancer and the lack of treatment. Tanner had been able to paste on a smile for most of the day. But here with me, he let out all the emotions that he'd been bottling up since they received the news a few weeks ago.

They hadn't told anyone outside the family yet. Leah wasn't ready for everyone to run at her and give her advice. She didn't want treatment; she didn't want to risk any harm to the baby. But Tanner and Leah knew that people would advise them to end the pregnancy, take care of the cancer, and then try again. Leah of course couldn't even think of doing that. Like Tanner said, she'd rather die than abort the baby or cause him or her any harm from treating the cancer.

I left that weekend with a heavy heart. My mind and heart were reeling from all that had happened in these two short weeks. I'd spent some amazing time reconnecting with my dad and brother. And I'd received Josh's forgiveness and understanding and had come away with a better relationship than we'd had in years. But I'd also received the worst news of my entire life. I almost felt worse than the day I found out I was pregnant after being raped. Because this time, the news affected Tanner. And Tanner didn't deserve this. He was an amazing man of God; he'd been a faithful follower and servant of Christ for his entire life, never once wavering in his faith. If anyone deserved to live a happy life full of blessings from Christ, it was Tanner. Instead, he was facing the bleak reality that he might lose his wife to cancer and be left to raise a baby on his own.

Tanner had said he didn't think he would make it through this. I was beginning to believe that. I just wasn't sure how he would be able to sit back and watch cancer drain the life from his wife simply because she couldn't treat it due to the pregnancy. And if Leah *did* pass away and the baby survived, I worried that Tanner wouldn't be able to forgive his child—there was a very real possibility that he would blame the baby for her death. After all, if Leah wasn't pregnant, the cancer would be much more treatable.

The only thing any of us could do now was wait. It was in God's hands, completely beyond our control. We were at the mercy of whatever it was that he decided was best. I was terrified of the possibility that God's plan could include taking either Leah or the baby though. It would be very near impossible for Tanner to survive the loss of either one of them. Because he'd already lost one love—me—after I'd run away and refused to contact him. Then he'd lost my baby, the baby that wasn't biologically but emotionally his.

It just didn't seem fair that he was facing such similar circumstances again.

FOURTEEN

※

Molly

JULY

Delilah and I were out in her backyard breaking our backs pulling weeds from the vegetable garden, the sun beating down on us and sweat pouring down our backs when Greg came running out of the house with the phone. "Lilah! Molly!" he shouted.

We both whipped around from the panic that dripped from his voice. Delilah shaded her eyes with her hands and shouted, "What's up, honey?"

He closed the phone and let his arm fall in defeat. Then he slowly walked across the yard to us, and we both looked at each other with dread in our eyes. This was surely bad news; as if we hadn't been getting enough of that lately.

"What happened?" I asked, not really wanting him to tell us but knowing that facing whatever had happened was necessary. I'd tried to run away from bad news before. Not a smart plan. You have to face it head on and *deal* with it. So I steeled myself for the news to come.

"That was your mom, Lilah. It's Albert. He had a heart attack this morning. He never came in for work, and she got nervous, so she called the neighbor and asked if she would check on him. I guess he fell and hit his head on the kitchen counter too. It...it doesn't look good."

Delilah's hand flew to her mouth, and she immediately started crying. I felt my throat begin to close up and my heart dropped. Just weeks ago, we'd had the best conversation we'd ever had, and now he was lying in a hospital bed fighting for his life. This all was happening much too fast. He'd *just* received the news of his failing heart. And now…now it looked like he wouldn't have much more time to spread his love and joy to all of us. Soon enough our pockets would be empty of those little caramel candies, and someone new would be lugging the dishes around at Mary Beth's little restaurant.

We didn't bother changing clothes or cleaning up. We just grabbed the kids, piled into Greg's car, and rushed to the hospital. Mary Beth was already there pacing, looking rumpled and completely overwhelmed. Her cheeks were tearstained, her face was beet red, and her cell phone was clamped to her ear. She was calling Rachel and Hannah to let them know the bad news. They both had young families and wouldn't be able to rush out here like we had, but they were sending up prayers and wishing they could be here. Albert was like a grandfather to the three of them, and their hearts were breaking right now.

Albert had told Mary Beth a few weeks ago that he didn't want the doctors to try and save him if something like this happened. He didn't want to be opened up and operated on. And Mary Beth made sure that the nurses and doctors understood that, even though Delilah strongly disagreed. But this wasn't about what any of us wanted. It was about what Albert wanted. He'd lived a long life, a long life full of trials and hardships. And although he'd lived out these last twenty years loving Mary Beth and her girls, living life to the absolute fullest, now he was ready to go home to his own family.

The doctors weren't too thrilled with Albert's wishes either, but after Mary Beth drove home and got the signed piece of paper from Albert saying that he didn't want to be operated on, they caved. Those were his wishes, and they had to respect them.

So they started pumping medication into him with hopes that he'd pull through. His head injuries weren't helping his chances though. After his heart attack, he fell and gouged his head on his kitchen counter, then hit it again fairly hard on the floor. Those three things combined made his prognosis pretty bleak.

The six of us sat in the waiting room, silent. Even the kids were quiet and still. Luke loved Albert so deeply; he had been the only male figure in his life up until Greg. He'd been there the day Luke was born, and he used to babysit him all the time, letting him play with the wooden toys he'd played with as a child. Albert had taught Luke about Jesus. He'd taught Luke how to love and to forgive, how to look for God even in the bleakest of circumstances. Albert was probably the reason little Luke was so wise beyond his years. Luke would never have another mentor like Albert for the rest of his life; he was beyond blessed to have had the opportunity to learn from him for these seven years of his life. Every once in a while, Luke would sniff, and we knew he was trying to hold back his tears. He wasn't ready to give Albert up yet, not when he had so much more learning to do.

Delilah crouched down in front of him and took his little hands in her own. He looked down and sniffed again, harder, but she gently lifted his chin so that he was looking in her eyes. His eyes were shining with tears, and he began to blink furiously. We all about lost it when his chin began to quiver and the tears finally slipped down his chubby, little boy cheeks.

"It's okay to cry, baby. Boys can cry too. This is a sad day. We all feel sad right now, and we all feel like crying. So you cry if you want to, okay?" she assured him.

He nodded, unable to speak, and I felt my own tears escape from my eyes. My heart broke for Luke, so young and tender and not ready to face something as final as death. It's too much for any adult to wrap their mind around, let alone a seven-year-old. To have someone with you one day and then to have them gone the next is mind-boggling. It happens fast; it happens when you're not ready. But it happens, and there's no stopping it.

Mandy was too young to fully understand what was happening, and she didn't have a strong connection to the man lying down the hall like the rest of us did. But I think she could sense that what had happened was serious and that this wasn't a time to be running and playing like she usually did all day long. This was a time for sitting quietly and respectfully.

The hours dragged on, but eventually, the staff decided to let us come into his room to see him. He was unresponsive, none of the medications seemed to be helping him, and they feared he only had hours left. They wanted us to be able to say our good-byes to him while he was still alive.

I let Mary Beth and Delilah go in alone at first because Albert was family to them. They deserved to say their good-byes to him on their own. When I did go in later, I almost wished I hadn't. My breath caught in my throat when I saw his broken body lying in that bed, hooked up to wires and tubes. He had a bandage covering his head, and one side of his face was bruised and purple from when he'd landed on the floor. The rest of his face, as well as his arms, were deathly white. We could see his veins through the skin. He looked nothing like the vibrant, young-at-heart Albert we all knew and loved.

I resisted the urge to turn and walk right back out the door and instead walked up to the bed and took his hand in mine. It was cold, but he was still alive, probably not for much longer though, and I wanted to say what was on my heart before that happened. I really didn't want to be holding his hand when it happened either. So I took a deep breath and tried to put into words all that Albert meant to me. Not an easy task. *How do you thank someone for helping save your life?*

"Albert," I began timidly, not sure if I would be able to get through this without completely losing it. "You became part of the family I so desperately needed when I first moved here.

From that first day I started at the diner, I felt your love, your total acceptance of me, even though I was so broken. But…after hearing your story, I realize that we're all broken in some way." I swallowed the marble in my throat and rolled my lips together, trying to stay composed. When I restarted, my voice was quavering uncontrollably.

"Thank you for sharing your story with me. Thank you for teaching me that no matter what happens in our lives, it's because God has a bigger plan for us than we have for ourselves. Even if we don't agree or understand…what happens to us is always for the best. Watching you live out each day with so much joy and peace even after all you went through gives me hope that one day I'll be able to do the same…that healing and moving on really *is* possible. So thank you, my sweet friend. Thank you for these priceless lessons. Now go and meet Jesus…laugh and smile with your family. They've been waiting such a long time to have you in their arms again. And…" I choked on a sob and looked to the ceiling. "Say hi to my baby for me, will you? Give her a kiss and let her know I love her and can't wait to meet her one day, okay?"

I leaned over the bed and gently kissed his head, then gave his hand a gentle squeeze. When I turned around, both Mary Beth and Delilah had tears streaming down their faces. We then quickly brought Luke in next so he could say good-bye.

He kept it short. "I love you, Papa. I'll miss you, but I know Jesus wants to hang out with you too. Have fun up there. But not too much fun. Wait until I get there too."

Delilah wiped her cheeks and lifted him up so he could give Albert a kiss. She and Mary Beth each took their turns whispering their last good-byes to him as well. Then we listened to his heartbeat slow, holding our breaths as his heart finally stopped beating. No one spoke; no one let their sobs escape. We just looked at each other and reveled in the fact that we had been in the room with him as his spirit left his body and traveled to Jesus.

Mary Beth was the first to move. She went up to Albert's body and smoothed his hair away from his face, then placed his hand on his chest. "Good-bye, dear friend. Until we meet again," she whispered, sealing her good-bye with a kiss on his forehead. Luke then ran up to her and buried his face in her middle, his little arms thrust around her and hanging on tightly as he finally let his sobs escape. She rocked him gently and whispered soothing words into his ear, and we all let the tears flow unashamedly. We'd lost a great soul, a great friend.

Eventually, a nurse came in and covered his body with a sheet, and after all of us were ready to let Albert go, we let them wheel him away. And just like that, he was really gone.

We wasted no time planning the funeral. Two days after he died, we held a prayer service, where almost every single person in Green Lake showed up to support Mary Beth and her daughters. Rachel and Hannah both brought their families back for the service and the funeral. There was simply no way they would allow themselves to miss these events. The same people packed into the church the next day for the funeral; they had to set up chairs in the fellowship hall and prop open the doors because the pews were jam-packed. And there wasn't a dry eye in the building. Albert had truly touched the lives of each and every one of the people in attendance with his incredible life of faith. It just went to show that it really is *how* you live and how you treat people. I'd heard it said once that as Christians, we're the only Bible some people will ever read. So we have to live out every single day of our lives for Christ because people are watching and listening. That's exactly what Albert had done, and it was evident from the stories that people got up and told.

I sat in amazement as I listened to those stories. Albert had left out so much of his life that day we talked, I suppose out of humbleness and the fact that he knew he didn't need to go around telling people all that he'd done for others throughout his life. Because as Jesus had said in Matthew 6:3, "But when you give to someone in need, don't let your left hand know what your right hand is doing. Give your gifts in private, and your Father, who sees everything will reward you." Albert had certainly done that. All that he did in his life, he did not to impress people but to serve the Lord. He knew that the only opinion that mattered anyway was the Lord's.

It was wonderful to hear about all that he'd done now though. When Albert first moved to Green Lake, he'd worked as a carpenter and handyman doing odd jobs around town. One man told about how Albert had fixed his roof after a tornado ripped it off, free of charge. The man and his wife had just had their third baby girl and were strapped for cash, and when the storm took their roof, they weren't sure they could afford to have it fixed. Albert drove past one day a few weeks after the storm however and saw that their roof was still missing. They'd covered it with a tarp, but there had been a few other bad storms since the tornado hit, and Albert knew they had a new baby to care for. So he came out one day and got to work, then refused to accept any money from them when the job was finished.

Another lady stood and said that Albert had once shown up unannounced on her doorstep with two weeks' worth of groceries for her family. She was a single mother who'd lost her job, and after her last paycheck, she was unable to refill her shelves. She never told anyone that the cupboards were bare because she was embarrassed. But when Albert showed up with the groceries, he simply shrugged and said that God had told him her family needed help. He then proceeded to land her a job the next week, a job with benefits and insurance. In the following years, he continued to stop by occasionally with treats for her kids. Their pockets were never empty of those little caramels.

One young man shared with us the kindness and love he'd received from Albert during the years Albert drove a school bus. He'd gotten too old to do construction but was too young to retire, so he drove bus for seven years. The young man came from a troubled home and was insecure and shy, which caused kids to pick on him. But every day when he left the bus, Albert would slip one of those little caramel candies into his pocket, give him a smile, and say, "Tomorrow's another day, kid. Another day to show those kids you won't let them get the best of you. Keep your chin up, and trust that God's got it all under control."

Story after story about how Albert had spread God's love continued to come for almost an hour and a half—stories that made us laugh, stories that reassured us that from the way Albert had loved others and loved God that he was enjoying the Lord's presence now. It gave us the closure we needed, and we left that day with light hearts. It was hard to be sad after hearing how Albert had cared for the people of this town, how he'd changed and molded so many hearts for Christ. We knew he was with the Lord, so we had peace. It hurt, and we missed him, but none of us wished him back. His work here on earth was done, and it was up to us to carry on his legacy of love now. He'd done more than his share of serving. It was our turn now, though he'd left some very big shoes to fill.

Albert gave one more gift after he died—a gift for me. As the final guests hugged Mary Beth and slowly shuffled out the door, I collapsed into a chair and pulled my knees up to my chest, wrapping my arms around my legs and not caring that I was wearing a dress. I rested my cheek on my knee and closed my eyes, completely drained from this exhausting day and wanting nothing more than to collapse into my bed and sleep for hours. Delilah joined me, and we sat in silence for a few minutes before she slid an envelope across the table for me.

I cocked my head in confusion. "From Albert," she whispered, standing up to leave so I could read it.

My name was scrawled across the tiny, coffee-stained envelope in Albert's cramped handwriting. I thought about tucking it in my purse to read later in the privacy of my apartment, but curiosity got the best of me, and I flipped it over and gently pried it open. My fingers trembled as I unfolded the single piece of paper nestled inside.

Molly.

I know my days are numbered. The doctor said it doesn't look good for me. But I've lived a long life, and I'm ready to go home.

I write this note just hours after our talk. I'm happy that I got to share my story with you. God will take care of you, Molly, just as he took care of me. Don't let the troubles of this world drag you down, sweet girl. You have your whole life to live out, and I want you to live it out in a way that shows the world what a powerful God we love and serve.

I want you to do that so much, and I want to help that happen. I don't have much in this world. I have worked hard all my life, but I have never been a rich man. That is fine with me. But what I do have, I want you to have. Use it to go to school. I know you want to help other girls heal just like you have healed, so go do it. And don't you feel guilty about it, you hear? This is my last wish, Molly. All my life I have tried to help others. I have tried to live out my beliefs. Keep doing that for me, and use my money to do it. When we meet again one day, I want to hear all about how you used my money. So don't try to give it back to Mary Beth. Take it with my blessing and go bless others for me when I'm gone and unable to do so any longer.

Albert.

I bit my lower lip and began to blink furiously. He knew I wouldn't want to take it, and he was right. I didn't want to take it. I didn't feel like I deserved it! I'd only known him a few short years. Mary Beth or one of the girls deserved it, not me. And yet, I couldn't *not* take it. He insisted that I do! He wanted to hear all about what I'd done with it when I joined him in eternity one day. Once I showed this to Mary Beth and the girls, I knew they'd agree with Albert's last wishes though. They would refuse to take it if I tried to give it to them.

So instead of feeling guilty, I celebrated. Not only had Albert completely changed my attitude about the way my life was currently going, he had given me the opportunity to chase after my dreams without worrying where the money would come from. That had been weighing heavy on my heart lately too. I'd been working super hard these past few years, but simply paying for rent and groceries depleted my savings quickly. Now, though, going to school wasn't just a distant dream for me. It was a reality.

I pressed the letter to my chest and whispered, "Okay, you crazy old man. I'll take it. And I promise to use it in a way that will make you proud. I'll try my hardest to bless others just as you did."

I curled up in my bed later that night completely overwhelmed with the way things had turned out these past few weeks: first the news of Leah's cancer, then the sudden death of Albert. His gift was the one ray of sunlight in this otherwise dark time however, and I fell asleep with a smile playing on my lips, beyond thankful and so ready to go out and bless, serve, and love others in the way that Albert had. And one day I would join him and tell him all about it, just like he wanted me to. It was a little scary but very exciting, and I knew that Albert's legacy of faith and love would spur me on when it seemed like the waves were getting the best of me and making me feel as though I was drowning. Because like Albert had told me just weeks ago, even in the toughest circumstances, God is faithful. He takes us into the rough waters not to drown us but to make us better, to cleanse us.

So with Albert's help and God's hand supporting me, I took my first faltering steps into the waves and scheduled my GED test, ready to conquer that and move on to college classes. I realized now that each day I waited, more girls were suffering and hurting. I needed to get this done so that I could begin to love and serve them like Albert wanted me to. All I could do was keep stepping out onto the waves and trusting that if I began to lose my faith and sink, all I had to do was look up and reach out. Christ's hand would pull me up, and I'd keep going, always, for Albert and for all the girls who needed to hear about forgiveness and healing but, most of all, for Christ. Because in the end, it was all about him and giving him the glory he so deserved.

PART THREE

Second Chances

For you have been born again, but not to a life that will quickly end. Your new life will last forever because it comes from the eternal, living word of God. As the scriptures say, "People are like grass; their beauty is like a flower in the field. The grass withers and the flower fades. But the word of the Lord remains forever."

—1 Peter 1:23–25

FIFTEEN

※

Delilah

AUGUST

Every day that passed after Albert's funeral, I felt myself getting angrier and angrier. It seemed like everyone had moved on from his sudden passing, like they didn't even care that we'd lost such an important person.

Mom had gone and done the unthinkable. She went out and hired a bunch of snotty teenagers who came in and messed up the orderly system that she had worked so hard to keep in place since she opened the restaurant all those years ago. When I started working there, I hadn't even lasted a full month! She had started me out as a waitress, but apparently, I was too slow and I always messed the orders up. So she moved me to the kitchen, but again, I was too slow and kept messing things up. I couldn't even do the dishes right! She got so frustrated with me that I finally told her I didn't want to work there anymore. She acted sad, but I could tell that secretly she was relieved.

The day mom called and told me that she had hired a new girl named Molly, my jaw had hit the floor in shock. I knew she really needed the help, but I never actually thought she'd let anyone in. I was skeptical at first that Molly would make it, but she had two years of waitressing under her belt, and she was amazing at it. Mom even let her help with the cooking and the baking too, which had and still kind of did cause a bit of jealousy to well up inside me. I hadn't been good enough to fit into my mother's little world, but Molly fit in beautifully.

When Albert worked there, he took care of the dishes, Mom did most of the cooking and baking, and Molly waitressed and helped Mom in the kitchen whenever she could. The diner was open Monday through Saturday, 5:00 a.m. until 9:00 p.m. Mom usually got there around 4:30 a.m. to start baking pies and cakes and to make sure everything was ready for when the old men would come in for coffee around 5:30 or 6:00 a.m. Albert usually came in around 8:00 a.m., and Molly came in whenever Mom told her to come in. The mornings and afternoons weren't so busy, but around 5:00 p.m. until almost 8:00 p.m., it picked up, and it was pretty chaotic at times. But Mom and Molly were pros at taking care of people, and they could usually handle it fairly well. It was just so much work for two people though. The extra help would be great, and Molly wouldn't have to come in so often, but it still felt weird. Albert and Molly were like family, and now there would be a bunch of strange teenagers working in our family restaurant. It just didn't feel right to me, even if Mom *could* use the help.

The diner would never be the same with Albert gone. I used to love bringing Luke in for lunch when things were slower so we could spend some time with him. It was evident that even at his old age, he valued hard work and always wanted to do the best job he could do. It broke my heart to see him lugging around that heavy bucket of dishes, but he never wanted any help. He refused to use the cart that Mom got for him, saying it only got in the way and slowed things down for Mom and Molly. So we all stood back and let him lug that stupid bucket around, even though we all knew it wasn't good for him. You couldn't stop him though. He was the world's nicest guy, but he was also the world's most stubborn guy. You couldn't talk him out of anything or change his mind once he had it set on something.

Not only did Albert take the dishes off the tables and bring them to the kitchen, he sent them through the dishwasher too. Mom had splurged after a particularly good year and had a state-of-the-art dishwasher installed, which Albert absolutely loved. But there were some pots and big cookie sheets that couldn't go in the washer, and he insisted on scrubbing them himself, which we also didn't like very much. And at the end of each day, before my mother could stop him and do it herself, he'd put all the chairs on the top of the tables and mop the floors until they shone. At least he wasn't there in the morning when Mom opened because he'd probably want to take all the chairs back down again himself.

Albert did a lot of other little stuff around the diner, stuff that no one else thought about doing. He checked the smoke detectors regularly and took the broom and swept out the tops of the doors where the cobwebs like to hide. He repainted the flower boxes hanging on the windows each year. And every once in a while, he'd polish all the silverware up until they sparkled and looked like new. With Albert around, everything always looked in tip-top shape because he cared about the little details.

"The little things always add up to be the big things, little girl," he'd say to me when I asked why he spent so much time taking care of the things that customers don't really care about. "You can't just make sure the things they *do* see look good. Maybe they can't tell that I polished up that spoon they're eating their soup with. But *I* can tell. And God can tell. He knows I work hard for these people. That's all that matters to me."

Priceless words of wisdom. That's one of the things I would miss most. Albert always had a little lesson, a little piece of gold that he'd share each time we talked. Since he'd been the only male figure in my life as a kid, all I learned about life and hard work, I learned from him. He taught me to never take the easy way out. Because if you cut corners now, you'd have to travel a longer distance later when those shortcuts eventually came back to bite you, which they usually did. He taught me to work hard even when nobody watched you. He told me over and over again that human approval always fades away, but God's approval is everlasting. If we work hard on this earth, always being truthful, honest, and loving, we will be rewarded in eternity.

I snapped the sheet I was folding, breathing deep the scent of fresh air and fabric softener. Greg had taken the time last weekend to construct a clothes line for me, something I'd always wanted but never had the room for. The little house Luke and I lived in before I got married to Greg had a tiny backyard barely big enough to fit one of those blue plastic wading pools in, let alone a clothesline. I was thoroughly enjoying having one now.

Things had calmed down around here, even though Luke wasn't away at school during the day. I found though that Luke loved helping out with Mandy, plus he entertained her during the day so I could actually get stuff done around the house. We'd spent the morning playing in the little wading pool in the back-yard and running through the sprinklers. They were both wiped after that so I plopped them in the living room with a Disney movie with that hopes that they'd fall asleep. If Luke didn't take a nap, I didn't mind, but I really hoped Mandy took a nap, even a small one. She was quickly outgrowing the desire to take a nap, which caused me to panic a little bit. She'd get cranky so early in the evening if she didn't take a nap, yet she never wanted to go to bed earlier than Luke. She lasted longer and was much easier to handle if she took a small nap in the afternoon. That's why I always tried to tire her out by swimming and playing outside in the morning.

Even though things were better at home, I still felt discontented. Greg and I had been married for almost four months now, and we still weren't pregnant. Molly tried to tell me that it was still too early to get panicked, but she was wrong. I had gotten pregnant with Luke the very first time David and I slept together. I knew this because that first time we had felt pretty guilty about what we'd done. We decided never to do it again and to focus on other things. A few months later though, I found out I was pregnant, so to me, it didn't seem to matter when he wanted to do it again. It felt good to be in his arms, and the danger of getting pregnant was already gone. So why not?

With Greg and Sophie, it had happened almost the same way. They used birth control at first, but when they finally felt ready, they stopped, and it had happened almost immediately. Clearly, something wasn't working between us if both of us had gotten pregnant so quickly with other partners. I guess I'd always thought if I'd gotten pregnant once, it wouldn't be a problem getting pregnant again. Oh, how wrong I was though.

Of course, I turned to the Internet for answers. But it didn't seem like any of the things I found related to us. We were both young. We didn't smoke, we weren't overweight, and we hadn't been exposed to any harmful chemicals or been treated for cancer. My first pregnancy had been smooth sailing and problem-free, including the delivery. And I wasn't currently taking any medications that might interfere with my ability to get pregnant and neither was Greg. So I tried to swallow my fears and convince myself that the timing just wasn't right. Maybe like Molly had said, God knew I wasn't ready. While I was nowhere near as overwhelmed as I was in the beginning, it was still tough. Maybe in a few months when I could do all this in my sleep, he'd bless us with a little bundle from heaven. In the meantime, I would continue trying to work through the mess of emotions that had attacked me after Albert's death.

I guess Mom had some big plan for all the kids she hired. She'd only hired Molly on because she felt God tugging at her heart, telling her that Molly needed to be around me and my mom so that one day she'd see that running away from God wasn't solving any of her problems. She'd seen it as an opportunity to win over a soul. She was trying to do something like that with these kids because most of them came from broken homes where either the parents were divorced, the mom never got married, or the parents were still together but the situation was less than ideal. She wanted the diner to be a place where the kids were exposed to God's love. She wanted them to see that not all adults are messed up and would mistreat them.

I was skeptical that simply working at the diner would help any of these kids. They'd lived their whole lives surrounded by hardships; they'd had almost two decades of bitterness harden their hearts and make them doubt God's love and existence. Working with Mom and Molly, though both of them were strong in the faith, probably wouldn't do much. They were *teenagers* after all. They'd just roll their eyes at the verses hanging on the walls or the encouragement that Mom and Molly would try to give.

Molly, however, strongly disagreed.

"This is exactly the type of thing that a broken teenager needs, Lilah! *I* needed it as a broken teenager!" she insisted.

I made a face at her. "Yeah, but you were already a Christian. Who knows what in the world these kids believe!" I argued.

She made a face right back at me. "I might have been a Christian for the first eighteen years of my life. But during my 'running away' years, I didn't really consider myself one anymore. I *hated* God. I wanted nothing to do with him. I was convinced that if he was real, he must hate me because of all that bad stuff I thought he was doing to me. I'd always been taught that God has good plans for us and well…the plans he had for me didn't seem so good, so I dumped him. Really committed follower, huh?" she challenged.

I sighed. "Well. Who cares that for a few years you had a problem with God? It was just a few years! But these kids…they've probably had a problem with God for their *whole lives!* That's a long time to have a problem. And the longer you have a problem with God, the harder it is to convince them that he's real and that he cares."

Molly sat back in surprise. "So you're saying that we shouldn't even try?"

"Well, no," I stammered, feeling like she was backing me up into a corner. "I'm just saying that its' gonna be a lot harder than I think you're ready for. Both you and mom."

Molly paused to think for a moment. "You're right. It *is* gonna be a lot harder than we think. But if we start getting discouraged before we even try, we'll fail for sure. Your mom and I have been doing a lot of thinking, and a lot of *praying* about this. When she first told me her idea, I was just as skeptical as you. But she's doing this to keep Albert's legacy alive. This is something that we should have done long ago so that he could have helped too. Because they could have learned so much from him, more than they'll ever learn from us. But we can't go back, we can only keep moving forward. He'd want us to do this, Lilah. You know that."

I did know that. Albert would have loved this idea. I didn't know why I was so hesitant about it—it's not like I'd be the one dealing with those kids day after day!

I think maybe some of my problem came from the fact that Albert had left most of his money to Molly. She shared the letter he'd left her, and after reading it, I tried to react positively even though I was really upset. Albert had only known Molly for a few years! He'd known me and my sisters much longer than that, and all of us could have used that money in some way. But Albert wanted Molly to use it to go to school. And you can't go against a person's last wishes, especially someone like Albert. Besides, everyone else was ecstatic for Molly: Mom, Rachel, and Hannah. They were beyond excited for Molly to finally stop wasting time on her GED and get moving with college classes. With the money Albert left, she'd be able to pay for it all no problem and use the money she earned while working to keep building up her savings. It really was the best use for the money, and yet it bothered me. My *head* knew that this was best, but my heart was fighting it.

Lately, I was feeling more and more bitter, and I hated it. The happily ever after I'd dreamed of while I was dating Greg hadn't turned out like I pictured. There just wasn't as much "happy" involved as I thought. Not that I didn't enjoy being married and having a family. I loved having someone to hold me, someone to whisper sweet things in my ear and really mean it, unlike David who had just done it so I would keep sleeping with him. I loved rolling over and seeing his messed up hair in the morning. I loved the security and the companionship after being on my own for all these years. And I loved Greg with all my heart. He was everything I'd hoped and prayed for during all my years as a single mother.

But in the movies, the fairy tale stops after the wedding bells ring. The happily ever after only goes as far as the big frilly dress and the fancy shoes and hairdo. After that, you never know what to expect! They never show crying three-year-olds or piles of laundry. Those things don't make for a good fairy tale because in fairy tales, the dreams just magically come true. You don't have to work for happiness and joy because it just comes bubbling out of you. In real life though, sometimes you have to work really hard to feel satisfied. And right now, I clearly wasn't working hard enough.

In the past, it had been so easy for me to count my blessings, to realize that there were so many people in the world whose situations were far worse than mine. I had a roof over my head, food on the table each night, two beautiful kids, and a husband who adored me. Surely that should be enough to keep me satisfied, right?

But then it hit me. Other people have all those things and aren't happy. And it's because they don't have Jesus. I tried to think back to the last time I'd cracked open my Bible to let God's word penetrate my heart, and I was ashamed to admit I couldn't remember. I had no excuse for that, not really. Sure, I was busy during the day but not too busy to sit and read for even a few minutes. Luke and Mandy spent the early mornings watching cartoons anyway, and I always seemed to find time to sit down with a book or a magazine during that downtime. *Why not swap my magazine with God's word?*

When you stop letting God's word soak into you, things change in a hurry. It's so easy to become discontented and unsatisfied in life because you're not filling up with what you need the most: Jesus. I knew that my discontentment would probably fade very quickly if I devoted myself to reading the Bible more and allowing the peace and love of God infiltrate my heart and soul. So right then and there, as I sat gritting my teeth at the giant pile of laundry I needed to do still, I made a promise to God that I would work harder at our relationship. I would be thankful that I had a house I needed to clean and clothes I needed to wash instead of getting frustrated. I would be thankful that I had two healthy kids running around instead of wishing I had another one. And I would make a conscious effort each day to open up my Bible and let God work on my heart. But I wouldn't be frustrated and feel guilty if I honestly didn't have time to do it. In high school, I used to feel really guilty if I missed a day of reading my Bible. Back then, I had thought that being a Christian only meant reading my Bible every day and going to church. As I grew in faith, I realized that being a Christian was so much more than that; it was a lifestyle. I had to live out my faith. I had to love and serve like Christ commanded.

And that's when it hit me. Mom and Molly were planning on doing just that. They wanted to live out their beliefs, not just go to church, read their Bibles, and be filled. They wanted to go out into our community and *pour out* all they were being filled up with from church and their own personal Bible reading. It was what we were all supposed to do as believers. That's why I think so many nonbelievers have such a big problem with the church—we haven't been doing what we've been commanded to do. We haven't been loving people and serving them to the best of our ability. Too many of us just sit back and assume others will step up and serve, but when we all start thinking like that, then nothing ever gets done. We have to step out of our comfort zones and do hard things, things like ministering to broken teenagers and stop just sitting back and hoping the world can see we love Jesus. Because that's when the church gets a bad reputation. *That's* when people look at us and think that all we do is talk about our beliefs, not live them out.

As the weeks went by, it was like I was falling in love with Jesus all over again. Passages that had once been so familiar to me were like new; it felt like I was discovering the power of the Bible for the very first time. And for the first time, I really felt like God was working and moving in my life, that he was leading me to follow in my mom and Molly's footsteps and serve like Albert always strived to serve. I wanted to do my part in keeping his legacy of love and service alive just like they were doing.

I found that I didn't have to do much searching to get connected to some sort of a project. After Albert's death, our little church suddenly came alive, empowered by Albert's life of faith. We all felt that it was our duty to make sure his life wasn't forgotten and that we carried on that faith to reach others for Christ.

Since Albert had lost two children of his own, much of the ministries that were popping up all over the place were focused on children. One program served free lunches to the kids whose parents worked during the day or who just couldn't afford to buy good, healthy food during the summer. Then each Friday, they'd send food to last the weekend with a few kids they knew probably weren't getting enough at home. Another program, the one I was getting involved in, was a free day care program at the church. A few of the stay-at-home moms launched the program so that kids could have a safe place to play while their parents worked. They wanted to share Jesus with these kids in the hopes that they'd go home and tell their parents too and maybe start coming on Sunday mornings. I brought Luke and Mandy with me when I went two times a week, and they loved it just as much as I did. Both of them got to play with kids their own age, and I got to pour out all my love onto kids who probably weren't getting enough love at home from their own parents. It was a simple way for me to actually live out my faith instead of cooping myself up at home and feeling sorry for myself. I found that the more you give of yourself, the more blessed you begin to feel.

These kids were blessing me far more than I was blessing them. I think that's how Albert had looked at it too. He served others because not only did he get to complete God's work and bless people, he was blessed in return. That's exactly what I felt like. I was growing deeper in my relationship with Christ, but I was also falling more in love with my husband. Now that I had something to focus on, I stopped focusing on all that was weighing me down. I didn't freak out anymore at the little things, like his inability to keep track of his expenses or his sloppiness in the bathroom. I was making the choice to focus on more important things, like serving the kids and serving my own family. I was more relaxed, which made our conversations much more relaxed and fun. It almost felt like we were first dating again because we'd flirt with each other and tease each other. So maybe now that I was more relaxed, we'd get pregnant. Maybe now that I stopped freaking out and worrying that it'd never happen, it would.

Because even though I was pouring my love out into these kids who so desperately needed to be loved, I still wanted a baby to pour out all my love into. I wanted my child to have two parents ready to love and cherish it because that was something I hadn't been able to give to Luke. He'd been born into a family that loved him of course but one that struggled to provide for him. He didn't have the stability that a child needs.

My arms still felt empty, my family incomplete. But like Molly advised, I decided to trust that God had a plan for all of this, even if I didn't agree or understand. His timing was ultimate and perfect, and though it was hard, I wanted and desperately needed to trust his will.

SIXTEEN

❖

Molly

AUGUST

We who are strong must be considerate of those who are sensitive about things like this. We must not just please ourselves. We should help others do what is right and build them up in the Lord. For even Christ didn't live to please himself. As the Scriptures say, "The insults of those who insult you, O God, have fallen on me." Such things were written in the Scriptures long ago to teach us. And the Scriptures give us hope and encouragement as we wait patiently for God's promises to be fulfilled. May God, who gives this patience and encouragement, help you live in complete harmony with each other, as is fitting for followers of Christ Jesus. Then all of you can join together with one voice, giving praise and glory to God, the Father of our Lord Jesus Christ. Therefore, accept each other just as Christ has accepted you so that God will be given glory.

I sat back and let those words soak into me. I was doing a Bible study on Romans, and this passage from chapter 15 was really hitting me hard this morning. I knew I wasn't loving and building Delilah up like I should be doing. But ever since her wedding, Delilah had been constantly grating on my nerves, something I just wasn't used to in our relationship. In the beginning, we had connected right away simply because we had struggled through much of the same stuff. We understood each other's pain and were able to help each other in ways that others simply could not. It was a friendship built off love and deep understanding, one that wanted to help bring healing to the other in any way possible.

It was still like that, sort of. But so much time had passed for Delilah, and she didn't struggle as much anymore. The pain never really goes away when something big like that happens, but it gets easier as more time goes by. I knew she still struggled; I knew she still felt guilty and unworthy. The pain of what I'd gone through was fresher for me though, and while I'd worked through many of my issues, they were a bit deeper than Delilah's. She didn't harbor the shame of sexual abuse, the regret of taking the life of her child. If you took our struggles and lined them up side-by-side, hers seemed nothing when compared to mine. Her mistakes just weren't as large.

Not that I was feeling sorry for myself. I'd done enough of that during the years I ran away from all those problems. It was just taking me a bit longer than her to get past all my mistakes and come to a place where I felt truly satisfied.

During the past month, I'd watched Delilah go out and do just that—which was great, and I was happy for her, but I sort of envied it. She absolutely glowed from the love of Christ now that she was volunteering at the free day care program, something I wished others could see in me. I *hoped* others could see it in me. *But was I really doing a good enough job?*

Delilah recently shared with me how wrong she'd been to try and discourage Mary Beth and me from hiring all those teenagers. She felt at first that having them at the diner would have caused more harm than good. She didn't think that just working at the diner would change their hearts.

In the beginning, I worried that she might be right. The kids we hired on came from very rough situations. You wouldn't think that anything bad could happen in a tiny, little town where most people go to church on Sunday mornings, but it does. After all, just because someone goes to church doesn't necessary mean they are a Christian. I was finding out that far too many people attended church as a cover up; they wanted people to believe they were good so they wouldn't question their lifestyle. Because of that, a few of the girls that came in were very bitter and unopen to any talk of Christ at all. They came from hypocritical homes, homes that *said* they believed in God but that abused them both physically and emotionally.

One girl we'd hired, Chelsea, was a beautiful sixteen-year-old girl, on the outside, at least. She had jet-black hair that fell in perfect ringlets all the way down her back, and her creamy skin was flawless; something every sixteen-year-old girl would be envious of. It was something *I* was envious of, with my plain brown hair and eyes, my simple looks. Her eyes were an unearthly shade of green, a color I'd never seen before. When I asked her if she wore colored contacts, she got all defensive about it, saying how much she hated that everyone just assumed her eye color wasn't real. So I took that as a no and never asked again.

But those eyes did more than just make you question if they were real. They were like a window straight to her soul. At times, you could look in her eyes and see all the emotions running through her mind, all the pain and confusion and anger at her situation. At other times, they were like a steel door, sealed up tight and unwilling to let anyone in. On the rare occasions that she laughed, her eyes sparkled and crinkled at the corners. But when she was angry, they were piercing and cold. It was like a roller coaster with that girl and her emotions. We never quite knew what to expect.

It had only been about a month since we hired her on, and not much had changed in her attitude. She'd responded pretty much the way that Delilah had predicted. She rolled her eyes at the verses Mary Beth had on the wall and didn't want anything to do with the encouragement we showered upon her. She shut down at the very mention of God, unwilling to hear anything we wanted to share with her. In a few weeks, Mary Beth would propose the idea of starting a Bible study to the teens, then invite all of them to join. I already knew Chelsea wouldn't want to participate. The others, though, would probably join with a bit of coaxing.

In addition to Chelsea was Jess and Alexa. Out of those three, Chelsea was the most angry, the most unwilling to share any part of her story with us. Jess was similar to Chelsea, just a bit softer. Her emotions weren't all over the place either; we pretty much expected that she'd come to work with that sullen look in her eyes. She'd do the bare minimum of what we expected of her, never going above and beyond to get the job done or satisfy the customers. And as cliché as it sounds, her hair matched her attitude perfectly. She had a head full or fiery, red curls, curls that refused to stay put no matter how hard Jess tried to pull them back into a pony tail. And although she sought to hide her pain from us, her eyes betrayed her. I'd catch a glimpse of fear in her eyes at times, especially when it got closer to closing time. I started to wonder if things at home were rougher than Mary Beth and I knew.

I swallowed all my fears one night and decided to ask Jess about it. And instead of blowing up like I expected, her eyes fell and her shoulders slumped. "My life sucks right now," she opened up. "My mom took back my loser father, the guy who ran off three years ago with a girl half his age. It amazes me that she let him back in the night he showed up on our doorstep, wasted and completely broke. But she says she loves him. Now me and my little brothers are suffering because my mother is an idiot."

I cringed at the harsh language she used. Even though her mother sounded like an awful woman who was unconcerned with the well-being of her children, I didn't like the fact that Jess called her mother an idiot. I guess I'd just grown up being taught to honor your mother and father, even if you didn't agree with them. Clearly, this girl had grown up far differently than I had.

She went on to tell me about how her mother was now working two jobs to support her father's alcohol addiction. She was
gone all day and all night working, leaving her two brothers, ages
seven and nine, to fend for themselves all day, their drunken father
yelling and threatening them while nursing his endless hangovers
on the living room couch. Jess said they usually tried to sneak
out while he was sleeping so they could spend the afternoons in
peace before they had to head back for dinner. I was thankful that
at least they were getting fed at the free lunch program that had
started a few weeks ago.

Jess said that all the money her mom brought in was barely
enough to cover all the bills and groceries each month. Any
money that was left over was used to buy more alcohol for Brett,
Jess's dad. That's why Jess had applied for this job in the first
place. She was tired of never having enough money to buy new
clothes or the little extra things each month. She was tired of her
brothers never getting any new things either. And most of all,
Jess hated that her dream of going off to college in a few years
would probably never happen. Her family couldn't afford it. My
heart went out to her because I had just been in that situation.
Only with Albert's help had I finally been able to go out and
take my GED, which I'd passed with flying colors, and enroll in
classes for the fall. I knew the stress of not having the means to
pay for school.

Out of the three girls that we'd hired, I connected with Alexa
the most. She was much softer than the other girls. And she
reminded me so much of myself. She was the most willing to
open up and talk about the problems she was facing. She was the
most willing to sit down at the end of a long day and talk over
coffee. But what I appreciated the most about Alexa was her good
attitude. She came in each day with a smile on her face, despite all
that lay back at home. And it truly seemed like she cared about
the people she was serving, like she wanted to do her best and

please both Mary Beth and myself. She was a breath of fresh air in our tension-filled, little restaurant.

Over coffee one night, she shared her story with me. "My mom died a few years ago in a drunk driving accident," she said with a quaver in her voice. "I'm an only child, so once my mom was gone, my dad started pouring out his entire life into me. It sounds cute, but...it isn't. It feels like he's smothering me most of the time."

I nodded and sipped my coffee, encouraging her to continue. "Anyway, even though in the beginning my dad was getting really annoying, things were okay. But then he had some sort of mental break down...he told me he felt like he was wasting his life and that he wanted to do something important. So he decided to start taking in foster kids."

"That's great," I said enthusiastically. But from the sad look on Alexa's face and the slow shaking of her head, I knew that it hadn't turned out great. "What happened?" I whispered.

She sighed and closed her eyes. "I was thirteen when my dad started taking in foster kids. It was really weird at first, but after awhile, I got used to it. Sometimes sibling groups would come in, and that was really fun. In the beginning, we only took in little kids, but then my dad decided to take a risk and start taking in older kids, which again, was fine in the beginning. But then these two brothers came in, Ethan and Weston. Ethan was sixteen and his little brother was six, and Ethan seemed very nurturing. That's why my dad trusted him so quickly...it seemed like he was very responsible for his age."

"Not the case?" I asked, expecting her to tell some story about how he threw a wild party while her dad was away or something along those lines. I never in a million years expected her to tell me whatshe did.

"No. One weekend my dad went away. My aunt needed his help to fix her car because she had an important job interview the next day. She lives a few hours away, so my dad just decided to stay the night and come back in the morning. That turned out to be the biggest mistake of his life though, because while he was gone, Ethan attacked me."

My jaw dropped, and my eyes widened. "Like…he raped you?" I whispered, my head spinning. I was quickly realizing that sexual abuse was much more common than I had once thought.

She quickly shook her head. "No, thank God. But it was just as ugly. He had me all tied up in my bed." She closed her eyes as those painful memories came flooding back like they always do when you share your story. "I won't go into details, but it was nasty, Molly. Weston was locked in the other room, and he was screaming all night because he was hungry. Eventually, Ethan got tired and fell asleep, and that's where my dad found us in the morning."

I imagined my own father walking in on what Jason had done to me that cold, rainy night in November all those years ago. My face burned with embarrassment just thinking about it. I couldn't imagine what Alexa had felt when her dad walked in to find her tied to the bed, probably not fully clothed.

"Needless to say that was the last time my dad took in foster kids," she said with a weak laugh.

I gave an exasperated sigh. "Well, I should hope so! Did you get the help you needed after the attack?" I asked, concerned that she had tried to deal with it on her own like I had done.

She nodded, and I felt the relief spread throughout my body. At least some girls had the common sense to deal with their issues, unlike me. "But," she said sadly, "word somehow spread around school that I had gotten Ethan kicked out of my house. A bunch of kids thought I was just making it up. They basically made my life a living hell until Ethan finally graduated and moved away. Then it died down a little…but a few people still call me ugly names and refuse to have anything to do with me."

I hated that sexual abuse got turned around like that. It always seemed like the girls got blamed for what happened, though that was hardly ever the case. It certainly hadn't been the case with Alexa; she'd been thirteen years old when she got attacked! No thirteen-year-old girl would ever ask for something like that to happen; she wouldn't have been flirting with him or encouraging him to have any contact with her. It just didn't seem fair that when a girl was sexually abused, she not only had to deal with that pain, but she also had to deal with the pain that came from people taunting her and calling her names. What a messed up world we lived in.

Alexa never said anything about being a Christian, but she also never rolled her eyes at the verses hanging on the wall or told us to stop shoving our beliefs down her throat when we talked about God around her. She seemed very passive about faith, not really embracing it but not completely against it like the other girls seemed to be. I had hopes that in a few weeks when we started the Bible study up, Alexa would want to attend. Maybe she'd give her life to Jesus and discover true healing from her abuse.

I hadn't connected much with the two boys we'd hired to do Albert's old job of removing dishes from the table and sending them through the dishwasher. But from the looks of it, Mary Beth was doing a great job connecting with Jake and Phil. She teased them constantly, and their laughter echoed throughout the diner, which of course only caused Chelsea and Jess to roll their eyes even more. Alexa would only smile at their laughter, shake her head, and keep doing her job. It was a crazy mixture of people, and even though it was stressful at times and seemed like their attitudes would never change, I was clinging to the hope that God would give me and Mary Beth a miracle. I kept praying that God would do something big, that he'd change and soften these teenagers' hearts and allow his love to infiltrate their lives.

That's why this passage in Romans was hitting me so hard this morning. My heart was heavy with concern for these teens, and I was still battling frustrations with Delilah. I needed to remind myself over and often that just as this passage said, I was to bear with the failings of the weak. I needed to build up those who were struggling and not let myself get frustrated with their bad attitudes. After all, Jesus had died for the sins of the world even as so many rejected him. I knew that I myself often had a bad attitude, and yet each day Christ's forgiveness was still present. "Accept each other just as Christ has accepted you." I couldn't think of a more fitting passage for my circumstances at the moment.

The ringing of my cell phone jarred me out of my peaceful Bible study. My heart skipped a beat when I saw Tyler's name on the screen, but then I remembered the emptiness our last conversation had left me with.

"Hey," I answered, not wanting to sound too overly enthusiastic to hear from him. Suddenly, I became painfully aware of the fact that I hadn't called him when Albert died. I wasn't sure why I hadn't turned to him during that sad time. I'd even sent Tanner a Facebook message letting him know, and he called me a few days after the funeral to see how I was doing. We'd only talked for a few minutes though because he was about to take Leah to a doctor's appointment. They were still struggling to figure out the best way to handle Leah's breast cancer. Things would be a whole lot easier if a baby wasn't involved.

Tyler wouldn't be happy that I hadn't called to tell him about Albert. He wanted to take our relationship to the next level, but if I couldn't even call him and let him know that a close friend had died, what did that say about our relationship? It wasn't that I didn't trust Tyler; it was just that I wasn't so sure I was ready for things to move this fast. When he'd reached out to me for the first time after we'd broken up, he said he'd wait as long as I needed. But once Jenny's situation worsened, he changed his mind pretty quickly. And I just wasn't sure if his heart was in the right place. I was pretty sure he had feelings for me, but I wanted those feelings for me to be the *only* reason he wanted to speed things up and move on to the next step. I didn't want Jenny to be the only reason Tyler wanted to marry me.

"Oh, Molly. It is so good to hear your voice," Tyler responded, sounding genuinely happy to hear my voice. He didn't sound stressed like last time we'd talked. He sounded warm and relaxed. He sounded like the Tyler I'd fallen in love with in Minneapolis.

So I allowed myself to relax as well, settling into my seat to enjoy this conversation. "It's good to hear your voice too," I said as my smile stretched across my face. I couldn't help feeling like a sixteen-year-old girl falling in love for the first time whenever I talked to Tyler. No matter how complicated our relationship was, he still made my stomach feel all warm and fuzzy.

"So what's new in your world since we last talked?" he asked innocently, expecting me to answer like I always did…that nothing was new and that all I was doing was working and studying. But my entire world had flipped upside down in the weeks since we'd talked, and I didn't know how to tell him without upsetting him. If the tables were turned, I'd be mad at him for not picking up the phone and allowing me into his world. This was just the type of thing I'd done to him in Minneapolis—I'd refused to let him in. That's why we'd broken up in the first place, and I knew he'd remember that. And I worried that he might start having doubts about starting things up again if he thought I was the same closed up, hurting soul I'd been back in Minneapolis. I knew I had to be honest with him though; I had to come clean about not calling to tell him about Albert.

I took a deep breath and then sighed. "Tyler…I'm sorry. I should have called you and told you sooner. So much has happened since we last talked. It's just that you kinda freaked me out with all the pressure to make a decision about us, and I've been trying to work through that as well as work through all that's happened too—"

"Whoa, whoa, whoa. Slow down, Molly! You're talking a mile a minute!" he said with a laugh.

I shook my head and took another deep breath, forcing myself to calm down and speak slower. "Sorry. I'm a tad overwhelmed right now."

"All right. Well…tell me what's been happening."

I poured it all out to him—Tanner and Leah's battle against breast cancer while their first child grew inside Leah, Albert's death, getting my GED, and my struggle to love the teenagers and my best friend Delilah. After I had spilled the entire sad story, Tyler was silent. I cringed inwardly, regretting it all the more that I hadn't just called him while all this was happening.

"Wow," was all he said after those excruciatingly long moments of silence. "Wow," he said again, clearly not knowing how to respond. "That's uh…that's quite a lot to deal with, Molly girl. How you holding up?"

I sat up in shock, surprised that Tyler hadn't responded in anger like I'd expected. The Tyler I knew in Minneapolis would have been outraged that I'd shut him out like that. But I suppose he wasn't that same Tyler anymore. He was a new creation, a newborn son of God and brother in Christ. Of course he was responding differently this time around! This time, he understood that I wasn't trying to shut him out; it was just that when I was trying to work through big issues I needed time and space to do so. So maybe I was overthinking our relationship…maybe things *could* work out between us.

"I'm doing okay," I said, not wanting to lie and say I was doing well. Because I wasn't doing as well as I wanted to be doing. I missed Albert. I missed his smile and his little caramel candies. I hated that Tanner and Leah were suffering during this time that should be so joyful. And I didn't like dragging around a heavy heart…it was getting increasingly more difficult to face those girls at the diner and their sad stories. It was so much to deal with right now.

"Yeah…well, okay sounds about right with all that going on. But hey. This is perfect timing! I was calling to see if you wanted to spend a weekend in Minneapolis with me…you know, to meet Jeff and Julie and Jenny."

My heart leapt at this opportunity. "Really?" I asked excitedly.

He laughed. "Nope. Just teasing. What I really want you to do is make the biggest decision of your life without even meeting Jenny."

"Oh, stop it," I laughed, knowing that if we were talking face-to-face I would have reached out to slap him playfully on the face.

"I'm serious, Molly," he reassured. "I want you to come up. I miss you."

My heart melted. "I miss you too," I whispered, grateful that at least part of the reason he wanted me to come up was because he wanted to see me. I knew a big part of why he wanted me to come up was to meet Jenny…but it was nice to know that he just wanted to see me too.

"Well! What are we still talking about this for? I think it's been decided that you need to come up for a visit."

I giggled. "I think you're right."

And that was that. I called up Mary Beth and told her I would be leaving on Thursday to spend the weekend in Minneapolis with Tyler. It wasn't a huge deal for me to leave now that we had extra help. Granted, it would be a little overwhelming for her to handle all the girls on her own, but she'd be fine. She did, however, have a few concerns.

"Now, where will you be sleeping, Ms. Molly?" she asked like a concerned mother.

I smiled and tried not to laugh. I appreciated her concern, but things weren't like that with Tyler and me anymore. "Not sure yet. I might stay with Tyler—"

"Molly!" she interjected.

I laughed. "It's not like that! He'd let me sleep in the bedroom, and he'd sleep on the couch in the living room. There will be no sleepovers on this trip. Or I could stay with Julie and Jeff too, whatever is easiest for Ty."

"Well, I'd be more comfortable with you sleeping at that nice pastor's house. But you do what you think is best. You're an adult, after all. You have to make those tough decisions on your own, you know."

"Yes, I know," I said, stifling another laugh.

The drive from Green Lake to Minneapolis was a little over ten hours, so I'd get there late on Thursday evening. The entire time I was driving, I couldn't tell if my stomach was tying in knots—nervous to find out if Tyler wanted to pursue a deeper relationship because of me or only because of Jenny—or if it was doing little flip flops out of excitement, ready to see his face and fold myself into his arms after all these months. Maybe it was a little of both.

I pulled into Minneapolis, amazed at how quickly the drive had gone. But I suppose driving has always calmed me down, so it wasn't too surprising. I wasn't expecting all these weird emotions to come welling up inside me however. But all of a sudden, my mind was racing back to that spring when I'd first come here, back when I'd been pregnant, alone, and completely scared out of my mind, back when I'd been a fresh victim of sexual assault, still so raw from the pain of my abuse.

I squeezed my eyes shut, trying my best to block out those early memories of Minneapolis. And yet when I drove past the section of road where I'd pulled over to try and change my tire, I could still see Melissa sashaying over to me to offer her assistance. I could taste the cheap burger and coffee I'd inhaled later on at Frankie's. And I could feel the uncomfortable lumps that made up my little bed in Melissa's cramped apartment, how alone and unsure I'd been back then on that first night with the girls.

Some memories are just too hard to shake.

Maybe it had been a horrible idea to come here. I had no good memories whatsoever of this city. None. Of course, all the terrible feelings would come rushing back at me! *What had I been thinking, coming back here and inviting all that pain to come rushing back?*

I know Tyler really wanted me to meet Jenny, but was meeting her worth all this? Would I really fall in love with her as quickly as Tyler said I would? She was just a little girl, after all. How much influence could one child have over my life?

Guess I'd just have to wait and see. For now, I swallowed all those memories, pushing them deep within me to deal with at a later time. And much of it I'd already dealt with. I'd worked through forgiving myself for the mistakes I'd made. But sometimes, even though I know I've forgiven myself and that God's forgiven me, I still struggled. Sometimes, I can't stop the horrible memories from popping into my head. Every once in a while, I'll get flashbacks to that rainy night in November, that night where I'd allowed myself to be alone with Jason, where he'd stolen my innocence, my life. And those feelings of shame and embarrassment continued to well up in my mind, even though I knew without a shadow of a doubt that it hadn't been my fault and that I couldn't have seen it coming. Because no matter how much of a bad guy Tanner and Kristina had thought he was, none of us had thought he would ever do something like that.

Flashbacks of the abortion are much vaguer because while that had been happening, I almost completely blocked it out. I had walked into the clinic that morning confident that abortion was the right choice for me and my baby. I thought I couldn't take care of her, and I thought that I was saving her from the cruel realities of this world. But when the doctor started, I knew immediately that something wasn't right. It wasn't one of those "oh no, I've made a huge mistake" moments. It was more of a "something doesn't feel right about this" moment. I wouldn't fully understand what I'd done until later, until I was completely empty and unable to move forward in my life. After my fight with Tyler, I had finally realized that something needed to change in my life. That's when I'd left the second time and ended up in a tiny, little town in Kansas…it was like I'd finally realized that running and hiding wasn't helping me at all. What I needed was to be found, and I'd most certainly been found in Green Lake.

I calmed down a bit once I was driving downtown to Tyler's apartment. Memories of this part of town were a bit happier. With Tyler, I'd felt something close to happiness. He'd made me smile and laugh; he'd made me feel like it was worth it to keep getting out of bed in the mornings.

As I walked up the stairs, I expected to be bombarded once again by bad memories. Because no matter how many happy memories this place held for me, it also held its fair share of bad memories as well, memories of me throwing my morals out the window and sleeping with Tyler like I hadn't been raised to believe that sex was sacred and only to be shared between a man and his wife, memories of me shutting down and Tyler getting frustrated and angry that I wouldn't—couldn't—let him into my world of pain, and memories of Tyler giving up and letting me walk home, our relationship over and done.

I was surprisingly at peace as I climbed the steps to his apartment. When I made it to his floor and turned to walk down the hallway, I took a deep breath and closed my eyes, choosing to forget about all the awful things that had taken place in this city, in this building. Those dark times were behind me, and now that I'd rejoined God's family, I had nothing but bright things ahead, filled with all the good plans that God had in store for me. Sure, there would, no doubt, be more dark times, but nothing compared to the darkness that I'd been walking through during those years. Back then, I'd had no hope of ever walking out. I was just stumbling along, hoping that things would get better but never really doing anything to make that happen. Now though when I walked through the darkness, I knew I had a hand to hold, someone to bring me through to the other side. I had Jesus, and that's all I needed to make it through the ups and downs of life.

I knocked on the door, which opened while I was still knocking to reveal an ecstatic Tyler, who then proceeded to swoop me up into a hug. He pulled me in and spun me around. I threw my head back and laughed, enjoying all the silliness of the moment and relishing in how good it felt to be in his arms again.

I just couldn't decide how I felt about him! One minute, I was doubting his intentions, sure that he was only using me so that he could adopt Jenny and give her the life she deserved. But after moments like this, when he said sweet things or attacked me with a hug, I was sure that he had fallen back in love with me and that Jenny had nothing to do with his sudden interest in speeding things along.

Maybe this weekend was just what I needed to make up my mind. Maybe everything would become very clear to me after I met Jenny and had some good time to reconnect with Tyler. I could only hope so, because I didn't want to return to Green Lake with a clouded mind, unsure which path to take in my life. I wanted to *get* there—wherever there was. So as I stepped into Tyler's apartment, I silently prayed for God to give me direction, because I still had no idea which way to turn.

SEVENTEEN

✤

Molly

AUGUST

"Seriously, Molly?" Tyler exclaimed, very excited. Talk had turned to spiritual matters as we sat chatting in his living room, talking about what God was doing in our lives and what he was using to make us grow deeper in faith.

I laughed. "Yeah, why? It's just the passage of scripture that's been speaking to me lately…what's so special about that?"

Tyler unfolded his legs, leapt off the couch, and ran to his room. When he came out again, he was holding a leather Bible and had a big grin stretched across his face. "It just happens to be the very same passage that's been speaking to me too. Weird, huh?"

"Not really," I said with a shrug. "God does stuff like that all the time. That's what's so special about the body of Christ. We can help each other and relate to one another."

He plopped beside me again and dropped a kiss on my head. "Well, all righty then, Ms. I've Gone to Church My Whole Life and Am Clearly Way Smarter Than Tyler!"

I gave him a playful shove. "Stop it."

"Just teasing," he said, shoving me back. But then he grew serious as he flipped to Galatians. I was surprised at how quickly his fingers found the book; he'd only been a Christian for a few months. He must really be digging into the word and getting to know Christ better through reading scripture. It truly was the best way to discover what Christ was all about.

Tyler cleared his throat and began reading from chapter 6, verses 7–10.

> Don't be misled—you cannot mock the justice of God. You will always harvest what you plant. Those who live only to satisfy their own sinful nature will harvest decay and death from that sinful nature. But those who live to please the Spirit will harvest everlasting life from the Spirit. So let's not get tired of doing what is good. At just the right time we will reap a harvest of blessing if we don't give up. Therefore, whenever we have the opportunity, we should do good to everyone—especially to those in the family of faith.

"*Hmm*," I murmured, closing my eyes and taking a sip of my iced tea. It was so nice to sit in this apartment and talk about our faith, to read the Bible aloud together. We'd never done anything like that before in this room. It was a pleasant change.

"What does this passage mean to you?" Tyler quietly asked.

I thought for a moment, chewing my lip. "Well," I said hesitantly, still feeling a bit weird discussing things like this with Tyler. It was all so new, Tyler's faith. It would take some getting used to. "I've kind of been struck lately at how much I've been selfishly sowing."

He cocked his head. "What do you mean?"

"I mean…after I went through all that I went through, I think I developed this mindset that I deserved all the good things life had to offer. I felt that I'd been through so much bad, that it was time for some good, you know?" He nodded but remained silent, wanting me to further explain what I was feeling. "So while I've been making good changes and figuring out how to heal from my mistakes, I haven't been sowing to please the spirit. I think I've been sowing to please my flesh, like the passage says. I haven't been investing in others, not really. Sure, I've been helping Delilah through all her issues. I've been listening to her struggles. And I've been helping Mary Beth with all those messed up teenagers. But…I've been doing it to try and fill some big hole. I've been doing it to try and make *myself* feel better. And that's not right."

Tyler shook his head.

"What?" I asked, confused at his reaction.

"I don't think I'd be able to see that in my own life. I mean, you've been through so much. Personally, I think you *do* deserve some happiness. You deserve for things to start going your way, don't you think?"

"Well yeah, of course I do. But I think I'm going about it the wrong way. I want to stop investing in myself and trying to make myself feel better. I think if I really invest in others, if I start sowing to please Christ, *that's* when the good will start happening."

He nodded. "Gotcha. Makes sense."

Both of us related to verses 9 and 10 so much right now.

> Let us not become weary in doing good, for at the proper time we will reap a harvest if we do not give up. Therefore, as we have opportunity, let us do good to all people, especially to those who belong to the family of believers.

We were both so involved in service right now, Tyler with volunteering at the children's home and me with the teenagers at the diner. It was so easy to become weary in doing good because the results were not instant. I wanted the girls to realize that their lives were pointless without Christ. I was tired of them showing up to work day after day with those empty looks in their eyes and sassy comments on their lips. I just wanted things to change!

Things weren't much better for Tyler. "They found family in South Korea, but her grandparents don't want to send her over there. I guess there are some deep family issues that never quite got resolved," he said with a shrug. "Which I thought was good news at first, but her grandparents decided to release her into the foster care system. They're just too old to care for her themselves, and there's nothing else they can do. The state steps in at this point. She gets placed in her first home at the beginning of next week," he said sadly.

This wasn't the plan that Tyler had in mind for her. I think deep down, he wanted us to get married and adopt Jenny before she was placed in any homes. Not that he had to be married to adopt her, but he thought it would be more stable. He wanted her to be loved by two adults, to be nurtured by both a mommy and a daddy. He admitted to me that he was tired of going to the home each week and helping the kids when they'd all end up in foster care eventually. He was growing tired of pouring himself out when in a few years, after they'd been shuffled around from home to home, they'd most likely become jaded and hard if no one ever adopted them.

"You know what?" I asked gently, taking his hand in mine. "I think we're overlooking the last part of this passage. 'So let's not get tired of doing what is good. *At just the right time* we will reap a harvest of blessing.' We can't give up, Ty. We have to keep doing good, knowing that at just the right time we'll finally reap the results. Maybe we're not seeing the results yet because there's still more work to do."

He nodded and sighed, then ran his fingers through his hair in frustration, giving him a wild man look, which set my heart pounding. I still found him so attractive; it would be a battle this weekend to focus on reconnecting and figuring out what to do about Jenny. And being alone in his apartment like this…it would be quite a struggle, especially considering how before we'd always given in to our desires here. This time, we had high standards and strict boundaries. But I knew all too well how easily good intentions could go horribly wrong. Just look what had happened to Delilah! She'd been dating a nice boy from her church, but she'd wound up pregnant and alone, left to fend for herself and her child because of a moment of weakness and desire—for a few moments of pleasure. I'd found that it doesn't matter how strong you think you are or how tall you think you stand. You can still fall to your knees; you can still make huge mistakes.

I didn't want this weekend to be tainted by that kind of mistake however. So I made a promise to myself to be strong, to refuse to give in to any kind of desire that might burn deep within my heart. But then he turned and faced me, brushing the hair out of my face and running his finger down my cheek, which sent tingles rushing up my spine, and I shivered, scared at how those old feelings of desire welled up inside me.

Tyler must have sensed too how the mood of the room had changed, how the air all of a sudden seemed charged with electricity, so he suggested we go out for a walk. It had been a scorcher today, but the air had cooled off a bit as the sun started to disappear. I quickly agreed, and we took off down the street, feeling good about removing ourselves from a potentially dangerous situation. That was something I'd never done before. With Jason, the first time we'd been alone somewhere together with any possibility of falling into temptation, he'd raped me. And with Tyler, neither of us had really cared about purity or what God thought about us sleeping together. I had cared a *little*, but not enough to stop. The main reason I hadn't really enjoyed sleeping with Tyler is because it felt shallow, empty. I'd known that eventually I'd leave, so it wasn't meaningful for me; I didn't feel any more connected to him during sex. It really wasn't like how the movies portrayed it to be. It didn't seal a bond between us; it didn't make us fall more in love, at least not for me. It felt cheap and dirty. Maybe if I kept reminding myself of how sleeping with him out of wedlock had made me feel, we could avoid falling into temptation this weekend. It'd make it so much easier to say no.

We walked down the street with our arms hanging loosely at our sides, both of us waiting to see if the other would eventually make the move to connect our hands. I wanted him to initiate that though, so I waited. And as we turned around to head back

225 ❖ AN OPEN WINDOW

to his apartment in the dwindling sunlight, he finally took my hand and wove his fingers through mine. I gave him a timid smile and squeezed his hand, letting him know that I was okay with this, that I wanted this to happen.

We made plans to get up around nine o'clock the next morning to get ready for the day. Tyler wanted to take me out for breakfast—at a restaurant we'd never gone to before so that no bad memories would taint our special weekend. After breakfast, we'd head over to the children's home to meet Jenny, which I was still incredibly nervous about. I wanted her to like me, and I wanted myself to fall in love with her like Tyler said I would. I wanted to see Tyler interact with her and give me a glimpse into what my life *could* be like, with the three of us living together as a family.

But what if I didn't fall in love with her? Or what if she didn't like me? Tyler's dreams rested upon our meeting tomorrow, and I really didn't want to mess anything more up for him. Before I wandered down the hall to bed though, Tyler pulled me close and held me. I felt my heart begin to pound and my stomach start to churn with all kinds of emotions and feelings, which of course intensified when he angled my face up to meet his and gently brushed his lips against mine.

"Molly..." he murmured, desire dripping from his voice. He felt it too. All those old feelings and wants bubbling back up after all these years apart. He put his hands on the side of my face, drawing me closer and kissing me like he used to when we first started dating, full of passion and desire, kisses that said he never wanted to stop, that he never wanted to let me go again. My body was telling me that this was fine, but my mind was screaming at me to run away. And for once in my life, I listened to that inner voice instead of shoving it away and ignoring it. So I pulled away and kissed Tyler's cheek. "Good night," I whispered, then turned and retreated to the bedroom.

Once I was behind the closed door, I sighed, closed my eyes, and flopped onto the bed. It was going to be much harder than I anticipated to stick to my morals and not let things get out of hand this weekend. Perhaps I should have listened to Mary Beth's advice and slept over at Jeff and Julie's place. I simply hadn't expected things to be so electric between us, so charged with these intense desires.

I smiled to myself though, as I snuggled into Tyler's bed, the bed I'd never slept in alone before. With things so charged between us, it erased all fear from my mind that he was after me only for Jenny. Granted, a deep relationship can't be built off of physical attraction and desire. I knew that all too well because of how things had turned out for us the first time around. This time though, it *was* deeper. We'd spent the whole evening discussing our faith and our dreams for the future, for goodness sake. *Everything* was different this time!

But a successful relationship required *some* kind of physical attraction, right? We definitely had plenty of that! We'd just have to take special care to keep things pure between us this time around. Because if things worked out for us and we got married, we'd have a lifetime to express our love to each other in a physical way.

After breakfast the next morning, we headed to the Children's Home, and the entire drive there my stomach was tying up in knots. This was a big moment for all three of us. If we didn't connect, then Tyler would have to make a choice: me or Jenny.

I clutched his hand as we walked across the street to the home. He gave my hand a gentle squeeze, reassuring me for the millionth time that I'd absolutely love her and that I had no need to worry about meeting Jenny. Still, my heart was about to burst out of my chest as we walked through the doors, still hand in hand.

The building was nothing like I imagined it to be. It wasn't a huge, cold building filled with little metal beds covered by ratty cotton blankets all lined up and little runny nosed kids running wild. It was actually a large house, and it was cheerful and happy, full of love and hope, not despair like I'd anticipated. There was a large dining room where all the moms and kids ate together, a cozy living room complete with a brick fireplace and a bookshelf overflowing with all kinds of reading material, and an amazing playground out back. There was no television anywhere in the house, which I thought was a great idea. This was a temporary living place after all. The workers probably didn't want to create a place that the women never wanted to leave. This was a place for healing, a place where their kids could be safe and have fun playing while they figured out what to do with their lives. For kids like Jenny, there was a wing especially for them, a place where they felt safe and loved while they waited to find out what would happen to them next.

Jenny lived in a room with a few other girls, and the room was absolutely adorable. It was painted a lovely shade of lavender, and there were bunk beds on three of the four walls. The fourth wall was a little play area for the girls, complete with a toy chest full of cuddly stuffed animals and a little toy kitchen for the girls to let their imaginations run wild.

There was a wing for abused mothers and their kids, one for teenage girls, and one for pregnant teenagers. A nursery was available for the girls to use when their babies arrived, but Tyler said the girls couldn't stay there long. They were encouraged to set up a place to live before the baby got there, but if they were unable to do so, they could stay for up to six months. After that, the workers stepped in and helped the girls find a place to live and a job. Then they checked up on them for a few months, making sure they were adjusting and their babies were being taken care of. Overall, I was very impressed with the Children's Home. The workers and volunteers seemed to be doing an excellent job creating a safe, loving environment for mothers and children but then encouraging them to get their lives together and move forward.

When we peeked into the craft room where Jenny was con-structing some kind of treasure box, her face lit up in excitement. She sprang out of her chair and rushed over to Tyler, and he swooped her up into his arms and swung her around, making her chortle in glee.

"How are you, princess?" he asked as he settled her onto his hip. I couldn't get over her precious face, her delicate china doll looks. Her skin was creamy and light; her jet-black hair was cut short and swept to the side with a tiny blue bow. She had deep, dark eyes, huge and filled with wonder. And her tiny pink lips, they were just perfect. I felt all my fears slip off my shoulders and roll right out the door because Tyler had been right all along. There was no way you could look at this angel child and not fall hopelessly in love with her. It just wasn't possible.

"I'm good," she replied properly, sounding much older than her four years of age.

"Good," he said, setting her back on the ground. Then he crouched down so that they were eye level. "I brought a friend who really wants to meet you. Remember all the things I've told you about Molly?"

She nodded seriously and looked up to me, slipping her pointer and middle fingers into her mouth, suddenly shy. "You're pretty," she mumbled around her fingers, and I broke into a smile. I crouched down too. "Thank you. You're very pretty too."

She ducked her head. I looked over at Tyler with panic in my eyes, but he shook his head. "She was like that with me too, at the beginning," he whispered. "She'll warm up to you."

We took Jenny out to play on the equipment out back, but the day was hot, sticky, and uncomfortable, making me more nervous and unsure of myself. But Jenny ran and played, shouting and letting loose like Tyler said she would. So I let go of my fears and chased her right alongside Tyler, and at the end of the day, she'd definitely softened up to me. She hugged me tight and even gave me a sticky little kiss on my cheek, making my heart melt and Tyler grin like a teenage boy on his first date.

He sighed and swung my hand happily as we walked back to the car after our visit with Jenny. Things had gone so well, and I definitely felt a connection with Jenny, maybe not enough of a connection to make the decision to move things along with Tyler, but that would probably come the more time I spent with her. For now, I was pleased with the wonderful time we'd all had today, and I smiled at all the future might hold for the three of us. I could easily picture all of us living and loving together as a family, maybe one day welcoming a little one in, a playmate for Jenny. *Who knew what was in store for us?*

We were so exhausted that night from our day with Jenny; when we got home, we whipped up some spaghetti and put in a movie, but both of us fell asleep before it was over. I woke up around 12:30, kissed his forehead, and padded down the hallway to his room. Although it probably wouldn't be a big deal to snuggle together all through the night, I felt better this way.

We spent Saturday hanging out with Jeff and Julie and their two little girls, Annabelle and Claire. Jeff took us out to Centennial Lakes Park, a twenty-four-acre park and pond, which was absolutely gorgeous. There was a paved pathway that meandered around the pond, and the whole thing was beautifully landscaped, complete with swinging benches and bubbling fountains. Our afternoon started out with a paddle boat rental—Tyler and I in one boat, Jeff and Annabelle in one, and Julie and Claire in another. Tyler suggested we try some fishing after that, but I opted out and just watched the girls throw their lines into the water. Tanner had tried to take me back in high school a couple times, and I hated it. I hated baiting my hook, I hated that it took forever for a fish to bite, and I hated the way the fish squirmed and flopped. But most of all, I hated the way fish smelled. *Yuck.*

We ended the day by watching a remote control sailboat race that was taking place at the park. Annabelle and Claire were enthralled with the race; they clapped and cheered on their favorite boats. The adults all settled onto benches to rest from our long day in the hot summer weather.

Jeff leaned forward with a mischievous look playing in his eyes. "So you two. Have you been enjoying your weekend together? Tyler's told me quite a bit about you, Molly. He can't stop talking about how pretty you are, what a committed Christian you are. And you know a man's in love when he talks about a girl constantly."

I felt the heat rushing to my face. "Jeff!" Julie exclaimed, swatting her bold husband on the back of his head, which of course only made him laugh. "Please excuse my husband. I guess he forgot to replace his filter this morning."

Tyler chuckled and settled his arm around my shoulder. "That's okay, Jules. He's right...I can't stop talking about this great lady. She's...something else," he said tenderly, looking deeply into my eyes and dropping a light kiss on my forehead.

"Yup. I knew it. See, hon?" Jeff teased, and Julie shoved him playfully, then folded her arms, giving up on trying to control her husband. But she too had a mischievous little smile on her lips, happy that Tyler and I seemed to be reconnecting so well and falling in love again, the *right* way this time.

"We'll just see what happens in the next few weeks. See what Molly's comfortable with. We want to make sure this is the right thing for us. I lost her once before...and I don't want to do that again. So we're gonna do it right this time, right, hon?"

I nodded, my heart soaring that once again Tyler seemed willing to wait for me to figure out if this really was the best thing for me. This weekend had been magical, but I didn't want to make a decision after a weekend so charged with emotion. I needed a little bit more time to figure out what I wanted to do with school, and I wasn't quite ready to leave Mary Beth and the girls at the diner just yet. Tyler had *said* that he'd move to Kansas, or anywhere, really, if only he could be with me. But I wasn't so sure about that after this weekend. He *loved* it here. He loved his apartment, and come on, who wouldn't? It was gorgeous, it had character, and it was so *him*. And he loved Jeff and Julie and their girls too. It would be beyond difficult for him to pick up and move, leaving his entire life behind him. I couldn't blame him. He'd made a great life for himself here, a life that would be hard for anyone to walk away from.

I tried to process all this on the way home, but it was overwhelming and I ended up just sticking in one of my favorite CDs and blaring my praise music the entire way home, singing at the top of my lungs to keep my mind off of all that had happened this weekend. I knew sooner or later I'd have to make a choice, but I chose later.

My voice was hoarse by the time I pulled into Green Lake late Sunday night. I fell into my bed completely exhausted, once again refusing to think through my crazy, mixed up feelings. Tomorrow I'd go into work; then, I'd probably head over to Delilah's place to tell her all about my weekend. Hopefully, she'd have some advice for me, an outsider's opinion free from all these conflicting thoughts and emotions.

But once again, my carefully manicured plans crumbled when I received a frantic phone call from my mother just as I was leaving work on Monday.

"Hi, Mom!" I answered cheerfully, only to be greeted with my mother's tear-filled voice.

"Oh, honey. How soon can you come back?"

My heart dropped, and I immediately thought that something had happened to Dad or Savannah. "Why? What's going on?" I asked, panicked and suddenly extremely nervous.

"It's Leah, honey. She went into early labor, and well. It doesn't look good, not for either of them. I guess the cancer's been much more aggressive than the doctors thought, and her body's rejecting the baby. Tanner asked me to call you…he wants you here, Molly."

My head began to spin, and the keys shook in my hands as I tried to turn them in the ignition. I took a deep breath and commanded myself to calm down. "Really?" I asked, completely shocked that of all people Tanner wanted to be beside him during this traumatic time, he'd chosen me. And while I wasn't sure if it was appropriate with my lingering feelings for him, I headed to my apartment and packed for a week back in Iowa, knowing that I had no choice in the matter. Tanner wanted me there, so I had to go, whether it was appropriate or not.

The five-hour drive to Iowa wasn't nearly enough time to prepare myself for what lay in the hospital though. I don't think any amount of time could have prepared me for that however. And I just wasn't sure if I was strong enough to be of any help to Tanner during this difficult time.

EIGHTEEN

❖

Molly

AUGUST

I sat beside Tanner in the sterile hospital waiting room, rigid and unmoving. The bright florescent lights didn't help relax me at all, and I had no idea how to begin trying to comfort Tanner, not after all that had happened in the last few hours. So I just sat beside him and fiddled with the ring on my hand, knowing too that he probably didn't want me to talk, to fill the quiet room with idle chatter, not when he was still trying to process what had happened.

He sat slumped in his chair, his whole body just wilting with sadness. His head was hanging, and he kept working his eyes with his hand. I'd never seen him like this before, so dejected and weighed down with sorrow. Tanner's the type of guy who likes to face difficulty head on, standing tall and knowing that whatever he walked into he'd be able to tackle it with Christ leading him. But nothing this big had ever happened to him before. Besides a distant great-aunt, Tanner had never lost anyone before; he'd never had to deal with the overwhelming sense of loss that follows after someone dies.

I, however, had experienced this twice already in my short life. The first had been my tiny daughter, her life snuffed out by my own hands, and Albert, his loss still so fresh in my mind. Now this—it was just too much death for me to handle all at once.

I'd rushed into Oak Ridge just hours ago, not sure I would be able to handle what lay inside. And I was right. I was nowhere near prepared enough for the events that quickly spiraled out of control, leaving Tanner standing alone in the aftermath, wondering how it had all happened so quickly.

Leah had gone into labor Sunday evening a whole two months before she was due. She hadn't been doing well at all because the cancer had spread like wildfire due to lack of treatment. But even after doctors told Leah that chemotherapy would be safer the farther she progressed into the pregnancy, she refused. She didn't want to risk anything, didn't want to harm her child to save herself. So Tanner had sat back helplessly, unable to convince his wife to fight for her life. He watched her body waste away while she fought only to feed the growing baby inside her. He watched her steps slow and her eyes struggle to stay open from lack of energy. He held her hair back as her body began to reject all food she tried to pump into her body.

Finally, her body had enough. The baby was stealing nutrients that she so desperately needed herself, and as they relaxed at home on Sunday evening, she felt the first pangs of labor pains… weeks before they were supposed to come. Tanner was glad it happened during the afternoon, and not during church where they would have had to rush out and cause a big stir.

Though a C-section might have been wiser, Leah desperately wanted a natural labor. Knowing she only had so much time left, she wanted more than anything to experience giving birth to her precious baby, and doctors respected that. Though she was weak and tired, her body seemed to handle labor just fine. They pulled Tanner aside while Leah was resting, however, and told him that if things took a turn for the worse, they'd do a C-section anyway, just to make sure Leah would at least get to meet the baby before her body gave up completely.

God must have known how much Leah needed to do this however because for the most part, her labor went okay. It was long though, lasting just over eighteen hours. Minutes after one o'clock in the afternoon on Monday, a screaming baby Elysa made her entrance into the world. She was premature, and even though they knew Leah probably didn't have much time left, for the baby's safety, they had to rush her away to be checked out. Tanner stayed by Leah's side, stroking her face and holding her close, savoring his last few hours with her. Finally though, just as Tanner felt Leah's body draining of all life, they brought Elysa back. She was perfectly healthy, a gorgeous little bundle straight from heaven.

The nurse placed the tiny baby girl into Leah's arms, and she melted with pleasure. "Sweet baby," she crooned, showering her face with light kisses. She continued whispering sweet words to her perfect baby while Tanner's tears wet her shoulder. Leah's parents snapped as many pictures as they could, but no one took Elysa from Leah. They all knew Leah's time was quickly running out; they wanted her to have all the time she could with her before Jesus welcomed her into his arms.

She lasted a short three hours, her body simply unable to recover from the long labor. Hours before, while Leah had been in labor, Tanner knew she wasn't going to make it. So, out of desperation, he wanted someone to be with him during those first difficult hours as a widower. That's when my mother had called me. He hadn't told my mother that he knew the end was near, though, not wanting to freak either of us out. All too soon though, Leah's body grew limp and cold, but she died with a smile playing on her lips, snuggling her daughter close to her side.

The first time Tanner held his daughter, he'd been taking her away from Leah's body. He left as they were removing Leah's body, and doctors took Elysa back again for a more thorough check, to which Tanner didn't object. He told me later that it wasn't like he was angry at her; he didn't blame Leah's death on her, but the joy of Elysa's birth would always be tainted by his wife's death.

I had gotten there a little after six o'clock the night of her death, not a single clue that she'd died. So when the nurses directed me to Leah's room when I asked where Tanner was, I walked in expecting to see her pale, limp body fighting to recover after birth. *Not the case.* I peeked in to find Tanner curled up in the little bed all by himself, clutching a shirt and sobbing uncontrollably.

I stopped in my tracks and retreated, my heart pounding out of my chest. I rushed back to the nurses' station, and I didn't even have to ask. My face said it all. "Oh, honey. I'm sorry! I thought you knew!" the nurse explained apologetically.

"No," I breathed, not knowing how to react. "When?" I asked numbly, unable to form a complete question out of my intense shock.

"Earlier today, 'bout four o'clock this afternoon," she said quietly. I could see the shine in her eyes. This was a small town; everyone knew each other. The sudden death of a woman so young would rock Oak Ridge to its very core. Leah had been born here, had gone to the Christian school since she was five. She had been very involved there, playing volleyball, writing for the school newspaper, and snapping pictures for the yearbook. While she hadn't been in the popular crowd at school, she'd still been well-liked and certainly well-known.

The nurse sensed my deer in the headlights look though, so she pulled herself together and stood to help me out. "Let me tell him you're here, Molly. Your mother told me you'd be in today at Tanner's request. I'll come get you when he's ready, okay?"

I nodded and sank into an uncomfortable chair in the waiting room. After what seemed like an eternity though, the nurse came back and beckoned for me to follow her. I stood hesitantly and crept down the hall once more, still not wanting to face Tanner and his out-of-control emotions, justifiable emotions, yes, but still hard for me to handle.

He was sitting in a chair in the corner this time. The nurse, whose name I finally found out was Bethany from the nametag hanging from her scrubs, gave me an encouraging squeeze as she left us alone. My stomach tightened, and I wanted to run away again, back to Green Lake and all its familiarity. I wanted to turn back the hands of time and make sure that Leah had found the cancer earlier so she could get treatment before she'd gotten pregnant. I wanted things to remain the way they'd been, with Tanner and Leah happily married and healthy, still young and in love and excited for the bright future ahead of them.

Instead, Tanner was alone, and Leah had only gotten to live a few years as a married, working woman before the cancer stole her life. She'd experienced so little in life, and it didn't seem fair. Someone like her should live a long, happy life. She was a good girl! She hadn't made mistakes like me—she'd been nothing but faithful to Christ during her short life. But life rarely works out the way we think it should. The good don't always win like we want them to.

Tanner looked up when I finally took my first faltering steps into the room. While his face didn't exactly light up when he saw me, I did see the relief spread through his body. He stood up quickly and covered the short distance between us in a few swift steps, and suddenly, he was in my arms, almost knocking me over with the force of his grip and taking me completely off guard with this physical contact. Luckily for me though, my body responded appropriately; the hug didn't cause my heart to pound and my stomach start fluttering like it would have done if the circumstances were different. This was strictly a hug to comfort him, to soften the blow of all that life had thrown at him in the last forty-eight hours and nothing more. So I didn't feel awkward letting him hold on for much longer than was probably appropriate. He needed me, so I let him hold on.

Any words that my brain might have come up with would have stuck to my throat, so I remained silent. Tanner pulled back and wiped his eyes, then heaved a giant sigh. Raking his hands through his already disheveled hair, he murmured, "Well, kinda creepy to hang out in this room all day, huh?"

I nodded and shuddered, realizing for the first time that this was where it had happened, in the very bed that Tanner had just been lying in.

"Just, uh, let me say one last good-bye, okay? Meet you in the waiting room?"

I nodded again, feeling beyond stupid at not being able to even say one word to him. So I turned and retreated to the waiting room once again and waited for him to come out. He dragged himself out twenty minutes later and fell into the chair beside me, looking like the entire weight of the world rested on his shoulders, which made sense; he'd just lost his entire world after all.

So that's where we sat for the remainder of the day, under those glaring florescent lights. Tanner's parents sat watch behind us, their presence offering quiet strength as they allowed me to support Tanner during this heart-wrenching time. Leah's parents watched over Elysa down the hall.

Tanner's body sunk a little further with each passing hour, the tears welling up in his eyes again and again, probably reliving this entire nightmare of a day in his mind. That's the thing about traumatic experiences though—it's entirely way too difficult to try and erase them from your memory. They seem to burn themselves into your mind, then jump into your dreams at night and your thoughts during the day, tormenting you with all the ugliness when the only thing you want to do is forget those moments ever happened. Try as hard as you might to block them out or run from them they're always there, ready to attack just when you think you're starting to forget.

This would be one of those memories for Tanner, I was sure of it. *How could he ever forget his wife's fragile body working so hard to give life to their tiny daughter? Or that first moment the doctors placed Elysa into Leah's arms, her face lighting up at the sight of the one person she'd sacrificed her own life for?* I'm sure he had been feeling an extreme range of emotions—joy at the sight of their child, intense pain when he realized that this was their first and last day as a family of three.

I finally got brave and stretched my arm across his back, lightly running my hand across it in a lame attempt to provide some sort of comfort. Tanner had always been a physical person, always welcoming and giving away hugs and scratching my back. His body responded to my touch, and he sat up a bit, seeming to enjoy my gentle circular scratches. He glanced back at me, and his mouth twitched up the slightest bit, hardly a smile but close enough. I didn't expect that crooked smile I'd come to love so much over the course of our friendship.

A nurse suddenly appeared, and Tanner shot up. "Mr. Walters? Would you like to spend some time with your daughter? She's doing quite well. Perhaps you'd like to give her a bottle? It's about time for that." She smiled encouragingly at him, coaxing him to really meet his daughter. He'd only spent a few hours with Elysa earlier that day as Leah held her, only holding her himself for a few brief moments before the nurses whisked her away again.

I saw all the oxygen escape from his body; I saw the battle between his head and his heart almost like it was playing out right in front of me. His brain was telling him no, that baby had taken Leah away from him far before it was her time to die. But his heart was telling him that inside the very room that his brain was telling him to avoid lay a little piece of Leah, the very reason that Leah had fought so hard for her life. Mom told me Leah had been experimenting with her diet, eating strictly organic and also trying other crazy methods people said helped. I guess it had held her over just long enough to meet Elysa though. And that was the only thing that mattered to her from the very first day she found out she had cancer. Her entire being was focused on staying alive long enough to experience this day. So he couldn't really avoid interacting with her because Leah wouldn't have liked that.

She'd want him to be pouring out all the love *she'd* wanted to pour out on her. Now that she was gone, it was Tanner's job to love her, to tell her all about the remarkable woman who'd given up her life so she could live.

So while Tanner heaved himself out of the tiny chair and slowly followed the nurse, I remained in my chair, unable to ignore how much Leah's sacrifice reminded me of Christ's sacrifice.

Leah's life had been picture perfect; she had a wonderful husband and a great job. She was pretty and well-liked, her future stretching out in front of her enticingly. But things had taken a drastic turn for the worse when the cancer struck her body without warning, advanced and spreading like wildfire through her tiny body. And if her body had been baby-free, they could have done surgery and started pumping her body full of drugs to kill the invader. But she refused all forms of treatment only because she knew it would compromise her child's life. She could have easily aborted Elysa and avoided the difficult journey she'd just suffered through, but there was no way Leah could have convinced herself that the baby was just a clump of cells like I had. Instead, she'd bravely chosen the tough road, knowing that in the end, it wouldn't work to her advantage. Deep down, she'd known she wouldn't make it; Tanner had told me that hours ago. Even then she kept walking down that rocky road, each mile more exhausting than the last and draining another ounce of life from her already weakened body.

Leah hadn't needed Elysa, but she *wanted* her. She knew in the end that she'd have to give up her own life so that baby Elysa could live, just as Christ had done for us. He didn't need us either. But I knew without a shadow of a doubt that he wanted us just as much as Leah wanted Elysa. And like Leah, Christ had done the unthinkable so that we could live. He'd stretched out his arms on a rough, wooden cross and allowed the blood to flow from his beaten and weak body, knowing at any moment he could have summoned the angels of heaven to rescue him. Like Leah, there had been a way out, an escape. But Leah didn't want out because that option didn't give her Elysa. Christ didn't choose an escape either, knowing that his blood, his death, was needed to pardon the ugly stains of our sins. We needed him to die so we could live.

Hot tears meandered slowly down my cheeks. My heart hurt for Tanner, but my breath caught in my throat and goose bumps rushed up my arms just thinking about the beautiful picture Leah's death painted. There was no denying the similarities between what she had done for her daughter and what Christ had done for me. Because while her body wasted away during her pregnancy, while it twisted and contorted during labor, she knew in the end she'd get Elysa. That had spurred her on when things were rough, no doubt about it. I bet there had been times she wanted to throw in the towel and take the easy way out, but she stood her ground and fought for her child, just as Christ had fought for us. During his thirty-three years on this earth, I bet Christ had faced similar circumstances, times when he got fed up with how broken and messed up our world was, how we as humans had this need to fight and hate each other instead of love and care for one another like he wanted us to do, and especially when he was beaten and flogged, forced to carry his own cross, then nailed and displayed as a criminal when he had not a single sin tainting his record. I bet he had wanted to call it quits in those hours where death laughed in his face, when Satan sneered and taunted, no doubt jumping up and down for joy, thinking he'd won.

But he never called on the angels. Because as he walked down the long road that led to the cross, he saw the faces of his children, the ones he needed to die to save. He saw how we were utterly incapable of saving ourselves, how desperate we were for his blood to wash over us and blot out our ugliness and bring the needed purity. Without his suffering, blood loss, and death, we would be stuck muddling through the mess of our sins. But with his death and later his resurrection, we are free from the entangling grasp of sin and death. We are pure. We are ransomed. We live because he died.

I took a cleansing breath, spent from this exhausting day. I wiped the tears from my eyes and leaned forward, resting my elbows on my knees and letting my head fall forward. *Oh Lord,* I prayed. *How our hearts hurt today. We need you now more than ever. We need the overwhelming peace that only you provide. But even as we mourn, I can't deny the beauty of Leah's sacrifice, how it reminds me of what you did for me. So thank you, Lord, for that reminder. You are good, even in the bad times. Help me remember that…help me remind Tanner of that as well.*

The nurse wandered out later, and I realized how late it was. Not a soul was in the room with me, not even Tanner and Leah's parents. They'd gone long ago, promising to be back bright and early tomorrow morning. I'd probably crash here for the night, not wanting to leave Tanner here alone.

"He's asking for you, Molly." Her soft voice cut through the silence and made me jump, but I nodded and quickly made my way down to Elysa's room. My heart just about melted when I walked through the door, and I stopped to absorb the tender scene playing out in front of me, straight out of a Hallmark movie.

Tanner had Elysa snuggled securely in the crook of his arm as she sucked away contentedly at a tiny little bottle. He gently rocked her, his face angled down to her.

"You're a hungry little girl, aren't ya?" he asked, a small smile playing on his lips. It's hard not to smile while holding such a precious little one. "That's good. Means you're healthy. And trust me, after the road I've just walked down with Mommy, I could use a healthy woman in my life."

I tiptoed across the room and gently cleared my throat, not wanting to disturb this tender moment but not wanting to eavesdrop either. He looked up in surprise, and this time, a real smile stretched across his face, though the tears were beginning to fill his already red eyes again.

"She's so perfect." He choked, unable to control the over-whelming emotions warring in his heart. "And she looks like her, has her nose, her ears."

I nodded and swallowed, once again not knowing what to say. "Want to hold her?" he offered.

My heart dropped to my toes, and the blood drained from my face. Leah's death had distracted me from my own pain, but now, alone here with Tanner and his baby daughter, it all came rushing back at me. Ever since the abortion, I tended to avoid babies like the plague, newborns especially. Toddlers, I could handle a bit easier, though it still made my throat close up with regret. And even as Tanner looked at me expectantly, offering up his precious baby for me to meet, I couldn't do it.

"I'm sorry, Tanner," I managed to croak. "I...I can't."

For a moment, fresh pain welled up in his eyes, but just as soon as it appeared, it vanished again as it clicked in his brain. It was so easy for others to forget what I'd done. It was next to impossible for me to forget. Holding this tiny gift from God would only make me think of my own baby, and that's something I didn't want to do right now. I wanted to be here for Tanner, to support *him*, not have another breakdown in the midst of all this turmoil.

"Hey," he said gently. "It's okay. I just forget. I'm sorry."

I gave him a half-hearted smile and dragged a chair as quietly as I could across the floor next to the rocking chair. I settled in, then gave his arm a small squeeze, reassuring him that I wasn't hurt by his oversight.

"You know what?" Tanner said with a bit of excitement. "I bet Leah's up there taking care of your little girl, Molly. Why wouldn't she? She wanted to be here so badly to take care of our baby..." He let his thoughts trail off, but I considered carefully what he'd suggested. It *did* make sense. She'd never gotten the chance to shower Elysa with love, but up in heaven, she had the opportunity to love *my* little one.

"That's a sweet thought, Tanner." I gave him a bigger smile and reached out to caress Elysa's perfect skin. "I bet you're right."

I fell asleep later that night in a stiff chair, unaware that in the coming weeks, I'd be battling my past demons harder than I ever had before. Because while Tanner clung to the hope that somewhere up in heaven Leah was adopting and caring for my baby, I'd soon have to make a similar choice with Elysa. And I just didn't know if my heart was capable of opening up and loving like that.

NINETEEN

❖

Molly

NOVEMBER

I bustled around my tiny kitchen, hiding clutter and wiping down every nook and cranny that looked even remotely dirty or grimy. Tanner and baby Elysa would be here any minute, and I'd put off tidying all day simply because my mind was buzzing. Tanner's call two weeks ago left my brain spinning with all sorts of different scenarios. I just didn't know what to make of his request to spend the weekend down in Kansas with me.

Sure, he'd been calling me a lot more since Leah's passing. But I figured that was just because he missed the companionship of marriage. At home alone with a three-month-old, he didn't have much opportunity for adult conversation. Our calls always focused on my classes at the community college or the teenagers at the diner, whom Mary Beth and I were still struggling to minister to. And we talked about Leah too, of course. He missed her and still didn't know what to do with himself now that she was gone. *How do you move on from something like that though?* Leah had been much too young to die of breast cancer.

So maybe this weekend was just an extension of the phone calls. After all, they provided comfort and distracted him for a bit. He probably figured a weekend away with me would do the same thing. Most likely, he wasn't looking forward to it in the same way that I was. Because darn it if my heart wasn't playing tricks on me, convincing me that I still had feelings for Tanner even as things were going so well with Tyler. I hated myself for having feelings for both of them. But I just couldn't help it! Why did I have to have two wonderful, *available* Christian men in my life?

Well, Tyler was more available than Tanner was, I supposed. It had only been three months since Leah died, and Tanner was probably far from ready to even begin thinking about dating and marriage yet. He needed more time to process, to grieve. And besides, he had a new little lady in his life—his adorable little daughter. She took up all his time now. Yes, Tyler was clearly the better choice for me.

And yet…I couldn't ignore that little niggling feeling at the bottom of my heart. Tyler was a great guy, and I was pretty sure he loved me. But the fact that I had to keep beating that into my head wasn't exactly giving me the most confidence in our relationship. I shouldn't have to constantly tell myself that he loved me; I didn't want to be pretty sure that he loved me. I wanted to be absolutely, 100 percent sure that he loved me, no doubts. But I *did* have doubts, and that scared me.

The physical attraction was definitely there; the chemistry between us was unquestionable. But a successful relationship required more than just a physical attraction. And the more time I spent with him, the more I became uncomfortable, remembering back to how he always needed to be in charge, how he needed to have the final say in everything. That caused my dander to act up because as an oldest child of three kids, I had the exact same personality. Throw two people with that need to be in charge into a pot, and it begins to simmer in a hurry, threatening to boil over and ruin all good intentions. With all the decisions that needed to be made concerning Jenny, I wondered when the pot would boil over.

He was really getting pushy with the whole Jenny ordeal. She was in the same foster home; they kept her there knowing that

Tyler and I were seriously considering the idea of marriage and then adopting her. He'd met the foster parents and said they were great people, but they had kids of their own plus a few other foster kids in the home as well, and Tyler worried she wasn't getting all the attention and love she needed with them. More than anything, he wanted to swoop in and yank her out of the foster system, to love her and call her his own. The bond they shared was strong, their connection deep and intimate. All he wanted was to be her daddy…and for me to be her mommy.

But too often, I got the feeling that he wanted Jenny to be his daughter more than he wanted me to be his wife. It was as if marrying me would be good, but being a father to Jenny would be the chocolate fudge icing on the bland white cake, the cherry on top of the plain vanilla ice cream. And no woman wants to feel like that! I wanted to be desired in a special way. I wanted him to want me more than anything else in the entire world, and right now, I couldn't say with confidence that he wanted me in that way.

But in the weeks since Leah had passed, it was beginning to sound more and more that Tanner wanted me in that way, just like he used to. And this surprised me a bit because just months earlier he'd been happily married, memories of our lost love long since dealt with and filed away in the recesses of his mind. *Why in the world would he come back to me after all the pain I'd put him through?* It just didn't make sense, and I didn't know how to deal with it.

It's like in the spring, when the weather's finally getting nice after months and months of bitter cold. That first day you can fling the windows open to let the spring breezes in is a call for celebration—it can melt the winter blues away in minutes. There is simply nothing like breathing in the scent of spring on that first day, enjoying the way it tickles your nose and sends your hair gently flying in the breeze.

But sometimes we open our windows too soon, so eager to let the sunshine and warm breezes in that we forget that too often, storm clouds are building up in the distance, ready to blow in more cold and rain. When it finally comes, we must run around the house, slamming shut the very windows we were once so eager to open up before the rain comes pouring in.

Should I open up the window of my heart to Tanner once again? I wondered. I had been hesitant when Tanner admitted his feelings to me for the first time, knowing that I also loved him, yet feeling unworthy of him. It was like that now too although I was more worried about what other people would think if we hooked up so soon after Leah's passing. *Would they shake their heads and cluck their tongues in disapproval, or would they smile warmly at us and wish us all the happiness that we could gather up together? Surely everyone thought that after all we'd both been through we deserved to be happy together...right?*

I wasn't so sure. People are quick to judge and even quicker to cast disapproval on the happy plans of others if they don't agree. And that's why I wasn't sure if I wanted to fling the window open just yet and let in the happy breezes that Tanner would surely bring into my life. Because the dark clouds were probably just beyond the horizon, far enough away where I couldn't see them to prepare myself for the storms those dark, angry clouds always bring. How disappointing it would be to have to slam the window shut again if things didn't work out between us for a second time, and how humiliating too.

I was about ready to pull my hair out because of my warring emotions. When I'd decided to settle in Green Lake, I figured my life would calm down considerably. I wanted to be able to fall into a predictable rhythm, to fall asleep each night knowing exactly what lay ahead for me in the coming day. Of course, that hadn't panned out. Only months after moving back I found myself riding a roller coaster full of twists and turns, dramatic uphill climbs and terrifying free falls. Falling for Greg and then watching him go out and marry my best friend, Tyler's sudden reappearance into my life, my baby brother's wedding, finding out about Leah's pregnancy and then later her cancer, and then finally Albert and Leah's deaths…it was all piling up on me now. I looked back at this past year and wondered at all that had happened, marveling at how differently things had turned out than what I expected to find here. *Was it possible for someone to endure all these things?* It must be because here I was, giddy as a fifteen-year-old girl before she goes out on her first real date. I really shouldn't be so excited with all the turmoil in my life right now. And yet I couldn't stop myself from pacing in small circles in my little living room. My heart felt like it was about to jump out of my chest, and I willed myself to calm down. I didn't want to give myself away…not yet. I would first test the waters this weekend, just barely putting my pinky toe in the cold water to see if Tanner felt the same way I felt.

Because really, I could wait. For Tanner, I would wait a lifetime. I still deeply regretted walking away from the beautiful relationship we'd finally found after twelve years of friendship. I think deep down, we both had known for years that there was something more, but each of us had been scared that admitting those feelings would ruin the great thing we had together. I was beyond grateful when he'd thrown his fears aside and finally told me he loved me because it had unlocked the rusty lock holding my heart captive. And yet what had I done? Run away and relocked it, then buried it so deep I had to dig and dig and dig to find it once more.

In Minneapolis, I was convinced my heart had disintegrated altogether. That would explain my ability to walk into an abortion clinic and do the very thing I had once thought undoable and beyond forgiveness. It had been why I'd let things with Tyler get so wildly out of control and why I hadn't been able to share my feelings of unworthiness and deep regret with him. It had doomed our relationship from the start. Yet I'd been so happy at the possibility of a second chance with him. For a while, it seemed like Tyler held all the dreams I ever dreamed. But I wondered if my feelings for Tyler were based just on that—on his ability to make me a mother and a wife, just like I always wanted. I knew that with Tanner, it was much deeper. My heart couldn't help but love Tanner. It had to really work on loving Tyler.

I would be at a crossroads this weekend. And I needed to decide which path I would travel down, even though I wasn't sure what was in store for me at the end of those paths. I assumed that if I chose Tyler, we would get married and adopt Jenny, then start a family of our own soon enough. *But would I be truly satisfied with that life? Would I never cease to wonder and dream about Tanner?* That wouldn't be good for a marriage, not in the least bit. But I had absolutely no idea what would be in store for me if I chose Tanner. If I told Tyler I couldn't be with him, there was still the possibility that Tanner wasn't ready for a relationship with me yet...or ever. With all I'd put him through, it was completely understandable. The uncertainty was killing me, so I continued to fret and pace, surely wearing a path in my carpet. It wasn't until my phone buzzed in my hand and I read the text from Tanner saying he'd be in Green Lake in fifteen minutes that I finally forced myself to stop and sit for a while. I needed to prepare myself for a weekend of more emotions, more decisions. I hoped my heart and my mind would stop arguing and start working together so that I knew without a doubt which way to go. I'd wasted enough of my life sitting around waiting for the answers to just fall into my lap. I wanted to take action and start living my life, for real this time. I couldn't afford to waste any more time, because if Leah's passing had taught me anything, it was that death didn't care how old you were or how many dreams you still had left to live out. It came unexpectedly, and I didn't want to have regrets when the end came for me. So it was time to stop playing these frustrating, little waiting games and time to start living out the dreams that swirled in my head.

And oh, how my heart soared at the possibility of sharing them with Tanner.

TWENTY

❖

Tanner

NOVEMBER

It was a long, boring drive from Oak Ridge to Green Lake—five hours in the car with Elysa, who was sleeping peacefully, thank goodness. So I had hours of uninterrupted thinking time; just me, the open road, and memories of my young wife who'd been snatched away from me way too soon. Three short years is all that we'd enjoyed together as man and wife, four years as a couple...four. Never in a million years would I have imagined being alone at age twenty-three, alone with a baby too. The weight of my situation was still pulling me down, the waves beginning to crash over my head, even after three months had passed since she'd slipped away from me. I just hadn't had any time to really grieve and process all that had happened because I had to take care of Elysa.

I wasn't ready for her. Once we found out about Leah's cancer, *that* became my main concern. I wanted to figure out a way to keep her healthy and strong so that maybe, just maybe, she'd get through the pregnancy, and then we'd be able to do some treatment. Of course, that hadn't panned out. But those stressful seven months were spent frantically trying anyway, and I hadn't prepared myself for fatherhood. I was completely and utterly unprepared to care for Elysa.

My mom stayed with me for a whole three weeks, day and night. We'd take turns getting up and feeding her, and she taught me how to correctly change a diaper. I was a bit shaky at first and incredibly grossed out, even gagging a little my first time, but I was an old pro now. Leah's mom, Heather, was going to stay for a few weeks too, but it was incredibly awkward for me and much too sad for her. She ended up staying for only two days before she physically and emotionally could not handle it anymore. So I hugged her good-bye and promised to bring Elysa by to visit as often as I could.

After six weeks of struggling through my new life as a single father, I broke the promise that Leah and I had made to each other. We absolutely did not want to put our kids into day care, but I had no other choice. I had to start looking around for childcare so that I could go back to work. I had a mortgage and utilities to pay each month; I simply couldn't stay home with her. My mom saw how much this decision was killing me though, so she volunteered to watch her during the day. At first, I refused because my mom still worked three days a week at the school as a teacher's aide, but she insisted that taking care of her family was more important to her than working. She'd stayed home with me and Ellen when we were little, only going out and getting a job when we hit junior high.

"Really, Mom," I tried to argue after Sunday dinner, juggling Elysa in my arms to quiet her whimpering. "I'm sure I can find a nice in-home day care for her. I don't want you to give up your job for me...you *love* working with those kids!"

She reached over and took Elysa from my arms and quickly replied, "Yes, well, I'd love working with *this* kid even more, Tanner! You know that! Family first," she said, wagging a finger in my face.

Family first. It's something my mom had said many times during our growing up years. When my dad was held up at the office and missed supper, she'd just shrug and say, "Family first," knowing that he didn't often miss supper, and when he did, it was because he was working hard for us. He worked extremely hard to provide for us, and my mom respected him and knew that everything he did, he did for us. And when Ellen and I tried to get out of doing chores, she'd remind us again in her familiar chide, "Family first." We had to care for and help one another out.

So it was pretty much ingrained in both Ellen and I that family was always first. That's why it was killing me that I couldn't stay home and care for my own daughter. But on the other hand, I needed to be working and providing for her. The clash tortured me, but then my mom stepped in, and there was no way I could talk her out of it. She wanted to do it, and if I didn't let her, it would hurt her feelings. So I dropped her off bright and early that first day back at work and let my mom once again take care of me.

I really *did* feel better leaving her with Mom. And I knew it made her happy to help me out. But it was bittersweet each morning because I shouldn't have to take Elysa somewhere else to be cared for. I *should* be leaving her in the capable, loving hands of my wife. I should be kissing Leah good-bye and promising to give her a break over my lunch hour and when I got back at night. It just didn't feel right, taking care of her all by myself at night and then dropping her off at Mom's each morning. Leah and I should be doing all this.

But instead, Mom would be the one to witness all Elysa's milestones. She'd be the one dealing with the constant crying when Elysa started cutting her first teeth. She'd hear her first words and watch her progress from crawling to walking to running. She'd be the one that would understand her little toddler chatter better than anyone else, simply because she'd be with her all the time during the day.

Sure, I had her at night and on the weekends. But Mom had her more, and that bothered me. I loved hearing stories about the cute things she did all day, but I wanted *Leah* to tell me about it. I wanted to see the pride and love shining from *her* eyes, not my mom's. The whole situation was just overwhelming me, especially when I was still getting the hang of my new job. I'd only graduated in May and started this job at the end of June, right when things with Leah had taken a turn for the worse. My coworkers were beyond supportive and understanding, but they still expected me to do my job and do it well.

I enjoyed my work. I was a computer analyst and although I have always enjoyed working with technology my heart wasn't in it anymore. What had once been a burning passion had cooled into hard, little lumps of coal with hardly a glimmer of heat left in them. It was simply a job for me, something to pay the bills, which were now beginning to pile up on me. I'd had to start paying on my student loans in October, an extra expense I didn't really need. Then there were the hospital bills and the cost of the funeral, both of which my parents and Leah's parents had helped out with. Still. There was so much to cover each month, and once again, I felt like I was being sucked into the cold, violent ocean, my head bobbing in the crashing waves, water rushing into my mouth in big, unmanageable gulps. I needed to get out. Fast.

Of course, I called Molly. She was a few months into her classes at the community college close to where she lived, but even though she was slightly overwhelmed with balancing school and work, she was ecstatic to host me and Elysa for a weekend.

"I just…really need to get away from it all," I explained sadly to her, feeling lame for inviting myself to stay.

"It's no problem, Tanner. Really. I'll just take that weekend off from work and chill with you two. I could use a break myself."

"No, no," I insisted, the guilt really starting to kick in. "I don't want you to miss work for me. It was rude of me to call and ask that of you." I knew full well that she needed money just as much as I did, especially since she was in school now.

"Tanner," she said forcefully, getting angry that I was making excuses. Couldn't fool her; she saw right through my little game.

She knew I really needed this but that I had overactive guilt. "Stop it. You need this. Money isn't an issue for me, not after Albert died and left me all that money to go to school. I have plenty each month to pay for my apartment and groceries. So you have no excuse. You're coming, and that's that."

Can't argue with Molly. She usually had the last say in our decisions, but that came from being the oldest sibling out of the three of them. I was the oldest too, but Ellen was quite a bit younger than me, and we didn't play together much as kids. I didn't have the need to win each fight, to come out the victor like Molly did. So I let her make the final call and decided not to feel bad about this. She probably would have invited me out sooner or later, sensing that I needed an escape from the roiling storm that was now my life. Treading such violent water gets exhausting in a hurry though; I was glad I'd taken a leap and asked if I could stay.

I leaned forward in my seat, scanning the low clouds that hung in the sky, the threat of snow imminent. I'd checked the weather before starting out this morning, and while the forecast did call for snow between Iowa and Kansas, it wouldn't be much. The clouds didn't look dark and menacing, the kind that would open up and dump without mercy, carpeting the ground in a matter of minutes. And it wasn't too windy either, a rarity in the Midwest. Any snow that fell would be light, more like rain than snow, especially when the temperature was hovering right above freezing. I speculated that it would melt the second it hit the windshield and not cause any problems.

I turned around to check on my sleeping baby, catching her right as she was waking, her face scrunching into a scowl. I knew that face all too well; she'd left me a present to open up and discover. I decided to pull over and check her diaper now, before any snow did decide to fall. I slowed and pulled into the shoulder, then flipped on my hazard lights and jogged around the car to take care of Elysa.

I got her changed and resettled into the car in record time, proud of how good I was at changing her. I hoped that the rocking of the car would lull her to sleep again because we still had a good two and a half hours of driving left; I didn't want to spend the remainder of it listening to her crying. Thankfully, her eyes closed again, and she was in dreamland, a small smile tugging at her delicate lips. She was so unaware of the fact that her life was already so much different than other children, so much more difficult without a mother to care for her and provide loving guidance. It was probably good that she'd never gotten the chance to know her mama, to fall in love with her like I had. Loving someone made losing them that much harder, I knew all too well.

As the first flakes of snow began to drift lazily down, I sighed and settled back into my seat, allowing myself to relax for the first time since Leah had died. Molly and I had both enjoyed taking drives as teenagers; sometimes we'd pile into my little car and just take off for the day, driving to the tiny towns around Oak Ridge to hit the antique stores and little cafes. I'd forgotten how soothing it was to set the cruise control and just sit back, taking in all the scenery and letting nature soothe my aching, cracked heart.

Not that my heart would ever heal from the trauma it had endured in the last year. It had been such a roller coaster year for me, the excitement of becoming a father soured by the discovery of Leah's cancer. And before I could even formulate a plan or prepare myself for fatherhood, she was gone. Like the soaking of the first rain of the spring…here one minute and gone the next. But at least after a spring rain, there is the pleasant smell of thirsty land, the lush green grass and the blooming of the flowers. There is the new hope that comes with the faint rainbows that stretched across the sky. With Leah's passing, I could find no good. I could see no rainbow, could taste no hope.

I couldn't help but feel sorry for myself. After all, I'd lost two women in my lifetime, in the span of five years, no less. With Leah I'd been slightly prepared; I'd known that sooner or later she would slip away from me. The cancer was too aggressive for her to fight off without treatment or surgery. So while I hadn't been ready to release her to Christ, I'd known I had no choice in the matter.

We'd been able to hold each other and cry, heartbroken that Leah would miss out on so much. We'd wept for our unborn child, knowing that her mama wouldn't be there to drop her off at her first day of kindergarten…teach her how to put on makeup…talk about boys…to help her through her first love, her first breakup. Not only would Leah miss out but so would Elysa. She wouldn't have a mother to make a Mother's Day card for in school, no one to teach her how to bake or to chase all the boys off that would no doubt come running after her in the years to come. And if she was anything like her mother, she'd be drop-dead gorgeous, a prize that all the boys would compete over.

Molly's disappearance had been quite different. That had been like a violent summer tornado, ripping through my life and leaving it in shambles. Clouds had been building that night she ran off; our fight had been heated and angry like the building of the clouds that leads to a tornado. I had felt the warm, sticky stirring of the air but ignored it, sure that Molly would come around after our fight. But oh, how wrong I'd been. Walking into Molly's room and realizing that she'd run, the tornado had hit me full force, knocking me to my knees and sucking all the air out of me. After the initial shock, I had to start picking up all the pieces of my shattered life, somehow figuring out how to get over her, to convince myself that she was never coming back and I needed to move on, to rebuild.

And even though death was permanent, I couldn't decide which loss had affected me the hardest. Leah was gone forever; there was no hope of her ever showing up so unexpectedly in my life again, like Molly had done. Still. Molly had been my first love; she'd been my entire life for twelve long years. The bond we shared was deep and full of history. We'd slept in each other's beds as kids, snuck out as preteens to explore the bike trail behind our houses at night. We'd made the decision to follow Christ together as kids at vacation Bible school the summer before fourth grade, then helped each other grow as young Christians. Many nights I'd crawl through her window, and we'd talk about our developing faith, helping each other through the ups and downs of middle school and high school. I could spill my heart to her so easily, share every secret, desire, hope and dream with her, never fearing that she'd laugh and think I was silly...because our dreams were very similar. Molly and I never dreamed of adventure, never wanted to travel far out of Oak Ridge. Mostly, we talked about love, about finding the one that Christ had in mind for us and starting a family. *I* talked about such things with her in mind though it never seemed like she included me in *her* dreams. She'd been oblivious of my love up until our senior year, never allowing herself to picture us together until I finally took that leap and told her I loved her.

Once I had crossed that line, she caved. At the time I didn't know it, but she had felt so undeserving of me after her abuse. I would never quite understand why Molly still felt that the rape was partly her fault, but that's the sad reality of sexual abuse, I mused. It would haunt her forever, and a piece of her would always blame herself though she'd told me she worked through those feelings and was more in control of them now. At the time when the abuse was so fresh, she was hesitant to allow herself to love me. She admitted to me that she knew of my feelings before I'd told her, and before the rape, she was simply ignoring them because she didn't want things to get awkward between us if we broke up. She'd even begun to feel the same way about me too— but then Jason swept in and stole her away from me.

His name still caused my blood to boil. If he hadn't come back to Iowa, Molly and I would have become a couple, no doubt. I would have eventually told her how I felt about her, if I sensed that she was starting to feel the same way about me as well. But he'd stolen her away before the feelings had a chance to develop, and there was nothing I could do about it. I hadn't wanted to chase her away from me by shaking her and telling her what a lowlife Jason was. I'd thought she'd see what a jerk he was on her own and break up with him, realizing that I was a much better choice for her. Once I heard the whole story about how she'd become pregnant, I began to suspect that her feelings for me came from fear of being alone. Jason had abused her, then cast her aside without a second thought. Then I had come galloping in, promising to stay with her and raise the baby with her. Of course she'd fallen for me so quickly! Even *if* she had any sort of feelings for me before Jason, I had to wonder if they intensified just because I promised to stay with her after Jason dumped her so cruelly. Surely that romance had just been a hope for Molly to cling to, the only certain thing in a rather uncertain time.

That's why I wasn't concerned about spending a weekend alone with her at her house. I was absolutely positive that Molly had no feelings for me whatsoever. Our love had been short, built off of fear and desperation. *My* feelings had been real, but I doubted Molly's ever were. There was just no way, not with all she had been going through. Besides, she'd recently shared with me her blossoming romance with Tyler, a young man she'd dated in Minneapolis. From the way it sounded, he'd propose here shortly; then they'd adopt the little girl who'd stolen his heart. No, I was certain that the window was shut tightly between us, and there would be no more sneaking into each other's lives like we had snuck through each other's windows as kids.

For a while there, it had seemed like I'd come out the winner, not that our lives were any big competition. But Molly had run off just months before graduation; she'd lied about her age and gotten a job to support herself. Meanwhile I had gone off to college as planned and gotten my education; I'd gotten married. I'd moved on. In the midst of all the tragedy, the swirling mess the rape and abortion had left behind; I'd come out pretty good in the end. Molly on the other hand...well, up until now she struggled. She was just now starting her college education; she'd delayed getting her GED for much too long, still feeling unworthy of being happy and successful. And she couldn't have much money saved up, not from waitressing in that tiny little town. But oh, how the tables had turned on me. I could look at her life now and think *that's not too bad.* Considering all she'd been through, she really was doing remarkably well. She had a steady job and was working to earn her education. And from the way she talked about Tyler, it sounded like she really liked him and was excited about their future together. For once, it sounded like things were going much better for her than they were for me.

What did I have now after all? My wife was gone, and I was taking care of a newborn all alone. I had a college education but an education that I was still trying to pay off. And other than my job, I had nothing. Molly's future stretched out brightly in front of her... but what did I have to look forward to? Who would want to marry a single man with a child? Would I ever love again?

I shook those thoughts from my head. I wasn't that old yet... surely I could find love again. I looked back at Elysa once more and smiled, knowing that for at least the next ten years she would love me unconditionally. For a short period, I would be her super hero, I would be capable of doing no wrong. I knew this because Ellen had been that way with our father. She was his little princess, and she knew it. I'd make sure Elysa knew that too, because right now, I needed that type of love. My heart was empty and aching, but all it took to make me feel better was to pick up my baby and snuggle her close, smell her sweet baby smell, and look into her trusting, loving eyes. She had no idea the power she had over me, how simply holding her lifted my spirits and made it possible for me to drag myself out of bed each day. She was the only reason my life was worth living right now—the only good thing I had in my life.

If God brought another woman into my life, I would welcome her gladly. But for now, Elysa was enough. At least that's what I kept telling myself. For a moment, Molly's face flashed in my mind, but I pushed it away just as fast as it entered. We were an impossibility now. Surely she had moved on—*if* her feelings for me were ever real at all. I knew that when she'd come back from Minnesota, she had hoped I'd still be there to take her back, but again, that could have been out of desperation. She had probably tricked herself into thinking she still loved me. Those feelings had probably faded quickly when she returned to Kansas, especially when Tyler reentered her life.

Still. Molly had rushed back to Iowa on my request as Leah fought to give life to Elysa. I'd known her time was limited, and I needed someone who really knew me to be there with me. I honestly hadn't expected her to drop everything and come, but in she had walked that day, unsure how to handle the situation. I would have done the same for her though…even after all these years we still had a bond so strong and deep. I doubt anything would ever break that, not marriage, not death.

And she'd stayed for an entire week. She helped me through it all, helped me pick out the casket and plan the funeral. Leah had drawn up a basic idea for us, nothing too detailed because it made her sad that we had to plan a funeral the same time we were planning for a birth. But she had a nice list of songs she wanted played and scripture she wanted read.

That had been the absolute worst day of my life. Not even Molly's running away had been that difficult. Sitting in the front row of the church while my wife's dead body sat just feet from me had been torturous. I didn't sing one song…couldn't, really. My throat had closed up, and my eyes burned with unshed tears. So I just stood there and tried not to sprint out of the room and drive away in my car, far away from the heaviness that filled the sanctuary, which was packed. Leah was loved by many; her death had sent our community falling to its knees. To lose one so young to cancer was unthinkable.

I wanted Molly to sit with me during the service, but she felt that was inappropriate. I argued that no one would care. They'd know she was just being there for me. But still she refused, saying she'd be by my side the rest of the day offering her support. She sat with her family a few rows back, and my parents and Leah's parents sat with me although Mom left with Elysa during the middle to feed and change her.

I didn't like all the pity, all the sad eyes and people coming up and shaking my hand, wishing me God's peace in this difficult time. It seemed like all their prayers and well wishes were falling on deaf ears, however, because it never got easier. The waves never stopped crashing over me, never stopped sucking me under and filling my mouth with the salty bitterness of anger and desperation. Not once had I felt the comfort and peace of God even though I knew that my entire church was praying for those things to settle in around me.

Maybe it was my own fault. I wasn't really angry at God, but I was confused. I kept asking the age old question, "Why do bad things happen to good people?" I just couldn't wrap my mind around the fact that I'd lost so much at my young age when I'd been nothing but faithful to God. And all around me, people who deliberately disobeyed God's law seemed to be prospering. *Where is the justice in that?*

Surely I deserved to prosper after faithfully following Christ for my entire life. But then I stopped, knowing that my thinking was skewed. My youth pastor used to talk about the prosperity gospel; televangelists often spread this false gospel in the hopes that they'd win over the hope starved people they targeted—people who'd start shelling out money because these phony pastors said God would bless them if they only gave their money. Lies were spreading all over the country, all over the world, lies that said, "Love Jesus, and he'll give you the desires of your heart.

Love Jesus, and you'll have the best of the best. Love Jesus, and he'll bless your socks off." Of course in our day and age, being blessed means being wealthy; it means driving expensive cars and dressing in luxurious clothes. It means having a big, fancy house full of fancy toys. I felt foolish for thinking that simply loving Jesus meant I'd live a comfortable, hardship-free life. Loving Jesus actually put me at a greater risk of running straight into hardships. It meant I'd walk a rockier road than people who rejected Jesus. *That* road was wide and smooth from the hordes of people who'd chosen to walk down it. The road *I* walked on was narrow and rocky, full of roots that wanted to grab my ankle and pull me into the mud. But the thing that makes that road bearable is knowing where it leads. It leads to Christ. It leads to a world that is perfect; the way God always intended things to be. I could keep walking on this road as long as I knew where I was headed. I shuddered thinking about where so many other people were walking toward.

A verse that I'd memorized in my youth flashed in my brain, and I rolled it around in my mind for miles, comforting myself with the familiar words. It was from Psalm 73, verses 25–26 that said,

> Whom have I in heaven but you? I desire you more than anything on earth. My health may fail, and my spirit may grow weak, but God remains the strength of my heart; he is mine forever.

I felt the guilt begin to creep up, because my greatest desire in life was that people would see Christ through me. I didn't want to spread some false gospel, leading people to believe that Christ was just a convenience for me, someone to give me all the good things I wanted in life. I knew that in this world I'd walk through trouble, I just hadn't been prepared for it. Now that it had come, I wanted to be able to say, "God is enough. He is good. He will satisfy me and get me through this." And I knew that God would be most glorified in me when I was most satisfied in him. There was no way that people would see how good God was, how loving and capable of providing satisfaction, if I couldn't face this loss and still say, "God, you are good." In the midst of loss, in the midst of suffering, I needed to say that. I needed others to see it, to wrestle with it like I was wrestling with it.

Because if I walked away from God now, right when something awful happened to me—no matter how unfair it seemed—I was sending a message to all nonbelievers that God *wasn't* enough, that he *wasn't* capable of giving me all I needed or providing satisfaction. No, I'd be spreading the message that God was cold and unloving, that he left us to figure out everything for ourselves, which I knew wasn't true. Because if God took care of the birds, if he gave them food to eat, I knew he would take care of me. That was another favorite verse of mine, found in Matthew 10:28,

> Don't be afraid of those who want to kill your body; they cannot touch your soul. Fear only God, who can destroy both soul and body in hell. What is the price of two sparrows—one copper coin? But not a single sparrow can fall to the ground without your Father knowing it. And the very hairs on your head are all numbered. So don't be afraid; you are more valuable to God than a whole flock of sparrows.

I sat back in wonder as I watched the tiny snowflakes melt on my windshield. I thought of myself as the sparrow, the insignificant little bird that didn't matter in the grand scheme of things. And yet my creator knew me inside and out; he knew every detail of my life. He knew the exact moment in time that I'd taken my first breath; in fact, more amazingly, he knew the very second my heart began to beat inside my mother's womb. He knew the very number of days I'd walk upon this earth. It was amazing...no, it was more than amazing. I just couldn't come up with a good enough word to describe how wonderful it felt to be known so well, better than I even knew myself! So how could I sit back and accuse God of not caring for me, telling him that he wasn't giving me what I deserved? I didn't deserve *anything*! Really, what I deserved was death, punishment for being so sinful, so ungrateful. And yet I knew that even as I doubted and accused, he loved me still. His arms were still flung open wide…he was just waiting for me to turn around and run back to him. Running away was tiring, and he knew it. So he'd wait until I came to my senses and let him take control again. He knew where we were headed anyway. When I drove I tended to crash and burn, so unsure of the twists and turns. Yet God could drive the twists and turns with ease, and still I struggled to let him drive.

I made a vow to release my grip and surrender the wheel to my creator. If I wanted to be a witness, I needed to show the world that I didn't have control of my life. Yes, God drove me through hardships. But he knew that those hardships strengthened me and made my faith blossom into something beyond beautiful. I just needed to trust in the roads he drove me down and say, "God is enough. I will get through this with him."

All of a sudden, I was pulling into Molly's sleepy, little town, unaware of how I'd mindlessly driven the rest of the way and arrived without even realizing where in the world I was! I was also completely surprised to find Elysa still sound asleep. I squinted at the crumpled up paper that was my directions to Molly's apartment complex. She lived in a newer part of town in a building only a few years old, so I assumed it would be quite easy to find in this little, aging town. While it was a nice, clean community, it was tiny. I'm sure it was a bustling little hub years ago, but today, it was quiet, and it showed its age by the peeling paint on the buildings, the sagging of the roofs on a few particularly old ones. Just as I imagined, Molly's building stuck out like a sore thumb in this town.

My heart surprised me by picking up the pace of its beating, and I ordered it to stop. Because this wasn't just the fast-paced beating that came from my excitement to see my old friend again. I felt that when I saw Molly's number pop up on my caller ID. This…this felt different than just excitement. And my suspicion was confirmed when I caught a glimpse of Molly standing outside the building waving to me, that silly grin stretched clear across her face.

Somewhere deep within me, the dead coals were catching fire again, reigniting with the same passion that once burned deep inside my heart. Because if just one look at her brown waves fluttering in the sharp November breeze and her rosy cheeks sent my heart exploding inside of my chest, I knew without a doubt that somehow I was still in love with Molly Taylor, the girl of my childhood.

I rolled into a guest parking space, and she hurried over to open the door for me. As she pulled me into a hug, I knew there was no way I could escape it. All those old feelings came rushing back to me—I loved her, and yet I felt I couldn't tell her because she was with someone else. I didn't want to complicate her life any more than it already was. So I was stuck, once again knowing that I loved her and yet unable to tell her. I'd lost her once, and now it looked like I was going to lose her for a second time, which caused my heart to lurch and twist with pain. All because she'd run off. If she'd only stayed put and waited things out for a few weeks, things would have smoothed over. We'd most likely be together right now if not for her rash decision to run away and leave my world crumbling around me.

When she drew back and smiled into my eyes, I had to pull myself together and smile back. I couldn't let her see the depth of my feelings; I had to somehow convince her that our relationship was nothing more than friendship. And I'd just lost my wife, so she wouldn't be expecting these feelings out of me. *I* wasn't expecting these feelings! I figured I was safe for now, as long as I could keep up this act. I'd just keep telling myself that Molly had finally moved on; I'd remind myself that this would probably be the last weekend like this. For in a few months, she'd probably be engaged and planning her life with Tyler. That thought alone was enough to keep me quiet. She deserved things to start going her way for once; she certainly didn't need me waltzing in here and messing things up for her again.

TWENTY-ONE

❖

Molly

NOVEMBER

"So good to see you!" I gushed, holding Tanner at arm's length away by his broad shoulders. I was still struck by how much he had changed since our senior year—seeing him that first time back in Iowa had shocked me; he no longer was the gangly, awkwardly, developing teenager. He'd filled out into a man, someone I barely recognized—though I only had to look into those blue eyes to know for sure it was Tanner. Those eyes had always been a source of comfort for me; they'd shown with love and fierce protectiveness for all the years I'd known him.

When I looked into his eyes on this dreary November afternoon, all I saw was sadness, emptiness. His smile was forced, and it didn't light up those familiar eyes like usual. But I couldn't expect him to be the same, not after these last few months. Of course his eyes were full of pain. Anyone's would after enduring what he'd endured.

"Let's get you two upstairs into the warmth. That's a long drive, and I bet you're both exhausted!" I waited as he wrestled Elysa's car seat from the buckle; then, I grabbed the diaper bag and suitcase before he even had a chance to reach for them. "I've got it!" I sang cheerfully, trying to bring some life back into his eyes. He rewarded me with a small smirk and a shake of his head, no doubt remembering back to the silly days of our youth, back to when he thought I was the weirdest creature on the face of the earth, always cracking jokes and trying to make him smile.

We finally made it up the three flights of stairs and entered into the cozy warmth of my apartment, no small task with the bulky suitcase and car seat. While he rolled his suitcase down the hall and tended to Elysa, I began preparing hot chocolate. I started to gather supplies for tea, then remembered that Tanner hated tea. Hot chocolate would be perfect on a day like today though and especially after a long ride in the car. He padded back down the hall in his socks, and I smiled as he entered, jostling baby Elysa. He had a soft, pink blanket in one hand, and he motioned to the living room floor. "May I?" he asked.

"Oh yeah," I agreed. "Go ahead and put her down. Just vacuumed before you came."

He smiled, spread the blanket on the floor, then gently set his daughter on her tummy. Her neck was just getting strong enough to hold up her head, and it was beyond adorable to watch her kick and stretch her legs, to grab and roll around. He dumped some small toys out for her to reach and grab onto, then stood to join me in the kitchen.

Tanner sat across from me and wrapped his hands appreciatively around the steaming mug, inhaling the rich aroma of the hot chocolate. I didn't mess around with chocolate, this stuff was handmade, a recipe that Mary Beth gave me when she tired of me constantly begging her for it. It was by far the best hot chocolate I'd ever had, and from the look on Tanner's face after his first sip, I could tell he thought so too. I'd even added some minimarshmallows, a favorite of his. We used to sit around his mom's table drinking hot chocolate with minimarshmallows, but of course more marshmallows always got flung in my face than made it into his mug. I thought about flinging one out to him, but a quiet awkwardness settled over the room, and I wasn't sure that a marshmallow in the face would be the best way to break it.

271 ❖ AN OPEN WINDOW

"Who named her?" I blurted, asking the first question that popped into my head. Her name started with an E of course—Tanner's family had a thing for Es; it surprised me that his name began with a T. Evelyn had told me once that Brian had had the name picked out before he'd met her and refused to name his son anything else. So I figured Tanner had named her, trying to keep the legacy of the E names alive.

"Leah did," Tanner answered with a smile.

"Really?" I asked, totally surprised.

He nodded and took another long sip from his mug. "Yup. We changed the spelling up a little bit. Originally, it was going to be spelled E-l-i-s-a, but we swapped the *I* for a *Y*. It means "Consecrated to God.""

"Wow," I whispered. "That's...that's really special, Tanner."

He nodded again and looked away, composing himself. "Yeah," he said with a small laugh. "Even after all she went through, she was still able to see Elysa for the absolute gift she is. And she wanted to give that gift back to God...she wanted to devote Elysa's life to Christ. I think she picked a perfect name, don't you think?" he asked wistfully.

"I really do."

A sudden blast of wind rattled the window, and I hurried over to peek behind the curtain. "Looks like the wind picked up quite a bit. It's snowing pretty good now too."

Tanner joined me at the window, his nearness causing a surge of energy between us. He moved away quickly, and I wondered if he felt it too. "Wonder if we're gonna get an early blizzard," he commented, sounding a little worried. He'd taken this Friday off to drive, but he wanted to be back on the road Sunday morning. Since he was still new at his job, he didn't have much vacation time built up, and he'd already taken quite a bit of time off after Leah died and when Elysa was still too young to be dropped off at day care. This would be a short, little break for him, and he couldn't afford it to be lengthened because a blizzard trapped us inside and forced him to stay off the road.

But I guess the weather didn't care about Tanner's carefully laid out plans because a half hour later, the sky opened up and emptied all its contents onto the earth below, which the wind then whipped around, leaving us blinded in the sudden blizzard. Tanner began nervously pacing before the window, worry creasing his eyebrows. Then the inevitable happened; the power cut off suddenly and left us in the dark. Luckily for me, Mary Beth had just come over the day before and stocked me up with candles, blankets, flashlights, and canned food, claiming she could feel in her bones that a nasty storm was headed our way. Of course I hadn't believed her, instead trusting the forecast that only called for light snow. I hadn't checked it in a while though, and surely, they could have seen a system this big moving across the country. Guess I should have paid closer attention. But things can change in a hurry, and there was nothing we could do now but wait it out and hope it didn't ruin our entire weekend.

I pulled out two flashlights, handing one to Tanner and keeping one for myself so I could begin lighting candles around the apartment. Normally, I wouldn't be allowed to burn candles in here because it was a fire hazard, but I figured a raging blizzard that left me with no power was an exception. I set them up strategically around the apartment, keeping most of them in the kitchen and living room area because that's where we'd be spending the most time, but I left a trail of them down the hall to the bathroom so we wouldn't trip or stumble in the darkness.

The candles were calming; the flames danced along the walls, their flickering soothing and warm. But I knew that in a few hours the room temperature would drop, so I began pulling out blankets and piling them in the corner so we could bundle up when it got too chilly for comfort. I was thankful we at least had our warm drinks still, keeping us toasty for a bit longer.

Tanner fussed over Elysa, worried that she would get too cold. Luckily for him, he was an overprotective daddy who'd packed much more than she needed for such a short trip. She had plenty of sweaters, socks, and fuzzy blankets to keep warm if the power was out for longer than we expected.

An hour passed slowly, and the power remained down. I could feel the temperature dropping, but even as the blizzard continued to rage all around us, I could see Tanner beginning to relax, settling into my secondhand sofa and closing his weary eyes.

I folded myself into the overstuffed easy chair adjacent to the sofa. I didn't even have to ask; he knew before the words were even on my lips. "This is the first time I've been able to just sit. There's nothing I can do…she's fed and changed, and I have nowhere to rush off to, no work that needs to get done," he explained, sounding oddly at peace with this situation.

I gazed around the room, soaking in the calming atmosphere that the candles created. I guess it wasn't too surprising that he could sit back and feel so at peace here, even as the wind and the snow howled outside and trapped us in my little apartment.

I shivered a little and grabbed a blanket in the corner, wrapping myself in its snuggly warmth. Tanner did the same, and for a while, we just sat in the silence, the only sound the rattling of the window as the wind tried to make its way inside. But it wasn't an awkward silence caused by a loss of relationship between us. No, the bond between us was just as strong as when I'd run away four years ago. One of the best things about a relationship as deep and connected as ours was that you could sit in silence, not feeling the need to fill the air up with useless chatter. We could communicate silently that we felt at ease right now, content even though the situation wasn't exactly ideal.

A smile suddenly brightened his face, the first genuine smile I'd seen since my brother's wedding back in June. I knew that smile—I could see a plan swirling around in his mind. "Let's play a game," he suggested cheerfully, that familiar twinkle of mischief I knew so well once again visible in his blue eyes. When I came back that first time and saw him again after three years, that twinkle had been there, yet it was diminished in a way. I once thought that Leah had stolen his twinkle, but she seemed like a fun, loving girl. She wasn't *that* serious; she couldn't have stolen his twinkle. Then it had hit me...*I* was probably the one to blame for its diminishing. My running off with Jason against Tanner's wishes, my pregnancy, and then my disappearance had all piled up on him, stealing the joy that always shone from those eyes. The fact that I was just now seeing it return—as he spent time with me—made my heart flip-flap wildly inside me, unsure if it was just coincidence or if I really did have something to do with it.

I realized I was just staring at him, so I snapped out of my daze and jumped up. "Sure," I said, embarrassed that he caught me thinking so deeply but grateful that he had no idea that I'd been thinking about him. "What do you want to play?"

He got up and followed me to the closet where I stashed my limited supply of cards and games. "Something we used to play as teenagers..." he trailed off, eyeing the one little shelf I had the games stored on. "Aha!" he exclaimed, excitement ringing in his voice. "This one."

"Phase 10?" I asked, surprised. The card game was a variant of rummy, named after the ten phases that a player must advance through in order to win. Tanner always seemed to get the right hand of cards, beating me to the phases and leaving me in the dust as he advanced on and on and on.

"Yeah! Don't you remember how we used to play this pretty much every weekend in the winter?" he asked.

"Well, yeah," I admitted. "But the last time we played..." I trailed off, not wanting to revisit the last time we played our favorite game.

He nodded slowly, also remembering. "It was the night before you left, wasn't it?" he asked sadly.

I didn't say anything, letting the silence confirm for him that he was indeed right. It had been a Thursday night in March 2008, and for some reason, neither of us had had much homework to do. To kill some boredom, he'd brought out the deck of Phase 10 cards, our favorite game, to play together. Of course he beat me soundly each and every time we played, which infuriated me to no end. I was never *really* mad at him, but I wondered how he did it. On that night though Lady Luck was smiling down on me, and I beat him for the first time in months. Of course I'd gloated all night, teasing him that he was losing his edge. But the lightheartedness of that last night in Oak Ridge had quickly dissipated by my running away the next day. The memory of our last night together was tainted by that forever.

"I believe I won the last game we played together," I teased, trying to lighten the mood that memories of that night had dampened. I grabbed the deck and headed for the kitchen table, bringing a few candles from the hallway with me so that we could see a little bit better.

"I let you win," Tanner replied with a smug look on his face as he leaned nonchalantly against the kitchen wall.

"You did not!" I squealed.

"Did so," he insisted, pushing off the wall and joining me at the table. "You were really getting mad that night cause I was ahead of you by two or three phases. So I pretended to get stuck on a phase to let you catch up. Bad idea though because then you started drawing all the cards you needed!"

"Well then, I can't help that it backfired on you...I probably would have beat you anyway if I was drawing all the right cards," I countered.

"I don't know," he teased. "You're kinda terrible at this game."

I threw him a saucy look and started shuffling the deck. "Come and get it then. I'll prove you wrong."

He accepted my challenge, and we fell back into the game as easily as if we'd never stopped playing. It didn't feel like four years had passed at all. In fact, for the hour and a half that we battled back and forth, we were transported back to Iowa, back to Tanner's cozy kitchen table where we'd played all throughout those dark winter days, back to a time where things were simple, when we hadn't had to deal with death and lost love, back to a time where all we needed was each other.

"How are things between you and Tyler?" Tanner asked quietly in the middle of the game. My heart squeezed in protest, not at all wanting to discuss this with him.

"It's going great," I lied, knowing that things were far from great since I couldn't seem to stop thinking about Tanner.

"Things are...getting serious between you guys?" he asked hesitantly. My heart perked up at that hesitancy.

Could he be upset about the possibility of losing me?

I nodded. "Yeah. We've been talking marriage. But I'm not 100 percent sure if we're ready for that or not." Actually, I knew Tyler was ready. He'd been hinting at how close he was coming to asking me. *I* was the one who wasn't ready. And it wasn't just because I still couldn't get Tanner out of my head. It was how deep Tyler was in Minneapolis right now. Months ago, he'd said he'd move here in a heartbeat if it meant we could be together. Now, though, he didn't seem like he wanted to move anymore. He would miss Jeff and Julie and the girls too much. He was stubborn and always liked things to go his way, and when it seemed like things weren't going his way, he poured on the charm to swing things back his direction. That's what was happening now—he was trying to charm me into moving to Minneapolis. Honestly though, I didn't think that would be the best thing for me. I had such an awesome support system here that I didn't want to lose. I still had so much more healing to do, and removing myself from my support would hinder my progress drastically. Plus, I was in the middle of school. And yet no matter how much I tried to explain that to Tyler, he never seemed to get it. He was still dead set on staying in Minneapolis.

I didn't really want to explain all that to Tanner, so when he cocked his head and asked why I thought we weren't ready for marriage yet, I just shrugged. "It's a big step for both of us. I've been having doubts for a while now, and I don't think that's the best way to start a marriage."

He nodded and dropped the subject of Tyler, picking up my little hints that I didn't want to discuss it. We continued playing, and I played as strategically as I could, trying to outsmart him. But in the end, it didn't matter. He beat me just as badly as he used to do all those years ago, and I felt that familiar irritation well back up again. Tanner had always been better at everything; he beat me at every game we played, got grades that were always slightly better than mine, and even though he hadn't played organized sports in school, he was very athletic and could easily outrun me, outhike me, and outplay me.

It wasn't real anger of course; it was just my competitive edge coming out in me, my need to be the best. I shook it off and focused on enjoying this time with Tanner because in a matter of days, he'd be back in Iowa, and I'd be stuck back in my normal routine.

By now, it was nearing suppertime, but since the power was out, I couldn't cook anything, and I didn't have much else to offer. "You hungry?" I asked him, knowing that the only thing I had was canned fruit.

"Little bit," he replied. "Whatcha got?"

I rummaged around in my little pantry and pulled out a few cans. "Canned peaches...pears...more peaches..." I laughed. "Looks like all I have is peaches and pears. That okay?"

"Oh I suppose," he said, mocking disappointment. "Figured you'd feed me better while I was here, but I'll make do."

I swatted him, and he laughed, the sound a healing balm to my soul. Even though the weekend wasn't turning out the way I'd planned, it seemed like this was just the thing that he needed to get his mind off his troubles back home. But then again, we'd never done anything really spectacular when we hung out as teenagers. Mostly we played card games and watched movies together, so it didn't surprise me that this was calming him down. Too bad the electricity was out though; it would have been nice to hunker down and watch a movie.

An idea popped into my head though. "Hey. Let's watch a movie."

He raised his eyebrows at me teasingly. "And how will we do this with no electricity?"

"I have a portable DVD player that Mary Beth gave to me. It's fully charged because I hardly ever use it, and it lasts for about one movie without needing to be recharged. We'll just set it on my coffee table and sit on the couch."

The smile that used to haunt me in my dreams stretched across his face, sending a rush of electricity up my spine. "Sounds like a plan. But only if I can choose the movie."

So we settled down with our cold fruit in front of the tiny DVD player after Tanner got Elysa quieted down and snuggled into her little car seat for the night. It would be warmer for her in there anyway since the temperature continued to drop inside the apartment. I'd already had to go pull on some thick socks and added an extra layer of sweatshirt over my two long-sleeved T-shirts. And even with all those layers, we still needed my thickest blanket to keep warm as the movie began.

Originally, we sat side by side on my little couch, our arms touching because we had to squeeze to fit comfortably together. Though no skin was touching, my arm was still burning from his nearness. I couldn't understand this rekindled attraction, my sudden desire to restart a relationship with him. His wife had just died after all. And too much time had passed; things were too complicated now. Then there was Tyler. When I was with him, I felt the same way. His touch sent tingles up my spine, and I was happy; I looked forward to a future with him, even though I had doubts. Still, with Tanner, the attraction was stronger, and I found myself longing for things that could never happen between us. There was just no way we could pick up where we left off... right?

I pushed those thoughts out of my head and focused on the movie. It was a total boy movie, complete with car chases and dramatic crashes, guns and blood and scantily clad women. I didn't even know why this movie was part of my collection. It must have been a gift from someone though because I'd never opened it until now.

Hours later, a loud knock on the door jolted me awake, and I shot up, confused and groggy from sleep. The DVD player was now dead, and I realized that Tanner and I had fallen asleep on the couch together. From the way he was lying on the couch, it looked like I'd been sleeping on his chest. One arm was flung above his head and the other was resting on his leg...I suspected that arm had been wrapped securely around me though because my middle was warm from his touch.

My face burned in embarrassment, but I shrugged. It felt nice to wake up in his arms, so what harm would it do if I just went back to sleep and pretended I'd never woken up and discovered it before Tanner? So I snuggled back into his warmth and sighed in contentment as his arms instinctively settled back over me, closing my eyes again and savoring how it felt to be wrapped in his arms. Sleep was quickly closing in on me, but I heard a faint jiggling at the door. I ignored it though, figuring it was the wind playing tricks on my mind.

But suddenly the door opened, and I shot up again.

"Molly?" a familiar voice called out into the cold darkness that was my apartment.

My heart lurched within me. It was Tyler! *What in the world was he doing here, in the middle of a blizzard no less?*

I flung the blanket off me and jumped off the couch, waking Tanner in the process. "What are you doing here?" I demanded a bit too harshly, and even in the dim lighting of the apartment, I could see the shock spread across his face.

"Well," he stumbled awkwardly. "I came to surprise you."

I could see from his expression that his plan had backfired cruelly onto him. I was the one surprising him, with Tanner here and all. And of course he'd walked in and immediately seen us sleeping together on the couch. I felt the heat spread through my cheeks again, and I was glad for the darkness so he couldn't see it.

Tanner was just waking up, rubbing sleep from his eyes. Elysa still slept soundly in her seat, so we all just stood and sat there awkwardly, no one knowing what to say to break the silence.

"Well. I, uh…can I talk to you for a minute, Molly?" Tyler stammered.

"Sure," I gulped, suddenly feeling guilty. It was wrong of me to lead Tyler on when I clearly still had feelings for Tanner. This was all just too confusing…I hated that I felt so strongly for both of them. I wanted to be able to make a choice and feel good about it, instead of always second guessing whether I was walking in the right direction.

He followed me down the hallway to my little bedroom, then gently closed the door behind us. "What's going on here?" he demanded angrily, the hurt and disappointment burning in his eyes. He folded his arms and waited for me to explain myself, but I felt my guard fly up in response to his anger.

"I invited Tanner over for a weekend away," I began, not feeling like explaining the real situation. Tanner had kind of invited himself over, but I didn't want to make him the bad guy. After all, I had agreed without a problem. Now Tyler was angry, and it was only fair that I take responsibility. "He was overwhelmed and sad," I explained, my words coming out in a jumbled, confusing mush like they always did when I was upset.

"Did you really think that was appropriate, Molly?"

"Yes," I snapped defensively. "We're friends, Tyler. He just needed some time away."

"Yeah, well he could have taken a cruise or something. Gone to stay with another friend."

"Like he can afford a cruise," I snapped. "Look. I think you're overreacting Tyler."

He snorted. "Not really," he retorted. "Not when I walk in to find you cuddling together on the couch."

"We fell asleep watching a movie," I explained lamely. It might have been an accident at first, but when I woke up, I hadn't moved away like I probably should have. I'd known what I was doing, and I knew Tyler was partly right although I wouldn't admit it to him.

"Whatever." He looked away sharply and sighed.

"How *did* you get in here anyway?" I asked, suddenly curious as to how he'd let himself inside. I never gave him a key.

He shrugged. "Nice hiding place you have. Took me all of five seconds to find it under your welcome mat," he smirked, loving the fact that he'd outsmarted me.

"Shoot," I mumbled, embarrassed at my lame attempt at hiding my spare key. I was always locking myself out though so I'd hidden it outside the door so that I could get back in without having to call the only locksmith in town. I'd figured that out after having to call him three times. It was an expensive accident, but my hiding place wasn't too hot.

He softened and took a step toward me. "I missed you," he whispered, gathering me in his arms. I let him, even though his arms were the last place I wanted to be right now. He hugged me close and stroked my hair, inhaling the scent of my berries and cream shampoo that I knew he loved. I knew he wanted me to say that I missed him too, but the words stuck in my throat. Up until this weekend, I'd missed him too, but now…I just wasn't so sure about us anymore. If one night with Tanner was causing me to doubt my relationship with Tyler, something wasn't right. And I just wasn't sure if I could keep leading Tyler on if I thought there was something between Tanner and I now even though there probably wasn't. Still. I couldn't ignore the chemistry we still shared or the fact that his very presence caused my heartbeat to quicken. Something was there; it had to be. I needed some time to figure out if Tanner felt the same way or if he was just enjoying our time together because he was lonely and craved a relationship with a woman.

He felt that I was stiff in his arms, suddenly realizing that my own arms were hanging limp at my side instead of wrapped around him like he wanted. He pulled back and searched my eyes.

"Something's up," he said flatly.

I shrugged, unsure what to say. He sighed and released me, then sat down on the edge of my bed. I stood there stiffly, wondering what to do next. Tanner was just down the hall; this felt beyond awkward to have both of the men in my life in the same building.

"Want to know the real reason I came all the way down here to see you?" he asked quietly, sadness seeping from his voice.

I nodded, choosing to remain silent out of fear that my emotions would betray me and I'd begin to cry, overwhelmed from this crazy twist of events.

He rummaged around in his pants pocket and pulled out a small velvet box. My breath caught in my throat, and my heart slammed against my chest. There was no denying what lay inside that little box. He'd come all this way to propose to me, only to find me in the arms of another man.

"I...I don't know what to say," I stammered. I felt my entire body begin to tremble, and my stomach was tying up in knots. But that confirmed the suspicion that had been nagging at me all night. I wasn't reacting out of excitement; my heart hadn't started pounding because a proposal was imminent. Instead, I had felt panic, dread. Surely, if I loved him, it wouldn't be like this. Surely, I would have responded the way he dreamed I would.

"Well. That says it all, actually," he answered dully. He stuffed the box back inside his pocket and hung his head. I really started panicking then. I'd just broken his heart right in half! I could almost hear it ripping in two; I could almost see the blood dripping out of his chest and onto my white carpet. This is not how I'd wanted things to end between us. Just weeks ago, I'd thought we'd never have to face a breakup again! I'd thought that we'd get married and adopt little Jenny, finally starting our happily ever after together. Sadly, it looked like things were headed sharply in another direction. I knew we were facing the end once more.

"I'm so sorry, Ty," I whispered.

He looked up and shrugged. "It's better I found out. I wouldn't have wanted to have you accept and then leave me at the altar."

I wanted to protest, to defend myself and argue that never in a million years would I do something like that. But I knew he was right. If Tanner hadn't been here and Tyler came to propose, I would have gladly accepted. *But what if things with Tanner started blossoming later? What if I'd discovered my feelings for him in the midst of planning a wedding with Tyler? Would I have tried to stuff them away and continue on…then realize that a marriage with Tyler was wrong? Would I have gotten all the way to the altar before finally figuring it out? Possibly.* I had to admit. Decision making was not my strongest trait. I hemmed and hawed over decisions for an agonizingly long time. So I knew Tyler was right. It was better he'd found us this way because it confirmed what I would never had admitted—that I still loved Tanner, that I would always love him.

"I'll just be going now, I guess," Tyler stated. "I don't want to stay here."

"But the blizzard! It knocked the electricity out," I protested.

"It's died down quite a bit…I bet the power will be back on soon. I'll stay in a hotel for the night and head back in the morning."

"Why don't you stay here and wait for the power to come back?" I pleaded.

He shook his head. "No," he replied firmly. "Too awkward. Really, Molly, it's not too bad out there anymore. I'll be fine."

I sighed and felt my entire body deflate. "Okay," I finally agreed in a whisper.

I walked him down to the lobby and gave him a hug good-bye, hanging on longer than he was comfortable with. "Guess this is good-bye for good, isn't it?" he asked.

"Yeah. Guess it is," I agreed.

And with that, he was gone. Just like the first time, he left and never looked back. It was better that way really. We didn't want to complicate things. Knowing him though, he'd probably send me a deep letter in a few weeks, to which I'd need to reply to. I needed to thoroughly explain my sudden change of feelings and to say good-bye properly. I needed closure this time.

I found Tanner feeding Elysa when I returned from saying good-bye to Tyler. He looked up with concern in his eyes. "What happened?"

I sat down beside him and sighed. "He uh…came to propose," I said, fiddling with my fingers and burning with embarrassment.

"Wow. Really?" Tanner asked, trying to act surprised.

"What?" I asked, confused. "You're not surprised?"

He shrugged. "Not really, Moll. The way you talk about that guy…I figured it was just a matter of time, even if you *did* have doubts. Obviously things didn't work out though…what happened?" he repeated, hungry for the details.

I ran my fingers through my hair, trying to figure out if I wanted to be honest with him or not. I wasn't sure how he would respond if I told him I refused the proposal because of him. *Because what if he didn't feel the same way about me?* His wife had *just* died three months ago after all. I couldn't expect him to feel the same way about me when the death of Leah was still so fresh and painful. Suddenly, I felt like I'd just made a huge mistake in saying good-bye to Tyler. I probably should have just stuck with him, a guy who adored me and could give me everything I wanted in life. I just wasn't sure if Tanner could give that to me anymore, not after all that had happened between us.

But then again, something else would have probably changed my mind down the road. Sooner or later, I'd realize that it wouldn't work out between us. I didn't really love him, not if I didn't immediately know in my heart when I saw that ring box that he was the one for me. Tanner couldn't be the only reason I hadn't been able to say yes. I remembered back to how he'd wanted to rush things along when Jenny was scheduled to go to her first foster home. I remembered how even back then I had doubted his feelings, how I'd always had to fight to make myself believe that he loved me only for me.

So I decided to take the risk and tell the truth. "I couldn't say yes, Tanner. Just couldn't do it."

"Why not?" he asked gently.

I looked him square in the eye and took his fingers, wrapping them in my own. "Because, Tanner, I'm not over you."

His eyes widened in shock. "You're not...over me?" he stammered.

I shook my head slowly. "Nope. It's always been there, Tanner. I've just always realized it too late."

Silence fell over the room. Suddenly, the lights flickered back on, which broke the awkward silence. But we stayed put, and his hand opened up, and he wove our fingers together and gave them a squeeze. "Never in a million years would I have guessed that you felt this way about me still," he said quietly, his voice barely a whisper. "But I guess I never expected myself to feel the same way about you too," he admitted, causing my heartbeat to once again pick up speed.

"Really?" I asked, sure I was dreaming.

"Really."

And suddenly, I was in his arms. He held me close and rocked me gently, stroked my hair, and breathed in the scent of me. I closed my eyes, but the tears leaked out anyway, wetting his shoulder. For once though my tears were happy, and I couldn't stop the ridiculous grin from spreading across my face. After years of friendship, after all I'd put him through, we were finally back where we belonged: in each other's arms. It's where we'd always belonged; it had simply taken us longer to realize it. We'd had to walk through hardships and trials, happiness and triumphs to finally make our way back to each other.

He pulled back and searched my eyes, and my heart melted at the love I saw shining from his own eyes. He took my face in his hands and stroked my cheeks with his thumbs. And then he brought my lips to his and kissed me the way I always dreamed he'd kiss me if we ever found our way back together again. My heart responded in a way that confirmed what it had just rejected with Tyler only minutes ago. It was telling me that this was right, that this is what I wanted my future to look like.

So I let his lips continue to cover my own, kissing me hungrily. Something deep within me told me that this wasn't just a byproduct of his loneliness. He wasn't kissing me and admitting his love for me out of fear that he'd be alone for the rest of his life. I knew Tanner much better than that; I knew he'd never allow himself to deceive me like I'd deceived Tyler for the last year. His feelings were real…they'd always been real. And I absolutely couldn't wait for the road ahead of me, because I knew that now I'd be walking beside Tanner, holding his hand and facing every obstacle and celebrating every victory together.

Finally, after all these years, we were finally where we were always supposed to be.

TWENTY-TWO

✦

Molly

DECEMBER

Molly,

I'll keep this short, because I don't want to make this any more painful than it already is. But I'm not gonna lie either. Walking in and finding you in Tanner's arms was just about the biggest blow I've ever received in my lifetime. But like I said before, it's better that I found out. And even as I write this good-bye letter to you, I wish you and Tanner the best. I'd like to know what happens with the two of you; I want to make sure you're taken care of. From how you've described Tanner to me, he seems like a great, God-fearing man. Just tell him I said he better take good care of you. You deserve that, Molly.

I should be honest with you though. Even as I drove to Kansas to surprise you, I was having doubts of my own. I know I said months ago that I'd move anywhere to be with you, but I think we both know how wrong it was of me to make that promise. It's not that I don't love you enough to leave Minnesota; it's just that I hoped you'd fall in love with my life there too and want to stay. I just don't know if I could walk away from Jeff and Julie and their girls… and you know I can't walk away from Jenny. I know she'd be fine moving…but I guess I'm just selfish. I'm sorry for that. Please don't think you weren't good enough. If anything, you're too good for me, and I don't deserve you.

The other reason I was having doubts about us is because I sort of feel that God is leading me in another direction…a different direction than you're headed in. I'm so proud of you for finally getting your GED and starting your college career, but I feel God calling me into ministry. If we got married, I'd want you to follow me too, but since you're now in school, that would have been next to impossible. Right now, I'm in the middle of launching a new program to help the Children's Home. I want to start photographing the kids and spreading the word to the community that the kids there need love. And I think I'm going to start going with Jeff on some of his mission's trips…documenting the trips to show other churches how God is working and what else needs to be done. Maybe I can start selling pictures and raising money for the home. I'm not sure yet where God is leading me, but I'm going to step out in faith anyway and trust he'll get me where I need to get.

I think God knew all along that things wouldn't work out between us. To others, it might seem like a waste, but I don't think it was. I love you, Molly. I always will. And I know in your own way, you love me too. Just because things didn't work out exactly like we'd planned, I hope we can still have a relationship. I think we're good for each other. We help each other heal. So I'll be content just being your brother in Christ.

I'll keep you updated with what's happening with Jenny.

Tyler

Delilah set the letter down and raised her eyebrows at me. We were sitting in a booth at Mary Beth's empty restaurant, our hands wrapped around steaming mugs of coffee. Everyone else had long since left for the evening, leaving a calm, quiet place for us to catch up in. "You're sure you want to let this one go,

Molly? Seems like a great guy to me…you break his heart, and he still says he loves you." It was a mixture of seriousness and teasing. We both knew things would have never worked out between Tyler and me. Yet it was impossible to overlook what an amazing guy he was. This letter made me want to cry. I'd hurt him so much, and yet he still loved me and wanted a relationship with me. He wasn't the charming, young man I'd fallen for as a scared eighteen-year-old runaway—he was a strong, mature Christian man who was handling a second breakup with me far better than he probably should be.

"I think I have to." I said with a shrug. "I'm in love with Tanner. I never stopped loving him. I might have told myself when I ran away that I hated him, but deep down, I knew that wasn't true. I never thought we'd have this second chance…but now that we do, I can't run away again. I can't make the biggest mistake of my life twice."

She grinned at me and shivered. "You gave me goose bumps! It just feels…so right. I didn't get that with Tyler. I mean, don't get me wrong. He's a nice guy, just not the one for you."

I nodded my agreement. "I know. It's like God is finally giving me a clear answer. I've been wasting so much time sitting around waiting for him to tell me what to do, and once I finally just decided to *do* something, he definitely affirmed it!"

That's the biggest lesson I'd learned this past year. When I moved to Green Lake last December, I was still so tender and bruised from my stumbling around in the desert. I thought the best thing to do was just sit back and listen for God's voice, but really all I'd done was waste time. I should have been able to take my GED test much sooner than I did, but for some reason, I always found something else that needed to get done. I think I was just scared. The future held so many uncertainties, and working at the restaurant and studying was so familiar, so safe. It was what came *after* the studying that scared me. Entering college was foreign, and it stripped away the familiarity. I should have known, though, that that's what living the Christian life is. It's not always safe and familiar. Sometimes we have to take a step into the darkness and trust that God will guide our footing. We have to open up the windows knowing that if the storms are building up in the distance, God is still looking over us and protecting us. We can't be too scared to open the windows of new possibilities. We miss out on so much that God has to offer if we leave them shut tight.

That Sunday, I pulled Greg aside while Delilah was frantically searching for Mandy, who'd wandered off again. "Thank you," I said gratefully.

He cocked his head, confused. "For what?"

"For doing the same thing I had to do with Tyler."

"Which was…?" he asked, still not quite understanding what I was getting at.

"For knowing when to step away and end things with me. I mean, when you place our situations side by side, they're pretty similar. I fell for you so fast and had our future all planned out, just like Tyler did with me. But you didn't ignore that little feeling in your heart…the feeling telling you to pursue Delilah," I explained, trying to put into words what I was feeling.

He nodded slowly, finally starting to understand. "And even though you had to hurt me in the process, you still did it because you knew God had something different in store for you. That something just happened to be Delilah."

A grin split across his serious face. "I thought you've been faking liking me for this entire year," he admitted sheepishly. "I know how much it hurt you even though you pretended to be so excited for us. That killed me, Molly. I knew I was doing the right thing…but gosh, sometimes doing the right thing really hurts."

I laughed. "Exactly! And hey…I *was* excited for you guys!" I argued. "Yeah, it hurt. But I knew too that you needed her. And she needed you. God knew what was best," I said with a shrug. "And he's doing the same thing for me. I thought I would be with

Tyler, but I had that same feeling that you had. Even as I was making plans with Tyler, I was thinking about Tanner." I paused and ran my fingers through my hair. "Was that what it was like for you?" I asked, somewhat not wanting to hear the answer to this one. No one likes to hear that they weren't really wanted.

"Yeah," he admitted slowly. "I did. And that's why I had to tell you. I didn't want to. I knew it would hurt your feelings. But I already had one failed relationship…I wanted to do it right the second time around. And lying about how I felt definitely didn't feel right."

I let that truth sink into me all throughout the week. But soon I was caught in another fierce battle—a battle with myself. Here I was, at the beginning of something absolutely beautiful with Tanner. But the doubts, insecurities, and fears came welling up in me with such a force that I could only put my arms over my head and shield my face from their stinging cold lies. I felt like I was being transported back to Iowa, back to the darkest, scariest time of my life. I felt like I was eighteen again, trying to figure out my feelings for Tanner instead of pushing them down and ignoring the reality that I loved him.

Facing those feelings meant facing my shortcomings. I felt unworthy of his love. Back then, I felt I didn't deserve his love because I had ignored it when it was right in front of me, choosing instead to run after some wolf dressed in sheepskin—the very devil in disguise. How could I have wanted Jason over Tanner? Sweet, sweet Tanner, who loved me despite my running around and mixed up actions. Surely, I didn't deserve him now, what with me being already twenty-three years old and just starting my college education! Someone who hemmed and hawed, unable to make choices, to make up my mind about who I really loved. And I couldn't forget the fact that I was still dragging around baggage from Jason…from the rape, the unwanted pregnancy, the abortion, and my sexual sinning, from two failed relationships with the same guy. My record was ugly, stained and ragged and probably too filthy for Tanner to even write his name on, if there even was any room at the bottom of my long record of failings.

Tanner's record, however, was spotless. He'd never done anything wrong! How could I weave our two very different lives together and expect them to mold and fit nicely? I would only taint his clean, orderly life and mess it all up. I was very good at messing things up.

Each phone call, text message, and Facebook post was making me feel guiltier and more unworthy by the second. It got to the point where I'd "accidentally" miss a call from Tanner, then claim to be too swamped with homework to call back. He texted every morning and night, and I responded only out of guilt; I rarely texted him first anymore. And Facebook? I avoided it at all costs, only booting up my computer to complete homework assignments and do research online. I was avoiding him; there was no way to deny it. But I was known for running away from problems, too terrified to face things head on and deal with the feeling of not being good enough. I'd run away before…what was stopping me from doing it now?

Tanner would be fine. At least that's what I started convincing myself of. Sure, he'd been heartbroken when I left him the first time. But he'd gotten over it back then; he could get over it now! He'd found love in Leah; surely he could find love in another woman this time. Tanner was still very attractive and very charming. Plus, he loved God and sought to follow and honor him in every area of his life. Any young Christian woman would drool over the chance to date a guy like Tanner. He'd have no problem starting over without me.

And he had Elysa. The very thought of her still stole the breath right out of me. She held a part of Tanner's heart that I could never compete with…she was a part of Leah, and if Tanner and I got married, I would never escape the fact that Tanner had loved another after loving me for so many years. As ridiculous as that sounded, I couldn't get it out of my head. Deep down, I knew that Tanner deserved to love again after losing me, but it would always sting knowing that I had been replaced so easily. *Sure, I'd messed up big time. But didn't I deserve to be waited for? Had it been crazy of me to wish that when I came back, I'd find Tanner waiting for me?* If I closed my eyes, I could still feel the weight of the crushing disappointment from that day I found out Tanner had married Leah, that he'd put the memories of me behind him and chosen to forget about the love we shared, though it was short and rocky, that he'd replaced my baby with a baby of his own.

Elysa wasn't mine. I didn't love her. I didn't *hate* her, but her existence was painful for me to accept. I knew it wasn't exactly fair for me to feel this way, considering all the trauma that Tanner had experienced the week of her birth. But when I walked into the hospital room to see Tanner rocking and cuddling his daughter the day Leah had died, a little part of me died too. My pregnancy had been unwanted—a nightmare, really. The situation only became hopeful when Tanner decided to stick with me and supported me. When I pictured Tanner rocking and cuddling my baby, the road became possible to walk on. There were still rocks to climb over and holes to fall in, but I knew Tanner would be helping me through those obstacles. Only things hadn't turned out that way, through no fault but my own. It hurt to see Tanner holding his baby when all I had ever wanted was to see him holding and loving mine.

All of a sudden, it hit me. Tanner must have struggled with the exact same feelings back in the spring of 2008. How terribly difficult it must have been for him to watch me go out and pursue another guy while he waited for the right time to tell me he loved me. When the time finally came, it probably wasn't exactly what he had been dreaming of for so many years. His admittance came at one of the darkest days of my life; it hadn't been the joyous celebration it should have been. I just couldn't get over the fact that'd he'd stayed with me—most guys would have thrown in the towel and let me figure out a way to deal with the mess I'd gotten myself into, but not Tanner. He was able to overlook the fact that I was having a baby with another guy. His love was that deep.

So I wrestled with that for a few days, well aware of the fact that with time, I could come to accept and love Elysa as my own, just as Tanner had done with my baby all those years ago. One day, I could come to love her as a daughter. But the doubts lingered, and I fought with my emotions—yes, I loved Tanner, and I knew one day I could love Elysa. But nothing could change the fact that I was far too messed up and weighed down with heavy baggage to saddle Tanner with. I wasn't good enough for him.

"I'm calling things off with Tanner," I declared to Delilah one snowy afternoon at the diner. It was only a little after three o'clock in the afternoon, and things were slow, but Mary Beth expected things to pick up quite a bit later in the evening. She was running a special Christmas deal; seniors got a half price meal if they came in and ate with their grandkids, something to try and encourage kids to spend time with their families. That's why Delilah was here—normally she never came in to help, but Mary Beth was holding out for a packed house later. She was drying a glass when I dropped this news on her, and I watched her eyes widen in shock and her mouth fall halfway to the ground.

"What?" she exclaimed, slamming the glass down with so much force I was surprised it hadn't shattered right in her hands. "Are you kidding me, Molly?" she demanded, her face turning red. I wasn't expecting her to get so angry over this.

By now the few people who were in the restaurant were staring at us with shock on their faces, knowing full well it was rude to eavesdrop but being unable to ignore the drama unfolding right in front of them. Chelsea, Jess, and Alexa also stopped in their tracks and craned their heads to see what the fuss was all about. I felt the heat flame up my neck and cheeks and gave Delilah a pointed look.

"Calm down," I hissed. "People are staring."

"Let 'em stare," she said just as loudly, angrily picking up another dripping cup. She shoved the dishtowel down the cup and forcefully began drying it. "You're being stupid."

Her blunt words sliced through my heart, and I took a few stumbling steps backward. "Excuse me?" I croaked, trying to figure out if she really had just called me stupid. Delilah had some fire in her, but she'd never called me stupid before. Our relationship wasn't like that; we hardly ever had outbursts or called each other names.

She huffed. "Molly. God's giving you this beautiful second chance, and you're throwing it in the dirt and stomping on it like some ungrateful little girl. Don't you see?" she said a bit softer, taking my hands in hers. "You're doing the same thing I did earlier this year. You're telling yourself you're not good enough, when God is clearly saying 'I don't care! This is my plan for you...this is where I want you to go.' Who are you to decide what's best for your life? How well has that worked out for you in the past?"

I swallowed. "Not very good," I admitted quietly.

She gave me a small smile. "That's right. Things never work out when we try and do God's job. Now. A month ago, you were on cloud nine, so excited that you were getting a second chance with the only guy you've ever really loved. But I've sat back and watched you beat yourself up and convince yourself that you don't deserve this for too long now, and I've had enough, Molly."

"I know, but—"

"Can I say something?" a small, clear voice asked out of the completely quiet dining room floor. All talking had ceased as me and Delilah's conversation got more heated. We both whirled around at Alexa's question.

"Sure. Go ahead," I said, surprised that Alexa had spoken up. She was a soft-spoken person, rarely volunteering information or starting up a conversation. If you kept asking her questions and prompting her, she'd eventually speak up, so this was weird.

Alexa wiped her hands on her apron and stepped behind the counter. Everyone returned to their meals and pretended we hadn't caught them all listening to us talk. Soon the sound of clinking silverware and quiet conversation filled the floor, and Alexa cleared her throat.

"For the past few months, all I've heard from you and Mary Beth is that God has good plans for each of us. You've said over and over that God loves each of us the same, that no one sin is worse than another in his eyes. We've all messed up. We all deserve the same punishment. But if we choose to accept the forgiveness he offers us, our record is wiped clean. We can live the life that God has in store for us even though we've messed up."

I blinked back the tears forming in my eyes and swallowed the marble stuck in my throat. "You *have* been listening," I croaked, touched.

She nodded and smiled. "Of course I have. But you're not really living out what you've been preaching to us."

I took another step back, unsure if I was able to handle all these two were accusing me of all of a sudden. "What do you mean?"

"I mean, if all sins are equal in his eyes, why do you keep punishing yourself for whatever it is you did? Because whatever you did, I'm sure you've dealt with it. Haven't you asked for his forgiveness?" she asked expectantly.

"Yeah," I admitted.

"So he forgave you then, right? And he doesn't hold it against you?"

"No," I whispered, a single tear sliding down my cheek.

"So why are you still holding it against yourself?"

"Because she's scared of change," a deep male voice answered for me. My heart responded immediately to that voice, and I turned to see Tanner pushing his way through the swinging kitchen door, a small smile on his face.

"Tanner," I breathed, my knees practically giving out on me right then and there. "What are you doing here?"

"Not letting you run away from me again." By now, everyone had given up on pretending not to hear us. The entire restaurant was silent, every eye on us. "I'm not blind and deaf, Molly. I could tell something was up. When you stopped responding to pretty much all forms of communication, I decided to take matters into my own hands."

"Where's Elysa?" I asked, still trying to recover from the shock of seeing him here.

"Don't try and change the subject here," he said with a hint of laughter in his voice. "She's with my parents. This isn't about her. This is about you and me." He took a step closer and reached for me, but I recoiled, like a turtle retreating into his shell when something scary and unfamiliar gets in his path.

"There shouldn't be a you and me, Tanner."

"And why not?" he asked.

"Because," I whispered. "I'm not...good enough." By now the tears were falling off my cheeks, and I could barely see through the blurriness they caused.

He took another step closer to me and took me by the shoulders, ignoring the fact that I was as rigid as a board and folding me into his arms.

"Don't ever say that again," he commanded, a hint of anger tinting his voice. "Why in the world would you think that?"

I threw out a sad laugh and withdrew from his hug. "Haven't you seen a single thing I've done in the past four years? I'm a wreck, Tanner! You have your life all together, everything all figured out...and I'm just some used up, dirty, time-wasting twenty-three-year-old who has no clue what she wants to do with her life!"

"Oh, you think I have it all figured out?" he threw back. "You think I have my life all together? Think again, Molly. I have no clue what I'm doing either! I'm a widower at twenty-three, taking care of a baby all by myself, and going to a job every single day that I'm not even sure I like anymore. Stop thinking of me as that cocky, eighteen-year-old guy who thought he was better than everyone else just because he didn't go out and party every weekend. I've made my fair share of mistakes too, Molly. I'm *not* better than you. I'm not something you deserve…I'm just a messed up soul who happens to be in love with another messed up soul."

"But why?" I demanded. *Why couldn't he see how terrible I was for him?*

"Because when I look at you, I don't see all your mistakes. I don't see all the bad things that you've done, all the crap that's happened to you. I just see *you*. I see the girl pinned down by her little pink bike with her knees and elbows all scraped up. I see the awkward preteen trying to figure out math homework with me. I see a confident young woman willing to take risks and follow God wherever he leads. And guess what, Molly?" he demanded.

"What?" I croaked.

"I think he's leading you to me. As crazy as that sounds, it's true. And you know it. So stop punishing yourself, okay, and do something for me."

I felt myself cracking. *What wouldn't I do for him?* "Anything," I replied.

"Marry me." And suddenly he was down on one knee, opening up a small black velvet box. Inside the box lay a ring I recognized immediately as Tanner's great-grandmother's ring. It was a ring we'd both admired as kids, loving the intricate crisscross and wheat patterns on the slender, white gold band. The diamond was a one-fourth carat, tiny but lovely. Tanner's mom let me try it on a few times as a kid, and we always marveled at how perfectly it fit me.

"Your great-grandmother's ring?" I breathed, in complete shock.

Tanner let a small chuckle escape from his lips. "Yes. When I told my mom I wanted to ask you to marry me, she insisted.

Now…are you going to leave me on the floor? It's kind of cold down here."

My mind processed a million things at once. I knew Tanner and Alexa were right. It was silly of me to think I was a worse sinner than him. It was wrong to punish myself after God had forgiven me. Still. I was scared. After everything had gone wrong in my life, the future terrified me. And yet I knew that if I said no, I'd walk around for the rest of my life miserable. I needed him. And he needed me. Without each other, we were just half of ourselves, wandering around trying to function as broken people.

"Of course I'll marry you," I whispered, a smile widening across my face. He jumped up, slid the ring over my finger, which still fit perfectly, and scooped me up into his arms. "Thank you," he breathed into my ear as the diner exploded in applause. When he released me from his arms, I turned to see Delilah wiping tears from her cheeks.

"Did you know he was here?" I asked though I could tell from the smug look on her face that she had.

"Yes. That's why I got so angry! He could hear every word we were saying from inside the kitchen! You were messing it all up. You know he had this cute proposal all planned out. But I think it turned out just fine anyway," she beamed.

I cocked my head and asked, "What were you planning on doing?"

Tanner shrugged. "I was going to text you to come outside, saying I sent a surprise package for you that you needed to make sure got inside before it started snowing too hard. When you walked out I planned to be on one knee, blah, blah, blah. But I was freaking out. I was sitting in there waiting and preparing myself. Then I heard you say you wanted to end things with me. You can bet my ear was glued to that door! But I agree with Delilah. This worked out well."

"I guess," I said with a laugh, admiring the beautiful ring gracing my hand.

SARA WHITLEY ❖ 300

Later that night, we snuggled into my apartment, all cozy and safe as the snow swirled down to the ground. "Know why I wanted to use this ring so badly?" Tanner asked.

"Why?"

"Because it reminds me of you," he explained, tweaking my noise. "This is an old ring. My great-grandfather gave it to my great-grandmother in 1927…right before the Great Depression hit. This ring has seen a lot of struggles and hardships, yet it is still beautiful. And it was a reminder to them that even in the middle of craziness, they loved each other. That's what I always want you to remember, Molly" he said gently. "Even in the middle of craziness, I still love you. When you fail me and mess up, I still love you. To me, you'll always be as beautiful as this ring… nothing could make you less beautiful to me."

I swallowed hard and pushed back that awful "not good enough" feeling. "You mean it?" I whispered.

"With all my heart."

I closed my eyes and sent a silent prayer of thanks up to my wonderful father in heaven. For the past four years, I was convinced I was going the wrong way, trying to fight my way through a crowd of people who only wanted to push me down and see me fail. It was only now becoming clear to me that even though the road had been hard to travel on, I'd always been on the right one. It had just taken me a bit longer to travel it than I wanted.

I knew I still had a long way to go. Because really, we're all just passing through this world. It's not our real home, and the journey to our real one is long and extremely difficult. But it was days like this that made the walk enjoyable. And for the first time in a long time, I could look up and smile at how far I still had to go.

Because now, the one my soul had always longed for was right beside me, holding my hand and helping me maneuver all the valleys and mountains along the way. The verse in Ecclesiastes 4:9 was starting to make a lot more sense to me now.

> Two people are better off than one, for they can help each other succeed. If one person falls, the other can reach out and help. But someone who falls alone is in real trouble… A person standing alone can be attacked and defeated, but two can stand back-to-back and conquer. Three are even better, for a triple-braided cord is not easily broken.

After all the brokenness I'd endured the past few years that was just the kind of promise my heart needed.

EPILOGUE

❀

June 2013

Sunlight streamed through the open window in our new bedroom, and I breathed deeply the scent of the early morning fresh air. Tanner still snored lightly beside me, and I resisted the urge to reach out and poke him so he could enjoy this gorgeous morning with me. Instead, I rolled onto my back and closed my eyes, savoring the sweetness of this moment. My heart was about ready to burst, so full of joy and wonder at how things had turned out for us.

We wasted no time with the wedding. We'd been waiting our entire lives to get married; we couldn't stand the thought of waiting much longer. My mother had wanted to throw a huge, extravagant wedding for us, but we declined. There was no time to wait for all those little details, not when there was so much life to be lived. Tanner and I knew better than most that time is not guaranteed to us. *Every second is precious—why waste it on the insignificant details that would soon be forgotten?* So we got married in March—on the anniversary of the weekend I'd run away from home. That weekend had always been tainted by my actions, and we both agreed that it was time to fix that and make it a happy memory instead. So on a rainy March Saturday, we joined our life together…finally. After all those years, after countless heartbreaks and disappointments, we had found a way back together again.

I rested my hands on my belly, on the growing life inside me. We'd wasted no time with starting a family either. I was only about eighteen weeks along, but I knew what a milestone that was for me. My first pregnancy had been cut short before it ever really began, and I thanked God every second I could at this second chance. Soon our daughter Elysa would have a baby brother or sister to play with. While it still felt strange to think of her as a daughter, every day was easier than the last as I constantly reminded myself that Tanner had been more than willing to accept Jason's child. My love for her grew daily, and my heart soared at the fact that Elysa was no longer without a mother.

A strong breeze fluttered the curtains, and I glanced at the window again. I was so thankful that I'd taken a risk, that I'd opened my window just wide enough to let Tanner back in. Just as he'd done as a teenager, he climbed into my life and changed everything all up. I shuddered to think of where I'd be right now if I'd panicked and slammed the window shut again, too scared to take a risk and let Tanner love me. But I *had* taken the risk, and here I was, married to Tanner and expecting a baby. We'd chosen to make Kansas our home, neither of us wanting to live out the rest of our lives in a town that held so many sad memories for both of us. So we were starting over here, living out this beautiful second chance and grabbing as much happiness as we could.

I'd made a decision recently—a decision that changed my entire outlook on life. I knew there would always be storm clouds building up in the distance. There is simply no escaping them, but keeping the window shut out of fear is stifling. Keeping it shut keeps the storm's out, sure, but it keeps the warm breezes out too. We limit the possibility of God's blessings if out of fear we keep our windows closed up tight. So while shutting the window may at first be seem like the safest thing to do, it isn't necessarily the case. So why not keep it open? Any storm that might blow my way in the future no longer scared me because I had Tanner by my side to hold me and see me through the other side.

But far greater than that, I had Christ. With Christ by my side, I could weather any storm. So let the winds howl and try to shake me, let the rain try to squelch the fire burning bright within me, for my foundation was secure and steady. And that was more than enough for me.